AUGUST IN TWILIGHT

William Fricke

This book is a work of fiction. Any references to historical events, real people, or real places are used fictitiously. Other names, characters, places, and events are products of the author's imagination, and any resemblance to actual events or places or persons, living or dead, is entirely coincidental.

KDP ISBN: 9798585899409

For my father

1

Williams stood in the bathroom mirror brushing his teeth, staring at an aging picture of his wife, Janet, and his ten-year-old son, Danny, in a baseball uniform. Danny had worked hard, really hard, to improve his batting during the season that year. In his last game he went four for four with a triple, two doubles, a single, and five RBIs. He came off the field beaming. Williams could still remember the day, a warm summer day, clouds lazily moving through the sky. Younger and older siblings were running around in the parks as their brothers played the all-American pastime. Parents lined the field with folding chairs and blankets. Dads cracked peanut shells while the moms chatted away, holding their cooler cups filled with iced tea.

Williams sat, yelling, "Go! Go! Go!" as Danny rounded second on his triple. He hoped for a lazy throw from the outfield so Danny could round third for his first home run. The throw hit the cut-off, who whipped it home to the catcher — a stand-up triple was good in any league. After the game, Janet was the first to greet Danny out of the dugout. Holding the game ball with a smile as wide as the Grand Canyon, Danny couldn't utter a word. Williams snapped several pictures, the best one was of Janet squatting down, looking Danny in the eye. She was about to tell him how proud they were of his hard work, which had brought his success that day. We always praised the effort, not the accomplishment, Williams thought. For the last thirty-three years, that was the image Williams saw before he went to bed at night and the first picture he saw each morning when he woke up. It was the last picture taken of them together.

Not two days after that season ending performance, Williams wanted to take Danny to get a new bat. He had used his teammate's bat for the last few games, with much more success. The bat was a new model by Easton. The local sporting goods store was having a season-ending sale, so Williams decided to take Danny one afternoon. However, Janet stepped in. She said the boys always bought all the sports stuff together, but moms could do it too. She had played sports in high school and she was still fit as a fiddle. She could take Danny; she wanted to take him. Williams relented, a choice he has regretted every day since. He worried about whether she would get the right model with the correct length and weight that was certified to be used for this year's playoffs and next year's league. Janet laughed at him and his worrying. "Gus," she said, "I am a college educated woman with one son and one husband. I know how to take care of both of them. We will get the right bat."

"Okay," Williams said, "just don't take the plastic off until you get home and I check it. I think it has to be broken in a certain way as well." Williams always worried. Janet hugged him, kissed him on the lips —a kiss that still lingered just out of reach— and called Danny to the car. Williams gave him a high five and a rub on the back of the head. The last words he said were, "Have fun with your mom, buddy. We'll break that bat in this afternoon." They pulled out of the driveway with the latest Top 40 blaring from the radio — both Janet and Danny singing along. They loved the current hits, but Gus, not so much. He was more of a blues fan.

Many times over, Gus recreated every detail in his mind from the moment he turned from Janet and Danny in the driveway to the moment when his friend Officer Wilson showed up at his door. He kicked himself for not going with them. He had nothing else to do. If he had been in the car with them, or driving, things could have been different. They could all be here now or they could all be gone.

After they left, he went inside to fix a big jug of water and put on his lawn mowing clothes. He turned his attention to the yard. He spent the first few minutes picking up sticks from his big shady oaks, then he weed-whipped around all the trees, fences, and landscaping. Then he took a short break with his ice water. He mulched that day, so he had to take the bag off the John Deere, but that didn't take much time. Finally, he topped off the gas, put on his ear covers, and pulled the crank until the machine roared to life. He marched around the yard for an hour.

When he was done, he took another break, sipping on his water from the porch swing. His focus then shifted to the gardens. He hated tending the gardens, but he liked how they looked, so he pulled weeds, little budding oak trees growing from acorns, chickweed, and creeping lawn grass. When he finished bagging his weeding, he took another break to enjoy the fruits of his labor. At this point, he checked the time and noted that it had been 11 am when they left and now it was close to 2 pm — they should be back anytime. He thought maybe they would have gone out to lunch as well. If he hurried, maybe he could get a cup of coffee and read a chapter before they returned. He remembered wanting them to not come back yet. He's ashamed of those thoughts now. He put the coffee on and rushed upstairs, shedding his clothes as he went to the shower.

He can see the steam coming off the cup of Folgers, the swirl of the Half-n-Half as he tipped it into his mug. He settled into his lounge chair in the backyard with *Something Wicked This Way Comes* by Ray Bradbury. He was about to grab another cup of coffee when the doorbell rang. Danny always rang the doorbell when he wanted to talk when he came home. Sometimes he would just barge into the house to do whatever, but when he had exciting news to share, he would ring the doorbell and wait eagerly for him or Janet to answer. Williams smiled through the kitchen, dropping off his cup on the counter before he hustled to the door.

He could see that it wasn't Danny, but there was a looming figure. When he opened the door, the look on Officer Wilson's face told Gus that something was not right. Williams stepped out to meet him and was immediately hugged by Wilson. While in an embrace, Wilson told him that there had been an accident. Janet and Danny were hit by another driver; they were both killed. Then there was a sinking feeling, a slow and gradual downward movement. Wilson must have guided him to the porch swing because he doesn't remember walking or falling or sitting, only the empty, sinking feeling.

Williams has felt that sinking feeling ever since.

His son's room, still untouched after all these years, remained open, waiting for Danny to return. Gus stopped for a moment to take another look. Danny's baseball uniform was still laid out on his bed. His comic books splayed across the dresser and baseball cards were taped to the wall next to *Star Wars* and car posters. Williams closed his eyes; he could hear Danny running through the hall, tossing things haphazardly in his room, and laughing. His laugh, bigger than his body, pulled everyone in earshot into the joy. Williams pulled the door closed; he could have remembered for hours. It was all he could do.

Williams took the long way to the doctor, to the scene of the accident. The spot was not picturesque and no one else remembered what had happened there that day except him. He parked his car in the Causeway Bay parking lot facing the intersection. Images from the newspaper coverage of the accident flashed through his mind. The Chevy truck must have been going nearly 70 through the light. The driver was grabbing a Whopper, not paying attention as the light turned yellow and then red. Janet was the first car at the light, she had accelerated just enough to put her driver's side into the path of the barreling truck. She had been killed on impact. Danny, who sat in the rear on the passenger side, had a chance to survive, but the force of the impact slammed his head through the window, breaking his neck and killing him. The truck's steering column crushed the driver's sternum, killing him. He died with a mouth full of his flame-broiled lunch.

The pain in Gus' chest, a hollow ache, had never gone away. When he visits this intersection, his heart beats faster, heavier. He often clutches at his heart. He wonders if he should tell his doctor about the feeling, but he would probably want to prescribe anti-depressants again.

Williams pulled out to the intersection, to the same spot where his wife was killed, breaking as his wife would have done at the red light. Then with his eyes closed, Gus took his foot off the brake, easing his car into the intersection before the light turned green. He hoped someone would be on their phone, not focused on the road.

A honking horn startled him to attention. His heart jumped, his feet tingled, and his sweaty palms gripped the steering wheel. The car drifted into the median; he jerked the wheel back to the right and into his lane, toward his doctor's office. Another day, Williams thought.

2

Dr. Roberts had been Williams' doctor for the last thirty years. They both joked that when one retires the other will as well. Roberts only worked two days a week, seeing his long-time patients. He didn't take on any new patients in his practice, but his younger doctors in the office were full. He built the practice from nothing into a sprawling campus that was first bought into by several other doctors. Roberts said he made enough money on that deal to retire to Mexico and live like a king, but he kept working. He said he liked helping people. A few years ago, Roberts and his doctor group sold the practice to the regional hospital, who built the complex into a state-of-the-art campus. Roberts said he could retire to the coast of Italy and live like a king for the rest of his days, but he kept working. Williams always joked with him, saying that he would retire when he could take a trip to Italy and live like a tourist. The truth was, neither would retire unless forced to do so.

Lately, Williams felt like hanging it up. He had taught kids, their parents, and their grandparents in school. He thought about calling it quits at the end of the last school year, but he didn't know what he would do with himself. Then the district hired a young hotshot that he was supposed to mentor this year, so he put it off again, an easy excuse. Over the summer he did some research into traveling abroad. He had saved enough to see the world before his body or mind gave out.

Dr. Roberts entered the room with a sour look on his face. Williams started feeling that hollow feeling again. He could tell something was amiss with his lab results. "Well, spit it out, Doc. Are you going to lose another patient and get another step closer to retirement? Or are you just not caffeinated enough?"

"My face gave it away, didn't it?"

"Shit, you're serious. It's not the lack of coffee?"

"No, I'm afraid not. I thought I would be better at hiding my concern."

"Doc, I see emotional boys for nine months who try to hide their feelings because they are afraid. I can read faces like an open book. Just hit me with the news."

"You do know a thing or two about hiding emotions, putting them away so no one can help you."

"Let's just get on with the results before you ruin this happy annual reunion we have going."

"Ok, Gus. The tests show low levels of red blood cells and your urine test came back abnormal."

"Low red blood cell count, does that mean cancer or does low white mean cancer?"

"The low blood cell count is just an indicator that something is wrong within the system. We have to do some more tests to identify exactly what is going on, but I have a few more questions to ask in order to identify what tests we need done."

Williams tuned out the next ten minutes of questions. He answered, but remained in a fog. They scheduled him for a battery of tests over the next week. They suspected he had something called multiple myeloma, a bone cancer. He needed to have a skeletal scan, a bone marrow biopsy, and more blood and urine tests. Once those tests were completed, it would confirm what Dr. Roberts already knew; Williams had cancer.

3

Williams sat in his car, holding a file folder full of information. He began to read through the information then tossed the entire packet onto the passenger seat. Time. Williams needed time to think. He headed for the state park in North Wellington, his favorite.

The Dune Ridge Trail wandered through a marshy area before turning sharply straight up to the peak of a dune. Trees hung over the trail until the last possible moment when the canopy opened up to a view of Lake Michigan. A well-loved bench was atop the hill under the shade of a few ash trees. Lately, kids had started to go hammocking along the ridge. They would stay for hours, laying in the hammocks, smoking grass, and sometimes drinking. Williams shied away, he didn't want to spoil their good time nor catch one of his students breaking the law.

But today, no matter who was up there, he would not turn back. His destination wasn't the first lookout on the trail, but the third bench that sat further into the dune. Thirty years ago, he had carried the bench there in pieces, with cinderblocks and a heavy chain for anchors. No one goes that far out into the dunes. For the number of times he has hiked the trail every year, he could count the people he has seen on one hand. Most of them are geocachers looking for a drop. But he and Janet would hike to that spot to put a blanket on the sand and watch the stars come out, which was why thirty years ago he built the bench with the park's approval. Then in the middle of one cloudless night, he climbed the ridge to the bench, to their secluded spot, and buried Janet's and Danny's ashes. This was their grave, marked only by a small engraved steel tag riveted onto the bench. Williams visited often.

Williams pulled his water bottle from his backpack and took a long drink of water before settling his gaze on Lake Michigan. The waves lapped at the shore, boats sped past into the channel, some sailed out into the great lake. When his sweat began to cool, he pulled a small bouquet of flowers from his pack. He took two zip ties from a small zippered pouch then attached the flowers to the back of the bench.

"Well, Janet. I have finally met my match. Roberts thinks I have multiple myeloma - cancer in my bones."

Williams sat until twilight, talking, telling her all about the disease he had just learned existed. He told her about his plans to travel, to go to Europe and ride the rails to see all the hangouts of authors he has read, to visit famous museums, to see the most respected art in the world. He had planned to take a safari through Africa to see lions and rhinos and gazelles. He wanted to hike Mount Kilimanjaro and to make it to Mount Everest base camp. He told her that he was finally ready to retire, but now, now that he was ready, he wasn't likely to travel anywhere.

The thoughts swirled. He could call the superintendent tonight to call it quits. Skip the treatments and live the next year or two like a king. If he had just a few years left, he could live in style instead of in pain. But he heard Danny's voice telling him, "But Dad, you promised you would help the new teacher," and he thought of Janet saying to him, "Gus, the doctor said you could live another ten years or more if the treatment worked. You are a fighter, don't quit now."

Alone on the bench, as the stars came out one by one, Gus wept. He hadn't fought for thirty years. And now that he was ready to move on, the universe was telling him that it was too late. The one thing that he would not do was let his son and wife down. He would fight this disease, help this young teacher, and finish living life the way he wanted to live it.

4

"Mr. Williams," Principal Anderson said opening the office door, "I would like you to meet your mentee for the year, Mr. Stacy Adams. I will let you two get acquainted and then I will see you in the cafeteria for some networking."

Behind Anderson was a young twenty-two year old with dark simmering eyes and jet black hair styled with edge-like perfection.

"Welcome to North Wellington, Mr. Adams," Williams said from his spot on the old wooden benches near the front of the school. "I'm Gus Williams, your mentor for the year."

Adams immediately thrust out his right hand in a formal greeting. "Nice to meet you, Mr. Williams."

Williams shifted his shoulders a little, feeling the lack of warmth. "I teach Senior English, AP English, and then whatever else they throw my way." Gus pointed to the box of supplies sitting on the bench, "I have taken the liberty of pulling together some desk supplies for you. I know it isn't much, but by the time your school order arrives, you will either have to spend a small fortune at Meijer or do without."

"Thank you for the supplies. I'm sure they'll be fine," Adams said moving to pick up the box of supplies.

Williams turned to walk with Adams up to their rooms. "You are on the second floor, and I am right across the hall from you, in case you ever need anything."

"I believe I have all that I need now, Mr. Williams," Adams said moving toward the stairs. "I appreciate you meeting me, but I have been in and out of the building for the last few weeks."

"Yes, well. Teaching English isn't all that difficult, it's the kids that need all the help."

"Right, the kids," Adams said focusing on the walk.

"More of an art than a science," Williams said. "Do you like art, Mr. Adams?"

"I do like art. In fact, I had several classes in art history. My favorite artists are Rothko and Pollock. What about you? Do you like art, Mr. Williams?"

"I love all art — music, performance, painting, writing, modern, post-modern, contemporary. What I 've discovered recently is James George. Have you heard of James George? He just blows my mind."

"I haven't. I will have to look him up." Adams continued toward his second-floor room. Williams just tried to keep up.

"We will have a few short meetings today, but often we have built-in time to work in our rooms. I am sure you are eager to get things going as a first-year teacher."

"Yes, I am eager to get working," Adams said stopping at his door.

"Well, yes, I see that you already know your way around the school. I am right across the hall here," Williams said pointing to his room, "if you need anything. We have about an hour of time to 'network' before the Professional Development starts, so if you would like, we can use that time to talk about Wellington and get you settled."

Adams slipped his key into the lock, "Well, if you don't mind, I think I would like to get some things settled on my own first. I always seem to work better when I can focus on the tasks at hand without trying to have a discussion on the side."

"Sure," Williams nodded. "I will be across the hall if you need anything or have questions."

Williams couldn't help but feel a little put off by Adams' demeanor. How could a new teacher not want to know about the community where he'd be teaching? Or about the procedures of the day or the quirks about what was coming next? Adams sure seemed full of himself.

Williams didn't waste much time. His lessons and handouts were ready to go for day one. The copy machines ran full time during the first two days — making the copy process twice as long as it needed to be. Years ago, he started coming in the weekend before school started to change his syllabus, print copies, and check class rosters. Usually on those first days, he would spend the time checking over the lessons before tweaking the next week's plans but, for today, he had research to do.

First, he looked up Rothko. He had heard of him, but knew very little. He discovered that he was of Russian descent, had a serious illness then slit his wrists over the kitchen sink. On the other hand, he knew Pollock. Famous for his large-scale paint drop, splatter techniques and his excessive drinking. He died in a car accident. Both artists seemed to have a simmering anger that underlined their work. He wondered if this was what was lying under Adams' demeanor — a slow-burning anger.

Williams dug out Adams' resume from his stack of mail from the summer and punched the family name into Google. His address, an Ann Arbor school system, the school Ann Arbor Prep. He interned at a law firm, one in which his mother was a partner. He would be a surefire candidate for law school then a job at the law firm then partner if things were to work out right. Why was he teaching here, three hours away from his home, barely making any money by his standards, when he had earned a 4.0 at U of M, had an in at one of the best law firms in the State of Michigan, and had a future as bright as any young person in the country? Williams could tell something was amiss.

Across the hall he heard tables being moved and the radio playing classical music. Williams sauntered back over. "Can I help move anything?"

"All done Googling me, are you?" Adams asked.

Williams felt a pang of guilt at the truthful comment. He wandered to the desk, surveying the meticulously placed piles of documents ready for the next day. "All ready for the first day?"

"I like to be prepared for whatever task I'm given. In this case, I'm readying myself to teach. The more prepared I can be prior to the kids' arrival, the more likely I will be able to handle the situations that arise that are not ideal."

"Well, that is a good plan," Williams said picking up one of the papers from the desk. "Do you have any questions about the classes or taking attendance or anything of the sort? I'm here to be your mentor and help you in any way that I can."

Adams quickly crossed the room, grabbed the paper from Williams' hand and placed it back on the desk with the other copies. Now in close proximity, Williams could feel Adams' tension flowing from his every movement. Adams straightened the edges of every pile on the desk. Williams watched the compulsive behavior with concern.

"Mr. Williams, I believe I have been briefed via computer on the procedures for attendance. I have also had courses in teaching that have prepared me for the first day of school," Adams said coming around the end of the desk, straightening the last pile. "But I do have one question, however."

Williams broke into a smile, "Shoot partner, I am here to help."

"I want to know if you feel out of touch with the younger students?" Adams crossed his arms in front of Williams. "You are by far the oldest staff member at North Wellington and English is most often the course that requires teachers to be relatable."

Williams felt that verbal attack from Adams. His mind shifted to defense, ready to strike back at the young punk standing before him. He knew, however, that Adams was trying to push him away. The walls around this young man were so thick that no one was welcome within their confines. Williams wondered if Adams even understood who he was as a person. Williams' thoughts jumped to the ACEs training he had last year. What sort of childhood trauma brought about such vitriol in Adams? If he responded with anger or frustration, he would successfully push Adams away and lose any chance to make a connection.

"Kids relate to all different types of people," Williams said leaning back on a desk. "For example, I am the same age as many of their grandparents, so they see me as a safe figure. Grandparents are really only good for the occasional babysitting, trips to the ice cream stand, and random wacky presents, so telling me about the party last Saturday is really not a big deal." Williams wanted to continue with this dialogue; he had caught Adams off guard with his response. "Now, your age can be easy or problematic."

Adams unfolded his arms and returned to stapling the border on a bulletin board. "Oh, yeah, why is my age a problem?"

Williams knew he had won that round. "Well, students identify with young teachers. You are five to six years apart in most instances, share the same interests in music, clothes, activities, and popular culture. The girls can see you as a love interest, which by the way you should take a keen interest in not pursuing, and the guys can see you as a buddy, which you are not."

Adams didn't turn to acknowledge Williams, but continued to staple butcher paper onto the next bulletin board. "You seem to have put quite a bit of thought into rationalizing your age and relationship with students. Did you have a little trouble with students when you were younger? Is that the reason for the warnings?"

Williams started to wander around the room looking at more of Adams' work on the bulletin board. He had never been one to decorate or use his boards with regular success. He had hung inspirational posters and cheesy teacher posters. His favorites were ones depicting an otter floating in the water reading a book titled *The Ottersey* and the other was of a squirrel reading a book on *Nuts: How to eat them and where to find them*. Those two posters always brought a little joy to Williams and a good chuckle for the students as well. Eventually both were ripped by a passing shoulder and had to be recycled.

"Relationships with students are the most important thing, Stacy," Williams said moving to the back of the room next to several boxes of binders waiting to be shelved. One binder was laid out on the counter, its tabs full of handouts and written paper samples. Williams began to leaf through the binder.

Suddenly, Adams' phone blasted a few lines of upbeat piano and guitar, a sharp contrast to the classical music playing from his computer speakers. As Adams hustled over to retrieve his phone, the song continued to play.

"Is that the 'Bitch is Back' by Elton John on your phone, Mr. Adams?"

Adams slipped a sly smile at Williams before answering, "Hi, Mom."

Williams knew he should leave, but he kept flipping through the binder: a meticulous collection of notes organized by subject, model papers, and writing prompts, all with examples.

"I am preparing my classroom. This is what you do as a teacher." Williams saw Adams building a wall around himself again. He had moved to the farthest corner away from Williams. "This may not be for one year. I do not want to follow you into the family business… Yes, I know my law school acceptance has been deferred for a year. It may be deferred for longer than that… You did what? …… Why would you buy a membership to the Wellington Country Club? Is that even a thing? … You know I am going to be paid a salary. I don't need you to send me money…I am fine. I do not need you to put money in an account for me at the country club, I am not eight years old and need to be fed and babysat…You also have me set up to receive shipments from the Meijer Shipt program. Who is doing the ordering? You? …"

Williams was intruding, he knew the conversation was something that Adams would not want him to hear. He closed the binder, slid it back into its exact place by the others, and sauntered to the rear classroom door. He paused briefly, taking one last look at Adams. He had settled into his high-back desk chair and rolled it to the corner of the room. He was hunched over with his phone tucked to his ear. Adams had made himself so small that Williams could hardly see him around the chair. He wondered if his mother was the one who had forced him to build defenses, to fight everyone who tried to take an interest, to push out his own personality as a defense mechanism.

"Mom, this is my life," Adams said loudly into the phone. "I am allowed to choose any profession. ... How will you know that I won't like it?"

Williams stepped out into the hall, closing Adam's door so others wouldn't be able to hear the conversation. Returning to his room, he couldn't help but be preoccupied by thinking about Adams. This year was going to be a tough one for him, Williams thought. Teachers shouldn't go into any year with too much personal baggage in the area of relationships. The personal stuff always came out in their teaching. Adams had so many defensive measures that the students would start pounding at the castle gates just because they existed.

Schools are little societies themselves. Williams didn't quite see the dynamics until several years into his career when he finally recognized all the cogs and wheels in place in a school system. Each school has a few linchpin teachers, who guide the rest of the staff in attitude or moral or spirit or culture or the newest buzzword. These teachers can be helpful for the school community or caustic. Williams had seen both. He liked to think that now he was a linchpin, maybe on the backside of his influence, but still able to exert pressure on the staff as well as the administration.

But the faculty was not the only group with leaders; students had linchpins as well. The seniors, if they had strong personalities, set the tone for the rest of the school. If their focus was on athletics, the student body would rally behind the success of sports. If a particular group was focused on the arts, a different culture would emerge from the student body. Creativity would become the norm and small projects would flood the hallways, social media, and stages. If students were intensely focused on academics, study groups would form in the halls, there would be discussions about works of literature and early college apps, and students would find self-worth based on SAT scores. Each personality wasn't singular, but a focus for the entire cohort. This was how things were at North Wellington, a small high school comprised of nearly 400 students. Certainly, the combination of staff and students could make for a truly engaging and pleasant teaching experience — or some years, it could seem like nine months of medieval torture.

Back in his room, Williams surveyed the last forty years of his life. The first ten were a blur — getting married, having Danny, figuring out how to build a life with another person and then having it all ripped away. The next five were a dark, brooding affair — hours and days spent peering into the darkness that surrounded his heart. Williams drank and drank and drank. At first, every few days he'd pick up a fifth of bourbon whiskey, Wild Turkey was a favorite. Then he would shift to Maker's Mark, Four Roses, Jim Beam, Old Crow, Old Forester, and Old Grand Dad. He sampled them all. In five years, he was buying cases out of the back door of the local liquor store. The owner began to think Williams was running a speakeasy.

During the first year of his drinking, Williams would play the TV, any channel, any channel with noise. He would sit at his kitchen table reliving the last ten years over and over in his mind, trying to hold on to what he had, his life. The TV would play in the background until a bottle and a half into one evening, he heard the sounds of a father hitting his wife and kids on some show. He doesn't remember throwing the bottle through the screen or taking the sledge hammer to the entire entertainment center. But the aftermath remains vivid. Sobered from the exertion, Williams stood before a pile of shattered plastic, glass, particle board, and TV guts. His shoulders ached, his brain sloshed in his skull, but he was not sorry about the TV, and he hadn't owned one since.

5

The staff members filed into the auditorium two by two. Coming down the hall, some staff members were laughing, some griping and clearly frustrated, others animated with stories from the day or the shenanigans from the night before. The district meeting was a monthly occurrence with little pomp and even less circumstance. The current administration's take on sharing news was to use base directives hidden in veiled threats. The current catchphrase was, "We are not out to whammy anybody!" Williams wasn't sure if he should imagine he was a participant on a game show or watching a Nixon impersonation without the air quotes.

The agenda for the day listed a presentation regarding the new teacher evaluation criteria that had been finalized by the state during the last lame duck session. Now, nearly six months later, it had been deciphered by the local intermediate school district for all the other schools in the county. The state's plan called for all teachers to be labeled in one of four categories: Highly Effective, Effective, Minimally Effective, Ineffective. Student test scores were now counted as 25% of a teacher's evaluation along with another 25% being district determined student growth, and the remaining percentage being principal observations.

Williams saw no problem with the system for himself

personally. If things went south, he could always retire, but the system wasn't really teacher friendly. His younger colleagues would have a tough time with a hard-nosed principal or with a tough group of students. Schools were not like businesses. If parts were defective, they could be sent back, but the school couldn't send their students back. Instead they had to educate them according to the guidelines defined by the district and state.

Young people need teachers dedicated to their well-being, to their needs outside of the home. Especially the ones whose homes were often a chaotic mess of debt, divorce, and distractions. Now more than ever before Williams saw more students with personal stress in their lives. Kids used to worry about playing sports after school, hanging out at the movies, and what to wear to the next dance, but now they were worrying about college debt, parental distress, and having the perfect body. Technology had laid bare the perfect life on Instagram and Snapchat. What kids didn't realize was that anyone could have that perfect life in a single picture. What happened before or after that picture was the real life. But students didn't get to see that. They only saw the carefully crafted photo, which added to the personal branding. Nothing else was broadcast across social media platforms. Today's children saw either a perfect life or the world airing its dirty laundry. On top of that most of them tended to take on too much responsibility because so many parents were afraid to parent and just wanted to be their child's best friend.

Certainly, the parents struggled too. Williams had seen it. The stereotypical parental role was a thing of the past. The stay-at-home moms were becoming a thing of the past too, thanks to women's empowerment movements and the economical need to have two wage earners in the home. Stay-at-home dads were still taboo in many families and communities. What was lost in the mix was the parent who knew what their child was doing, who was present when help was needed, and who acted as a role model. Why couldn't parents just be parents, Williams wondered. Forget about trying to be a YouTube star or an Instagram influencer or a Twitter demagogue, just parent.

The evaluation system was set up to allow the principal to tip the scale in the district's favor. Any observation could be marked ineffective or effective depending on the opinion of the principal. The principal could set the criteria of the teacher's performance based on the prerogative of the administration.

Williams remembered John Warner, the principal who helped him recover from his wife's and son's death. Warner could have easily broomed him out the door like dust on the floor. Williams would have been done teaching, and most likely done being a productive member of society. A career change wasn't in the cards. He could barely hold on to the successful career he had before the accident. Principal Warner had saved his life.

Williams wasn't so sure about Principal Anderson's compassion and willingness to help a colleague in need. The only neck he would save from the noose would be his own, probably at the expense of the others. Superintendent Snyder was even worse, catering to the needs of the board and their individual whims. Anything to save a dollar to bargain for another personal benefit, to degrade the teachers, to place the blame directly in their lap, to make them feel lucky to even have a job, to deny raises but take personal bonuses in the face of budget cuts. The tip of the iceberg. Williams wasn't so sure he would live to see the end of his reign.

Other superintendents at North Wellington involved themselves in the day to day operations of the school -- subbing for a classroom, acting as principal when the principal was away, participating in school-wide activities. But not Superintendent Bart Snyder. He sat behind the phone in his office most of the day or met with other superintendents or tried to meet with local government representatives. He didn't cover for his principal and didn't move from here to there to defend a teacher against a disgruntled parent. But, of course, in the public eye, he was all glad-handing, agreeable smiles, and nondescript answers. Williams, as well as others, saw through the façade, but kept their distance and their mouths shut. He knew enough not to get into a pissing match with the boss. Power always wins.

"I would like to start by thanking you all for coming to this meeting today, and I hope you enjoyed the end of your summer," Snyder said.

Williams heard someone behind him say, "Does that mean we didn't have to come?" and he chuckled at the wry wit.

The administration carried on, "Teacher evaluations are not any fun to talk about, but it is something that is required for us to do. If we think about evaluations as tools to help teach children instead of pieces of judgment, I think the whole process will hold much less stress and more promise." After a few smiles and awkward eye contact around the room he continued, "Now my piece of this process is complete, I am going to turn the reins over to your principals who will outline the evaluation process for you and then will answer questions you may have regarding the new procedures." Without further thought to the process, Superintendent Snyder, with careful precision, picked up his 8 oz white styrofoam cup filled with coffee and slid off to the corner to watch his principal work.

Williams listened as the high school and elementary principals, Anderson and Smith, droned on about the ratings and the categories and the testing and the nuances of observations. They showcased the new app the district had purchased in order to give real-time feedback as well as electronic storage lockers for all professional goals. The PowerPoints were packed so tightly with text that Williams couldn't read any of the slides. He wondered who had taught those two to make presentations. The handouts weren't much better; printed six slides to a page, he would need more than his readers to magnify the text to a legible size.

Williams doodled little arabesque patterns as the principals pontificated about each category, six in all, and the five benchmarks for each. He wondered about the cancer in his bones. Could he will it away? He read books where the main character changed his lifestyle and miraculously became better, living happily ever after. Could he do that? If he did, would he even live happily ever after? Williams drew one final swirl in the corner of his paper, completing the border with a dense pattern of curly-cues, sprouting vines, and floating amoebas. Principal Anderson was coming to the end of his presentation.

"In order for any teacher to be rated 'Highly Effective' in our district, they will need to document all thirty benchmarks for the six categories and submit the documentation by May 15th each year in order to receive the rating. This documentation must also be supported by principal observations and student test scores. Any one area dipping below Highly Effective and the total rating will be 'Effective'."

Overboard, Williams thought.

As the superintendent took to the stage again, the staff, who had been ever so quiet for the preceding sixty minutes, started to stir. Williams thought about the categories of teacher evaluation, specifically about the engagement of students in a lesson. Surely today's lesson would not fall under Highly Effective or even Effective. The lesson was all "Sit and Get" as they say or "Sage on the Stage." How could the district ask for one thing but present it in the very opposite manner of the target goal?

"We hope that wasn't too confusing for anyone," the superintendent said with a chuckle. "Clear as mud, right?"

Williams closed his pen, slipped it and the agenda back into his bag.

The superintendent continued, "We are all in this together and will do our best to iron out the wrinkles as we go. No one here is getting whammied."

Williams turned to Pete Jorgmander, the union president and AP Government teacher. "So, who is getting whammied this year, Pete? The good 'ole super has used that term twice so far in this meeting which usually means somebody was going to get bulldogged out the door."

Pete looked around and then leaned over to Williams and said in a whisper, "You better watch yourself, Gus. They are trying to force Beth Mitchelson to take over the DK position next year, hoping she will quit instead."

"Beth has taught second grade for thirty years. She is one of the best teachers down there; that's ridiculous."

"We all know that, but she is one of the highest paid teachers and says she never wants to quit. Her husband passed away five years ago, her kids are all living on their own, teaching keeps her sharp."

"Well, they won't make her change, will they?"

"Not if we can help it," Pete said putting away his folder.

The superintendent finished his comments about the new evaluation process as the two principals stood just off stage in the shadows of the curtain.

"Are there any questions about the process? Or about the rest of the day? Or anything for the good of the cause?" Principal Snyder stood with his hands in front of his chest, slowly working them together.

Jorgmander unfolded himself from his spot next to Gus. "I just want to clarify. As a teacher, we can't be evaluated as Highly Effective, but we must submit documentation of our own Highly Effective rating for nine months in a row. Then, and only then, if our documentation coincides with the one or two observations of the principal and student test scores, we will be rated Highly Effective. Did I get that right?"

"Yes-Yes," Snyder said. "You hit the nail on the head there, Pete."

"What if we show that we are Highly Effective and our observations show we are Effective, are we Highly Effective then?"

"Not necessarily," Snyder said, looking a little red in the face. "The criteria must match in a way that signals to your principal that what he sees and what you see and what the test scores show equals Highly Effective." Jorgmander still stood, unwilling to relent on his questions. "What these scores look like to me are sort of like your gradebook in the classroom. We could sit together and change all the scores in order to figure out what is needed in each area in order for a teacher to be Highly Effective, but what would be best is for teachers to work at being the best they can be."

"Yes, certainly Mr. Snyder. We, the staff, just want to know what those targets are and how the categories all work so that we can do our best. Is it possible for a teacher to receive a Highly Effective mark?"

Snyder was really working his hands together. "This evaluation process is all new to us as well. As a board and admin team, we looked at the criteria for being Highly Effective and thought that it was damn near impossible. We feel that Highly Effective is a place we can visit, hopefully fairly often, but not live there throughout the year."

"So, no one will be rated Highly Effective?" Pete asked, finally taking his seat.

"No, no one will be rated Highly Effective by the administration alone. Being Highly Effective means working in conjunction with different stakeholders and members of the school community. Documentation needs to show those relationships." Snyder turned from facing Jorgmander to the other side of the auditorium. "Does anyone else besides Pete have a question?"

Pete looked ready to stand again, to continue the fight against the unfair burden that was being placed on teachers. Williams leaned over, tapping Pete on the top of the knee. "You made your point."

The superintendent clapped his hands twice and said, "Meeting dismissed. If you have any further questions please stop by, my door is always open."

Someone behind Williams mumbled, "Yeah, because you are never there."

Williams offered up a surprised chuckle and looked for Stacy in the crowd. He might have questions regarding the evaluation process.

A full day of professional development came and went with little excitement. Teachers were shuffled from one meeting to the next, from one speaker to the next, and then given breaks to stretch their legs and the use the facilities. Adams always wondered if administrators thought the sit-and-get PD was good teaching. In all the years of his teaching, not once had he been told to stand at the front of the room, talk for an hour, then send the students on their way. He had always been told to capture their interest, teach a small lesson, have the students practice, then assess. Wash, rinse, repeat this cycle until the end of the school year. If a teacher taught lessons like PD, they would receive an "Ineffective" rating and need to have a development plan.

But Williams had been through it before, forty-two times. He passed his time doodling away on his notepad. He might sketch a speaker or make arabesque patterns around the edges of his paper. Or jot lines from his favorite poems. The day passed. He caught up with colleagues. He learned about their trips, their children, and their grandchildren that filled the summers with laughter and fond memories. Williams recounted the books he read and the sunsets he had seen over Lake Michigan. The number of miles he logged on the trail was always a popular question. He had been slacking the last few years; this year he logged only 200 miles. When the meetings finally ended, Williams left his colleagues amid their conversations about last week's home football game and the next one coming up to return to his room.

At his desk, Williams made himself a cup of 3 o'clock coffee from his Keurig, poured a single mini-moo creamer and took a tiny sip. The last opening day of PD he thought to himself. Williams pulled out his journal from his messenger bag. He had been journaling for nearly thirty years, keeping a regular practice of writing after the last bell of the day to clear his thoughts and to take note of important events that happened in his life. Today he would write about Adams. He was sure it would be a familiar topic by the end of the year.

Williams fumbled his pen, dropping it under his desk. He pushed back his chair and eased himself under the desk on all fours to retrieve it. He noticed some graffiti adorned the underside of his drawer. Laying on his back to get a better look at the handy work, Williams's heart skipped a beat: "Hey dad! I bet you will find this someday and be sooooo mad :=) just wanted to say you are the best DAD in the whole world! Good Bye! Love, Danny. PS. Do you want to go to a Tiger's game with me this summer?"

Tears came at once, Williams laid there, pen in hand, the other across his heart. He never thought he would hear from his son again. Now from thirty years ago, he could see his son's face as he smiled from under the desk. He had always been full of good-natured mischief. Williams reached up, tracing each scraggly letter with his finger, remembering his son's heart, his passions, his everything. He laid there well after he heard Adams leave from across the hall and the doors of the other rooms close and lock. He didn't move until the cleaning crew started running the vacuums. He crawled out from under the desk, grabbed his keys, and put his journal back in his bag. The coffee sat untouched on his desk. He walked out of his room, flicking off the light switch.

6

Williams couldn't get Danny's graffiti out of his mind. As he walked to his car, the image spun round and round in his head. Williams' blue Ford Focus was one of the last vehicles in the lot. The rest belonged to coaches and custodians. Williams sat behind the wheel, hands at 11:00 and 1:00, forehead at high noon. His son, so silly, he thinks, how could he have expected Williams to find the note? He searched his memories for when Danny could have written the note. Anytime, he could have written it anytime. Did he take Danny to a Tiger's game? He did every year. Maybe that was the first one at age six. No, the writing was too good. It had to have been years later. It probably would have been the last note Danny had written to him. He would have to get a picture tomorrow, print it out, and put it on a shelf.

Williams started his car. He drove past his house, past the corner store where he used to buy bourbon, past where he used to buy ice cream for Danny with Janet. He pulled into the state park past the empty pass booth heading toward his favorite trailhead. He drove by a father teaching his son how to fish. The dad stood behind his son showing him how to cast from 10 to 2 and then point his rod down toward the water. All the while the dad's pole sat without bait in the grass — a parent surrendering his pleasure and freedoms for his child.

He drove past the picnic area full of parents sitting around a table, covered with chips, hotdogs, salads, and half-full juice boxes. The kids played on the playset, climbing and swinging, yelling not to touch the hot lava. They shouted to the parents that their feet were on fire because they were in a river of lava. A dad turned and shouted that he was drinking anti-lava juice and held up a can of Wellington's own Walter Blonde Ale from Pigeon Hill Brewery. Williams gave a small chuckle; the hot lava game was one of Danny's favorites.

At the end of the parking lot was the trailhead. He parked his car under a small flowering pear tree. He had always really liked that tree — the leaves formed a pear shape above a straight tall trunk - like it was shaped perfectly from pixels instead of by nature. The trail signage warned of ticks. Williams blasted past the warning without a look, knowing his way from years of walking the trail.

The first time Williams walked this trail after the accident had been later into the evening as well. He was drunk then. He had broken his TV, but the silence haunted him. Everywhere he went his memories came flooding back, in each room his wife and son were reading, playing, cooking, cleaning. Around every corner came a stabbing memory of something he couldn't have any longer, of something that was ripped from his life. He drank to forget, to numb the pain from those memories. The silence became so loud that Williams grabbed his keys, his drink, and left the front door wide open. He didn't know where he was going, but his car knew exactly where to take him.

Williams found himself on the Dune Ridge Trail, a bottle of Maker's Mark in his hand, stumbling forward, blind about his direction but guided by the well-worn path. A stick caught his pant leg, one foot missed its mark, the other tangled, and with bottle in hand, Williams splayed out onto the trail. A shoe came loose and tumbled down the hill. He kicked off the other and threw it down to its pair. A mile into the trail he was dripping with sweat, the Maker's clutched in his hand, burning each time he tipped it to his lips. People eyed him warily as they passed on the way back down to their cars, heading to their perfect homes filled with laughter and love. Williams hated those people; he leered at each one. His countenance filled with hate and unspeakable sorrow. He was soaked with fear about the future. His life no longer made sense. He let his thoughts drift back to the pain in his heart, the dreams filled with longing for the past. The whispers heard on the trail from other hikers. Unlike most, Williams felt like a hollow shell, an emptiness; they don't know, he thought to himself. They only saw a drunk. Williams poured out his family in the bottle but it didn't give them back.

Up the trail went and up Williams went, stumbling, tripping over roots and rocks. Out of breath from climbing 500 vertical feet to the top of a dune overlooking Lake Michigan, Williams paused against a tree. Kids had carved their initials as some token of their passing. "Idiots," Williams said running his hand against the trunk. Williams made it to the first bench, out of breath, and feeling woozy; he looked at the bottle as Janet's words popped into his head, telling him to stop, that could be dangerous, the broken glass. Instead he took a drink, put the cap back on the bottle and staggered on. He knew where he was going now.

He followed the meandering trail along the ridge of the dune. A deep ravine covered in pine trees fell to one side and the sprawling sand and dune grass fell to the other. The trail curved down into the dune. At the next bench, another swig from his bottle. The hike had sobered him up some even though the fifth was nearly gone. Williams lumbered on for another mile until he reached what looked like a bench from the 1800s. The wood was worn thin, cracked, and splintered. The metal braces had rusted. The entire bench was chained to a cinderblock, worn with age, poised for a visitor. Williams drank the rest of the bourbon in one long single drink. He was tired. Bottle after bottle, the pain never subsided no matter how much he drank. He was tired of the pain, tired of the ache in his chest. He shouted out to Lake

Michigan as it swallowed the sun, "Take me too, you son of a bitch! You have taken everything else!" His arm drew back, the bottle flew toward the sun, and Williams collapsed onto the bench, sobbing. He was so tired. He laid down for just a moment, he thought a short rest would be good before heading back to his car. The night enveloped Williams, the stars covered him with their cool blanket.

This time at the top of the hill Williams wasn't hurting because of his drinking but because of his myeloma. The aches he thought were because of old age were really points on his bones that were degrading, being eaten away. He paused long enough at the top to catch his breath then continued on to the next bench. He viewed the ravine, the dark place he had been. He has been all the way to the bottom, pitched his tent there for years before trying to climb his way out. Lately, he thought that he was close to the top again, ready to stumble into the sun-filled dune grass. But, he tumbled back down into that darkness again with this recent diagnosis. He felt like life might not let him out of that ravine.

Finally, Gus reached Janet and Danny Williams' Memorial Bench. He was exhausted. Lake Michigan tossed its white-capped waves to the shore, flexing its muscle, showing its power. The wind whipped through the dune, picking up sand, turning the cooling breeze into a cutting knife. Williams turned to avoid the sandy blast. It would momentarily subside; it always did. Too bad all things couldn't be that way. Once the wind died down, Williams could see a bit of red peeking out from one of the ridges of sand surrounding the bench. Could it be? He ambled over to the peeking color and dropped down to one knee. Using both hands to scoop away the sand, he discovered his old bottle of Maker's Mark. The red was the signature wax bottle top. He pulled the bottle from the sand. He thought someone had packed out the bottle long ago. He never found it on any return trip and he had returned to that bench almost once a week for the last twenty-five years. Today he was taking it home.

Twenty-five years ago, Williams had hiked up drunk on a five-year binge and hiked down shoeless with new determination. He had walked down the Dune Ridge Trail ready to get sober, and he hadn't touched a drop of liquor since that night. The bottle he now held in his hands served as a symbol of his understanding that the pain from the accident will never dissipate, will never subside, or ever leave him. The ache in his heart would be a constant reminder of what he had lost. No amount of drinking or brooding would change how he felt. Williams had decided during the hike down the trail that his life was going to be different. When he got home he had cleared out his broken TV, tossed away his empty bottles of bourbon, and gave the rest back to the liquor store. The owner took out a bottle of Pappy Van Winkle and made a gift to Williams. He said he had had the bottle for years, no one was going to spend $200 on a bottle of bourbon, not in this town. He said he would rather have someone who would appreciate what was in the glass rather than sell it to some rich yuppie who was just trying to show off. Williams tried to decline, but took the bottle to be polite. He had kept that expensive drink on his kitchen table for weeks as a reminder of what drinking would cost him. Then he put it on a shelf to strengthen his resolve on a daily basis.

7

Williams returned home, pulling his blue Focus into the driveway of his small Cape Cod. A row of hostas adorned the front walkway. The garage, set slightly behind the front of the house, had room for a single car. The lawn was well-manicured, a requirement of the social etiquette in the neighborhood. Inside, Williams had created his own personal library, each room adorned with books, some paperback, some hardcover, some rare, some mass produced. Today he walked through the door with the last bottle of bourbon he ever drank; twenty-five years ago he had walked through the door with a bottle that would prove to be either his death or his future. The bottle of Pappy Van Winkle had remained at the center of his kitchen table for days, calling to him in the morning, and throughout the night. When a memory of Janet and Danny crept into his consciousness, it called.

Williams didn't fill half the shelves with books and the other half with knick-knacks, but stacked book after book. Every shelf on every bookcase was chock full of books except one. On that one shelf at eye-level, Williams had placed the bottle of Pappy, a tattered copy of *Leaves of Grass*, and a family photo. Williams slid each item over, making room for the empty bottle of Maker's Mark. He ran his fingers over the worn and curled edges of Whitman's masterpiece. He drifted back to finding *Leaves of*

Grass on the floor on the day he kicked his drinking for good.

For five years after the accident, he drank every day for almost as many hours as he was awake. As soon as he pulled out from the school parking lot, he would take a swig from a flask. Never on school grounds, never before school, but when 3 o'clock hit, the booze hit his lips. For five years, Williams had lived by that routine. He shook his head in amazement that he kept his job, didn't die in an accident, or kill anyone in the process. It was a wonder he didn't die during those years or when he stopped cold turkey.

After coming down from the trail, Williams prepared for 3 o'clock when the bottle would come calling, Williams knew enough about withdrawal to know that the first day would be tantamount to his stopping drinking. He put a rubber sheet on his side of the bed, a sheet that Danny had used when he was a toddler. Filled a gallon jug with water. Found a bucket in case he threw up. Put extra blankets near the bed. Extra towels and toilet paper. Crackers, bananas, and a jar of applesauce. He switched the knob on the door and threw the key out of the window. He was locking himself in his bedroom. He had food, water, and a bathroom. He would kick his drinking.

The hours passed quickly as he prepared, but when Williams laid on his bed waiting for the worst to come, time seemed to stand still. The sun burned through the room, turning a window-sized square into the Arizona desert. The square crept throughout the room as the sun lowered itself on the horizon. Inch by inch, Williams watched the sun until sleep came upon him. He awoke suddenly with fear, a panic like death called to him in a nightmare. The sun had left. Darkness invited itself to stay. Williams grabbed for the lamp on the nightstand, knocked over his water glass, the light tumbled over to the floor, bulb popping. He scrambled over to Janet's side of the bed, found the lamp base first, seized it with both hands then reached up under the light for the switch.

He remembered each moment vividly, like an ingrained

memory, but the reality was more like a dream. The light burned his eyes, his head pounded, and he could feel every inch of his skin. The sensation was overwhelming. The clothes itched him, scratched his skin. It hurt. He stripped down. His throat burned. Williams greedily drank from the gallon. His stomach cramped. He ran to the bathroom. Cold. Williams wrapped himself in a blanket. Shivering, Williams laid himself back down on the bed, fighting the cramps, the thirst, and the cold. His mind began to wander. He held on for two days, waking, fighting, then sleeping. On the third day Williams awoke to the sun coming through the window, heating the room, burning small patches as it inched closer and closer to his foot. The sun could heal he thought, the sun could help me to get better. Williams crawled down off the bed, curling himself up in the small patch of sun. He soaked in every ray. For the first time in days he wasn't cold, he didn't feel like he had to run to the bathroom, and his head didn't feel like it was being smashed by Gallagher and a giant mallet. For the first time in two days he slept a restful sleep. When he woke up, next to his head laid a paperback edition of *Leaves of Grass* by Walt Whitman. Inside the cover was a note, "Remember to 'leave' time for yourself this fall. Love, Janet." It had been a back-to-school gift. He must have unknowingly knocked it off his nightstand and kicked it under the bed.

Laying there in his room, naked, smelling of three days of sweat, vomit, diarrhea, and stale liquor, Williams cried, a full heart-wrenching mournful cry. He felt the pain of loss, the aching pain in his chest. He had real feelings again. He couldn't drown them out, not any more. Now was the test, now was when his will would be tested. The last three days were easy compared to what the next years of his life would be. He knew he would have to contend with the hurt instead of drowning it with a bottle. He would have to learn to live with the pain, recognize when it was coming, find ways to cope, to shield himself. The answer was in his hands. Reading. He would read instead of drink. He would take the time, the time he devoted to

Danny, to Janet, to building a family, and now he would read. He would "leave" time for himself. No more tears, no more drinking, only quiet memories.

Williams moved the bed back. Stuffed the sheets, leftover applesauce, crumbled crackers, empty water jug, and his clothes in the trash. He cleaned the bathroom with bleach and took a shower. In the shower Williams felt like a snake shedding his skin, peeling off the old constraints that had been hanging him up for the last five years. He felt like life might be ok after all. His first obstacle, the locked door. He had locked himself inside, making sure he would not run down to that bottle of Pappy.

The tossed key flashed in the yard, mocking him. He was only two stories up; he could jump. He remembered thinking what if he broke a leg or his arm or his back. People would say he tried to commit suicide by jumping out of his bedroom window. No. He couldn't jump. Even if he hung down from the ledge, he would fall into the landscaping, something would give. Then he looked at the bag of garbage in his hand. He would make a rope from his sheets. Taking the two sheets from the bag, he tied the ends together and then tied a knot in one end of a sheet. He closed the knot in the hinge of the bathroom door. After giving the rope a good tug, Williams felt like it would hold. He tossed the sheets out of the window. Looking down, the sheet only reached about three more feet below. It would have to do. Williams swung one leg out over the ledge and he pulled on the sheet one more time to test the strength. He held the sheet in one hand and the window sill in the other as he swung his other leg out of the window. Here he was with both legs facing the yard, his butt firmly planted on the window ledge. Now what? He would have liked to remember that he planted both feet on the siding and then repelled down like an expert mountain climber, but the reality was quite different. He tried to slowly lower himself, but his hand slipped off the window and he lost his grip with the other. His knot came undone and he tumbled into the azaleas, scratched, sore, but alive. Crawling out of the bushes,

Williams laughed for the first time in years. How his wife would have scolded him! She would have said to call to a neighbor, to break the door open, to not have turned the lock around in the first place. Even now, he smiled at the thought of her reaction.

After that day, Williams commissioned a neighbor to build him a bookshelf. He put Pappy on the shelf and saved a spot for *Leaves of Grass*. The first book he bought after that was *The Sun Also Rises* by Hemingway because he thought the title was fitting. Over the next few years he would stop at yard sales, used bookstores, and library sales to find books. He made his way through the Russians, Marquez, Hemingway, Fitzgerald, Steinbeck, Hawthorne, Poe, Twain, Faulkner, Orwell, Austen, Rowling, and Murakami. After he finished one book, it would go to the bookshelf, not to be reread or loaned out or shuffled into another order. The bookshelves were a living history of his reading life. Tracing back through the years, he could remember where he had found certain books, where he was when he read them, and how he was feeling. He remembered the winter storm of '95 that shut down North Wellington Schools for two days and the town for another. He read *The Brothers Karamazov* from cover to cover, sipping on coffee and tea throughout the day — sleeping when the need came over him, then waking only to read some more. His life and his reading were entwined, creating a lucid dream-state experience like he had never had before and has never had since. Even now, flipping through Karamazov, those images hop back and forth from Russia to his house. Then he had the fantasy period with Tolkien, Herbert, Heinlein, Goodkind. Then the dark winter with King, Stoker, Barker, and Lovecraft. The bookshelves were his living memories, traced back from the present through the years.

8

Standing in the open doorway of room 203, Williams felt giddy with excitement about the incoming students, "Good morning, Stacy!"

"Good morning," Stacy said with a small glance from his papers to the door.

"All set for today? The students should be arriving any time," Williams said with a smile. "Best to be jovial in your greetings."

"Thank you. I will channel my inner Santa Claus, but first I must channel my inner Henry Ford and put the finishing touches on this notebook for the ninth grade course, so if you don't mind."

Williams' upbeat smile turned down as he stood in the doorway. "Your sarcasm, while witty, is not going to win you any fans with the students. I would suggest you stick to straight instruction, respectful conversations, and concerned comments."

"Oh, yeah?"

"Yes. They will laugh at your comments at first, but then they will think you are cutting them down, causing them to look foolish in front of their peers, even if you are not trying to do that, and looking foolish in front of their peers is the worst thing that can happen to many of these students."

"Ok, thank you," Adams said turning his attention from his work to Williams. "I was wrong to say that to you. You are just trying to help and be friendly. I have been here on and off all weekend and someone, someone is always stopping to talk, to see the room, to offer help and suggestions on everything from what to do in the classroom, to where to eat, to beaches to visit, to ask questions, to … it just went on and on."

Williams remembered all too well the traps of working in the classroom the weekend before school. So many staff members, students, and parents were around the school that focused work time was hard to come by, which was why he had traded his weekends. He came in the evening the week before school and then didn't set foot in the building until after PD ended and the school year began. "Yes, I know that can be frustrating. You will find many more aspects of school teaching to be just as frustrating. You just have to roll with it."

Adams' face scrunched in disgust, "Roll with it?!"

"Roll with it," Williams repeated. That is the best advice I can give you right now, thirty minutes before the start of school. Students will start passing your room any minute. Staff members will come by to ask you about being nervous, if you slept. Then during the first period you will have students show up late. Some announcement will be made each hour of the day. Students will switch classes for the first three days. Some will have their computers, some will not. And on and on — just roll with it," Williams repeated as he headed across the hall to 206. "ROLL WITH IT, MR. ADAMS!"

Williams unlocked his door, flipped on his lights, and savored the smell of the first day of school. Before the students filled the halls, the lockers were stuffed, and the lunches were made, the school sat waiting, ready to receive and Williams was ready to give for one more year. He placed his messenger bag on the floor by his desk, a bag he had carried back and forth for forty years. As staff bought new bags with laptop compartments, then laptop sleeves, then bags with wheels, then backpacks with iPad sleeves, then messenger bags again, Williams simply carried his old leather bag. The edges were scuffed, the buckle straps had worn through, and the inside had a small snap-down pouch for pens and one for maybe paperclips or an eraser. The center was just one big cavern, ready to accept whatever Williams wanted to carry. Over the years, the bag had carried pages and pages of student work, a laptop, jackets, books, lunch bags, but the most important thing it ever held was the engagement ring for Janet.

He met Janet in college when she was studying to become a teacher as well. They fell in love listening to music on her record player, drinking sweet wine, and talking about the future. They took camping trips all over Michigan, from Tawas and Alpena to Mackinac to Walloon Lake and down to the small town of Wellington, trapped on the north and south by inland lakes and to the west by Lake Michigan. They loved their time on the beach in Wellington, the small row of downtown shops, and the small affordable homes with children running in and out of yards.

The beach linked with a campground where families set out their tents, cooked hotdogs over a fire, and walked to the beach and back all day long. On a trip to that beach, Williams made a connection that would lead to his first job. A small boy, no older than four years old, had wandered through the trees near the bathroom, crying and calling out for his daddy. Williams, waiting for Janet to come out of the women's restroom, didn't hesitate. He knelt down and asked the boy if he was lost. The little boy turned away, scared. Williams introduced himself and asked if he could help him find his parents. The boy nodded but stayed away from Williams. He asked if his dad was in the bathroom or at the beach or back at the campsite. The boy said, "campsite." The boy didn't know in which direction to walk in order to get back. Williams asked what color car the boy's family owned. "Brown," he said. Once Janet was out of the bathroom, they walked the campground looking for all the brown cars until they found the boy's campsite. He took off running toward his dad, who seemed to be searching for his son, going in and out of tents, walking around the car. His dad turned out to be on the local school board, so a few days later when Williams received a call from the principal asking if he wanted a job at the school, he couldn't say no.

Later that day Williams went to the local jewelry store searching for an engagement ring. The owner, happy to have a young person understand the importance of marriage and devoting oneself to a single person, found him a ring he could afford, albeit at a steeply discounted price. Williams, not wanting to argue with the man about the importance of a counterculture, about how the "hippies" allowed society to rethink their own wants and means, listened to the store owner carry on until, ring in hand, he slipped the ring into the bottom of his new "work bag" and retreated from the store.

The students started coming in droves up the stairs, down the halls, fidgeting with lockers, standing in groups checking their phones, taking pictures together, shouting out to one another through the halls. New students wandered around clutching their schedules, looking from room to room. Familiar students looked in on new teachers and spied on old ones, gossiping about what they had heard over the summer. There was a time when Williams was at the center of the rumors, but those years had long been over. Students and staff alike had been wondering if he would come back each year. Most teachers skedaddle as soon as their retirement requirements were met. They move on to do other things all the while collecting a paycheck. Others who love the atmosphere, the camaraderie, and the vibrant life brought to the school by the students, stick around until they are forced out by the school board that is looking to hire younger, cheaper staff members.

Williams was in that boat now. The past few years his schedule had been switched, giving him more prep time than before. Administration asked often about retirement and when he responded with not yet, they asked him about chairing a committee or covering an event or serving as a mentor. Williams knew the game, so he played along when he wanted, otherwise, he simply said no as kindly as possible. Now, in his last year, he basked in the young vibrant life that burned with passion and energy. Soon teachers would ask them to sit still, silent, and shore tight to the expectations of rigid learning. Some teachers branched out from the norm, incorporated more movement, freedom, and choice, but others did not because teaching that way was so much harder than just making them sit.

Williams learned long ago that forcing students to act like automatons was more stressful than allowing them to learn at their own pace, guided by their own interests. To expect all the students to learn from one prompt, with one reading, and from one lecture was like beating one's head against the wall. After all, teachers were no longer experts. YouTube was now the king of information dispensing. Williams turned himself from the sage on the stage, which he was never comfortable with being in the first place, to being an "organizer of learning opportunities." At first, the administration wasn't comfortable with his loose classroom environment. Then, as students talked more and more positively about his class to other teachers, the more the other teachers incorporated similar elements into their classroom. Eventually, the administration came to terms with how he ran his class, as long as the test scores were high. Williams hadn't concerned himself with test scores for years and years. The way he figured it, if the students were reading, writing and discussing, they were growing, and their test scores should improve.

Across the hall, Adams looked as uncomfortable as a criminal in a line-up full of orangutans. He nodded as each student entered his room, "Good morning, good morning, good morning."

"Are you ready for this?" Williams asked sipping on his coffee.

"I am prepared, if that is what you mean," Adams stated

matter-of-factly.

"No, what I am asking you is if you are ready." Williams smiled back. "Being prepared is only part of finding success. You have to get your mind and your spirit in line with the atmosphere as well."

Adams cocked his head sideways, the same look a confused dog might give its owner when asked to do something new. "Mind and spirit, huh?"

"Yes," Williams moved across the hall, shuffling between passing students. "Nice dress, Lillian. First-day outfit?"

"Yes," a blond girl said moving on down the hall. "See you sixth hour, Mr. Williams."

"Your mind and spirit are the most important aspects of this job," Williams said standing next to Adams. "Remember our conversation the other day? Teaching is more of an art than a science."

Uncomfortable, Adams shifted a step away from Williams. "Yes, I remember - James George blows your mind."

Smiling, Williams acknowledged the memory, "Every time, every time. And you like Rothko and Pollock, those abstract, crazy splotches."

"What most people don't understand about Pollock is the immensity of his paintings. People buy these little posters to hang on the wall but, in reality, most of his paintings wouldn't fit on the walls in most of these kids' houses. One was eight feet tall and nearly twenty feet wide."

"Yes, you are right about that, but we will have to continue another time because we only have five minutes before class and I need to use the restroom. I don't have the bladder of a twenty-five year old barfly anymore. Remember to get your mind and spirit right."

Williams left Adams to his own thoughts for the last five minutes. He made his way to the staff bathroom. Even though the student bathroom was closer, he liked to amble down the hall. He felt like those steps helped clear his mind.

9

After the syllabus talk, Williams slid right into conversations with some of the students. As a teacher of the oldest students in the school, he could take some things for granted, like not having to explain endless amounts of procedures.

"Mr. Williams, who is the new guy across the hall?"

Williams pulled out a chair next to the inquisitor, Jessica. "That is Mr. Adams. He is new this year from the University of Michigan. He was the best in his class."

"Well, he's cute. That is for sure."

Williams chuckled, "I suppose."

"Yo, Mr. Williams. Do you suppose that because he is so smart that he will expect us to all be super smart? Or is he going to be chill like you?"

"That is hard to say, Anthony." Williams moved from his chair across the row to another table. "Every teacher has their own teaching style and sometimes as new teachers we still need to discover what that style might be, just like young writers try to discover their voice. It can't be a copy of anyone else, it just won't work."

"So, my voice is like my style. I like that, Mr. Williams, always teaching us."

"Yes, well that is my style," he said with a wink.

Williams sensed something was amiss. A corner of the room

had gone quiet and the students shared nervous looks to where Williams was talking to others. He moved to the group of boys in the back of the room.

"Gentlemen, what seems to be the big to do?" Williams flipped an unused chair around from another table to join the circle. He straddled the back of the chair and leaned in to the group.

The boys looked from one to another with a worried look. They mouthed to each other not to tell, then looked down at the floor.

"Nothing, we are just unsure of what to do with the assignment," said one boy.

Williams' palms started to perspire a little. He looked down as well, rubbing his hands together. After forty years of teaching, he still got palm sweats when there was tension in a student conversation. "I don't think that is true, but if you would like me to explain syllabus bingo again, I certainly can."

"Okay, Mr. Williams, we know what we are doing," said Harry. "We know you are chill, but you're like a grandpa and stuff, so we don't know if you want to hear what we were talking about."

Williams felt like a weight had been lifted. He knew they were just talking teenage nonsense now. He chuckled and then straightened his expression to look each boy in the eye. "You boys never have to tell me or any other teacher your personal business. I respect you enough to have you keep that to yourself, but if you want to share those things with me, I would be happy to hear. Remember, I wasn't born a grandpa." A devilish grin spread across Williams' face. "I grew-up just like you, but I did it in the sixties and the seventies."

The boys grabbed each other by the shoulder, eliciting a collective "ohhhhhh - Mr. Williams was a hellraiser!"

The rest of the class turned to look in the back corner, where the boys were shouting. With a small smile on his face he walked toward the whiteboard. "The bell is about to ring, so let's make sure we finish our conversations and finish recording on the syllabus bingo sheet. Yes, I know it is the first day and working with procedures and rules for an hour isn't that fun, but it is important. We are here to learn, so we will do our best to learn a little every day even if it isn't entertaining!"

The bell rang, punctuating Williams' last statement.

"Have a great first day of school!"

A few thank you's floated from the students shuffling out the door. Some students were already flipping through messages on their phones, showing each other, giggling, rolling their eyes. Williams couldn't help but think of the students as one giant amoeba compressing itself to squeeze through the door before spilling out into the hall and attaching itself to a greater mass, then splitting off as it entered another classroom, growing smaller and smaller each minute until the next bell would ring. Williams followed the last of his students out into the hall. At the door, he greeted his students with a fist bump, a smile, and a good morning.

He noticed Adams was back at his door, greeting students by sticking out his hand in a formal handshake. He wondered about his first hour of his first day of teaching. Williams remembered back to his first day. How could he forget? He wore a jacket and a tie — the only one he owned. By first hour he was dripping with sweat and the sun hadn't even warmed the sky, let alone his classroom. His roll call each hour was a stammering, jumble of names. He talked so fast through his opening day lecture that he gave the students thirty minutes of time to discuss a story from the summer. Thinking back on that day, Williams laughed to himself.

"What are your laughing at, Mr. Williams?" Sam asked as he stood in the doorway to the room. "Did something happen?"

Slightly embarrassed, Williams turned to Sam for a fist bump. "No, nothing happened. Have you ever remembered something that made you laugh out loud to yourself?"

"I don't think I ever had that happen when I was all by

myself, no."

"One day you will and you should enjoy that feeling because if a memory elicits that strong of an emotion, it must be important."

"All right, Mr. Williams. So, what were you thinking about? What was your memory?"

Williams chuckled again. "I was thinking about my very first day of teaching and what a disaster it was for me."

"And that made you laugh?"

"What else can I do? It was so bad on so many levels. There is no use feeling bad about it or embarrassed or self-conscious — it's been over forty years."

"Now, I am interested in what made it so funny. Did you like get lost in the halls or did someone think you were a student or something?"

"No, no. Nothing like that. Someone did mistake me for a high school student that year though. I was running on the track before school started and the football coach came out to check on the field. A big, big guy, stereotypical football-coach size - Mr. Carsonelli was his name. He saw me sprinting my last lap, waited for me to stop then came ambling over. 'That was a great final lap, son,' he says. I was doubled over just panting, so he couldn't see my face up close. Then he says, 'Are you new here?' I was thinking that he's just being nice. I could tell from his North Wellington head to toe uniform that he was from the school. 'Yeah,' I said. 'Just moved in.' Then he starts going on and on about North Wellington's tradition of academic excellence, then he goes on to say that they have a pretty good football team too. They started practice a few weeks ago and they were going to have their first scrimmage that night. At this point, I am thinking like, 'Ok, buddy, I get it. You have North Wellington fever. I might too someday, but right now, I want to jog back to my apartment and take a shower.'

"Right," Sam said, "town super fan."

"Yeah, that was what I was thinking," but then he says, 'I

think you would be a good fit for the team.' I just started laughing. And he looked a little put off."

Sam's jaw dropped, "No way, what did you say?"

"Well, I wish I would have said sure, just to have some fun, but I told him that I was actually a new teacher at North Wellington, in the English Department."

"What did he say to that? Was he embarrassed?"

"I am sure he was. We talked for another thirty minutes about the school and community. He came to be one of my closest friends on staff. I called him Coach until he retired ten years later."

"Wow, good story, Mr. Williams."

"Yes, thank you. Now, I am going to check on Mr. Adams, who is having his first day of teaching. I do hope that it is going better than mine. See you in class."

"See you."

Williams shuffled through the passing students to stand near Adams. "Stacy, how is the first hour of the first day?"

Students came and went through the halls, peering at their schedules, at their phones, and at the youngest and the oldest teachers standing side by side. A more existential student might note this as the passing of the guard, from the old to the new, from the Greatest Generation to the Millennial. If one were to look closely, the oldest member looked comfortable surrounded by the teeming energy of the youth, while the younger looked out of place, tense, and defensive. While experience might make all the difference, so does deference to the situation.

"Fine, thank you. And how was yours?" Adams asked extending a formal handshake out to an incoming student.

"Great, I like to get them started right away with working together, skipping all of that lecture business." An extended fist swung over the outstretched hand to Williams, "Justin, how was the summer?"

"King! Mr. Williams, I got a job at Lee's Chicken, hung out at the beach all day, and got a new car!"

"What did you get? Honda Civic, Toyota, Ford Focus?"

Justin shook his head in disbelief, "Mr. Williams, I am not going to drive around in one of those little beaters. I bought a Jeep Wrangler. I've been cruising around all summer with no top, web doors, and a couple of speakers strapped to the back."

"Wow! Sounds like a great time." Williams glanced at Adams, who was pretending not to listen, but kept eyeing the discussion blocking his classroom door. "What year is that hoopty?"

"an '05."

"And did it come with full doors and a soft top?"

Justin's head dropped as a smile spreads across his lips.

"Justin! You bought a Jeep Wrangler with no top, no doors in Michigan! What are you going to do in a month when the temperature drops to 50 degrees and then a month later when the snow falls?"

Justin retreated into Mr. Adams' room, "Oh, come on now, Mr. Williams. I still have time to figure that out! When you start worrying about stuff like that, it means you are getting old!"

Williams shook his head as he walked back across the hall, marveling at the tenacity of youth, the ability to live in the moment, not to think about the next move before the first one had been made. Did he even remember what that felt like to live in the moment, to throw caution to the wind? His time was being cut short. He thought of his youthful dreams and now of his disease eating away at his bones. How he longed to see the world, to take his family through the great national parks of the West, to the bustle of New York City, the beaches of the Florida Keys, the history of Washington DC, the untamed Alaskan wilderness, the tropics of Hawaii, and the wonders of the rest of the world. Instead he read his way through his life, visited the local parks, taught kids who would forget him as soon as they donned their caps and gowns, and lived in the ten years of his happiness when Janet and Danny were still alive.

10

"Mr. Williams, you're not going to give us another lecture about the syllabus, are you?" Thomas shouted, waking Williams out his walking delirium. "We just had to sit and listen to Mrs. G. lecture about her bio-points, cellular makeup, and organic learning opportunities. I mean, she was really into it."

"Yeah," another student joined in, "all I know is that I will have to do a lot of evolution credits in order to pass that class."

"Well, Thomas, if I get a chance to start class, you will find out what I am about to do. Do you think I could start now?"

"Sure, Mr. Williams, I give you permission to start class."

"Thank you, Thomas, I appreciate the opportunity to teach you again this year. In this class we will be working on writing from the point of idea generation to the culminating product. This product will be ready for public consumption when we are finished ..."

Williams continued his speech to his AP Lang class, the same one he had given several times before. Each time he talked about writing, reading, and then finally believing in one's self. He found that most people, students included, believed they were terrible writers, writers of no consequence. He had tried for forty years to change their minds about their abilities. He started with the idea. Confidence and the willingness to work were the most important notions he asked the students to consider, but students often thought they had to create something unique with a great spin or twist. Williams tried to tell them the idea just had to be about themselves and their relationship to the idea. If they could show the reader how they related, then the reader would make their own connections.

So, he started with an idea and a belief. Then he moved on to the work, the slog, the long road, the journey of writing. He told them that most students would sit down to write their final draft on the same day, at the same time, as writing their first draft. This was not good he told them, knowing full well that most students would not heed his advice. The trick was to write early on, then let the words simmer in your mind and in your gut for a few days. Those few days of cooking time would loosen the message, create a tender juicy bite for the reader to digest. Finishing the paper after letting it marinate for a few days allowed the writer to spot all the awkward phrases, the digressions, and the terrible words from the draft before dressing it up on a platter with all the fixings. This, he said, was the writing process. Most students would not do it, but if a writer truly cared about getting better at their craft, they would.

Williams always finished his speech in about ten minutes and then turned the music on for ten minutes while the students wrote in their journals about their writing process. "This time," he said, "is sacred time. This time is for you to listen to what you have to say from in here," he pointed to his chest. "There is no need for your cell phone, playlist, or anything else. Work with your thoughts."

"That is some deep stuff, Mr. Williams," Thomas said from his seat by the window. "You old people are wise, like Gandalf or Dumbledore."

The entire class chuckled at Thomas' remarks and looked to Williams for a response. He knew this was a test, even if Thomas didn't. Certain students always tested their boundaries in the first few weeks of school. Williams knew that if he shut him down too hard, he would lose a student like Thomas for a long time. If he let him run his mouth rampant, the rest of the students, even the "good ones," would follow suit.

"Yes, well, our experience teaches us much, but much is still to be learned, Thomas." Williams pretended to pull a whiteboard marker from his belt directing it at Thomas. "Now, Silencio!"

The class chuckled. "He went Dumbledore on you, Thomas!" A student shouted from the back of the room.

"Now, enough games for the moment," Williams said, feigning putting back his wand in its scabbard. "Let's spend the next ten minutes writing, then we will have time to talk with our neighbors."

Williams was happy with his performance. He loved those moments as much as he loved the ones where he helped a student turn on the light bulb. Small individual moments were the ones he cared for rather than the big lectures, the info dumping. Before the research showed that students could only pay attention for ten minutes or less, he was cutting his lectures. He hated to listen to someone talk for an hour, so how could he expect a teenager to do it and get something out of it?

After the bell, Williams booked it to the staff bathroom. He had had too much coffee during the first two hours of the day. Now he was in trouble. Teachers weren't allowed to leave their classrooms unattended, so missed opportunities for bathroom breaks meant he had to hustle down the hall after the bell.

Third hour had been his planning hour, so he had a little time. But he was meeting with Principal Anderson to tell him about his decision to retire. The walk to the staff bathroom took him through the middle school hallway. He moved slowly, taking care to avoid the sixth graders who darted across his path, hustling to get to their lockers and then to their next class. Most of them would arrive two to three minutes before class were to start. If the teacher was still in the room, they would proceed to ask what they were doing during the hour. Or there would be a story about something that had happened the previous hour or the night before. Or their friends would arrive and the room would look more like a romper room than a classroom for learning. The boys would be wrestling each other, cracking jokes, and trying to talk to the girls without offending them in the process. The girls would be huddled around their phones or talking about what someone said or what someone was wearing or who so-and-so liked. Williams didn't miss middle school now that he taught seniors and AP English.

At the end of the hall he ran into Ken Walters, the junior history teacher. "Hi, Ken!"

"Gus, how are you this fine morning?"

"Good, good. How about you?"

"Well, things are just cooking along this morning! I have a little video for the students about history and then we start looking at our policies, grades, etcetera. You know, all the boring stuff that has to be done."

"Yes, right!" Williams nodded. "I do my best to cover that info too with a little bit of actual learning thrown in as well."

"Oh, yeah. You still got it. The kids still tell me about your class, say it is one of their favorites."

"Thank you, that means a lot for an old guy like me."

"Now that kid you're mentoring, what is his name again, Mr. Allen?" asked Walters.

"No, no, Mr. Adams," Williams said starting to get a little panicked about making it to the bathroom.

"Well, anyway. The students are already starting to complain about him and it is only the third hour of the day."

"No, that is not a good sign. What are the students saying about him exactly? He is pretty tight-lipped around me, says he 'has been trained'."

"Whatever he has been 'trained' in isn't working because they have every complaint under the sun — too strict, too boring, too dry, too hard, too uptight. The list goes on and on."

"Okay, well. I will have to talk to him." Williams started

jingling his keys in his pocket as he turned away. "Thanks," he called over his shoulder.

"No problem, I just want to make sure he has a good experience. We need more good young teachers."

11

The principal busily shuffled through papers at his desk. Williams wasn't the most organized person in the school, but he knew what being overwhelmed looked like and this was it.

"Just give me a hot minute Mr. Williams," he said.

"No problem, Mr. Anderson. You look like you have quite a bit going on. Would you like me to come back?"

"This is your planning, isn't it?" Darting from the room with papers in hand, Anderson could be heard giving directives in the front office. He came back empty handed, shut the door behind him, and decisively took his place behind the desk. "Now, what would you like to talk about? You said earlier that you wanted to have a word with me."

"Well, you said something was important, so why don't you go first."

"Okay, we are slightly worried about the Adams situation." Williams thought about the information he just received from Ken Walters, but he couldn't understand how Anderson would be talking to him about it already unless Adams did something really wrong.

"What situation?"

Anderson paused again, "His mother seems to be a high profile and very powerful attorney in the Detroit area. We don't want any trouble from her. The district cannot deal with a lawsuit from her or anyone else."

Williams chuckled to himself. This was the first time in forty years he had been called into the office to talk about the parent of teacher. Many times he had to talk about a student's parent, but never a teacher's parent.

"How, ahhh, let me backtrack. Didn't you know who she was and who Stacy was before he was hired? I found out in five minutes from a simple Google search."

Anderson shifted a little in his chair, like he had been sitting too long. His hand went to his chin, rubbing it a little. Williams could tell that Anderson was contemplating how much he should divulge.

"Yes, we knew who he was, we even knew who she was," he said leaning his elbows on his desk, clasping his hands together. "We were hoping that this was a lifelong job for him and that maybe with a little influence on his part, the district could benefit from such a relationship."

"So, what has changed now? It's the first day of school and everything isn't coming up roses?"

Anderson leaned back in his chair. Williams' questions were making him uncomfortable, to say the least.

"Yes, well. She called."

"What?" Williams laughed again. "What did she say, 'I am going to sue if something happens to my son' or something along those lines?"

"Ahh ... I'm not at liberty to say."

"She did!" Williams laughed a big hearty laugh, filling the room. "So, what do you want me to do, call her? Tell her that her son is doing well lecturing the students on the syllabus?"

"No, I don't think a phone call will be necessary at this time."

"At this time, so you might want me to call her later?"

"Well, yes, I think that might be a possibility in the future."

"Mr. Anderson, that is not going to happen. Stacy Adams is an adult. If he has any problems then we can work with him to solve those problems. We do not need to call his mom, plus, I don't think that he would like it very much if we went around his back to discuss his career with his mother."

"Uh-huh," Anderson nodded.

"In fact, he would probably be very upset if he knew the reason for his hiring had to do with his mother. I believe he went into teaching to break away from her influence."

"I understand your stance," said Anderson with a serious expression, "but if we feel a phone call is necessary, we would like you to be in on it, as his mentor."

"I think that is a very bad idea."

"Thank you for your time, Mr. Williams. Now, what was it that you wanted to talk about?"

Williams' face felt flushed, his pulse a little faster, and his palms started to perspire. He couldn't believe the district hired a teacher based on the occupation and reputation of the family. But he could see that in this age, with this board, with this principal, and with this superintendent, that education had turned from being just about helping kids into a business. Or maybe it always had been this way and Williams was just now seeing it. And it really wasn't their fault, but the fault of society's pressure.

Education had turned away from keeping students as the focal point to being the focal point of a business. Each new teaching methodology, technological advancement, or curriculum said students were the center of the plan, but often what was supposed to be true wasn't at all. More often than not, the reason was because funding was not adequate. The country spends more money on prisons and inmates than on schools and students. Each school in Michigan was allocated different amounts of pe- pupil-funding, which meant that not every student's education was worth the same amount. As a result, administration was having to do everything it could to raise money to educate students. And often the first thing that lawmakers and school boards wanted to do was cut the largest line item, namely the teacher salaries. What was most important in the school, however, was the teacher. They were the ones dealing directly with the students. Teachers organized the learning. When students had problems, they often went to teachers. Teachers were the people in a school who could educate, inspire, and save students. And if a teacher wasn't the right fit, then they could damage a student for life, not just academically, but in terms of self-esteem, self-worth, and self-perception.

Williams was upset. He wasn't going to divulge his plans to retire, not now. The administration would celebrate over the savings to the district as they pushed him out the doors. Anderson would probably be doing a little happy dance in the office once he left this meeting.

"It seems to have slipped my mind at the moment. Old age, I guess," Williams said standing to leave.

"Yes, well. You do have all your years in. I am sure you are looking forward to retirement."

"I don't know if I am ready to retire quite yet. I think I might take a big trip to Europe in the summer and then maybe Africa the year after, so I will have to come back one more year at least in order to do those things."

Williams spotted Anderson's jaw clench. A small smile lighted across Williams' lips.

"Well, we are lucky to have such a dedicated teacher," Anderson said standing up. "I do hope you will consider helping us with the present situation if the need arises."

Williams moved to the door, followed by Anderson.

"I will consider it," Williams said, "for the sake of the district."

"Great! I think it can be a win-win," Anderson said clasping Williams' hand. "Have a great rest of the first day of the year."

"Thank you, you too, Mr. Anderson."

Williams slid out of the office, thinking about what Adams would do if he discovered his position at the school was granted to him based on his name and family influence. If the conversation he overhead during PD was any inclination, Adams wouldn't be too happy with the news. How would he gain Stacy's confidence, build a trusting relationship, and then maybe have to talk to this grown man's mother about him?

Funny thing, Williams thought, was that he didn't have to do a damn thing any more. He had been in a position for many years where he wasn't afraid to say no to any requests by the administration. When he was younger, anything that was asked of him, he did. Then when he was struggling personally and the district helped him through, Williams felt like he owed the district. They could have fired him many, many times. The then principal, John Warner, covered for his classes when he wasn't feeling well. He stopped by to check on Williams, called him in the morning to make sure he would arrive on time, and even on more than one occasion, took him home before school because he smelled so much like booze.

When a boss, manager, principal, or supervisor does that for someone then they deserve undivided, unquestioning loyalty. Warner received that sort of loyalty from Williams during the last ten years of his service. If Warner needed a teacher on a committee, Williams would volunteer; if a teacher had to leave early, Williams would cover; if state reports had to be completed, Williams would help. Warner was Williams' saving grace and the day that Warner left the job, Williams nearly quite the profession himself. Now, the job has been like a revolving door, principals staying for a few years before moving on to higher paying positions, then on to retirement. Teaching in general had become so stressful that young teachers were moving on to greener pastures with more money, and more experienced teachers were taking positions just to boost their pensions. The recipe was not one that lead to success. Now with a bright young mind willing to work his ass off for his students, the district was jeopardizing it by positioning itself for a side deal with the kid's family. Williams chuckled as he headed back up the stairs, this was only the first day of the year.

"Mr. Williams, what are you laughing at?" Jessie asked bounding down the stairs. "Or are you getting a little senile in your old age?"

"Oh! Very funny, my young Padawan, but such quips are only the thoughts of a weak mind."

"Touche, Mr. Williams, touche."

"How was your summer, Jessie?" Williams asked pausing on the stairs. "You are a senior this year, is that right?"

"It was amazing, Mr. Williams. I visited U of M and MSU this summer. We also took a trip to Notre Dame. I don't think I will get in there, but I wanted to visit anyway."

"Well, that is great, all three are wonderful schools."

"Yes, it was nice talking to you, but I have to run - I am getting my schedule changed out of Mrs. Descartes class. There is no way I am doing that much work my senior year in French. She just gave us 100 flashcards to learn in the next week, plus we are all going to be on a Cabaret committee. No way! I need a little bit of freedom, and I am taking two AP classes and English 101 at the community college."

"I don't blame you one bit. Always give yourself some breathing room."

"I know, right! See you, Mr. Williams."

12

Williams had about ten minutes before the bell rang for passing to fourth hour. He hustled back to his room, pulled out the copies for the next class, took a look at his lesson plans, and checked his email, seventeen new emails since before first hour. He clicked through each one. An email from the superintendent giving everyone a little pump-up, one from the library clerk saying the library was still closed for books because of Chromebook disbursement, one from the head cheerleader reminding the school about the upcoming game on Friday, etc. Williams skimmed the details until he saw one about a former student, Nick Logan.

Nick had trouble with the formality of school. Williams had tried to help him find his way during his time at North Wellington. For one reason or another, Nick never really found his tribe at NW. He left the school during his junior year, took his GED, then went on to an art school in Chicago. Williams hadn't heard from him since he left. Williams knew that it wasn't personal, after all, if a person didn't feel welcome some place, the likelihood of coming back or trying to stay in touch with the people from there was slim to none. Williams had attempted a few searches for the art school and its students, but found nothing about Nick or his art.

Since then Nick must have found his niche and his tribe. But last week it all ended, a drunk driver hit Nick as he crossed the street in the Bridgeport area of Chicago. The driver, leaving a White Sox game to return to his home in Michigan, sped through a stop sign when Nick stepped out to cross the street at the same time. Nick left behind a large body of work. His small studio apartment was packed with canvas after canvas and only a small mattress in the corner as a token of domestic comfort. It seemed that Nick was out celebrating with his friends when he was struck by the car. One of his pieces had just been accepted by a major gallery to hang in an art show. Since his death, his friends seemed to have orchestrated a one-man show for Nick at the Hyde Park Art Center with notable attendees from the White Sox organization, the mayor, senators, and other prominent individuals.

A link in the email took Williams to the website for the art center where the show was being advertised. He clicked through a few of the paintings on the site, stopping at one of an older man kneeling next to a student at a desk. The boy's head was down, only his black shaggy hair was visible, but his shoulders were slumped. The scene denotes the boy was hurting. The older gentleman had his arm around the boy, comforting him. On the board, Williams noticed a name scrawled in half-print and half-cursive just like his own handwriting. It said, "Mr. Williams." The painting's title, *The Teacher*. When the bell rang, Williams was still wiping his eyes. No matter his age or his connection to the student, a loss of a bright future always stung. He made a note to attempt to attend the art show.

"Yo, Mr. Williams. What we gonna learn today?"

The bluster from the student body always shocked Williams back to the present, which was one reason why he may have stuck with teaching for so long. Young people are so enveloped in the present moment that anyone near them could be pulled into the vortex if they allowed themselves to be. Williams did. He lived in the moment with each class period, enjoying the time they had together, teaching, mentoring, bonding. When he went home, Williams lived in the past and he knew it, but he couldn't move away from the memory of his wife and son, nor did he really want to get away from it. He wanted to live it, with them.

"Hey, Williams, did you come to our game on Thursday night? We destroyed Pioneer! I had this tackle, oh man, should've been on ESPN it was so tight!"

"No, I am sorry I didn't make it, Brandon. I always forget that the first game is on Thursday not Friday."

"How long you been teaching, Mr. Williams? Shouldn't you remember that stuff by now?"

"Well, yes, I probably should. But for a long time, the school started before Labor Day, which meant students would be in class before their first game of the year. I could be reminded. And now I am old and I don't get reminders when I need them."

"True, you a funny old man, Mr. Williams."

"Yes, I am a funny old man who needs lots of help," Williams chuckled, knowing full well that students liked a little bit of self-depreciating humor. "In fact, I could use your help getting your friends to stop wrestling by the door. I do believe they are trying to knock each other in the privates."

"I got this, Mr. Williams," Brandon said as he charged to the back of the room. "Hey, my linebackers, save it for the practice field. Stop jackin' up Mr. Williams' room."

The linebackers reacted in kind before attacking Brandon with precision. One went high while the other went low. He couldn't block both. The result was one low-blow and then a retaliatory punch to the shoulder by Brandon. All three flopped into chairs at the same table giggling and in a little pain. Williams watched in amusement at the spectacle, but some of his students were not so amused.

"Mr. Williams, how do you tolerate those boys?"

Andrea took all things very seriously. Williams had seen her posting flyers about how the dress code was sexist, how the pep assemblies only recognized the male sports, how the academic awards were crammed into one assembly at the end of the year and after school, and, of course, how "the school" allowed the "in-crowd" to do whatever they wanted. Every class had an advocate that took on the establishment with gusto; sometimes they got results and sometimes they were just persistently annoying. Either way, Williams appreciated that the students were thinking for themselves.

"Well, they seemed to have solved the problem themselves. All I had to do was make a suggestion."

"So, you knew by telling Brandon to go back there that they would whack each other in the nuts?"

"Pretty much. See, Andrea, most situations repeat themselves every year with slight variations. The leader of the football team is one that is about as old as Shakespeare."

"I don't think they had football at the Globe Theater, Mr. Williams."

"Well, maybe it's not that old," Williams said chuckling as he walked to the front of the room.

"By now you have probably heard about three hours worth of lectures — all about the syllabus. You have sat, drifted off to sleep, or daydreamed about sports practice after school or the beach or whatever you have going on, am I right?"

"Yeah, we don't even listen to that syllabus stuff anyway, Mr. Williams. Why do you have to tell it to us, it's like wasting a practice listening to coach talk about 'the nuances of the offense' for an hour instead of just practicing the offense."

"Well, yes, maybe he is trying to get you to see the big picture so you can better understand your role in the offense versus just running the play, Cameron."

"Here is the best play, give me the ball and everybody else block somebody. I will take out at least one dude every time!"

The boys all started slapping hands and shouting "That's the truth! Give him the ball!" Slowly, Williams walked back to the corner with the football team. As he approached, they started to quiet down. Once he reached their table, he gave each one a high five then asked them to conserve some energy for football practice.

"Now, we were talking about not wanting to listen to another lecture about the syllabus, so instead, I would like to talk about safety drills!"

The class let out a collective grown. Andrea was the first to speak-up, "We thought you were going to have us do something exciting the first day that looked like learning, but no, we are going to walk down stairs."

"Right you are, Miss. Andrea. You are always right on top of things. One of your most endearing traits."

Cameron chuckled in the back. "Shut up, Cameron," Andrea snapped. "Using my head for something besides smashing into others doesn't make me annoying, it makes me smart."

"Okay," Cameron chuckled as he whispered to his friends. They all snickered as they covered their mouths.

"Mr. Williams, they are probably being nasty. You should tell them to be quiet."

"Andrea, I am not going to draw their comments out into the open." Williams moved over to his desk. "I would like all of you to look up here for a moment. This is the emergency binder the school has given us this year. Inside you will find copies of the protocol for such things as tornadoes, fires, internal and external lockdowns, bomb threats, etc."

"And why do we need to know where that is?" Alex asked. "Don't you just tell us what to do?"

"Well, yes, I do, Alex," Williams said handing the binder down the first row. "But I may not always be here to tell you what to do."

"That is something someone says when they are secretly dying, Mr. Williams."

Williams felt a little jolt in his nerves, his hands tingled, and his heart raced. He hoped no one noticed his reaction. "Well, that is not the case, but I am getting older, which means I am more susceptible to conditions where one of the symptoms is death or a long hospital stay, so if you will just bear with me."

"Okay, but I still don't get it," Alex said turning his attention to his lap, where he must have received a text or a message.

"In the binder is all the emergency information. When there is a drill, we all need to work together to make sure everyone is safe and accounted for in the classroom. So, for example, if there is a fire drill, where do we go?"

The class looked at Williams as if he was trying to bore them to death. "Outside," someone said.

"Yes," Williams said, "but where and how?"

"Well, we would probably go down the stairs and out the front doors, that is the most direct route to being outside," Andrea replied.

"And we would use our feet," Brandon shouted as his friends all chuckled and Andrea rolled her eyes.

"Yes, we would use our feet, Brandon," Williams knew that this would be his class for the term that made him earn his paycheck. "But we will also go quietly and quickly down the stairs, out the front door, across the street next to the stop sign. Once we are there we should line up in alphabetical order."

"Why alphabetical order, we ain't in kindergarten or nothin," Cameron said crossing his arms.

"No, Cameron, you are not in third grade, you know how to act in school," Williams said looking over his reading classes at him. Cameron knew he had gone too far, so he sat back in his desk, arms still crossed. "The reason we line up in alphabetical order is so that I can quickly tell who is not here. I can then relay that information to the office, which is one reason why we need you to sign out if you leave the classroom."

Williams surveyed the room, nearly all of the students were using the physical cues to show that they were listening. However, one student, Alex, was not. He was still staring down into his lap, which in this day and age meant he was sneaking a look at his cell phone.

"Now, you may be thinking that no emergencies happen at NW, but I would like to point out that it only takes one time for an emergency to happen for someone to lose their life because they weren't prepared."

Williams retrieved the binder from the last row. He showed the students the red and green card in the binder. "The green card is to show that all is well and everyone is accounted for in our classroom and the red card is to show that someone is missing. I would like to practice a few times."

Williams walked over to Alex, who quickly slid his phone further under the desk. "Alex, I would like you to lead us in the first practice exercise of the hour: the fire drill." Alex took the binder with one hand, still holding his phone under his desk with the other. Williams stayed right next to Alex to watch him struggle with one hand. Alex wouldn't put his phone in his pocket for fear of Williams confiscating it and offering a citation in its stead.

"We have to close the windows then exit out to the spot by the stop sign. Once we are there, we have to show the secretary the red or green card."

"Very good, Alex," Williams said returning to the front of the room. Alex quickly slipped his phone back into his pocket. "Let's all go down to the stop sign."

The rest of the hour was spent going through the drills for various emergencies including a defibrillation drill. Williams knew that it may be a waste of a day, but considering the constant jabbering about the syllabus, he couldn't help but try to get the students up and out of the building. He would switch the game plan tomorrow; his morning classes would go through the drills and the afternoon classes would play syllabus bingo.

During one drill, Williams didn't know exactly which one, Adams burst into the hallway to shut his door and gave Williams and his students a dirty look. Williams saw the look but let it go. Starting a ruckus with another teacher was never a good idea, but it would be even worse in front of other students.

Liz, a shy unassuming girl, came up to Mr. Williams after Adams slammed his door. "Mr. Williams, Mr. Adams just gave me a dirty look. What did I do?"

"Liz you did nothing wrong. I think the class was a little too loud for Mr. Adams. I am sure the dirty look and the door slam was directed at yours truly. I wouldn't worry about it."

"Well, he shouldn't be giving anyone dirty looks. We all need to practice these drills for safety anyway, right?"

"Yes, you are correct."

Williams would have to talk to Adams about the looks and the slamming and about all of the other information he had heard on the first day.

13

When the lunch bell rang, Williams was famished. In the future, he would have to bring a snack for his planning hour. As the students streamed out of the classroom, one student hung back, Alex. He looked like he wanted to share something, but wasn't so sure that he wanted to share it.

"Hey, Alex. Everything all right? I noticed you were a little distracted today during our safety drills."

"Yeah, I am sorry about that Mr. Williams. I just got this video post from a friend and couldn't help but watch it."

"Well, that's okay. We all make mistakes in judgement. Please don't let it happen again, okay?"

"I won't, but I think you should watch the video."

Williams held up his hands and waved off the suggestion. "Alex, I don't think I want to watch your friend's video. I bet it is more entertaining for you than it would be for me."

"It's not that it's entertaining, but it is about the teacher across the hall, Mr. Adams. He was lecturing on the syllabus and one of the kids started playing on his phone, so Mr. Adams snatched it away and tossed it, like seriously tossed it into a basket by the door. Only luck would have saved that phone from breaking. Then he went on this big loud lecture about being respectful, listening to teachers, and taking education seriously. Then the comments started to roll from students in other classes, all of them were complaining about him as a teacher."

"Well, I better take a look."

Williams watched in horror as Adams did as Alex described. He would have to have a talk with him about several things. Ken was right, whatever he was trained to do, it wasn't working.

"So, tell me about this video. Do you think we can have your friend take it down?"

"Well, Mr. Williams, he could delete it, but I am afraid that other students may have already taken parts of it for GIFs and memes."

"I understand, but let's start with what we can do first."

"Ok, Mr. Williams. I know Johnny eats lunch here, so you can go talk to him in the lunchroom. He would probably do it for you. He respects you as a teacher."

"Thank you, Alex, I will seek him out after I eat my sandwich."

"Ok, the sooner the better though because that will be blowing up at lunch."

After Alex left, Williams headed straight for the lunchroom. How could any teacher not understand the ramifications of throwing a student's phone? In this society, when everyone has a video camera attached to their hand, teachers have to be especially careful. At any given moment a student could decide to record a teacher during a lecture, a rant, a moment of distractedness, or even a moment leaving a group unsupervised.

He spotted Johnny in the lunch line about twenty students from the front. Johnny was a precarious little devil. He didn't necessarily stand out as a troublemaker, but he liked to stir the pot.

"Johnny, may I have a word with you?"

Although Johnny wasn't disrespectful, the shoulder droop and deep sigh signaled to Williams that Johnny wasn't too keen on leaving the line to talk with Williams.

"It will only take a moment," Williams assured him as he stepped to the opposite side of the hall, just far enough away from the other students so the conversation wouldn't be overheard.

Johnny shuffled over, clearly looking put upon.

"I have received some information within the last hour about your cameraman abilities. I'm inquiring about the video you took of Mr. Adams this morning and wondering if you would consider removing it from your website, social media accounts, etcetera?"

"Mr. Williams, I totally understand that the video in question paints said teacher in a bad light; I have, in fact, seen the video myself, but I am not the owner nor publisher of said video."

"You are not?"

"No."

"Is your YouTube username, JohnnyFireball69? And isn't that your picture as the account icon?"

"Yes, that's me."

"So, then this is your video showing Mr. Adams using poor judgment?" Williams showed Johnny his phone where the video was cued. The views had jumped by 100 since lunch had started. Williams needed to get the video down and down fast.

"Ok, so it's my video. Mr. Williams, it's going to make my account go viral. I will be able to make some money finally on YouTube. Can't I just leave it for like, forty-eight hours? " N o , Johnny. You are not allowed to keep it for even twenty-four hours. Please take it down and don't use other people's shortcomings to catapult yourself to local stardom. Your light might shine mildly for a brief time, but you can count on it being snuffed out by another story like monkeys throwing poop on old ladies at the zoo."

"Com' on!"

"Using other people for your benefit is only burning bridges and hurting their feelings. Neither of those things are good. I would like you to take it down right now while I stand here with you. That way I'm assured the video is taken down."

Johnny pulled his phone from his pocket. The new iPhone

was as big as a paperback book. Johnny zipped through several screens then showed Williams the message, video deleted.

"Are you satisfied now?"

Williams refreshed his phone and saw that he could no longer find the video. "Yes, almost. I would like you to delete it from your phone as well. I don't want it popping back up anytime soon or ever."

"Fine, but you owe me, Mr. Williams. I don't have to do this shit."

"Excuse me, Johnny. Please don't take that tone or use those words with me. You should have some more compassion for others instead of preying on their weakness. How would you feel if you were in his shoes in that situation?"

"I am not going to be a nine to fiver, so I wouldn't be in his shoes."

"Yes, well. In whatever way we choose to live life, we must have compassion for others. I sincerely appreciate your help in this matter."

"Done. Can I go now?"

"Yes, thank you, but let me help you out a little here since you just helped me." Williams guided Johnny to the front of the line, ahead of his previous spot. He asked for double the pizza and milk for Johnny. He added a couple of cookies on top of Johnny's tray, then asked for the entire amount to be taken from his personal lunch account.

"I do appreciate your efforts to be a leader in this school, Johnny. Remember that with great power comes great responsibility." With that Williams turned to retrieve his own lunch.

"Yes, Uncle Ben." Johnny shouted to the retreating Williams.

14

Williams strolled down the hall to the teachers' break room. Many of the teachers were close to finishing their meals by the time Williams arrived. His eyes swept the room, but no sign of Adams.

Williams sat next to Ken; he talked non-stop, so Williams would have a chance to think instead of interact. He would somehow have to get to Adams in the last two hours of the day or at least before he left for the day. If the students were revolting already, he would be asked to make that phone call to Adams' mother sooner rather than later. In fact, that video would probably do the trick unless the kid actually took it down.

"How's the new recruit? Did we get him straightened out yet?" Ken had finished his food, so now the non-stop talking would last the final fifteen minutes of lunch.

"Well, I think he is still ironing out some wrinkles in his delivery, but you know, I don't get to watch him teach."

"Well, from what I heard today, he is going to need a lot more than an iron, maybe a steam press or whole dry cleaning service."

"Now Ken, let's not label him just yet. It is his first day. Do you remember your first day?" Williams asked with a smile. Ken's first day was a disaster. Not so much as what Stacy's was adding up to be, but then again there were no cell phones to record Ken's nonstop talking. He would ask the students a question then immediately answer it without any wait time or even processing. He could have been an auctioneer.

"Well, you are correct on that account. No labels. The first day is always a little rough," Ken said. "Speaking of firsts, how about that first football game. What a doozy!"

Williams just let Ken talk himself through the rest of lunch. The sound was like white noise for Williams. He kept thinking that he had to figure out how to get Adams to loosen up a bit.

After lunch the kids were abuzz with the news of the video. Williams checked his phone on the way back to his room, then again as he set out papers for class. The video still seemed to be down, but who knew how many screenshots or downloads or copies were made before Johnny deleted it. He just hoped that Adams had reflected during lunch about his outburst and could self-correct.

Adams unlocked his door just before the bell, making Williams' goal of addressing the situation impossible. As soon as the throng of students filed through the door, the bell rang and Williams had his own class to teach. He hoped that Adams would understand that now, since a student was able to get under his skin, he would be a target for more.

Williams knew his students would be fine the first day. Most students were like deer in the headlights or were so tired from the early morning alarm clock that any sort of energy expenditure would be reserved for after school frolicking at the lake or on the practice field. After roll call, Williams directed the students to the class website and gave them ten minutes to read the syllabus and complete a bingo worksheet on the most important elements. Students were required to fill the board, so he knew he had time to kill. Each student would receive a piece of candy from Williams. Not only did the bingo board and candy make looking at the syllabus a little more fun, Williams didn't have to lecture for twenty, thirty, or sixty minutes. Usually he just let the students work independently while he walked around the room answering questions and directing the struggling students to the right spots. But this time Williams was going to slip across the hall.

Adams had left his door ajar in his rush back from lunch. He was at the front of his desk, moving slowly through the syllabus and rules of the classroom. The students looked bored. Williams leaned against the wall across the hall to watch Adams at work. He had some good ideas in his syllabus and unique procedures that allowed for students to succeed. He could be really good. The wild cards would be his temper and his reactions.

Adams glanced over at Williams. Without breaking from his lecture, the message from Adams' eyes told Williams that he knew he screwed up. Williams saw the look of regret, of recognizing that what had happened could be the end of a career that had just begun. Williams knew Adams wouldn't make the same mistake again. He had learned his lesson.

Williams nodded and with a slight smile turned back to his classroom. A few students were now in a frenzy trying to find the late work policy so they could be the first ones completed. Williams chuckled to himself. Every year students raced to complete the bingo board even though he clearly stated that everyone who finished would get a prize. He directed the students back to the homepage then on to the information section.

"Bingo!"

An entire table had just finished. Williams walked over to the table; he had a test for them. He pulled up a chair, straddling the back, and asked for their papers. He quickly looked them over to see that each one was complete.

"Mr. Williams, we are done too." A student said running up to him.

Williams didn't even know the student's name, he had forgotten to take roll call. He also forgot that he wanted to practice drills this afternoon and not do the syllabus. His brain was scrambled by this new mentee. "Yes, I will be with you in a minute. Please remain at your table."

Williams returned to his present table. They had their phones out, computers packed up, and were ready to go. "I would like to ask you four a few questions, if I may?"

"Sure," Jess said.

"Well, I wondered if any of you could tell me the process for turning in a late assignment - B4."

All the students looked at each other. No one had their paper and no one had their computer open. Williams gave them an uncomfortable ten seconds.

"Just give me the gist of it. In case you ever need to complete anything late."

"Oh, I do all my work on time," Michelle said. "I won't need to know that."

"Yeah, me too," said Jess.

"Well, I know none of you would have late work, but what if someone you know asks you about it? You know, because you are such good students, and the best students always get asked for help. Could you tell me just a few details?"

Megan responded first, "Well, first we need to talk to you about it then we have to complete some paper or something."

"Very good, Megan," Williams returned the papers to the students. "Use these papers as CliffsNotes to the class procedures and guidelines."

"Thanks," Megan said.

As Williams returned the chair to another table, he heard Jess ask Megan, "What are CliffsNotes?"

She responded, "Like a study guide or something. Probably a term from the 80s or something. He is so old."

Williams couldn't help but chuckle. He moved from group to group repeating the same message over and over again. Part of teaching was being able to do the same thing over and over again like Sisyphus. The last hour of the day went much like the fifth. Everyone in the building was tired from the first day of school or work. The students were ready to get out of the building, to have their freedom back, and the staff was ready to be responsible for only themselves again instead of twenty or thirty teenagers. Williams wasn't feeling so well. He wasn't so sure about his choice to continue this year. But he wasn't going to let it beat him on the first day.

As every other year at the end of the first day, Williams took out a new journal, turned to page one, and recorded his thoughts on the day. Since he had decided to stay sober, Williams had written about his days, his wandering thoughts, and his memories. The journal let him reflect and calmed his nerves. When he missed a day, he could tell his emotions were starting to build. His last year wasn't going to be the exception; no matter how sick or tired he felt, he would journal, he had to.

For Williams, September always flew by with few problems. Adams settled himself down, the students had come to terms with his exacting manner of teaching, and Williams didn't hear any more talk of making a call home to Ms. Adams. He was feeling pretty good considering his diagnosis. He had a visit to the doctor the following day. It happened to fall on the district's first professional development day. The students were getting half of the day off, while the teachers were to sit in meetings for the remainder of the work day.

Depending on the principal and the superintendent, professional development days could either be a waste of time, bearable, or somewhat enjoyable. Williams couldn't really remember when he had a professional development day that inspired him to work and allowed him time to dig into his material. Because Williams was near the end of his time as a teacher, he wouldn't have to make up any professional development time. His teaching certificate was permanent, unlike the new teachers who had to renew it every five years for $150 a pop. New teachers didn't even get a new certificate in the mail, just a link to print one out on a piece of paper. When Williams heard about the change from the state, he chalked it up as another way for the government to extract money from its employees. If the more than 86,000 teachers in the state had to renew every five years — most would have to renew five times over the course of their entire career — the state would make 13 million dollars every five years from the teachers. And yet the state was always cutting school funding. Williams never understood why certain government administrations and public opinions would want to cut school funding based on the idea the teachers were making too much money or the school district was wasting money.

School staff, teachers in particular, want students and communities to thrive. Teachers often live in or near their school communities and they care about their own children's education. Teachers are often labeled as lazy or called expensive babysitters, but the truth of the matter is that most teachers care enough to work extra time away from the regular school day to help their students succeed without being motivated by a sales commission, performance bonus, or other work incentives. Teachers simply want kids to learn because that is, at their core, what they feel will make the world a better place — and they enjoy it.

Missing this first PD wasn't going to make or break his teaching career. Certainly, he would rather miss a day with administrators than a day with the students.

15

"August Williams."

The nurse called his name. For the first time, he felt like he was a dead man walking. Never before had he felt that way but now, in this place, he felt like death had come a calling. He stuck a thin pack of sticky notes in his book, *Angle of Repose,* to mark his place. The sticky note bookmark was a practice he had started years ago. As he read, if something stood out to him, he would mark it with a sticky note then return to it when he finished the book. If the phrase or passage still resonated, he would copy down the saying on the sticky note and then transfer it to his journal, where he would explain why the phrase stuck with him. He loved it. He felt like he couldn't read a novel without the notes anymore and if a novel didn't move him to make a note, he wondered about the quality of writing, the story, and the plot.

Often he would find himself cruising through fantasy novels for fun, keeping the same note as a bookmark for each book. He wouldn't call them trashy, or good, or worthless books — he never understood why any reader would trash a genre. He himself knew how hard it was to write those books no matter the subject matter, and would always give them the respect they deserved. His latest fantasy book was *Staked* by Kevin Hearne. It was one of those novels that he didn't expect to offer up any nuggets of wisdom, but surprisingly, Mr. Hearne had upped the ante in this eighth book, writing a few passages about living in the past — a timely message for Williams.

The nurse interrupted his thoughts. "Hi, Mr. Williams. We are going to room number eight at the end of the hall and to the right."

Williams wondered about the closed doors. In each room was someone getting the news that there was no hope, that their life would be over in six painful months? Were their loved ones in the room with them, sobbing? Were patients getting the news that the treatments weren't working, that now all the doctors could do was make them comfortable in the last few months? Was someone hearing for the first time that their child had cancer? Williams thought about the stories unfolding in each room had. If the walls were alive, would they want to go on living after witnessing so much death and sorrow? Then he wondered about the doctors and the nurses. How many faces have they looked into and watched hope flutter away? How many times did the patient grasp for them, needing comfort from the harbinger of bad news? How many death sentences had each one handed down?

"Here we are, Mr. Williams," the nurse said from behind Williams. He slipped into the office, tossing his windbreaker onto the chair in the corner. He remembered getting that jacket with Janet. She joked that he was turning into a grandpa before her eyes. The thick elastic waistband and cuffs, the way the jacket would make noise as he walked, the collar the same as the cuffs. Williams had laughed, it was just ten dollars, an extra jacket he reasoned, but now he wore it all the time. He was always a little cold, and new jackets cost $250. He liked the memory, and the jacket.

"Mr. Williams, if you could have a seat on the exam table, I have a few questions before you get into the gown."

After answering what seemed like an inordinate amount of questions, he was asked to get into a gown for the doctor.

Williams hated perching on the exam table. The paper crinkling under his khakis. He always wore khakis. He didn't think jeans look good on older people. They were made for young people. With khakis he felt a little bit more distinguished, like people might see that he was still useful and not just some old guy in jeans and a T-shirt. By dressing the part, he looked as though he was still an active member of society not someone who was hanging on the fringes. He wanted to be in the middle. He wanted to keep death on the fringes. He needed to dress the part.

"Mr. Williams, how are you today?" The doctor asked as he breezed into the exam room.

"I would be better if I didn't have to be here."

"Yes, wouldn't we all." The doctor didn't even look up from his reading the lab results. He cycled through several screens on his laptop, clicking his mouse then squinting his eyes, pulling back then clicking and moving forward. Williams hoped that he was just refreshing his memory of the scans before proceeding.

"Well, Doc? How are the old bones?"

"Mr. Williams, you have early stage multiple myeloma, which means some cancerous cells have started to break down bones in various parts of your body. In this process, over time, those bones get weaker and weaker, eventually leading to breakage and the inability to heal."

"That is what the internet said," Williams lifted his gown back to his shoulders. "I have been doing a little research. It seems I have one of the slow painful types of cancers that breaks your spirit first before it kills you."

The doctor gave a slight uptick in his demeanor. Williams thought that he had the doctor on the ropes, almost through his defenses. If anything was certain, it was that Williams was determined to enjoy these appointments. He wasn't going to come in like he was picking out a casket. He would win this fight and had to make every appointment seem like visiting an old friend rather than a visit with the grim reaper.

"Yes, I think you are correct on that point," the doctor said turning to look at Williams. "Have you researched your options for treatment?"

"I read about a few, but none of them sounded too easy."

"Well, correct. The easiest course of action is to do nothing for a year or so then start treatment. Some research has shown that patients in the early stages of multiple myeloma don't get any better, live longer, or have any better quality of life if they start their treatment early. Another study shows that starting treatment early extends the life timeline when started on a three-prong approach to treatment. The experts are split at this point."

"What is your position? Take the drugs or just say no."

"Mr. Williams, I always advocate for taking the medicine that will get you back to the status quo. If a drug is out there that can eliminate the cancer then you should take it. With that being said, mostly with cancer, we must always do what we can to eliminate the spread of the cells. In the case of MM, we can never get rid of those cells, but what we want to do is to keep you in a healthy-as-you-can-be state for as long as possible."

"So, don't take the drugs?"

"No, I think we should try them to see how your body reacts. If we can give you a treatment over the course of three weeks for about three to four cycles and you feel relatively well and the numbers look good, we may be able to take you off the medicine for a few months."

"That is a lot of ifs, doc. What sort of drugs are we talking about, not chemotherapy, right?"

"Yes, one of the treatment options is chemotherapy, but it doesn't have the same side effects as the chemo that most people think of when they hear chemo. We would be giving you an injection of bortezomib and then prescriptions for lenalidomide, and dexamethasone. You will have an injection four times over the first two weeks, then a week with no injections. The rest is in pill form. We can start with the first injection today and monitor your reaction. We will have to put a port into your chest for the

IV."

"Well, you are the expert. If this is how we beat this thing, then let's do it."

"Yes, ok. We will set you up with an injection today. I would like to remind you, Mr. Williams, that you are you and only you can tell us how the injections make you feel. Feeling worse initially is one thing, but if you continually feel terrible, then we should stop the injections and try a different medicine."

"Yes, sir. Now what else can I do to help fight off this bone cancer? Should I take some supplements, lift weights, drink milk? I would like to know some other options to help heal me besides these drugs."

"As of right now, no clinical trials have been done to prove the safety and effectiveness of supplements for patients with multiple myeloma; however, we do have some information on certain supplements that are currently being investigated."

"What does, being investigated, mean?"

"Well, some studies have been done, but not enough to have scientific certainty. For example, patients who take calcium, L-glutamine, drink milk, eat beef and pork, and take a high quality multivitamin, usually see a significant difference in their health. But at the same time, some patients who take calcium will experience hypercalcemia because their bones are releasing calcium and the patients are taking too many supplements, which leads to a buildup of calcium in the blood."

"So, what should I take then?"

"To start with, you should not take supplements on days that you receive your Velcade injection. The supplements have often been shown to alter the effects of the medicine. On most days, take a multivitamin that has a high-absorption rate, a fish oil pill with at least 1400 grams of omega 3, and L-glutamine at thirty grams a day. If you feel any side effects from these supplements, stop taking them immediately."

"Multivitamin and fish oil is easy, but what is L-glutamine?"

"L-glutamine is part of the branched-chain-amino-acids. The

supplement helps build muscle, fight cancer, and strengthen the digestive system. You can find it at most health food stores, supplement stores like GNC, and online through Amazon."

"Ok, got it. I will stop on the way home for some supplements."

"I would also urge you to eat a balanced, whole food diet with plenty of leafy vegetables, lean red meat, pork, fish, sweet potatoes, berries, etc. The nutrients in these foods help boost your immune system and fight the cancer cells. If your body responds well, then you could live a long time without ever seeing symptoms of myeloma."

"Right! Well, let's kick this thing in the rear end then!"

"We have an opening for a port to be put in today. Your primary physician said you would be getting the treatment, so they made it for you."

"Of course he did," Williams said smiling.

"We won't do it here though, the nurse will show you to the other room."

16

At GNC Williams started in the vitamin section. Row after row of vitamins promised to increase energy, to be engineered specifically for men over fifty, or to enhance athletic performance. The branding went on and on. Williams wished he knew what a good mixture would be for his current condition. He decided on a bottle that said fast absorbing with a high dose of calcium and vitamin D. L-glutamine was even harder to choose. He looked at each bottle - Micronized, Free Form, encapsulated, pharmaceutical grade. He grabbed a small tub of powder that promised five grams for each scoop with a thirty day supply. Next he moved on back to the protein section. A worker with biceps bulging out of his shirt finally made his way over to him.

"Hi sir, can I help you locate anything today?"

"Sure, I am looking for a protein powder that doesn't have any artificial ingredients like sucralose or aspartame. If you could point me to that bottle, I will be on my way."

"Off the top of my head, I don't really know which one. If you look at the ingredients of each bottle, you can see if they have the ingredients you want or don't want. GNC Brand and EAS is popular as is Optimum Nutrition, I would suggest you start with those. Look here on the package to see the ingredients."

Williams smiled as the clerk returned to the desk. Shouldn't he know the products he was peddling? Now Williams was starting to feel tired from the medicine and wasn't really ready to analyze the ingredients of each jug. There were one hundred flavors, sizes, and varieties. A familiar voice came from behind a display rack of chewable vitamins, "If you want an all-natural protein powder, you will have to probably look elsewhere." Stacy Adams appeared from behind the rack holding his own bottle of protein and a bottle of Pre-Workout. "Nearly every one of those has sucralose. The one bag that doesn't is that small one of pea protein."

"Thank you, Stacy. Do you come here often for supplies? You seem to know your stuff."

"No, I tend to order most of my supplements from Amazon, but I needed a few things right now."

"What kind of protein powder are you getting, if you don't mind me asking."

"Well, I ordered some Optimum Nutrition Natural Whey from Amazon, but it won't be here for a couple of days, so I bought this two-pounder of chocolate. It has sucralose in it, but for two days, I think it will be ok."

"Yes, well I have to check out Amazon myself. I haven't used the service before."

"Well, it is great for books too. You can get almost any book for around five dollars from a used book seller. If you get Amazon Prime, which comes with some other perks, you also get free shipping for new books and everything else on the website that has a prime label."

"Well, I will have to check it out." Williams grabbed the small bag of pea protein and started heading for the register. "How was school and PD today?"

"So frustrating! I tested the kids again and they are nearly back to where they were at the start of the year. I pushed them really hard and now, now they are nearly back to the beginning. I feel like the other teachers are allowing these students to just coast along. We are a college prep school and those students need to be pushed."

"Well, I think some of the classrooms are a little less rigorous and are little more laid back, but I think all of teachers care about the students making progress."

Adams didn't miss a beat and said, "I think some teachers could do a little more."

"I wouldn't get too wound up in what others are doing at this point. Maybe you should focus on the students in your room and how you can help them retain the information you are teaching them."

"Well, that's the plan."

"Form relationships with them and they will want to come to your class to learn whatever you have to teach."

"Oh, yeah?"

The clerk interjected as he scanned Adams' merchandise, "I loved my history teacher, Mr. Colgan. He would dress up as characters in history or have us role play or we would watch these old videos about history and then he would give us articles to read that told the non-textbook version of the history. It was my favorite class because he was so chill and it felt like we were hanging out and learning at the same time and stuff. I still watch the History Channel all the time now because of it."

Williams looked at Stacy. Stacy furrowed his brow, mouthing "chill and stuff" to Williams.

Williams smiled and looked back to the clerk. "So, were the assignments rigorous?"

"I am not sure if the class was rigorous or not, mister," the clerk said. "But I do know that the atmosphere was very chill. He would let us bring coffee or hot chocolate to class or take a day off if we really needed to sleep. He would just hold us accountable for getting the work in on time and to the best of our ability."

"Sounds like an amazing teacher," Williams said smiling.

"He was." The clerk handed Adams his receipt and his bag.

"Any teacher that lets students sleep in class probably isn't amazing by teaching standards, but by student's likability standards," Adams said.

"Well, what matters most?" Williams asked. "If the students like the teacher, aren't they more willing to do the work, to try the hard tasks, to go the extra mile so as not to disappoint? Having a strong likability factor is more important than the drill n' kill, if you ask me."

The clerk looked from Adams to Williams and back again. He seemed to recognize that some sort of disagreement was taking place. Williams placed his basket full of vitamins and protein powder on the counter. Adams seemed to be unsure of what to do next. Williams was certainly tired enough for one day.

"We all have our ways," Adams said turning for the door. "I will see you tomorrow."

"Yes, have a restful night and a good workout." Williams returned his attention to the clerk, who had just finished scanning the products. After the clerk attempted to register Williams for a GNC club account and pushed the special of the week (Quest Bars), Williams paid and walked outside. He was wiped out physically. Between the stress of seeing the doctor, the port being put in, and the conversation with Adams, Williams was ready to call it a night even though the clock on his dashboard only read 4 p.m.; but he had one more stop to make.

17

At the top of the Dune Ridge Trail, Williams dropped himself down on the sand. Behind him a state forest was alive with all the wild animals an outdoorsman could ever want: bears, coyotes, snakes, deer, skunks, porcupines, rabbits, squirrels, bald eagles, ducks, swans, and maybe even a bobcat or two. To Williams, the state forest was special, a place where he could wander to collect himself, a place in between the parking lot and the dunes. A blanket of comfort that enveloped him as soon as he stepped from the parking lot to the trail.

In front of him, Williams watched as the sun washed everything in light. In the summer months the sun bathed the sand and trees and wildlife in a cleansing heat. He would have to dig his toes down into the sand to prevent the soft soles of his feet from burning. He would sit with his feet hidden underneath the hot sand and dig his hands down into the cool sand below. He would look out to the blue waters of Lake Michigan as they touched the horizon. Sailboats dotted the big blue lake, while powerboats zipped along the coast. The slight sounds of human activity would drift up from the public beach below. The rumble of a souped-up muscle car cruising the beach or a diesel truck pulling a fifth-wheel camper to the campground would break the ambient serenity of the moment.

In the fall the sun wasn't as warm, but the dunes held just as much life. With the open sand of the dune in front and the forest behind him, Williams could smell the decay of leaves, the decomposition of downed trees that built the new soil of the forest floor. The pungent smell of a world living under a canopy. The peaty odor a stark contrast to the dry, clean, barren breeze that blew through the dunes. The unforgiving sun relentlessly shined down on anyone and anything left out in the dune like the harshest spotlight.

Behind him, downed trees and memories were left to fester and mold over, a slow transformation from the living to the dead, fodder for another organism. A person could think something new was being formed, but it was only the beginning of total destruction. Living things needed the sun to grow, but out in the sun there was too much heat. It burned away the layers, exposing the core, the soft insides. Under the bright glare of the sun's rays, life was too hard to sustain. No wonder so many celebrities crack over time. The scrutiny was too harsh to sustain for long.

Williams wondered what he had been doing for the last thirty years. Had he been in hiding, festering on the forest floor, letting his life be the foundation of another, or had he been living in the sun, unable to grow because of the harsh light? His life had festered, decomposing in a slow rot like the downed trees and leaves on the forest floor beside him. As he sat in the shade of a giant oak with his legs stretched out into the afternoon sun, Williams knew right where he had been all those years. Right in the middle, with the darkness behind him and the light right in front.

For a few years Williams let the darkness grab hold of him, taking him further into the shadowy shell of his own life. But then he came back from the brink. However, he never really gave himself the chance to live in the sunlight, to have an opportunity for true happiness, to flourish and grow.

He was ready now, but the hourglass had been emptying for too long. His time was almost up. Wasn't that how it always worked in the movies and in books? As soon as a person was ready to move forward, to deal with their problems, it was too late. Life mimicked art and art mimicked life. Now it was too little, too late.

No one can live life over and Williams didn't want to live life over, he just wanted to live life now. The doctors had been optimistic with his treatment plan. He had been told that often times myeloma responds differently in different people. Sometimes chemo works, sometimes not; sometimes steroids, sometimes not. The goal was to fight to live and to fight and live. But Williams didn't really feel like fighting, not now, not here at the end of his life. What was the point? What if he said no to the treatment? He could live a few years traveling abroad and then return home to find comfort in his final days.

No, he was not done yet. Janet would be furious with him for quitting on life. Williams stood, careful to keep his balance so as to not pitch head first down the dune. He shouldered his light daypack then stepped out into the sun. Life could be good, life could still be good.

18

For Homecoming, Williams had been asked to be the Grand Marshal of the parade, riding in the first car, waving to all the people eager to watch their kids march the three blocks from the school to the football stadium, cheering in celebration of all of those who had come before. One day they too would return to North Wellington, to relive and relish in their youth. This time they would celebrate those who had returned.

Half the parents would drink in the parking lot after the parade passed, the other half would have already started. Williams knew many stories about homecoming games and drunk parents, drunk alumni, and bad choices. He remembered when he was barred from going into the game by Warner. "For your own good, Gus," Warner had said. Williams remembered turning toward home with his head down, sipping from a flask all the way. Another moment he was thankful for Warner. All of that is behind him now. This time he will be celebrated for his years of teaching service. Only a few alumni will remember his dark days and, hopefully, they were about to form a new opinion of their old teacher.

The student council planned all the homecoming activities or coordinated with the groups that did. Each class loved to have dress-up days at school. Monday's theme was BEACH DAY! Williams was up early to find his lightweight white beach pants with a drawstring waist. He pulled on a white tank top followed by a billowy hibiscus print shirt. On the way out the door Williams slipped on his sandals and donned his Panama Jack hat. He was ready for the day, ready to watch the kids get excited and giddy about their days and events. He learned long ago that whatever sort of school work was accomplished during homecoming week was a bonus to the curriculum. The kids were focused on building floats, training for powderpuff, getting dates to the dance, and prepping for the big game. After school last Friday, Williams had reminded Adams that the kids would be keyed up this week, and by going the extra distance to dress the part, he could lead some of the students back in his favor.

The loudspeaker played a mix of Jack Johnson and The Beach Boys during the opening thirty minutes of the day, small beach balls were batted down the hall and scooped up by teachers, and the kids dressed the part. Girls donned grass skirts with bikini-tops, made school appropriate by coverups. Flip-flops snapped up and down the hallway. Flowers were braided into the long hair of girls and boys. The boys wore their best board shorts and rash guard shirts. Some boys opted for sleeveless shirts and tank tops. Nearly everyone pushed sunglasses to the tops of their heads or let them rest on the bridge of their noses, sight be damned.

As for the teachers, they played their part as well. Williams looked ready for a Mai-Tai. Walters was dressed in a hula skirt with a t-shirt that had the body of a girl wearing coconut shells for a top and a lei around his neck. He would be full of inappropriate jokes for most of the day, at least to the teachers. Becky Evans was in Bermuda shorts with a billowing floral blouse. Even the principal put on a bright tie covered with surfboards. It seemed the entire staff was participating in the homecoming traditions.

Then Williams saw Adams turn the corner for his room. He was dressed in a white button down shirt, red power tie, and black pants. He looked the opposite of beachy. He looked ready for Wall Street, for a stiff meeting over the school's core competencies before discussing norms and lack of engagement in the bottom thirty percent. Williams cringed.

"Stacy!" Williams approached Adams through the mix of students in the hall.

"Mr. Williams, how can I help you this morning?"

"Let's talk in your room," Williams said following closely behind Adams then shutting the door so that no students could follow. "I thought we talked on Friday about dressing up this week. Y'know, getting in the good graces with the students?"

"Yes, well. I thought about it over the weekend, and I came to the conclusion that if I dressed up, I would be distracting the students. They would be more focused on my outfit than on learning the material."

"Of course!" Williams shouted. "Dressing up today wasn't about the learning that will be happening today, but about the learning that will be happening tomorrow, and next week, and the rest of the year. By letting the students see your fun side, they get to know you, feel comfortable, feel trusting, and then they learn."

"Well," Adams said, "they should trust me based on my position as a teacher that I am making the best decisions."

"They won't," Williams said turning back toward the door. "They won't trust you until they get to know you, and they definitely won't trust you until you try to get to know them."

Sounds from the hall, a cacophony of voices, cell phone rings, and lockers closing, filled the space left by Williams. Alone, Adams seemed to contemplate what Williams had said before turning to his desk, computer, and stacks of handouts. As the students started to filter into his room, he watched them from the corner of his eye. He saw the students look at him with anticipation before their countenance fell flat when they saw his shirt and tie. In the hall, he heard students shout to Williams. He returned their beach calls with his own antiquated, "Cowabunga, dude!"

Williams high-fived a few students in the hall and then slipped into his room. A few moments later the sounds of The Beach Boys came floating out of his doorway into the hall.

"Hey, Anthony! Hang ten, dude!" Williams slipped down into a surfer position pretending to ride the waves.

"Yo, Mr. Williams, that's pretty groovy!" Anthony said tossing his backpack onto the desk. "You should be careful not to hurt yourself. Those knees look like they could give out at any moment!"

"Fit as a fiddle, Anthony! Fit as a fiddle!" Williams said pretending to hang ten. "But the class is starting to fill up, so I better stop before someone gets hurt."

"Yeah, you, Mr. Williams!" Anthony said smiling.

Williams returned to the computer, turning down the sounds of summer. The students shuffled in one by one, checking their phones, scrolling through pictures of friends and strangers, checking stories, and posting updates. Williams was never sure what exactly needed updating between first and second hour, but something was always occupying the students' time on their 3x5 screens.

"Mr. Williams," Harry said pulling his headphones from his ears, "you should play some of this beach music. This is lit."

"Oh, yeah? More lit than Jan and Dean and Brian Wilson?" Williams said with a sarcastic grin.

"Uh, yeah sure, Mr. Williams. Whoever they are. Just have a listen."

Harry pulled off his white and gold headphones, extending them in Williams' direction.

"Just take a listen, Mr. Williams. I will even turn the music down so that it doesn't damage your old ears."

Williams hesitantly grabbed the headphones. "You might need it a little louder for my old ears," Williams said securing the headphones. The class was all watching now. Even though the bell hadn't rung, everyone was silent, phones poised, ready to record Williams' reaction when he put the headphones to his ears. Williams held the headphones, looking them over.

"They go on like this," Harry said motioning his hands over his ears. "You have to know how to use headphones, Mr. Williams."

"Yes, Harry. I know how to use headphones," Williams said smiling. "I was just admiring them. They seem like pretty nice headphones, leather ear pads, a good weight, strong wire connections."

"Those are Beats, Mr. Williams. You haven't heard music unless you heard it through Beats."

"Well, let's hear some music for the first time," Williams said placing the headphones over his ears.

Over the headphones, Williams heard somber melodies laid over a drum track and then he heard the rapper, "I been fuckin' hoes and poppin' pillies, man, I feel just like a rockstar." Williams started nodding his head. To chastise the student for having him listen to those lyrics would kill the vibe in the room. And why? Williams had heard it all before. In fact, the reason that Harry let him listen on headphones was because he knew that the lyrics were not appropriate for the whole class, but he trusted Williams to listen without busting him.

Williams started nodding his head to the beat, then bouncing his knees. His hands waved out in front of him to the beat and he grabbed Harry's phone. Williams moved his grooving toward the door, dancing between the tables. Students were filming him, he paid no mind as he danced out the door. Many of the students followed him to where Adams was back out in the hall shaking hands and directing students to bring their books. As Williams stepped out, he heard a roar go up from behind him.

"Yo, Mr. Williams is grooving to Post Malone! He a rockstar!"

As Williams danced in the hallway, others students stopped what they were doing to watch. Some students peeked from the door in Adams' room. He smiled and gave them a wink. As the song ended, Williams took off the headphones, the bell rang, and the students jumped into doorways to keep from being marked tardy.

"Thank you, Harry, for letting me listen to that new music. Is that what kids are listening to nowadays?"

"Yeah, that's number one right now on the charts."

"With those lyrics?"

"Well, there's a radio version, but it's not as good. Sorry about that, Mr. Williams."

"No-no-no, it was fine. I liked it. I would probably prefer to listen to the radio version. The more I hear cursing, the more I might feel inclined to use it. And, unfortunately. that is frowned upon in my world."

"Right."

"Those were nice headphones too. What did you call them again?"

"Beats"

"I liked those; I might have to get some. I don't have much use for headphones but I prefer those to the earbuds that I have to stick into my ears."

"Well, save your dollars, Mr. Williams. They will cost you a few bucks."

"But worth it, right?"

"Yeah, they worth it."

Williams played up the beach theme for the rest of the day. Each hour he would turn The Beach Boys back on in the classroom. Each hour brought new questions about his music. Was this what he listened to as a kid? How old was this music? Or statements like, "My grandparents listen to this." Or "This is pretty groovy." Or "I think I heard this in an 80s movie, is it from the 80s?"

Williams enjoyed every minute of telling the students about The Beach Boys and surf music from the sixties. Before the British Invasion, The Beach Boys and Brian Wilson were changing the music scene all on their own. Then The Beatles came to America and The Beach Boys took a backseat. Wilson went off the deep end for a little while and then the Vietnam war changed the tune of America's music.

As students were constantly checking out what Mr. Williams had going on in his class, they weren't digging what Adams had going on in his room. Each hour, student after student puffed out a big sigh, shoulders weighed down with stress and tension from the hour. Some, Williams could tell, were at a breaking point from the course. Students were supposed to feel some stress during school, but Adams didn't seem to understand that he had to let his foot off of the gas pedal at certain times. Although homecoming week isn't a no-school-break, students were usually given a little reprieve from the amount of work they had to tackle. Williams limited his work to in-class assignments only, along with some fun activities built into the week. After all, most students at North Wellington wouldn't finish the homework anyway this week unless it counted for major points on their grade.

19

As Thursday rolled around, the theme for the day was "movie characters." This day came about every few years. The students wore subtle costumes from recent dramas, superhero costumes, or even rented suits from the Rent-All. Williams had heard a few of the students talk about their plans for movie characters. One group was going to be the Avengers, another Justice League, and a few of the others were going to be the kids from *Stranger Things*. Williams was going to go the more subtle route, he was going as Clark Kent. He had found a light pair of reading glasses and a silky sweat-wicking shirt with a Superman logo emblazoned on the chest.

He tried talking Adams into dressing the part, any part, for the day. For the week, Adams had refused to participate — nothing for Beach Day, nothing for PowderPuff, nothing for Wild Wacky Wednesday. Williams gave Adams several ideas for simple costumes. He could simply wear a suit and put a fake badge on his belt. He could wear a dirty t-shirt, shorts, and a bathrobe and be the Dude. He could wear a suit and play the principal from *The Breakfast Club*. He could wear a sweater that matched Mr. Keating from *Dead Poets Society*. Williams gave idea after idea, but Adams refused to participate. Williams understood. Once he didn't dress on Monday, Tuesday, or Wednesday, jumping on to the bandwagon wouldn't be easy on

Thursday. But Williams had hope. As he walked into school, he hoped that Adams would finally take one bit of his advice and dress the part.

As he stepped through the door to the school, the junior and senior lockers stood before him. Students lined the hallways. Most students were facing their lockers, organizing for their day, placing their coats and backpacks on little metal hooks. Students were sprawled on the floor, legs protruding like hurdles for all on-comers. More were huddled in groups, engaged in various phone activities. One group was playing a game, the sound blasting from the center. Another was posing for pictures. Others were silently typing messages. A few were standing in mid-stride as if they were going somewhere, but the urge to scroll through their Snapchat stories stopped them. Williams had to navigate them all to get through to his classroom. His shortcut through the gym was blocked by a bucket lift left by the maintenance crew working on changing the lights and sound for the upcoming volleyball tournament in a couple of weeks.

"Mr. Williams, who is your movie character?" a student shouted from the crowd. As Williams turned to look for the owner of the voice, the student body turned toward Williams. He saw Johnny with his phone up, ready to capture the next few moments for his YouTube channel. Williams knew he could get back in Johnny's favor by putting on a little show. He slowly set down his messenger bag, stepped his feet a little further apart then looked majestically to the sky as he pulled open his dress shirt to reveal the superman logo stretched across his chest.

The students chuckled while Johnny recorded the bit. Then out from the crowd stepped Frank, a senior, dressed in a full Batman costume.

In a deep gravelly voice from the *Dark Knight* series he said, "Tell me, Superman, do you bleed? … You will."

Williams stepped forward, "The next time they shine your light in the sky, don't go to it. The bat is dead."

Batman started to circle Williams. Some of the students

started to chant "Batman" and others started the "Superman" chant.

"Don't do this, Batman," Williams said circling to his left. "I can take you in without killing you."

Frank didn't step out of character, "You say you want to help people, but you can't feel their pain, their morality."

Then Williams and Batman collided in the center, hands on each other's shoulders in a classic WWE style tie-up. Williams drew back his fist then swung slowly through the center, in line with Batman's jaw. Batman flew backward into the lockers, sprawled against them. He slowly slid to the floor.

Batman started to get to his feet, "It is time you learn what it feels like to be a man, Superman!"

"Don't do this," Williams said standing over Batman with his fist cocked, "If I wanted, you'd be dead already."

"STOP!" a shout came from the crowd and out stepped Liz, wearing knee-high red boots, a Wonder Woman corset, a sword strapped to her back, and her long wild black hair falling over her shoulders. The crowd parted as she slowly made her way toward Williams and Frank. "You know what they say is true about little boys, born with no natural inclination to share. There is room enough in this school for all of us."

As Batman stood, Williams positioned himself opposite Wonder Woman. "Is she with you?" he asked.

"I thought she was with you."

All three started to chuckle at their roleplaying, but then through the crowd stepped two of the biggest kids in the school, Big J and Little Kevin. As a pair, standing shoulder to shoulder, they blocked the majority of the hallway. Both would be getting some sort of scholarship to play football after the season was over, one was committed to Ferris State and the other to Central Michigan. But now they were dressed as Bane and Doomsday.

"But there is not room enough for all of us," they said in unison.

The crowd let out a collective, "ooooohhhhh!"

The three superheroes turned to face the two villains. All five crouched down in a fighting stance. Batman stepped to the front, "You'll never ...."

Just then the bell rang for students to get to class. And on cue, the students turned to their lockers, grabbing books and binders before hustling down the corridor. Williams turned to Frank and Liz. "Nice job, you two. That was fun!"

"Thanks for playing along, Mr. Williams," Frank said taking off his mask. "I don't know how Bruce Wayne does it. This suit is so hot, but not as hot as Liz here, Daaang!"

"Thank you!" Liz said flinging her hair back over her shoulder revealing her full corset- style top. "I do what I can. What do you think, Mr. Williams?"

"Well, you certainly look the part! I think the creators of Wonder Woman would be proud. Now if you'll excuse me, I must be getting to class." Williams grabbed his bag from the floor and quickly headed down the emptying hallway toward his room. Big J and Little Kevin were still in the hallway discussing some football issue. "You two look scary! If I saw you on the street in those get-ups, I would probably turn the other way."

"Thanks, Mr. Williams," they said in unison before slowly turning toward their classroom.

As Williams made his way down the hall, a hand tapped him on the shoulder causing him to stop.

"Mr. Williams," came Johnny's voice from behind, "do you think I could post that video online? It was really good and I think it will get a lot of views."

"Johnny, thank you for asking," Williams said turning to look him in the eye. "I think that is totally acceptable to use. Did you already ask the other two?"

"No, not yet. I thought I should ask you first. The others wouldn't care."

"But you should still ask, right?"

"Yes, probably. You know this legit filming business is more time consuming than just shooting and posting."

Williams could tell Johnny was getting frustrated with trying to do the right thing all the time. He always had the inclination to do first and ask for forgiveness later. "I know it takes more time, but building this habit will help ensure that you are not sued later for unlawful use of someone in a video. This is a good habit to start."

"Yeah, yeah. Thanks, Mr. Williams. I gotta run to get Frank and Liz before class, so I can post these videos during first hour." Johnny took off down the hall.

"Don't forget Big J and Little Kevin," Williams shouted. "You will need their permission too."

Johnny put a thumb in the air as he ran down the hall. Williams turned to go up the stairs to his room, wondering if Stacy had dressed up as a movie character.

20

In his room, Stacy was sitting behind his desk, working through a stack of papers. He wore the most nondescript ensemble, a white dress shirt and a dark, striped tie. He could be anyone or no one in a film with office workers. Williams knew that time was running out on Stacy to win over the students this semester. He would have to offer a little help for the day if Stacy was going to make any progress in forming relationships with his students.

Back in his room, Williams tossed his jacket and briefcase over the chair then called up Google to search for movie characters dressed like Stacy. The first character he remembered was from a movie long ago, *Falling Down,* starring Michael Douglas. In the film, Douglas' character snaps from the stress of modern society. His adventures take him throughout the city of Los Angeles as he confronts everyday problems that prove to be too much for him to handle.

Williams clicked the images tab, modified the search field to include only large images, and then scrolled through pictures until he found the one that would show Douglas' character in the same outfit as Adams; Douglas standing in a field, holding his black briefcase, and a baseball bat. He clicked print, sending it to the color printer in the library. Then he printed a copy of the movie poster. Williams dashed out of his classroom as students were filing in. He swung by the baseball coach's classroom; Pat Frissella also taught science, but he always had baseball gear laying around. Williams grabbed a bat, stopped in the drama room for a briefcase, and then cut through the crowd to the library to get his printout.

"Yo, Mr. Williams! Clark Kent had a briefcase but he didn't need no baseball bat!"

"Right you are, Ethan!" Williams breezed by him into the library for the picture.

On the way out he addressed Ethan, "Clark Kent didn't need a baseball bat. Only one negative per sentence, please."

"Right, Mr. Williams," Ethan tilted up his chin in response. "We don't want no misunderstandings."

Williams shook his head, "Maybe we need to review, why ..."

"Oh, I am just messing with you!" Ethan laughed, slapping Williams on the back. "I won't use a double negative in your presence, Mr. Williams, no worries!"

Williams smiled, "Very good, very good. You really had me for a second."

"Yeah," Ethan turned serious. "I am working on my 'code switching' for talk with my friends to my academic or professional interactions. How you think I'm doin?"

"That is some serious language ideas. Where did you learn about code switching?"

"I have been watching these videos about how a young black man can't be black in a white man's world. We need to switch from our culture to a white culture in order to be accepted and not deemed a threat."

"Wow! I would like to know more. Would you be willing to share the videos with me?"

"Yes, Mr. Williams. I can share the links with you but just to warn you, they don't really like white folks."

"I don't know what to say," Williams said. "I didn't think there was still such a problem."

"You wouldn't cuz you white." Ethan stood, ready for the

blowback. But Williams just nodded in approval. "Statistics show there is still prejudice against an African Americans in today's society. It is systemic racism. Most middle class white people don't see it because it is built into society."

"I am sorry that you have to go through that. I would hope that I never made you feel like I thought less of you because of your skin color."

"Nah, you straight."

"Thank you, Ethan," Williams said turning to go then returning to Ethan. "Ethan, I hope that you are true to yourself first. We all have to change how we speak for professional purposes. We make our speech and actions more formal. I wouldn't necessarily call it 'white,' but formal. This is why we don't swear, use slang, or too many colloquialisms. And be careful of extreme groups."

"Thank you, sir. I will keep that in mind."

"You're welcome and thank you for sharing all that with me." Williams turned to go. "Please don't forget to send me the links."

Williams hustled up the stairs. He had to find a way to tape the picture outside of Adams' door without him noticing and then drop the props in the room without being spotted.

In his room, Williams applied scotch tape to the back of the picture.

"Mr. Williams, what are you doing with a bat?"

Jessica stood before Williams, one arm across her stomach, the other holding her cellphone as she swiped through story after story.

"Well," Williams turned holding the picture up for Jessica, "I am helping Mr. Adams get in the school spirit."

"Yeah," Jessica said still looking at her phone. "How so?"

"If you put your phone down, Betty Cooper, and look up, you will get a clue."

"Harsh, Mr. Williams!" Jessica lowered her phone to look at the picture. "Who is that guy?"

Williams showed her the image of the movie poster.

"I've never heard of it before."

"Well, it came out before you were born. It is from the early 90s."

"Wow that is like, really old. Hey, do you watch *Riverdale* Mr. Williams?"

"No, I am not sure what that is."

"Well, how did you know I was dressed as Betty Cooper?"

"As with most things, history repeats. Your show must be based on the old Archie comics. I could tell from the crown on your sweater."

"Oh, cool!"

Williams turned to go, then stepped back to Jessica, "Would you like to help me put these props in Mr. Adams' room?"

"He doesn't know you are doing this, does he?"

"No, he does not." Williams stacked the images face to face, tape facing out. "You are very perceptive yourself, Jessica."

"So, what do I get to do?"

"Do you want to place the items or create a distraction?"

A huge smile bloomed across her face, "I would love to distract Mr. Adams."

"Okay, I am going to put up these pictures outside his room, then place the briefcase and bat in front of his room. I will need you to make a distraction toward the back of the room. I will pretend I am coming to get you for class after I drop off the props."

"Sounds like a good plan. Are we going right now?"

"Yes," Williams said motioning for her to head toward the door.

Jessica pulled up her skirt a tad bit higher to show a little more of her legs, violating the school's dress code by a good five inches. Williams shook his head — he hoped Adams didn't get himself in trouble. Then he laughed, Adams was so uptight, he probably would be stressed because she wasn't on his seating chart. As she crossed the front of the room, she greeted Mr.

Adams with a teasing little wave before stopping at a student's desk at the far side of the room. As he expected, Adams tracked Jessica across the room. He was probably trying to figure out why she was there and may not even have noticed her costume and short skirt.

Jessica leaned over her friend's desk to whisper something in her ear. She positioned herself so her backside was facing Mr. Adams.

Williams watched as Adams kept an eye on her; however, he was not looking directly at her. She was showing too much and he wasn't going to get distracted. The act was working on the boys however. Jake made eye contact with Martin, then raised one eyebrow before nodding in Jessica's direction.

"Hey, Jessica!" Martin shouted.

"Hi, Martin," Jessica said standing up, working her way to the rear of the class.

Martin started asking her about his English homework when the bell finally rang. Neither Martin nor Jessica gave any inclination of stopping. Not when Adams shouted to the back for Jessica to leave or when the rest of the class started getting out their work at the sound of his instructions. Adams got up from his desk to interrupt when Jake dropped his books in the aisle.

"Ooops, sorry, Mr. Adams!" Jake said.

"That's okay, Jake. We all have accidents," Adams said stooping to help pick up Jake's papers.

While Adams was distracted, Williams slipped into the room, putting the briefcase on his turn-in assignment table. He taped the picture to the briefcase and slipped back out into the hall. Williams then spun around calling from the hallway, "Jessica!"

Adams turned as Jessica turned, "Oh! Did the bell ring? Sorry, Mr. Williams," Jessica spun away from Martin. She slowly brushed past Adams, letting his tie run through her fingers. "Sorry to disrupt your class," she said in whisper.

At the front of the room, she looked over her shoulder at

Martin, then slid a soft glance at Adams. Williams stood in the doorway holding his hand toward his room, keeping his grin hidden.

Once in the hall, Williams turned to Jessica, "You went a little overboard, I think."

"You think so?" she said. "I think it was perfect. Mr. Adams was totally districted."

Williams chuckled, "Yes, Jessica. I think every male in the room was distracted."

"Even you, Mr. Williams?" Jessica said playfully.

"No, Jessica, not me." Williams pointed back to his room. "I'm old, like a grandpa. I view nearly everyone in this school as my own children." He paused, stunned at his own words. His eyes started to glisten, filling with remembrance of times past. "But let's see how that works for Mr. Adams. Now, let's go learn some English."

"Oh, baby! I can't wait," Jessica said with a heady dose of sarcasm.

"Me too!" Williams said trying to match her energy, "What do you like better, gerunds or infinitives?"

21

As the staff lunch room door opened, all heads turned to look at the late arrival. Adams stood in the doorway with a bat and a suitcase. He looked uncertain about what to do next as all the eyes bore down on him. Pat Frissella stood up, making room at the table with Walters and Williams.

"Well, come in and sit down," Pat said moving a chair over to the table where he was holding court. "That is an odd looking lunch box, I have to say. Where did you get it?"

The rest of the group attempted to contain their laughs but small smiles slipped from their lips. Williams motioned Adams over with a wave of his hand.

"Thank you," Adams said, "but I can't stay."

"Oh, come on now," Pat said with a grin. "I was only kidding." Up from his chair, he pulled a small bag of Fritos from his lunch box and grabbed a Coke from the refrigerator. He pushed the small offering into Stacy's hand, while grabbing the suitcase and the baseball bat. "Here now, come sit with us."

Stacy looked down at his gut wrenching lunch offering and slipped into the empty chair. Williams gave him a smile, "Thanks for joining us."

Pat set down the briefcase and bat next to Stacy. "You are really dedicated to your character today, sir," he said. "I wouldn't want to carry that briefcase around all day or that bat. I mean, you couldn't really do much with your hands."

Stacy looked at Pat with disdain, "You can give up the ruse now, Mr. Frissella."

Pat continued, "In that movie, doesn't Michael Douglas carry his lunch in the briefcase, like a banana and a sandwich or something?"

"I think so," Williams added. "He was let go from his job and he went off the deep end a little. He pretended to go to work every day with just a briefcase lunch."

"Yeah," Ken said, "he was wound a little too tight."

Stacy put his hands up in front of him, "I carry it around because I am not sure what to do with my hands."

Williams, Walters, and Frissella looked at each other in confusion. Cody, a teacher just a few years older than Adams, looked at them and then back to Stacy, "I think you just put them down at your sides."

"Oh, okay," Stacy said lowering his hands before he continued. "Things were just going real good today." His hands started to come back up in front of his face.

Cody reached over and lowered Stacy's hands, "down here."

Stacy and Cody started laughing then looked at Williams, Walters, and Frissella who were still looking a little confused.

"*Talladega Nights*?" Cody asked, "You three have never seen it? I fast-forwarded about years years on your movie time. Will Ferrell and John C. Reilly?"

Williams, Walters, and Frissella looked at each other. Frissella answered, "I think that I may have seen that one once. Is that the one with the drum scene?"

"No, that is *Step-Brothers,* also with John C. Reilly."

"I feel like John C. Reilly is one of those names that always has the middle initial in it. You know like how some people are called by their whole name," Williams said.

"Yes!" Cody jumped in, slapping the table. "So true. Like Steve Nash from the NBA was always Steve Nash, not just Steve and not just Nash but always Steve Nash."

"The opposite of Lebron and Beyonce and Usher," Frissella added.

"Like Bill Gates or Steve Jobs," Stacy said.

"I wonder if it has to do with the number of syllables in the name," Williams said.

"Could be," Stacy said. "We often remember things in groups of two, three, and four. Think about how as a society we group phone numbers and social security numbers."

"Life, liberty, and the pursuit of happiness," Walters said stuffing his last Hostess cake into his mouth before getting up to throw away his brown lunch bag.

The rest of the room started to follow suit. Adams looked to Williams. He was slowly finishing his carrots and hummus. "Time to go back to work," Williams said. "But if I eat these carrots too fast, I will get the hiccups. You take some."

Adams grabbed a few carrots as he stood to leave, "Thanks."

Williams gave a small smile and nod. Adams deposited the barely eaten chips into the garbage and took the Coke with him. Williams wasn't sure he would drink it, but the boy certainly knew his manners. Williams had a breakthrough with him today. Adams referencing a movie for a joke in the midst of the other staff members was a first. It was a good way to bring Adams into the fold.

22

After a long day at school, Williams didn't much want to go workout, but he did want to follow the doctor's suggestions. That feeling changed as soon he walked into Planet Fitness because he felt like a Los Angeles Laker. The colors purple and yellow were infused into nearly every aspect of the gym from the carpet to the walls to even some of the exercise equipment. He had completed a membership form online and was sent a key card in the mail, but he still felt like he should talk to an employee to tell them he was a member, to let them know he was there, to share that he was supposed to be there. As he looked around, he saw a young woman sitting behind the desk talking on the phone. She waved him over and pointed at a scanner on the counter. He swiped his key card, she mouthed "thank you," and turned back to her conversation. Williams gave a simple wave then meandered to the locker room.

Williams changed from his khakis to his sweatpants and from his quarter-zip to his old North Wellington t-shirt. He slipped his white New Balance onto his feet and placed his brown loafers in the locker. With a quarter, Williams locked his belongings into a cubby and went out into the rows of machines feeling a little out of place. The last time he was in a gym happened to be the early 1980s. He had always done a few push-ups and sit-ups as part of his daily routine, but never any heavy lifting. Now the doc told him that lifting weights would build strong bones along with a healthy diet and the right supplements. He was eating right, and he had just bought a stack of goods from the pill-and-powder store (as he now called it), so it was time to check off the last item on the list.

The speakers blasted some sort of bubblegum pop music that matched the sparkle coming from the glossy purple machines. Williams knew this was a sharp contrast to the Iron Bulldog Gym he had tried a few weeks back. At the Iron Bulldog, the speakers blasted angry metal, where the drums slammed with an unhealthy aggression, the guitar screamed in sonic pain, and the singer wailed or groaned or tried really hard to make his throat bleed. Several large men stood near their lifts, bars laden with several plates on each side. They took turns yelling at each other during each lift. The lifter replied with his own primal scream. Williams felt like he could be crushed with an accidental drop of the bar. After a few minutes in the Iron Bulldog, he knew that while in his youth the aggressive power-lifting gym may have been the place he would have wanted to go, but now he needed something a different speed. But looking at all the purple, he wasn't so sure about Planet Fitness either.

At Planet Fitness, more people his age were milling about. Some were walking on the treadmill, some were doing a fitness cycle in the Power Zone, and still more were just methodically moving from one machine to the next. Williams couldn't stand the thought of running or walking on a treadmill, not when there were trails and trails to cover in the wilderness. He slipped his yellow-and-white striped towel over his shoulder and headed into the city of purple machines.

He sat down at what he perceived to be one of the least complicated looking machines. The diagram on the side of the machine showed a man sitting with his arms at a 90-degree angle out in front of him. The man's chest was highlighted in a bright blue. Williams sat in the seat as the diagram showed. He pulled out the pin from the weight stack and inserted it into one of the lighter numbers. No reason to hurt himself on the first go-round. He pressed the machine a few times, but felt more stress on his shoulders than his chest.

He sat for a moment watching others fiddle with the machines. A rather tall man kept adjusting the seat of each machine to the lowest position. Williams fiddled with his own seat, pulling it up to a higher level. The handles of the machine now appeared in front of his chest instead of by his shoulders. This time as he pressed, the pressure was concentrated on his chest muscles instead of his shoulders. Success! Williams thought.

Williams pushed the bar twelve times then moved to the next in line. Down the row and back up the next – twenty-four exercises should be plenty. There seemed to be two or three machines primed to torture each body part. There was the chest press, the flies, the incline press, and a dip machine that said it was for the chest but seemed awfully hard on the arms as well. By the time he got to the shoulders, he knew these machines were enough.

Planet Fitness people moved in and out of machines, talking, listening to headphones, watching television, reading magazines, sitting, and staring. Williams took his time moving from one machine to the next, resting in between. A person moved from behind his machine, "Do you mind if I work in with you?"

"Oh! Hi, Stacy," Gus said with a smile. He stood and shook Stacy's hand. "There isn't really much working in with me. I just go from one to the next. Trying to figure out what I am doing as I go. I have never been much of a weightlifter."

"Well, I can help you if you'd like," Stacy said throwing his towel over his shoulder and plunging his Airpods back into their case.

"I wouldn't mind a little company," Gus said as he started to press the machine handles over his head. "Some of these machines are a little confusing."

"If you do them all one time, you'll get the hang of it," Adams said sitting down at the last of the chest press machines. He pulled the pin and ran it down the stack. He completed five reps before resting. "So what made you start to lift weights after all these years?"

Williams pondered the question as he finished his last reps. He knew that being open could really start to deepen their friendship. On the other hand, he didn't want any pity or some rumor about his cancer to spread at school. But nothing offered, nothing gained.

"Just before the school year started, I was diagnosed with a type of bone cancer called multiple myeloma." He turned to look at Stacy to gauge his reaction.

Adams looked sincerely to Gus, "I am really sorry to hear that. What is the prognosis? Is there a cure? I have never heard of that type of cancer before."

Williams, stared directly into Adams' eyes, "No cure. I will have it until it kills me."

"Jesus! How long do you have?"

"Well, they are not sure," Williams said standing and moving to the next machine. The machine looked like the fly machine but the big foam arm pads were stuck in the middle already.

Stacy recognized the confusion, "This is a rear fly machine. You put your arms in front of you like you are going to block a punch, then swing them back like opening two doors at one time."

"Oh, thanks," Williams said pulling the pin and trying the machine with no weight.

"So, could you, like, live a long time with myeloma? Or is it like pancreatic or lung cancer that is pretty swift in the end of life timeline?"

"Well, like I said, they are not sure." Williams began doing the reverse flies as Adams started his overhead press. "I really have to eat well and exercise -- they recommended lifting weights -- but they put me on some treatment plan."

"Oh, okay," Adams said pulling the pin out of his machine to add more weight.

"It all depends on how my body reacts to the medicine and the food and everything else."

Williams slid over to the next machine while Adams finished his set and followed his mentor along the line.

"Okay, so tell me," Williams said changing the subject, "how many times do you do each machine?"

"Oh, well, right now I am doing a couple of sets and moving along to work with you."

"So, if I weren't here, what would you be doing?"

"Most of the time I do a full body circuit of straight sets."

"You know that is like speaking a foreign language to me, don't you?"

Adams chuckled.

"Teach me about lifting weights." Williams looked Adams in the eye, "Teach me as if my life depended on it." A short smile crept across his face.

"Ok," Adams said. "First you should warm up each muscle group. You can do that by light stretching and light lifting. I would suggest doing one set of fifteen repetitions at really light weight to warm up, then add a little more weight for twelve repetitions, then add more weight for eight reps, and if you are feeling really good and want to push yourself, add more weight and do six more reps."

"Wow, that seems like a lot for an old man."

"I wouldn't suggest doing that to start."

"What you are doing is just fine for now," Adams said sitting at the reverse fly machine. "Once you feel like your muscles are ready for more, then you can add more weight or more reps. You may want to do research on what is the best lifting program for your condition."

"Yeah, my condition," Williams said sitting down at the next machine. "Where the heck are the handles on this one?" he said looking around.

Adams chuckled again, "You have to sit backward on the seat. This one has you pull the handles back ..."

"...to work your back," they said in unison.

Little by little, Williams could see the defensive walls Stacy had built start to come down. If he could create the bonds of friendship with Adams, then maybe he could teach him how to connect with his students. Connecting with students was the key to successful teaching. If there was one thing Williams had learned about teaching in all his years that the textbooks, pedagogy, and curriculum books didn't tell, it was that a child wouldn't learn from someone they didn't like.

As Adams and Williams made their way through the machines, Williams was doing one set of twelve and Adams was doing two heavier sets, they started to tell their personal histories — the first binding conversation of true friendship. Friends were made in many different ways, but one of the most time-honored markers of building a friendship was sharing stories from the past. These stories bound individuals together like a shared memory.

"Well," Williams said sitting up from his last leg curl, "I think that will about do it for this old man. Thank you for helping me today."

"No problem," Stacy said moving over to sit on the leg curler. "It was nice getting to talk to you about things. I am sorry that you have to go through this whole cancer business."

"About that," Williams said getting serious, "I would like to keep that between us for right now. I haven't told anyone else."

"Oh, okay."

"I don't want any pity or questions or strange looks. And I certainly don't want any comments from the administration."

"No problem," Adams said. "If you need any help with a doctor's visit or medicine or anything, don't hesitate to ask."

"Thank you. I will be fine."

Back in the locker room, Williams' muscles were so sore that he had a hard time changing out of his clothes. The other men looked at him with odd expressions as he waddled completely naked to the shower stall, carrying his towel in one hand and shampoo in the other. This, he remembered, was what they were supposed to do after gym class, take a shower. The boys would slip off their shirts and shorts and walk to the group shower. There would be some snapping of towels, but mostly it would be a quick shower and then out to get ready for class.

Now it seemed that the men might not shower at all. They simply threw on a clean shirt and headed for the exits, probably to shower at home. For what? He thought, too shy? He was too old to be shy. They could look at his old wrinkly ass. He saw some of the men wrap clean towels around their waists and then head to the shower. Some only took off their tennis shoes before heading in fully clothed. Times have changed Williams thought, times have changed.

23

"Stacy?"

Gus leaned casually on the front door frame, hands in pockets.

"Yes, Mr. Williams," Stacy said putting down his pen on the desk and swiveling his office chair toward the door, hands clasped together in his lap. "What can I do for you today?"

"Well, I was wondering if you had given any thought to parent-teacher conferences on Wednesday and Thursday."

"No, not really," Adams said. "I simply plan to hand over the pre/post-test information and then share the grade sheet. It should be sufficient."

"That sounds like a good plan. Do you plan to show the parents that you know their child?"

Stacy squeezed his hands together, turning his knuckles white. "What do you mean, show that I know their child? Isn't explaining their growth as a student knowing their child?"

"Well, in a way," Gus said, "talking about their skills shows how attentive you are to their needs academically, but parents only see that as one thing. They also see their joy and pain and frustration. They see the whole child."

"The data shows whether or not the student is successful in class. I am not their counselor or their friend." Adams swiveled back to his papers. "The data should be enough."

It was now Williams' turn to move. He slid into a front row

desk, looking intently at Adams working. The dance had begun.

"Data is useful, but my personal experience and some research suggests that the most engaged students are the ones who feel connected to their school, classroom, and teacher."

"Yes, well, I know the research, we had a whole lecture on it at U of M. But I wasn't hired to be their friend, Mr. Williams. Or their parent. Or their big brother. I'm their English teacher, which was what I will talk about with them. Now if you don't mind, I must finish these papers."

Gus knew he had pushed too hard, crossed a line. Now he was being shut out after making such progress in getting to know Stacy. As much as he wanted to stay and talk more, Adams was certainly not prepared to listen any longer. Lingering would only create a festering resentment.

Back at his desk, Williams Googled "Parent Teacher Conference Tips" and found sixteen million results. The first four pages didn't have a lick of what he was looking for, something simple. Something well written. He knew what he wanted to say, so he clicked over to a word document, straightened his back, and began to type.

The words flew from his fingertips, filling the page with his thoughts on what parents really desired from conferences. When the bell rang and students filled the room, he was still attentive only to his computer and his writing. Only when the second bell signaled for class to begin did Williams look up from his screen.

Glasses perched on his nose, he stood, drawing the class's attention.

"We are going to have thirty minutes of reading time today to start, please begin now."

He returned to his desk, lost in the labyrinth of his writing. He started with the idea for writing tips to teachers about PTC, but then he remembered past conferences that proved his points. He wrote one example after another, each anecdote illustrating a point or teaching a lesson about handling different types of parents and situations.

How simple, he thought at first. Share a positive trait, show you know their child personally, and give them a focus for the next few months of school. Keep it simple. He was only going to jot a few ideas down, but now he was pages deep and wanted to keep going. As the thirty minutes set to expire, Williams told himself just a few more sentences, finish the paragraph. By the end of the hour, students had been milling about and talking for at least twenty minutes, but he didn't care, not today. He was enraptured. He had never felt like this before. Put it away, he thought. But no. Another class had thirty minutes to read.

By the end of the day, Williams had written nearly thirty pages of reflection. He saved it all to his Google Drive then clicked print. As the pages shot out of the printer, Williams couldn't believe his production.

Tapping his reflection, advice, and memories on the short edge, then on the long to straighten the pages, Williams looked at his work with a bit of satisfaction. It felt good to share all those thoughts and feelings. He pulled his thumb back across the edges, flipping the pages forward. All of this was his work. He smiled.

Back home, after a simple meal of grilled chicken, broccoli, and quinoa, Williams took out his thirty pages of writing. Spreading the pages out on the kitchen table, Williams saw only a mess of ideas. Here he was a teacher of English, a good one, and he did exactly what he told his students not to do, write without a plan. This, he thought, was a free-write. A game of association. One idea led on to the next and that idea linked to another idea and before he knew it, he was way off track. Now he had to sort it out.

"Darn it, Williams!" He said as he slapped his hands together then positioned them behind his head. The papers stayed on the table, waiting to be stacked or sorted or read or put away. Williams headed to his bedroom, changed into his sweatpants and a t-shirt before wrapping a cardigan around his shoulders.

Back in the kitchen, the tea kettle whistled. He poured a cup of vanilla chamomile tea. He set the steeping tea next to the papers sprawled out on the table. He began to read, marking the points where one story started and another ended. The pages began to arrange themselves into sections. He grabbed a pair of scissors, cutting pages in half, removing paragraphs like a surgeon removing a damaged organ. He took a sip of tea, then grabbed a pad of sticky notes. He wrote little notes here and there, marking points that needed more, pieces that were missing. By 10 pm, his tea was gone and his eyes were closing. He left the papers on the table for another day. On the way up the stairs he remembered Stacy. He needed to make another attempt at talking with him time before conferences. Williams had a feeling there was a storm coming.

In the morning, Williams was tired from his late night. Usually he was in bed reading by 8 pm unless he was helping at an event. Missing two hours of sleep was draining on a body wracked with cancer. However, he was back on his lesson plans. The writing would have to wait. After basically a free day the day before, the students were eager for more.

"More reading today, Mr. Williams?" Antonio asked.

"Always more reading," Williams smiled. "Always more. What are you reading? Must be pretty exciting."

"Well, I am reading about the main man, Phil Knight in *Shoe Dog*."

"The founder of Nike, a brilliant business man, I hear."

"Well, we shall see. I just picked it up last night from Schulers."

"Schulers? I used to go there all the time," Williams said crossing his arms. "Is that the one in Grand Rapids?"

"Yeah, that's the one," Antonio said flipping to his place in the book.

"What were you doing over there on a school night?"

"I had an AAU practice over on Beltline by the colleges. My

dad wanted to grab a coffee and a book to read while I was at practice, so we left early."

"Your dad still goes with you to practice?"

"Yeah, he likes to watch and sometimes he says the sound of practice makes him comfortable, it fills him up," Antonio said putting up his fingers in air quotes.

"Well, we all have the things that drive us and we have things that comfort us."

"I guess," Antonio said hanging his head down.

"Antonio," Williams said dipping his head down to make eye contact. "Cherish the time you have with your father because next year you will be off to college and he won't be there anymore and you won't be there for him."

"Yeah, you're right, Mr. Williams," Antonio said. "You're spouting wisdom like Yoda, as usual."

To Williams, Antonio's choice to go to a bookstore to purchase a book that fed his interest was what he hoped and worked for every day. Williams kept his reading time sacred. Administrators and colleagues had balked over his fifteen minutes a day for independent reading. Some students came to class with never having read an adult or young adult novel on their own. Instead, every book had been directed by a teacher or a parent. Many left with renewed interest or at least a respect for reading. He knew from experience that sometimes finding a book was hard, especially for a non-reader. A reader who wasn't on level or was slower than others avoided reading like a bad chore. But he kept pushing the students to find their genre, their book.

He had his own reading drought in 1997. He had just finished *Gravity's Rainbow* by Thomas Pynchon, and he was tired of reading. He worked his way through the book, losing his place before finding the narrative again. He had read how *Gravity's Rainbow* was nominated for a Pulitzer but then turned down by the committee for being "turgid" and "unreadable." He thought that if a book was supposed to be the best book of the year, but then dismissed as "unreadable," what was the point of reading great books? In fact, the committee didn't even offer an award that year, so he stopped reading fiction for six months.

In that time, he worked in his garden and went on long hikes. He brought along poetry and magazines. He played with the new technology called the internet, where he could read about so many things.

Then came the publication of the Harry Potter books. He wasn't drawn in by the boy protagonist, who he envisioned looked just like Danny, although that helped, but the fantastic world of fantasy brought down to a playful level while maintaining the complexities of real life. The trope of good against evil was as old as time itself, but in this set of books, evil grew as did the boy. At each stage of his life, Harry Potter would have to defeat evil. While the book was complete fantasy, it also mimicked real life.

Each year Williams would preorder the next installment of Harry Potter. As popularity grew, the release parties grew more elaborate. The stores would be packed at midnight with children and teens and adults dressed in house robes, fashioning homemade wands, and pretending to fling spells at one another as they waited in line. Williams enjoyed the spectacle. Entire bookstores were alive with witches and wizards, barely able to contain their excitement, like an Obscurial ready to come undone. Williams enjoyed it all. He would walk to the bookstore cafe, order a hot tea, then find a corner table with a full view of the cashier's line, where the new books were being handed out upon purchase. He watched as the sleepy eyes all of a sudden grew bright with wonder. As he finished his tea, the line would die down and Williams would take his place among those waiting for their pre-ordered copies. After a long night of sleep, Williams would make himself a pot of coffee, recline in his reading chair, and read from start to finish.

His coffee would grow cold on the side table; he would be lost in the pages. Once the films started to be made, kids filled the theaters the same way they had filled the bookstores. Now the movies were all the kids knew. When he asks a student if they have read Harry Potter, they say, "No, but the movies are great!" He always replied, "Try the books, they are even better."

J.K. Rowling kickstarted his love of reading again, like she did for so many others. For this, he's forever grateful. On a shelf sits the first edition of each Harry Potter novel, read only once, along with a handmade replica of the Elder Wand. He couldn't resist buying the wand when he saw it at a craft fair in downtown Wellington.

24

As the bell signaled the end of class, Williams decided to make another run at Adams and his approach to conferences. "Stacy?" Williams said coming through the door, "I would like to ask you a couple of more questions."

"About parent-teacher conferences?" Adams interrupted.

"Yes."

"Mr. Williams," Stacy said adding an air of formality, "we have been over this. I am fine with my grade sheet and test data."

"Yes, I know you are," Gus said taking a seat at a desk in the front row. "I think what you are offering the parents is very valuable, but …"

"But what?"

"I know you are not happy with my constant suggestions, but hear me out," William said holding up his hands like they contained an idea. "Many of the parents that come to conferences are well aware of their child's ability and work ethic. Your data will only confirm what they already know."

"And this is a problem how?" Stacy said, brow furrowed. "I don't understand what you are getting at here."

"What will you say when the parent says they aren't worried about their child's grades and asks how they are doing? When they ask you if you know what they are reading? Or if they talk about their band concert? Or their basketball game? Or their robotic competition? What will you say?"

"I am not sure what those things have to do with me. I teach the students English, reading, and writing."

Williams stood up, "No, you don't." He started to pace. "You teach students, young people. Adolescents that couldn't care less about your theory or canon or essay prompts. Because they are more concerned about their appearance, their relationships with others, whether someone will laugh at them or with them. They worry if they will get mocked on for wearing the new style of pants or complemented. If Jimmy or Johnny or Jane or Julie likes them. Or maybe they need to tell someone that every night their parents are screaming at each other, fighting over money or infidelity or nothing at all. Or maybe they are too worried about their friend who is cutting or the friend who is really into pills or smoking. They wonder if they should go to the big party this weekend, where they can drink all night. In their existence, Stacy, you can either be a problem center or a safe haven. And the work you covet so much is just something they have to do. They couldn't care less about the assignment or your data. So, when a parent asks how their child is doing, they not only mean academically, but emotionally as well."

Stacy watched Williams make his way to the door. Then before he moved out into the quiet empty hall, Williams turned. "Just think about it."

Wednesday afternoon, two folding chairs sat next to each doorway. The principal stood at the front office greeting parents, the library doors were open for a small book fair, and the Spanish Club's concession stand was selling snacks to raise money for their upcoming trip to Spain. The volleyball team was in a full practice session, with the music pumping and the girls screaming. The teachers were all in their rooms, organizing student grade sheets and arranging a conference spot for parents.

Williams sat behind his desk, adjusting the volume on his computer so a soft murmur of classical music filled the room. He set his cup of tea on the table and worked his way through the writing samples for his scheduled conferences that night. He had a grade sheet too, but he knew that he probably wouldn't reference it. The parents enjoyed the student work more than the numbers.

Across the hall, Stacy Adams had three pages of data for each parent. He sat behind his desk and had two student desks arranged in front for parents. There was no question who appeared to be in charge. He wore a grey pinstripe suit with a white shirt and a green patterned tie to match the school colors. Williams, in contrast, was in everyday khakis and a thick fall sweater.

The halls sat empty, a calm before the storm. Then the slow murmur of voices drifted up from the first floor. Then parental voices became clear as they rounded the stairwell, looking for their first appointment. The teachers appeared outside their doorways, like candles appearing in windows at nightfall. Then one by one they disappeared back into their room followed by one, two, or three parents. Students sometimes followed behind, sometimes younger siblings sat through conference after conference. The only rule for conferences was the ten-minute time limit. No matter if the parents had more to say, they only got ten minutes. If more needed to be said, they would have to make a follow-up appointment.

One parent after another, like an assembly line. There would never be a line stretching down the hall nor a queue of parents waiting. In Williams' experience, a long line meant the teacher was having problems with the whole class, either with behavior or grades. In the old days, the teachers would sit side by side in the gymnasium and parents would mill about, talking to whichever teacher was free at the moment. Now, each parent scheduled ten minutes with the teachers of their choice. Williams wondered when the world became so scheduled.

25

Williams shook hands and sent a parent off down the hall to their next appointment. No issues for him tonight. He had a lull in the action, twenty minutes until his next appointment, the luxury of having senior laden classes. He heard the loud voice of a father coming from Stacy's room, "She works every night for your class, hours. Writing and rewriting. It's ridiculous her grade isn't better. I would like to know why her grade isn't better, does she do something wrong? Goof around in class? Not follow directions? Have several errors in her work? What?"

Williams slid over next to Stacy's door and had a seat in the folding chair.

"Mr. Montana. I am sure your daughter works very hard at home," he heard Stacy telling the father. "The grade is not based on her production but the quality of her work. Her writing is just not 'A' level writing. If you look at the data …"

"I don't want to look at the damn data!"

Williams shifted ever so slightly to see into the room. He took out his phone, pretending to check his notifications, so he could watch the interaction out of the corner of his eye.

"... I want to know what you are doing so that she can feel successful in your class. If she doesn't feel like all her effort is making a difference, she will be crushed. And besides ..." Mr. Montana's finger-pointed at Stacy, "... she has always received

As for her work. This, this right here, is bullshit!"

"I'm sorry, Mr. Montana, you feel she is not seeing the results of her efforts. Sometimes working harder isn't the answer, but working smarter."

Mr. Montana launched out of his seat, hands slamming down on Adam's desk. "Don't get fucking smart with me! I don't think you know what the hell you are doing!"

At this, Williams made his move, out of his chair and into the room toward Stacy's desk.

"Mr. Montana, how are you doing this fine evening? The demolition business going well this year?"

"Gus." Montana turned to nod in Williams' direction. "Business is good because I know what I am doing unlike this little punk kid here." Mr. Montana motions toward Adams. "Will you tell him how to do his goddamn job? He wants to shove all this data crap into my face. I am about to stick it so far up his ass that he won't be able to see anything but numbers."

Williams held back a small smile at the data comment, then looked to Adams who seemed ready to explode. Diffuse and remove, Williams remembered from some training.

"Tony, it seems like you are really frustrated with Mr. Adams," Williams said moving in between the two. "How about you and I go across the hall for a few minutes? Maybe we can sort some things out."

Tony snatched the data papers from where he was sitting and stormed across the hall. The tension was palpable. Williams stepped to the side, making a barrier in front of Stacy in case Tony came storming back. Williams watched as Mr. Montana went into his classroom, then turned to Stacy.

But before Williams could say a word, Stacy blurted, "That guy is out of control. I am calling the principal."

Williams held up his hand up, "I wouldn't make a big stink out of this. Mr. Montana is a good man. He can get kind of intense when he feels threatened or cornered."

"He's feeling threatened?" Stacy said flopping back into his chair. "I feel a little threatened right now."

"You have to remember," Williams said leaning against the desk, "he is only reacting this way because of the way his daughter is feeling about your class. Her emotional distress goes right to her parents. This is the same for all families."

"It is just school work. The data shows her grade exactly where it should be for her ability."

"According to whose standards?" Williams said pushing his thumb down on his palm. "This is English class, not math or science. This is the most subjective curriculum in the system. Did you ever stop to think you are putting the bar too high? They are not college students. And they are not one dimensional."

"What am I supposed to do, give them all As?"

"No, you are supposed to teach them so they can earn an A. This isn't about you or the curriculum, but the student. Each unique one."

"There has to be a standard, a baseline. I just can't be willy-nilly."

"If every student grows from the beginning of the year to the end, shouldn't that count? Shouldn't that equal an A?"

Williams turned to leave, feeling heated. At the door he turned, "Teaching is an art not a science. Keep trying to reach kids, meet them where they are, and help them gain more knowledge. It is never about the curriculum or the grade but their belief. If they believe in you, they will work their asses off for you without complaint. But you have to show them it means something to you. You have to give back."

Williams left Stacy alone for a few minutes until his next conference and sauntered over to his room where Mr. Montana was waiting. He wondered if the talk would have any effect on Stacy.

26

Parent-teacher conferences were always a little blip in the teacher's fall calendar. The extra hours and the face to face with parents made for a few long days. Even more so for the coaches in the building who had to teach, then coach, then return back to the school for three or four hours of conference time. Conferences also provided some staff team-building opportunities as they usually patronized a local bar afterward to trade stories about parents and let off some stress from the long work week. Lately, some of Williams' colleagues had been complaining how times had changed.

"It used to be that parents would come to see the teacher and if their kid was being a little turd in class, then the parent would go home and whip that kid into shape. Now, now, the parent stays right at school and tries to whip the teacher into shape. It's hard to stomach," Walters said sipping on a pint of Walter Gets Buzzed, a locally brewed beer that had nothing to do with Walters except that he drank it and then talked even more than normal.

"Well, I don't know, Ken," Gus said sipping on his Diet Coke, "Parents have always been protective of their children."

"Right, but don't you think that now more than ever before parents are looking to pin the blame on the teacher?"

"I think parents are more willing to see both sides of the story.

Think about it," Gus said. "Adults are no longer the authority figure by default. The new generation of parents have grown up told to question authority, so their children in turn question authority. Parent-teacher conferences are a way for those parents to question the authority for their children."

"It's just a mess."

"Well, I think it also makes teachers and administrators think about how they do things and how they treat people."

"True," Walters said sipping on his pint. "I would just like to feel a little more support from the community."

Pete Jorgmander walked up with a dark pint in his hand. "C'mon now, Ken," he said flicking him in the shoulder with the back of his hand. "We have it pretty good at North Wellington. Think about those poor bastards down in Wellington proper. They are getting screamed at by some ignorant sons-a-bitches all the time and then, and then, they have to worry about getting shot on the way to parking lot. It's like the wild west down there."

"No kidding," Gus said. "It seems like there is another report of shots fired each week."

"War zone. I don't even go down there anymore."

"I just go when I get my treatment," Gus said.

"Oh, yeah?" Pete said turning to Gus. "What are you getting treatment for, are you okay?"

Williams panicked a little, he had let his guard down, "Old age I think," he said laughing. "Speaking of parents getting hot. I had to calm down Mr. Montana tonight."

"Oh, was that who was yelling?" Ken asked "I heard a little bit all the way down the hall."

"What happened?" Pete asked, "I thought you and Montana were old buddies."

"He wasn't upset with me but with Adams."

"Jesus, is that kid here?"

"No, he wouldn't come out, said he was tired."

"Bullshit."

"What was Tony upset with him for? Adams better watch his ass. Tony is not one to mess with, fucking guy will put your body in the cement crusher and there will be nothing left."

"C'mon," Gus said laughing. "Tony isn't a gangster."

"Right, well," Ken said, "I'm not taking any chances."

A smile left Pete's face. "Is this something we are going to have to worry about? Unionwise, I mean."

"I don't think there is anything the union can do for Stacy anyway," Gus said sipping on his Coke. "He doesn't have the same protections that we have because he's not tenured."

"No, admin still has to follow the guidelines of our contract."

"Yes, I know, but they can can his ass whenever for no reason."

"True," Pete said looking a little less stressed. "So what did the kid do?"

"He just sat there and took it."

"No," Ken asked, "what did he do to make Montana so mad?"

"His expectations are way too high."

"Classic first year teacher," Walters said holding up his empty glass. "Either too high or too low."

"Speaking of the union," Gus said, "any word on negotiations?"

"Mums the word," Pete said. "We are dealing with a lot of bullshit right now from the state. We should be starting very soon here."

Walters was handed another full pint, "I need to go talk to a man about a horse."

"Alright, see you, Pete," Gus said backing up. Just then he felt a bump from behind and heard some jingling. He turned to see the choir teacher, Sarah Bilikin, a rather jolly, plump woman, making some dancing motions. She was always singing or humming a tune. If she was silent for a moment, the bangles around her wrist continue to jingle and jangle, making their own song. She seemed to be well in her cups.

"Hi, Sarah."

"Oh, hi, Gus," she said. "Sorry to bump into you."

"No problem. How were your conferences this fall?"

"Lovely," she said, "like a song." Then she let out a full note that drew some looks from the other staff members in the bar.

"That's great," Gus said chuckling.

"How were yours?" She asked placing a hand on his arm.

"Mine went just fine, thank you," Gus said stepping to the side, making it hard for her to hold his arm. "And your year is off to a good start I take it."

"Oh, yes," she said stepping closer. "We are about to start work on the Pops concert. It is going to be a-maaazzzing," she said singing the final line. "You want to know something?"

Gus was in uncharted territory. He hadn't really had many long conversations with Sarah and had never been in her presence when she'd had a few drinks. "Sure, Sarah, what's the news?"

"When I was in high school," she said with a slight hiccup, "I had the biggest crush on you."

"Stop it," Gus said blushing, "really."

"Oh, yes," she said putting her hand on his chest. "We used to walk by your room all the time to peek inside to see what Mr. Williams was doing."

"I had no clue."

"When we got the yearbook, we would pin the page so we could flip right to your picture."

It was Williams turn to feel a little flushed, "I don't know what to say. That makes me feel sorta special."

"Well, it should," she said with another slight hiccup. "You are a special man."

"Thank you," Gus said. "Are you all right?"

"Oh, my dear heavens," she said holding her hand to her cheek, "I think I am a little drunk." And then she stated to giggle.

Williams chuckled, "Yes, you may be on your last round."

"Oh, well, dear me. I am embarrassing myself."

"No, no," Williams said. "What you said takes courage."

"I have been a chicken, Gus, really. And all of sudden I feel sober as can be. But I know I can't finish this wine." Sarah held on to Gus' arm as she set the wine down on the bar, half of the Chardonnay still rested in the glass. She looked up to Gus, eyes full of emotion, "I have always thought you were a good man, Gus. Maybe, when you are ready, we can go have some coffee or a drink."

She left Gus standing at the bar, stunned. Teachers were dropping their empty pints on the bar. He put his Coke on the counter next to Sarah's wine. *When you are ready*? she said. Has it been that obvious to everyone else?

He followed the crowd out the front door into the brisk fall night. Leaves scattered through the parking lot pushed by an invisible wind, while the strong unwavering headlights lead the way home.

27

The coach yelled, "Help! Help!....You've got to help on the drive."

Williams sat back against the bleacher chair taking in his first middle school basketball game in years. The athletic director came to him last minute to help run the clock because the parent volunteer called to cancel just as the final school bell sounded. Williams was walking down the hall, ready to take a much needed rest, when Stuart Jefferies asked him for a favor. Williams couldn't say no.

On more than one occasion when Williams was supporting his share of the bourbon industry, Stuart's father, Marion Jefferies, grabbed him from the stands during football games. He would get Williams to sit in the press box with a paper for taking stats. Williams would get focused, the loud crass language would dissipate, and then before he knew it, the game was over and he was finding the sober end of the night. Or when Williams tried to pull a Shooter Flatch by walking out on the floor full of booze and belligerence at a basketball game, Marion always guided him to the athletic office for a cup of cold water or a hot cup of coffee. Then Marion would sneak him out the back door, where no students or parents or administrators would see him struggling to stand upright or speak clearly. On the short drive home, Marion would talk college basketball with Williams, particularly about a game that was playing on television that evening, hoping Williams would get excited about watching it and stay in his house for the night. Little did Marion know that Williams had destroyed his TV long before.

After dumping Williams at home, Marion would return to the school to finish his job at the game. And so went the five seasons of William's fandom under the influence. When Stuart took over for his father, he never pretended to know Williams' secrets or tried to use them as blackmail for helping out at athletic events. He simply asked when he needed help and Williams always said, "yes."

At today's game the North Wellington Warriors were hosting the Oakview Falcons. A town from just down the road, but drastically different. The hard-working families from Oakview were salt-of-the-earth type of people. Their hands were calloused and their bodies were muscled from manual labor. Their children would work alongside their parents in the summer and on weekends: landscaping, farming, construction, or machine shop work. The boys of Oakview became strong young men. They ruled the football field as perennial playoff and state champion contenders.

In basketball, North Wellington held their own with the best in their league. The program was strong all the way through the grades. As young as third grade, parents would start fielding teams to ensure their sons would be able to make the varsity in eight years. The varsity players would go to local colleges, continuing their sports dreams.

The buzzer sounded, signaling the end of the first quarter. Williams reset the score. North Wellington and the Lakeshore League ran a special quarter system for their middle school games where the winner of each of the first two quarters received two points to start the second half. The rules allowed coaches to play all players in the first half in order to develop skills and give all kids a good experience.

The second quarter began with Oakview running a press

against a more inexperienced line-up of Warrior players and quickly extended the lead by eight points before Frank Pearl, the North Wellington coach, called a time-out. Williams hoped he would let those kids figure out the game a little for themselves instead of bailing them out by playing the big guns. In the long run, the right call here would benefit the team— even if it meant losing the quarter.

Williams watched as Coach Pearl pulled out his whiteboard, "Listen boys, don't panic. Remember what we practiced yesterday."

The boys nodded their heads in agreement.

"Look at the board now. Tony and Jeremy, you are running a pick and roll to get open. Q, you are taking the ball out. Snap those passes. Sam and Wade, you are at half-court. Flash forward, Sam or Wade, to the middle if Tony and Jeremy don't get the ball."

The players nodded.

"Once we inbound, the opposite player, Sam or Wade, flashes to the middle of the floor. Then run your lanes. You can do this!" Pearl looked at them with fire in his eyes. "Well, can you do this?" he shouted.

"Yes, Coach!" The players shouted in unison.

"You have three minutes left in your rotation. Make the most of it."

The players shoved their fists toward the center of the huddle. "Team on 3, Family on 6!" Tony shouted. "1, 2, 3," he said.

"Team!" the players shouted in unison.

"4, 5, 6!"

"Family!"

Williams smiled as he smashed the buzzer to signal the end of the time out. Coach Pearl was letting them learn. That was a tough call for a coach to make. Parents may not quite understand, but youth basketball is about learning and that is what the special quarter system is all about. Paul turned toward Williams, puffing out his lips and running his hand through his hair.

"That's the right call, Coach," Williams said smashing the buzzer again to signal the start of play.

"Thanks, Coach," Pearl said. "I learned from one of the best."

Williams smiled, "I had my moments, but you must be thinking of someone else."

On the court Tony and Jeremy executed a pick and roll, the ball went in to Jeremy. Wade flashed to the middle to receive the pass. He pivoted to see Tony streaking down the opposite sideline. Sam was setting up on the block. His defender came off the post to stop the ball. Tony dropped a soft pass to Sam for a layup.

The boys on the bench shouted at the successful press break. After an Oakview turnover, the boys broke the press again, cutting the lead to four points. Tony decided to pick up his defense at three-quarter court. Oakview was not quite ready for the pressure and had no one back to help. As the ball reached half-court, the Oakview point guard dribbled out of control. Tony reached for the ball, knocking it loose. He was first to the ball and heading for the basket with a full head of steam. As he went up for a layup, the Oakview player tried to climb up his back for a block, sending Tony to the floor. Whistle. Foul. The crowd erupted as the ball spun around the rim and fell in. An and-one opportunity. His teammates ran to his aid, yanking him from the floor, patting him on the back, and bumping him with their chests.

The Wellington subs lined the scorer's table. Tony sunk the foul shot to give himself a three-point play and brought his team to within one point in the quarter. The subbing players all slapped high-fives as they came into the game. The second team now knew that they could play with anybody and win. Instilling confidence and teaching content was what middle school was all about.

When the buzzer signaled the end of the first-half of action, Williams stood to stretch his legs. The bleachers were not kind to his knees. He took a few wobbly steps before they loosened up and felt good again.

The referees jogged over to the scorer's table, placing the game ball by the clock.

"Did you switch the arrow, Gus?"

"Nope, that's all you, Randy."

"Ok, arrow switched. Oakview ball to start. Please put eight minutes on the clock for halftime."

Gus ambled over, punched the time on the clock and flipped the switch, "Got it. See you in a few minutes."

Some of the younger students found the extra basketballs and had taken control of one end of the court. Williams thought of Danny, just learning about the game before the accident. Williams would teach him games like Pig and Around the World. He would try to teach him and his friends to play Lightning and 21. Danny was just a couple of years away from organized basketball. Williams had been thinking it was time to organize a team, a team he could coach for fun, to not worry about winning and losing, but they didn't have out-of-season leagues then. Youth sports had yet to be turned into big business.

Williams could see Danny now, his hair drifting to one side as he pushed the ball up the court, the pull-up jump shot. His big awkward feet sliding around on defense. A block in the post. A steal on the wing. A dagger of a three-pointer. A long outlet pass for a layup.

A ball came careening off the rim toward Williams. He bent down to retrieve it for the boy hustling behind it.

"Here you go, Danny," Gus said. "Keep practicing, those shots will start falling."

The boy grabbed the ball, "Thanks, mister, but my name ain't Danny. It's Jerry."

The horn sounded, signaling the end of halftime. Williams snapped out of his reverie. He shook his head as he climbed back to his spot behind the scorer's table. The idea of calling that boy Danny lingered in his mind for the rest of the game, pestering him like a bad mistake.

The second half didn't bode well for Oakview. The starting group quickly jumped to a 16-2 lead on the back of their pressing defense. By the fourth quarter, up 32-6, Coach Pearl was subbing at will. The eleventh and twelfth guys were getting as much time as the starters. The starting five were working to get shots for the players who rarely got to play in tight games; some hadn't scored all year. Now was their chance, so each offense set was designed to get a shot for the twelfth man.

Pete hadn't scored all year. He was big but slow and his coordination really hadn't caught up with his size. Q drove the lane past his defender, Pete's defender came off to help. Q flipped Pete the ball on the block. Pete, keeping the ball above his head like he had been taught, shot the ball high off the glass, where it bounced once then twice on the rim before falling into the net. The crowd and the players erupted in cheers. Williams laughed, enjoying the excitement. The buzzer sounded and the team surrounded Pete as if he had just won the game with a last second shot.

Williams knew that basketball teams everywhere else weren't like teams at North Wellington. One reason he loved working at the school was because the students, for the most part, built each other up instead of tearing each other down. What a great feeling for Pete and the whole team.

Williams flipped the power switch on the scoreboard, bundled the cords with care, and placed the entire unit in the hard plastic briefcase. Williams delivered the case to the athletic director's office and then headed home for the evening. He was exhausted from his medicine and his cancer and his old age. The mistake of calling that boy Danny had shaken him a little. His mind wandered to the moments with his son. The laughing, rolling on the floor in a fit of tickles. The exuberance from hitting a trick shot — the granny shot or the behind the backboard shot — to the sweet talks lying in bed at night answering all of the day's unanswered questions. As Williams walked from the school, he could see Danny running across the playground, "Dad, can we stay for just a little bit? Come watch me on the monkey bars."

His breath left him as he reached his old Focus. He fell into the driver's seat gasping for air. The phone fumbled from his hand to the floor. He reached down to retrieve it but fell back gasping. His first thought was *this is it*. But seconds passed, then minutes. His breathing returned to normal. He had no pain in his chest or his arms. He knew he wasn't dying. A new form of anguish, despair, crept into his thoughts. His body was tense, clenched like a fist. He let out a deep breath, and then another. He let his head rest against the back of the seat. The playground sat empty. All life had fled from its borders. Tomorrow it would return. But not for Williams. He couldn't get his life back in the same way the playground got new life every day. No children. No wife. He could have remarried. No, he couldn't. His heart wouldn't let him. Always, just like now, his heart made him remember the pain of losing the ones he had loved the most.

The headlights from cars flashed past, showing a glimpse of Williams staring off into the night. In his mind he was watching Danny on the court. He would be grown now, out of college, possibly with his own family. But those memories had never been made. He would wait for his grandson to be a Wellington Warrior. Williams waited. He could wait all night, living in his dreams, living the life he so desperately wanted. He had been doing it for twenty-five years.

A knock on his window shook him from his visions. A high-pitched voice called out. "Mr. Williams! Are you all right?" The pounding intensified. "Mr. Williams! I am going to call an ambulance! Are you all right? Can you unlock the door?"

Williams turned to see Sarah Bilikin. She rapped on the window one more time with her fist, bracelets clacking against the glass. "Can you unlock the door?" She yelled exaggerating her words as if the car window was soundproof. "Okay, turn your face. I am going to break the glass to get you out."

Williams watched as she pulled some sort of gadget out of her handbag. He recognized it as one of those emergency car tools with a seatbelt cutter and a spike for breaking glass. She turned her face away and was about to swing when Williams realized she was really going to smash his window. He snapped out of his delirium. "Wait, Sarah! I am fine!" He yelled. Shit. He popped the door open, banging it into her backside.

"Oh! My goodness, Gus! You scared me half to death. I thought you were dying in your car," Sarah said dropping the tool into one of her totes.

"No, no. I am ok. I was just doing a little daydreaming is all," he said stepping out from his car. "I was at the basketball game and then I came out here to go home, but I guess I closed my eyes for a moment and went right to sleep. I will be on my way home now. Thanks for waking me."

Sarah eyed him with concern. "Are you sure? I don't usually see people sleep with their eyes open."

"Yes, I had just sort of come out of my slumber when you arrived," Williams said continuing the small fib.

"Well, I would be happy to follow you home, Gus," she said smiling. "I don't mind. I could stay with you for a moment in case you have another episode." She reached out touching his arm.

He remembered the conversation from after conferences. "That is very kind of you," he said. "I, uh, don't think I will have another episode. All rested. Thank you for asking, however. I appreciate your concern."

"No problem," she said. "If you are ever here late and something feels off, shoot me a text. I am usually here in the afternoons giving lessons or having evening adult choir practice. My number is on the staff list."

Bilikin turned with her bags toward her car, bracelets strangely in tune with her humming. She certainly was the living embodiment of a music teacher, filling life with beautiful sounds.

"Thank you," Williams said. "I will."

She turned, giving Williams a wave and small smile.

The short drive home had Williams contemplating so many things. Maybe it was time to return to his long time counselor. This new episode had shaken him, but then again, he didn't know how much time he had left to get things right.

28

After homecoming, the days passed quickly, like a tumbling rock cascading down a mountain. The kids saw an end to football and volleyball and then the coming of basketball season. The school play always fell between the sports seasons, garnering more patrons since there weren't any sporting events vying for attention. Thanksgiving offered a couple of days off from school near the end of the month. Then basketball games bounced the students into the holiday break and took them out of it again.

The beginning of November was also when students began to tire of school work. Their work ethic started to slip, their focus shifted as the routines became stale. This was when Williams changed the lesson plans, shifting to lighter fare — speeches, presentations, and fewer tests and formal essays. The students continued to work with the lighter load, not skipping a beat. However, across the hall, Adams still had the pedal to the floor with quiz after quiz, essay after essay, and test after test. Wash, rinse, repeat.

Coming into Thanksgiving week, Williams provided three days of simple daily assignments. Nothing a student couldn't miss if their family left town early, which was often the case in North Wellington.

"Stacy, what are you doing in class next week?" Williams

asked striding into Adams' room.

Stacy looked up from his desk and the stacks of papers. He returned to make a final mark on the topmost paper then turned back to Williams.

"We are doing a mini-unit looking at Native American and Puritan writings around the time of the first great feast. The culmination assignment is a short essay-style test on Wednesday. I thought it would be a great time for the students to make these connections."

"Well, I think you are right about the opportune time for the lesson, but do you think the students are in a position to do well on your essay test the day before break? Their first big break of the school year?" Williams moved from the door to the desk in the front row, taking a less authoritative position.

"They should be able to do school work in school. If we aren't teaching them, why are they here?" Stacy picked up a stack of papers in a file folder then tapped the edges on the desk to straighten them. He then moved the folder to the side, making room for the next, which he placed in the center of his desk blotter and opened.

"What are you grading?" Williams asked.

"These are papers analyzing themes in *The Scarlet Letter*. They had to write them in class today. Each essay had to cover one theme, one symbol, and analyze one passage that I supplied."

"Jesus!" Williams blurted. "And you want them to write more essays in three more days?" He stood, running his hand through his white hair. "You are going to burn yourself out, kid. The school year isn't a sprint, it's a marathon."

Williams moved toward the door, taking his steps slowly, for his hips had been bothering him. Adams began to grade his essays, but turned as Williams stepped out into the hall, "You know, Gus."

Williams turned, "What's that?"

"The best marathon runners sprint the whole race."

Williams turned back to the hall then paused for a moment to look back at Stacy, "You are correct, Stacy. But those are professionals, most of our kids jog or walk a 5k when it comes to writing." Williams threw a slight wave in the air then headed to his room across the hall.

The weekend was calling and so was the final book in the *Game of Thrones* series. George R.R. Martin shocked his fans by actually finishing the series. Being a teacher, Williams knew full well the effort and work that it took to write a novel. And writing such large, detailed books like the *Game of Thrones* series certainly would have its challenges. He had been patient and confident that one of his favorite modern writers had pulled through. He had been ecstatic when he heard the final installment was coming out. This weekend his preordered copy should be in at Barnes & Noble. Williams always liked to hit up the local book stores, even if it was a chain, as long as they had good coffee. There was no use trying to browse the stacks while suffering through a terrible cup of joe.

If Williams was a stickler about anything it was a good cup of coffee.

29

Williams maneuvered his car out from between the well-manicured homes and side streets. As he turned to cross over from North Wellington to Wellington proper, he could see the small changes happening. The cars became a little older, a little more worn out than those in the driveways next to his home. The landscaping around the houses became more haphazard and less of a point of pride. The homes themselves showed more distress than the ones he could see from his windows.

On the highway, Williams saw the basic tenets of a strip mall city. Each major exit saw two jagged streets reaching out east and west. Both directions were buffeted by one long row of stores, each anchored by a superstore: Walmart, Sam's Club, Lowes, Target. Or the exit dropped off into a turgid industrial park, where children road their bikes around parked semi-trucks on their way to convenience store with barred windows. Over the years Williams had witnessed Wellington moving away from manufacturing as its base to that of tourism and small business. The great port city used to be a major hub for lumber back in the 1800s, then as a port for its paper mill and foundry and textiles. Now the port was only good for dropping large loads of salt to cover the roads during the short Michigan winters.

Williams, like most other long-time residents, had initially been distressed about the closing of so many businesses that had provided the structure of Wellington for years. As the lean, empty years started to pass into the present, families chose to visit Wellington for vacation and more residents decided to stay and invest their time in Wellington. Eventually, a richer existence started to take hold for residents. The town was transforming.

The biggest bookstore in the area, however, was a Barnes & Noble, near the vacant shopping mall that was slowing becoming an eyesore. As online shopping took over, the anchoring stores had to shutter their support of the mall. Now the once proud gem that had provided Wellington residents and the surrounding community with a place to shop without driving to the bustling city of Grand Rapids, was nothing more than an indoor track for senior citizens.

The brisk November wind cut through Williams as he stepped from his Taurus. Maybe retirement to the South would be in order, he thought. As he walked through the scattered cars in the parking lot, he noticed a large black Escalade with darkly tinted windows idling in an empty row of parking spaces. Williams thought it unusual, but dismissed it as he stepped into the wood-paneled entryway stacked with clearance books. The smell of fresh coffee being brewed, the sharp hisses of frothing milk, and the soft chatter in the cafe drew all of his attention.

Williams ordered a tall coffee. He had been so drained of energy lately from his medicine that a coffee at 4 pm only meant that he would be more alert on the drive home. He would fall into an exhausted sleep tonight when he got home; something that wouldn't have happened just a few months ago. Just one more week was left of his treatment before being rechecked. He couldn't have been happier with how the medicine affected his daily life. He felt drained and that was all. For a guy in his sixties with no responsibilities but himself, he was able to rest when he wanted and to take time from school when he needed.

Williams wandered through the store with his coffee. He always liked to stop at the Buy- 2-Get-1-Free paperback table.

Often times he would find some of the former hardcover best sellers on the table or some older books that had slipped his gaze. Then he would browse the best seller and new releases shelves. He also liked to read the staff recommendations. He would read each tag, flip through the recommendations wondering if the reader's opinion would be the same as his own. When he finished, he wound his way through the discount section past the self-help shelves and into the history section before finding himself staring at the rather small travel section. Even though this small section of the store had probably been visited less and less since all the maps and tourist information could be found online, the store still kept a small table and two chairs ready for anyone who wanted to peruse a book of maps.

Williams found himself standing shoulder to shoulder with a dark-haired woman with sharp features dressed in what Gus could only imagine was a very expensive suit. He wasn't used to seeing someone dressed in such a manner at Barnes & Noble. She had taken great care to keep her age from showing through her features. Williams could see she was closer to his age than maybe she would want to admit.

"Good afternoon," Williams said reaching out for a Bill Bryson book, *Notes from a Small Island*. He set his coffee down on the ledge where he had pulled the book.

"Good afternoon," came the reply. "Are you planning on visiting Great Britain?"

Williams looked a little shocked by her comment, "How did you know I was thinking about visiting England?"

"Your book," she said pointing at *Notes from a Small Island*. "Bryson lived in Britain for many years."

"Yes, I suppose that did give it away," Williams said studying the woman. "And where are you planning to visit?"

"I think it is time to visit Africa," she said facing Williams directly. "Have you ever been?"

"No," Williams said chuckling. "I haven't been much out of Michigan in a long time, much less to Africa."

"So, your trip to Europe is a big event," she said.

"Yes, I suppose it would be," Williams said sitting down at the table.

Williams watched as the woman turned to look at the shelves. She didn't pull a book from the shelf nor did she step close to run her fingers along the spines to examine each title more closely. What was she looking for he wondered? He continued to flip through Bryson's book.

Then she pulled a large atlas of Africa from the shelf, along with a small volume on Kilimanjaro. She set both down on the table, took a small glasses case from her purse, removed the slim elegant frames, placed them upon her nose, and sat on the edge of the chair with her back as straight as a board. Williams watched from the corner of his eye as she used the table of contents to find the pages she desired. She sat looking over both of the books.

Williams returned his book to the shelf, retrieving his coffee. "Thinking about hiking Mount Kilimanjaro?" he asked sitting down in the chair opposite the focused woman.

"I think it is time," she said.

"Just like that," Williams said snapping his fingers. "It's time."

"Yes," she said looking at him over her reading glasses. "You sound like you may have an opinion on the matter."

"Well," Williams said, "I haven't been a world explorer but I have done quite a bit of hiking over the years. And hiking Mount Kilimanjaro has been on my bucket list for quite some time, so I know the challenges it offers."

"Tell me," she said focusing all her attention on Williams.

He felt a little uncomfortable under her gaze, but hiking, Williams knew, and he could hold his own with the best in the business when it came to discussing most aspects except maybe canyoning. He never felt too comfortable in tight spaces he couldn't get out of.

"First are the dangers of Tanzania, which has had several warnings in recent years to use extreme caution when traveling along. Next is that you need a guide to take you to the top. These guides can sometimes be dishonest. The expensive ones are not necessarily the most reliable," Gus said leaning forward, getting excited about the prospect of traveling.

"Those things are of no concern to me," the woman said, "most places, even in the US, can be dangerous. And as far as guides go, I will do my due diligence in vetting the proper service."

"Okay," Williams said, "now you have to worry about the actual climb."

"No technical expertise is needed for this summit," she said.

"Yes, but you are climbing to over 19,000 feet, which offers its own set of problems."

"Acclimatization?"

"Yes."

"I have been to the top of several fourteeners and have had very little effects from altitude. With a little medicine from my doctor, I don't think this will be a problem."

"As long as you take at least seven days for the hike."

"Is that the recommended time?"

"That is what I have read."

She closed each book before putting her glasses back into their small case and returning it to her purse.

"When are you thinking about going?" Williams asked wanting to continue the conversation.

"I haven't decided," she said. "I have read there are two seasons to hike, one in the winter and one in the summer."

"So, you had already done all your homework on Kilimanjaro," Gus said slightly embarrassed.

"Yes, but you seemed very excited to tell me about it, so I thought I would humor you." A warm smile spread across her lips.

"Well, thank you for that, it was rather exciting," Gus said. "Being a teacher, I can get quite excited about relaying information to willing listeners."

"A teacher," she said her tone shifting from playful to perturbed. "My son has decided he wants to be a teacher."

"And you don't seem to like the idea."

"It's not that I don't like teachers," she said placing one hand over the other on the table. "I think teachers are very valuable to society, but he has so much potential in other areas."

"Areas you feel are more suitable to him?" Gus said.

"Well, he has been rather sheltered from life's financial hardships, and I am afraid that he will regret his choice once he has to live within his means and the other opportunities are closed to him."

"Don't we all have to live within our means," Gus said, "no matter how much we make?"

"Yes," she said standing and replacing the books on the shelves before turning back to Gus. "We only know what we know. And I know my son, Stacy, doesn't realize what he is giving up."

Gus' heart skipped a beat. How many teachers in Wellington County were named Stacy? How many have mothers who want him to have a different career? Williams' pause signaled the end of the conversation for Ms. Adams.

"Have a good evening," she said pushing her chair under the table. "And enjoy your trip to Great Britain, it has always been one of my favorite places to visit."

"Thank you," Williams said as she walked away. "Good luck on your hike."

Williams didn't know what to think. He had just met Stacy's mother. She didn't seem like the cold-hearted controlling bitch he had made her out to be. She seemed more like a concerned mother who wanted what was best for her son. Maybe she didn't let him fail enough. In teaching, you have to let the kids fail at times in order for them to heed your advice. All he knows is that he didn't know how to play this one off. Should he tell Stacy? Should he try to make contact with Ms. Adams?

As he finished his cooling coffee, he no longer had any interest in reading about Great Britain. He needed to read something to temper his thoughts. He picked up *The Snows of Kilimanjaro and Other Stories* by Ernest Hemingway. The story of a dying writer should put his perspective straight. He went right to the checkout counter to retrieve *A Dream of Spring*. Between the two writers, Williams had enough mortality and contemplation to carry him through the weekend.

30

Williams arrived early to school after what felt like a long weekend waiting to see Stacy. He went to the gym on Saturday and Sunday hoping to see his teaching companion. But to no avail; Gus didn't catch a glimpse.

The halls were still dark in the upstairs corridor. He walked the familiar path lit only by the red glow of the exit signs. He pulled his staff ID and room key from his jacket pocket. As he turned the corner, blindly reaching to flick on the hallway lights, the glow from under Stacy's room drew his attention. The door was shut. No music. No noise was coming from within. Williams hesitated then turned to his own room.

He flicked the lights on, dropped his bag onto his desk, then hung his coat from the back of his chair. He took out his journal, laid out his dark purple fountain pen. Purple had been Janet's favorite.

He turned to his Nespresso machine. He poured too long shots, dropped two liquid creamers in his pocket and made a beeline across the hall to Stacy's room. Holding both cups by the handle in one hand, Williams knocked and pressed down on the levered handle, pulling the old wooden door out toward him. Stacy sat enveloped in his stacks of papers. He looked up as Williams entered, the bags and dark circles under Stacy's young eyes said it all.

"Early bird gets the worm," Williams said, "and a cup of coffee."

He placed the coffee down in an empty square of desk with two creamers stacked neatly beside it.

"Thank you," Adams said lifting the coffee with both hands to his lips. He took a quick sip then poured the two creamers into the cup in quick succession. He pushed one empty creamer inside the other before dropping it into the trash. Williams took his time, pouring one then the other creamer. He left the two creamer cups sitting on his desk.

"You are here early. Couldn't wait to start the short week, huh?"

Adams looked at Williams, took another sip from his coffee, "I couldn't finish my papers this weekend, so I thought I would get some done this morning."

Williams smiled, "Is it always nose to the grindstone with you? What kept you so occupied this weekend? Did you get distracted by a young lady friend? Maybe you took the foot off the pedal and decided to go out on the town?"

"Nothing of the sort," Adams said with derision. "Quite the opposite actually. My mother came into town."

"Oh!" Williams said feigning surprise.

"She sort of monopolized my time, as she has always done. Then proceeds to tell me what to do with my time when she is not around, like I'm a little puppet."

"I sense some irritation," Williams said. "I'm sure her agenda has your best interests at heart."

"Oh, of course," Stacy said leaning back into his chair. "Her agenda is always what she feels is best for me, but she fails to ask what it is that I want to do."

"And what does she want for you?" Williams was fishing. He knew Stacy was strained, he didn't fit the teacher type in many respects. Something was hidden down deep, guarded from everyone, most likely including his mother.

"What she always wants," Adams said looking up from his

coffee into Williams' eyes. "She wants me to do exactly as she says until I become the male version of her."

"You mean a lawyer?" Williams asked.

"Not only a lawyer, but a ruthless, self-serving, power-hungry, materialistic bitch of a lawyer."

Williams could feel the tension from Stacy. He was running hot but now was the time he could get Stacy to be forthcoming. "And you don't want to be a lawyer? You want to be a teacher?"

Stacy looked Williams in the eye then finished his cup of coffee. "Thank you for the coffee this morning, Gus. I have to finish this stack of papers before first hour."

Williams stood, tossing his empty creamer cups into the garbage. He took Stacy's cup from his outstretched hand. Without an answer, Williams already knew the truth. "Of course, you are always welcome to grab a cup anytime, whether you want to converse or just need a caffeine jolt."

"Thanks, I might need it today."

"Are you going to the gym later, or is your mother still in town?"

Stacy tapped his pencil on his stack of papers. "She is leaving this morning. A car is scheduled to bring her back to Ann Arbor."

"A car?" Williams said with an upward lilt to his voice, "Like an Escalade?"

"Yes, probably an Escalade. Only the best!" Adams said. "She always has a car drive her unless I'm around then I get to be the chauffeur."

Williams chuckled as he headed back across the hall, closing Stacy's door as he went. He had to find a way to continue the conversation about Stacy's future otherwise it would fade into the atmosphere like steam from their morning coffee.

As the bell signaled five minutes until first hour, Williams stepped out into the hall to greet his students one-by-one as they slid from the flow of the crowd into his room. Students bumped and shuffled from locker to friend to classroom. A single person joined the mass, becoming unrecognizable from the others. Then one would break free, then another, disappearing into a classroom, a bathroom, down the stairwell, or around the corner. Williams watched the bumping fists and smiles and nods and hugs and high fives. Adams never appeared. His room filled with students who smiled until they reached his door. Their shoulders slumped as they entered. Williams could hear condolences as one student entered and another shot off down the hall. Friends whispered good luck as they drifted away to their own rooms. Students entered with a heavy burden weighing on their shoulders. An old adage in teaching was that the personality of the teacher will become the personality of the classroom. If Stacy felt burdened by the weight of his mother's expectations, those same expectations were going to transfer to Adams' students.

Williams returned to his room wondering if Adams would stay away from the hallway and from him now that he had let his defenses down for a moment.

Williams began his lesson, "Today will be working with commas!"

The class collectively groaned.

"Yes! Yes!" Williams said, "I know that you all loathe the idea of writing and grammar rules, but a few comma rules will take you far in your writing game."

"Is that like the shoe game but with commas, Mr. Williams?" Tony blurted out. "You know, like coordinate the shoes with the outfit, like I got my tight red Jordans on right here with no creases."

"Uh?" Williams was a little slow to pick up on Tony's references. "Do you have rules in your shoe game, Tony?"

"Yeah, sure do," Tony said. "Only one rule, your shoes gotta look fly." He started slapping his friends hands as they laughed and pushed on each other's shoulders.

"So, I am guessing my white New Balance sneakers are not

going to make the starting lineup in the shoe game," Williams said chuckling to himself.

The laughter continued.

"Alright, alright," Williams said to quiet them down. "Our rules for commas are a little more defined than that, but on the most basic level, commas are used to avoid confusion." Williams paused. "Everybody, write this down in your notebooks. Number 1: Writers use commas to avoid confusion. Every rule, and there are lots of them, is designed to help the reader make sense of their ideas. We, as writers, put commas in for a reason. Commas are not just random decorations."

Michelle interrupted, "Aren't you supposed to use commas when you pause to take a breath?"

Williams turned back to Michelle's group, "No, not at all, but many people think that way. Somewhere along the line, people heard the wrong message — like in the game of telephone. A writer put those commas into their sentences for a reason, usually following a rule. But," Williams said, "but when we read aloud, we pause to take a breath at commas and all other forms of punctuation."

Williams heard a few "ohhs" from students who understood what he just explained, like a lightbulb had just turned on.

"Mr. Williams," Tony said raising his hand, "can we play telephone?"

"No, Tony," Williams said without a second thought to the question, "Nice try though. We are going to stay on task."

The students continued to take notes and write sentences. After every rule the students watched Williams write a correct sentence on the board then offer a few sample sentences to correct themselves. Then as the students became more comfortable with the rule, they wrote their own sentences correctly using the rule. Students then shared with an elbow partner to check their work. The hour went by in a flash, even though the students were learning grammar rules. When the bell rang, students were surprised. They quickly packed the notebooks, pens, and binders back into their bags.

Williams ducked into the hall away from second-hour students asking about the day's lesson plans. Adams was still a no show. Williams walked briskly down the hall joining the throng of students traveling from one room to the next in a regimented fashion. He nodded to the other teachers when they looked his way. Some were talking to each other in a closed circle, while others were talking with students. One teacher had a pair of pliers, helping to open a jammed locker.

31

The halls were empty upon Williams' return from the restroom. The one-minute tardy bell rang as he stopped for a drink from a fountain. Students hustled into various classrooms, trying to avoid the penalty for lateness.

He peered into Stacy's room. He was at the back already returning papers to students. The looks on their faces told Williams that the score didn't run in their favor. Adams did not look up to acknowledge Williams' presence in the doorway. He probably didn't even notice. His singular focus had taken over. Gus returned to his classroom, hoping it went as well as first hour.

"Hi, Mr. Williams?"

He turned to see a new face before him. A petite blonde with big green eyes. Her smile spread naturally, showing perfect rows of white teeth.

"Yes, I am the one and only Mr. Williams here at North Wellington. How can I help you?"

She stretched out her hand, "I'm Sophia Sternwood. I'm new to school today. I was just wondering where you would like me to sit?"

"Ah, and here I am tardy on your first day to class. Not my best first impression." He motioned with his hand toward the classroom. "Come this way. I will have to see what is open for you." He took a step then stopped. "Welcome to North Wellington. Are you from the area?"

"No, we just moved here from Cleveland."

"Well, I hope you find it enjoyable. You just missed the best seasons here in West Michigan, summer and fall."

As they entered the room, Williams turned to her again. "Do you know anyone in class? Some new friends maybe?"

"No, I'm afraid not. I traded the shores of Lake Erie for the shores of Lake Michigan," she said smiling.

Williams could tell she was putting on a brave front. He didn't know if it was from the nerves of the first day or if there was more of a story to tell. Moving was hard for anyone, especially for girls who could be cruel for little to no reason.

"Well, how about right up front next to Jessica. She can show you the ropes and help answer any questions."

"Ok, thank you, Mr. Williams."

As Sophia took her seat, he saw the boys whispering in the back, looking at Sophia and then back to their friends again.

"Ok, everyone. How about we discuss one of the most common misused pieces of punctuation today, THE COMMA!"

Williams thrust his fists into the air with a jab of excitement. The students groaned. Lessons are lessons he knew. But by showing a little enthusiasm, a pun, or a dad joke to the students a few times a week, he knew the atmosphere of the classroom would be a little lighter. Even as a senior citizen, Williams knew he must identify with the students.

As the lesson continued on, he wanted to slip out across the hall to make contact with Stacy again before his guard went back up. He peeked out the door but all was quiet on the Western front. Adams' door was closed and faint talking could be heard.

As the bell signaled the end of second hour, Williams followed behind his students into the bustling lanes of traffic only to be faced with a locked door. Stacy had either secured himself inside or outside of his room. Williams knocked and waited, but no response or sound could be heard from within.

As the bell rang for third hour Williams moved on.

Williams walked down the corridor and turned to the stairwell. Jorgmander side-stepped to be in close conversation with Terry James. Folders and notebooks in hand, Jorgmander looked like he was coming from or going to a meeting with the administration.

"Good morning," Williams said approaching.

"Morning," they said in unison before climbing up the rest of the stairs. Their voices still just a whisper as they rounded the corner. The hallways, suddenly clear of students, seemed strangely quiet to Williams, almost eerie. He wound his way to the front office where his mailbox was located. The principal's door was shut, but Superintendent Snyder, in a formal suit and tie, sat at a table with documents spread out before him and Principal Anderson. The elementary principal sat typing on the computer with an uncommon focus. From experience, Williams knew something had happened. If the super had called for a meeting with the principal, usually they would use the central office conference room, not the principal's office. In the past he would be worried and try to help but this time, he just wondered about what James may have done.

His mailbox sat empty, except for some promotional catalogs for new textbooks. Williams didn't need new American Lit textbooks. He chuckled to himself. What changed in the literature of the past 200 years of America? Nothing. How could it? Certain textbooks needed to be updated more than others, like when countries change names or science uncovers new answers to old problems. But textbooks with writing from the last 200 years aren't really going to change all that much. He tossed the catalog into Adams' box.

Williams turned to leave, then swiftly changed course back to Adams' box. He looked through the papers there. A small stack of referrals sat under an educational travel brochure. Williams flipped through them. Most of the referrals were for tardies, one for not turning in homework, and a couple for insubordination.

The students all received warnings or they were told to attend Saturday school. He slipped the referrals back into the mailbox. Adams had to learn how to deal with students without creating extra paperwork for the principal.

As Williams stepped back into the office, the principal's door opened and all three administrators filed out as they finalized their conversation.

"Whoa," Williams said bumping into the superintendent, a big heavyset man with a wispy combover. "Are all the world's problems solved?"

"We would need you for that, Mr. Williams," Superintendent Snyder said. "We would need your wisdom from the ancient scrolls of North Wellington. All your experience would come in handy to predict and rectify issues."

"Oh, that's a good one Mr. Snyder," Williams said clapping his hands. "Ancient scrolls, I like it. I did do some writing back in the olden days."

The men all chuckled and shook hands. The "old boys club," as it's called, still had its stronghold on certain places around the US. North Wellington was no exception. As the administrators flowed out into the hall, Williams stood back, waiting for Principal Anderson to return to his office.

"Can I have a word?" Williams asked following Anderson back into his office.

Principal Anderson looked at him with a worried brow. "Sure. Come on in," he said fighting with his cuffs and his suit coat. "What can I help you with today, Mr. Williams?"

Williams casually took a seat at the conference table, grabbing a handful of Peanut M&Ms from a candy bowl and waited for Principal Anderson to settle himself.

"I wanted to see if you have had any contact with Ms. Adams recently."

Anderson stopped what he was doing on his phone and placed it face down on his desk.

"No, why?" He said with a startled expression. "Is she here?

Is she coming? Have you talked with her?"

Williams was enjoying making Anderson squirm. It wasn't his intention, but now that it was happening, he was going to work it a little. He popped a yellow M&M into his mouth. "No, no," he said through the crunching of the candy. "I just heard that she had been in town this week and seeing all the suits in the office this morning, I wondered if it had something to do with my boy."

"Your boy, huh?" Anderson smiled. "You are really taking a liking to him, aren't you?"

"As much as I can anyway. He is still very closed off but I am making progress. So, the meeting wasn't about Mr. Adams this morning?"

Williams tossed another couple of M&Ms into his mouth, this time green and red.

"No, it wasn't and stop your prying, Gus. We don't want the rumor mill to start going around town that someone is getting fired or in trouble."

Williams continued to pop one M&M in after another, inviting an awkward silence, which he knew would elicit more information from Anderson.

"We had to discuss other issues."

Williams finished his last M&M then brushed his hands together. "Right, I did see Pete and Terry in the hall this morning in what seemed to be a very discrete discussion."

Anderson tightened his lips, "If there is nothing else, Mr. Williams. I have a parent phone call to conduct on a truant student."

"Oh, yes, of course!" Williams said grabbing a brown M&M from the bowl and tossing it into his mouth. "Thank you for the time and candy. And good luck with the parent phone call."

"Thank you," Anderson said picking up the desk phone.

Williams didn't find out anything new, but he did get confirmation that James was in deep trouble. Anderson was tightlipped about the issue. If the other administrators were involved, then students were bound to know something.

32

"Mr. Williams?" Sonya asked at the start of fourth hour. "What's going on with Mr. James?"

"What do you mean?" Williams knew it wouldn't take long before someone started talking about Mr. James, no matter what he did. The curse of the small town, everyone knew, or thought they knew, everything about everyone else. He turned, glasses perched on his nose, holding a stack of papers that were ready to be returned to students. "Has something happened?"

"Maybe," she said looking shyly around the room, "I shouldn't say."

"Well, whatever you have heard, I can neither confirm nor deny because I have no knowledge of the alleged situation, BUT," Williams said with a long pause, "I can determine if it is just a far-fetched rumor based on my vast amount of life experience."

Sonya stood from her desk and moved next Williams in the back of the classroom. She lowered her voice to a whisper and leaned in close to Williams. "Well, in first hour, Dylan Winkler had his foot out in the aisle in Mr. James' room. After Mr. James tripped on his foot once, he asked Dylan to move it. But he didn't, ya know, because Dylan is, well, Dylan. So, the next time Mr. James went by, Dylan yelled out that Mr. James kicked him. Then Dylan's friend, Trae, started yelling, 'why'd ya kick him,

Mr. James? Why ya kicking students?' Then they both stormed off, out of the room. Now Mr. James hasn't been in his class since first hour. Everyone is saying that Dylan got Mr. James fired."

"Wow, that is quite a story! Thank you for sharing." Williams shuffled the papers in his hands, noticing that students were starting to stare in their direction and get restless. "First, Sonya, Mr. James can't get fired in such a short time even if he did kick a student. Second, it sounds like Mr. Winkler and his friend are up to some hijinks. I bet their grades aren't too good and Mr. James keeps students a little more on the straight and narrow in class, am I right?" Williams handed the stack of papers to a nearby student and asked him to pass them out.

"Yeah," Sonya said. "He always calls them out and they never do well in class. But, Mr. Williams, Dylan also has this big bruise on his ankle and he has been limping all afternoon."

"I am sure there is a reasonable explanation for Mr. James' absence from class and Dylan's bruise," Williams assured her by tapping her on the shoulder. "Now let's get this class started."

"Yeah, I just didn't want Mr. James to be fired. He's a good teacher."

"Everything will be just fine," Williams turned to see his papers were almost all handed out. He began to wonder if everything would be just fine or if James was in real trouble.

Williams wondered why students acted the way they did. Why did they choose to be defiant, to disrespect a person being fair? Dylan wasn't working toward a future, a life. He was living in the present, caring only about his current emotions. How does a child grow up to focus on the destruction of authority just for the sake of doing so? Would Danny have been that way if he had lived another five or six years? He hoped not.

Maybe it was all the parents doing. Did Dylan's parents know the type of student and child he was becoming? Does Dylan mimic their behavior? Were they enabling him by not holding him responsible? Williams had experienced all sorts of parents over the years. The absent, the hovering, the lawnmower, the supportive, the gushing, the concerned, the clueless, the demanding, the expert, etc. By the time the parents reached him in high school, little could be done to change their view or the role they had taken. Yet, he always tried to show each parent that he cared about them and their children. But what about James? What was he thinking, Williams wondered? Even in the most frustrating moments, Williams never lashed out to strike a student. Something more must be going on to make James act that way.

As fourth hour ended, Williams headed across the hall to see Stacy. The door was open but no one was home. One student remained behind, Stewart, a tall cheerful boy who never seemed to lose a smile.

"Stewie, have you seen Mr. Adams recently?"

"Yeah," Stewart said sliding his computer into his case, "I just saw him for a whole class period."

"Of course," Williams said giving a small chuckle, "Let me rephrase to be more accurate. Did you see where Mr. Adams went after class?"

"Yes," Stewie said zipping up his case.

"Ok, Stew," Williams said crossing his arms. "Where did he go?"

"He went out into the hall right when the bell rang along with all the students that couldn't wait to get out of here."

"Thank you for your answer. Did he say where he was going?"

"No, but I am sure he will be back for the next hour." Stewart put his computer case over his shoulder and grabbed his books. "I wish I could be more help but I was busy talking with Megan. And no offense, she is way more interesting to talk to and look at than Mr. Adams."

Williams chuckled and shook his head, "Thanks, Stewart. Have a great lunch."

"See you later, Mr. Williams."

Stewart joined the flow of student traffic in the hall. Williams sat down at a student desk. Taking off his glasses, Williams rested his face in his hands. So many years ago, Williams was the scared new teacher. Where had the time gone? Thirty to forty years passed by him in the blink of an eye and what did he have to show for it but a room full of books, a handful of happy memories, and buckets of pain.

The memories came flooding back, Williams could see his first class of students with shaggy hair and tight-fitting clothes, much like today's teenagers. He remembered the smell of the school in the first week before the students arrived bringing all their baggage. The school was allowed to be itself. The smell of past lives, history, memories. For 100 years the building had grown and lived its own life.

The town lumbermen sent their children here. The town doctors. The farmers and the store owners. The owners of the mill and workers on the dock. As the lumber barons moved on, North Wellington became the bedroom community it is today. Small homes nestled between mansions on the lake. A place where up until twenty years ago, the school sent every child home for lunch because the school had no cafeteria. The students who brought a sack lunch would sit in the halls with friends as teachers huddled together in their staff lounge or in a teacher's classroom. Other students would make the trek home or to a friend's house or to the local store to buy a pocket full of snacks. Williams loved those days. He would steal home to make love to his wife in the early years, then later he would sneak home to hold his newborn son. Relishing the time he spent with his family.

Sitting at the student's desk, Williams' eyes filled with memories. He wiped the tears from his eyes with both hands. He was tired of searching for answers and searching for Adams. He took a note pad from Stacy's desk. He wrote in bold block letters: "Come see me to talk ~ Gus." He dropped the pad on the half-finished pile of papers, tossed the pen on the desk, and walked back to his room for lunch.

33

The oncology department at the Unity Health Center was a solemn place, full of weeping men and women. Visions of growing old with spouses were crushed under piles of statistics and survival rates. Technicians and nurses, doctors and pharmacologists, walked lithely from room to room, carrying data tablets, rolling IV stands and drug carts.

Williams had been here for his first round of treatments. His cycles had come to a close and today's visit was to get new scans to see if the treatment was working or if the doctors needed to increase his dose.

He had an X-ray to start and then an MRI in the afternoon. His day would be spent in one room, in one machine or another. At sixty-six, his age put him at risk of falling below the average five and one-half year survival rate. But he knew he could beat the odds; he could live out the remaining years of his life with dignity and respect. He could see the world. He could see the world that he had only read about in books.

If the treatments were working, he would make plans to retire and take that Alaskan cruise he had always wanted to take. Then maybe next winter he could take a trip to Hemingway's hideout in Key West and Cuba. After that to Russia to see the culture of his favorite authors. No more hiding. No more feeling sorry for himself. Life would get better in many ways if the treatments were working.

"Well, Dr. Fitzkowski, how are the X-rays? Tell me some good news."

"Mr. Williams, we cannot tell you much at this point except you still have myeloma present in certain parts of your body. We think with these scans that there is no more, but no less."

Williams didn't know how to react. "So, the same as before. Does this mean the treatment isn't working?"

"The treatments may be working, we are not sure. All we know is that the disease has not progressed. We did not find any place in which you have a lesion to be compromised."

"Meaning what, doc?"

"You have no broken bones or stress fractures or bones that look like they are going to break because of the cancer."

"Well, that is good news, right!? Does that happen often to patients with myeloma?"

"Yes, in some cases, but not for you at this moment."

"What do you mean, 'at this moment'? That seems rather ominous. Is that going to happen in the future?"

"Mr. Williams. With multiple myeloma, there is no cure." The doctor placed his tablet down on the counter and folded his hands into his lap. "We can only attempt to control the growth of the disease. We can get the disease to go into remission, but it will never go away. With the right treatment, we can have you live for ten or more years in relatively good health."

"I thought the timeline was five years," Williams said confused. "How do we turn five into ten? I am not very good at math. I need some help here."

"The first thing we have to do is find the right combination of drugs to treat your type of myeloma."

Williams noticed the doctor looking at Williams with an expectation of understanding.

"Have you told me all this before, doc?"

The doctor chuckled, "I am afraid so."

"I'm sorry," Williams said, "I must have blanked out during

that appointment."

"It's okay," Fitzkowski said. "I see it all the time. We drop this bombshell on the patients then expect them to be the best listeners. I don't think anyone really hears what we have to say after the phrase, 'you have cancer.' Which is why we advocate for a patient advocate."

"I understand," Williams said. "If you don't mind, could you explain it to me again? I know I just went through a regiment of pills and injections and all of that, is there more? Will I always be tied to the hospital?"

"The short version is that we find two or three different types of drugs that can hold the cancer at bay with minimal side effects. We use trial and error to determine the correct amount for each dose. We do the scientific part and you tell us how the drugs make you feel. Understand so far?"

"Yes," Williams said.

"You should tell us if the drugs adversely affect your quality of life. And we will tell you if the drugs are shrinking the lesions or keeping them the same or allowing them to grow."

"Ok," Williams said, "let's keep trying. I would like to enjoy my coming retirement. I don't mind taking pills, but I would rather not have to get injections in this port. In fact, I would like to get this thing taken out of my chest."

"We will see what we can do, Mr. Williams, to accommodate you. We will take the port out before you are given an MRI."

Williams was asked a litany of questions about diet, habits, and exercise. He explained his sleep, exercise, supplements, work stress, and sexual habits or lack thereof. All of this information was loaded into his file along with the medicine and vitamins and the reactions to the medicines. He was then taken to another part of the hospital to have the port removed, then to another part for the MRI. He had to be pushed in a wheelchair as per the hospital protocol.

He was wheeled through corridor after corridor. Around one blind corner after another. The orderly's badge zipped out from his hip to swipe the door open and then it quickly retracted, where it dangled from a Cialis sponsored key ring. Finally, Williams saw the sign above a door indicating Imaging: MRI.

Williams was asked to sign in at the window and then to take a seat. The orderly backed the wheelchair from the room and headed back in the direction he came from. Williams was given another pair of scrubs with a shirt that opened in the back and a plastic bag for his belongings. He saw another man come from the waiting room, a little older, shoulders stooped, bruises up and down his arms from IV sticks. He shuffled to a seat next to Williams.

"How ya doin', Sonny?"

Williams smiled, he was not often at a loss for words, but language seemed to have escaped his tongue. Sometimes, but not very often, even the most experienced in life can suddenly feel like a child.

"What's wrong? Cat got your tongue?" The old man was smiling at Williams now. "Well, I'll start, that will be a little easier. I have to get a scan to see if my cancer has come back. I get these tumors in my abdomen and they are trying to shrink them instead of constantly cutting them out."

Williams stared as the man pointed to his belly in all sorts of spots. Out of his stupor, Williams pointed at the IV marks, "How long have you been locked up in this joint?"

"He speaks!" the patient said. "My name is Rex Chamberlain. I have been in and out of here for ten years."

"And in that time have you ever felt as good as you did before you came in here?"

"Well sure, ah, Mr. … Mr. …?"

"Williams, Gus Williams," he stuck out his hand for a shake to make the greeting official.

"Williams Gus Williams, why that is a funny name. Is that like William Carlos Williams? The poet who wrote so much depends on a red wheelbarrow glazed with rainwater beside the white chickens."

"Does it?"

"Does what?"

"Does so much depend upon the red wheelbarrow?"

"I was simply making a joke, Mr. Williams."

"Our lives are no joke. Did you know that Mr. William Carlos Williams wrote that poem in a moment at the bedside of a dying child?"

"I have heard that rumor."

"I believe that is a fact."

"I know that it is false. He wrote it while visiting his friend Marshall, an old African American fisherman. In that man's backyard was a red wheelbarrow surrounded by white chickens. There was no dying child, although that is pretty poetic."

"I am sorry. I am just being …"

"Scared," Rex cut in.

Williams nodded his head.

"Listen, Gus, we are all scared every day of our lives, whether we know it, say it, or believe it. That is why we stay in the lines and follow the good book. Don't let cancer change the way you live your life. Fight it. Get sick. Get well. Live! Then do it all over again."

"Thank you, Rex," Williams said, "for giving me a little pep talk. I needed it."

A nurse appeared, "Mr. Williams, we are ready to have you change now."

Another nurse appeared with a wheelchair, "Mr. Chamberlain."

"That's my ride," he said. "It's not a figure shrouded in black with a scythe nor a white-robed man with wings and a halo, so I'll take it and I will probably be back."

Williams stood, shaking the old man's hand, "Shall we get some coffee some time?"

"Sounds lovely," Rex said as he sat down in the waiting wheelchair. The nurse turned him to exit the waiting room, "But I just want to say," Rex exclaimed, "that I have eaten the plums that were in the icebox .... Have a good scan, Williams Gus Williams."

Williams was guided by his nurse in the opposite direction to a changing room. That poem, he knew the end but right then it escaped him. He was asked to dress in his scrubs then lock all his belongings into a locker. At least they gave me pants, he thought to himself.

At the front desk, he asked for a piece of paper and a pen. He wrote his name and phone number then handed it over to the receptionist. "Please give this to Mr. Chamberlain. Thank you."

He returned to his seat, holding his locker key as if all the world might depend on it. He had been through this before, a surreal experience. Now the reality was there in front of him, in his hands. He had cancer, he needed scans, he needed medicine, he needed to do this for the rest of his life. One more thing in a long line of injustices. His past was locked away in a hospital locker. He would return in an hour to get his things, but life would not be the same.

So much wasted time, wallowing in self-pity, dreaming and remembering, wishing the past could be upended. A life full of sorrow for the time lost to him.

As the nurse wheeled him down the hall, Williams' vision faded, the past released, the future blurred. Halls, turns, rooms, one after another. Like life, we tend to follow the path set before us, rarely thinking we have a choice to make. Sometimes we can't see the light until we are in the dark.

Gus finally remembered the end of the poem Rex was quoting, "And which you were probably saving for breakfast. Forgive me. They were delicious, so sweet -- and so cold."

34

As usual, the office was busy with students signing in for the day and some signing out to attend local community college courses. A chattering of voices came from the conference room filled with counselors and therapists and psychologists discussing some child. The student aides filled mailboxes with flyers, textbook catalogs, and memos from various departments.

Williams held the door open for who he assumed was a 6th or 7th grader. The 4′ ½″ tall boy looked frazzled. His bright blue hair was a mess atop his head. He said, "Thanks, old guy!" as he charged down the hall on his Heelys.

Williams chuckled, "That kid is a hoot," as he thumbed the boy's way.

"Hi, Mr. Williams," said Dottie, the principal's administrative assistant.

"I am here for my ten o'clock with Principal Anderson."

"Yes, you can go right in. He is in the conference room with the Child Study Team, but he knows you have a meeting and should be right out."

"Ok, thanks," Williams said taking his seat in the guest chair across from the principal's desk.

He could hear the discussion from the conference room — sounds of frustration and questioning. The door opened and closed. Williams turned to see if it was Principal Anderson, but the door closed too quickly.

After five minutes, Williams stood, stretching his back by twisting it one way then the other. He moved over to the bookshelf where he eyed a neat line of books on leadership. Each one was filled with promises of success and triumph. His favorite title was, *Bruno the Leadership Bulldog*. Williams pulled the book from the shelf, turning it over in his hands.

"Follow Bruno the leadership Bulldog as he deals with frustrated employees and keeping the dog treat business competitive in today's marketplace."

Williams flipped through the first few pages of this graphic children's book. In the first few chapters Bruno leaves his wife and pups at home to go off to work in his Arfa-Romeo. The company Top Notch Treats was doing well and was ready to expand, which was posing a problem. The CEO and Board of Directors were thinking of building a plant overseas and shipping treats to the US. The union leadership became upset and fearful for the security of their jobs. While Bruno wasn't involved with the negotiations, he certainly had to deal with disgruntled workers in his department, Muscle Meat Treats. The health and nutrition sector had boomed in the last few years and Bruno was poised and ready. His department was one reason the company had to expand.

His signature line of Bow-Wow Pow health food ranked number one in the country. He had ambassadors all over the US using Twitter, Instagram, and Facebook to promote Bow-Wow Pow. The supplement powders, protein bars, and drinks all came from his department and the vision of his top people. The success also meant bigger bonuses and more pressure.

The door to the office suddenly closed. Williams, startled from his focused reading, turned to see Principal Anderson with a stack of file folders.

"Sorry to keep you waiting, Mr. Williams."

"Oh, that's okay," Williams glanced at his watch; he had lost 20 minutes of his planning time. "I was just looking at your leadership books here. This one about Bruno the Bulldog seems fairly entertaining."

"Yeah, that was a fun one -- not quite as valuable as others but a better read, as they say."

Williams placed the book back on the shelf as Anderson slid his files into a holder on his desk. Williams took his seat, "You wanted to meet to discuss Stacy and his progress."

"Yes, I just wanted to touch base, not take up a lot of your time. How is it going, is he making progress?"

"Progress as in what way?"

"In becoming a better teacher, one less prone to making students cry, or tossing their phones, or having upset parents call me about his unreasonably high expectations."

"Being a good teacher is not about keeping parents off the principal's back."

"Right, Mr. Williams, but if the students are so unhappy that their parents are calling me then there is probably a problem with the workload or the grading or something. Have you had a discussion with him?"

"Mr. Adams has high expectations to be sure, but only because he is trying to have all students reach those high marks and their potential."

"Well, his data better show he is being successful in getting those scores up to that high level."

"Or what will happen?"

"Mr. Williams, we needn't talk about that again. The district can live with a demanding teacher that doesn't connect with students if the test scores are high, but if that same teacher is just plain difficult and the scores are average, well, then what is the headache for?"

Williams knew that Anderson's reasoning was accurate. "He is making progress," Williams said clenching his jaw. "Is there anything else because I have some work to do before my planning time is over."

"Well, I was going to ask you how you are doing." The

principal leaned back in his chair drumming his fingers on his desk.

He's fishing. Anderson and Snyder constantly fished for clues for when the teachers on the seniority list would retire. The district would save some cash, just to spend it on themselves or something else. Williams wasn't going to give them the satisfaction. "I feel great. I am thinking about taking an Alaskan cruise this summer then hike Kilimanjaro the next year. I figure if I can take two big trips a year, the job is still worth it. I might be here after you're long gone!"

"Alaskan cruise, huh?" Anderson said gripping the chair arm. "Sounds nice, inside passage or outside?"

He's trying to catch me, Williams knew. "Oh, I was thinking of taking a big boat up from Seattle then taking a small boat on the way back along with a train across the country."

"Sound extravagant."

"Well, that is why I need to keep working," Williams stood to go. "Speaking of which, I better get back to it."

35

The late fall wind picked up. December had always been a fickle month in Wellington. Gus could count on snow before Halloween and some warm days after, but December could be a snow-covered wonderland or a mild grey month. Sure enough, snow had fallen in October for a single morning and again briefly in November but the weather had stayed mild, warm enough to get out on the trails one more time.

Williams knew his time on the trails grew shorter because of the weather and also his failing body. On the trail, Williams took the long route to Janet's bench. He skirted left of the Dune Ridge Trail. He followed the shoreline, avoiding the hardening muck. He then climbed from the forest floor up into the stiffening sand. He held out his hands over the tops of the dune grass, letting the sharp points drag against his skin. Lake Wellington pushed its edges up. No one was fishing, no one was sailing.

In a small clearing, Gus laid his accordion style mat down on cool sand. Clouds pushed through the sky and the wind pulled at his thoughts.

William thought of his former student. Nick's art show was approaching. He had so much life left to live. A shame that his life was snuffed out by a careless driver. The same pangs of anger that he felt for years started to resurface. If the driver decided against one more beer at the ball game, Nick would still be painting, still making art.

Nick, shit. Williams' thoughts tumbled. He sat in this same spot thinking the same thoughts about Janet and Danny. They too had so much life left to live. Then he realized that another life died that day, his own. Janet, Danny, and Nick all had their lives taken from them. They couldn't move on from their tragedies but he could have. He had so much life left to live, but squandered it all in grief and self-pity.

He sat up, looking out at the whitecaps rolling over in the lake. Winter was coming. No one can change time to reverse events that had already happened. But now there was a choice to be made. Williams was forced to deal with his own mortality. How would he choose to live the rest of his days? He stood, ready to move through cleansing sands of the dune.

As Williams rounded the dune to the campground, he saw a couple of families still camping, maybe even without a permit. The children, no older than five or six, rode their bikes around the empty sites, through fire-pits, kicking their legs out, tagging each other as they tried to stay upright. He waved to the man who was probably their dad. He struggled to light a fire in the blowing wind.

As he made his way through the wooded trail, Williams' thoughts turned to Adams. He didn't know what to do. Anderson was losing his patience. The district had done this before, fired a probationary teacher. Nothing could be done. A fired teacher would have a tough time finding a decent job again. A teacher with a tarnished reputation had a hard time staying in the profession. Williams had to do something.

At Janet's bench Williams stopped. He took a long pull on his water. Williams unzipped a side pouch on his pack and found a white macadamia nut Cliff Bar. Janet would be proud of his choices and his preparation. No Snickers or Paydays for Gus, not with his health teetering on the edge.

"I don't know what to do," he said out loud to Janet. "I have tried to really guide him, tell him how to work with kids, give him evidence to prove I am right, and I've even tried to cover up for his mistakes. I need some help here, babe."

He knew there would be no reply but the one-sided conversation comforted him. Gus watched as the sun set over the lake. Twilight in the dunes was one of his favorite moments. A time when nature stood still. The daylight creatures were finding their beds for the night, while the nocturnal animals awoke from their slumber but were not yet ready for the night's adventures. Twilight fell just in between. If you stop at just the right moment, the world seemed to be all yours, and you were a bridge to the other side.

Williams felt that way now, like a bridge between two worlds. The life that was his before and the life that it was becoming. Adams was in the same place, yet he didn't have a clue. Youth would do that to a person. Years ago, he couldn't handle it. He let the bottle be the bridge. A long bridge that he couldn't get off. Now, he could handle it. He had the strength. Adams needed him to be the bridge for him as well. But Williams didn't know if he was strong enough for the both of them.

36

Williams had never been to an art show, nor had he ever been to a fundraiser quite like this one. In the past he may have been somewhat reluctant to spend $200 on a fundraiser ticket, but now that his time seemed to be running short, he had no qualms. After Nick's death, his friends decided that his art should be sold at an auction, otherwise it may be destroyed by the school. But before they could hold an auction, they had to create a demand for the art. That was how this high-priced fundraiser came into being.

The Bridgeport Art Center was located near where Nick had been killed. Williams hadn't been to the Bridgeport area of Chicago, except maybe as a pathway to Magnificent Mile or as a wrong turn to a White Sox game. Until he drove the history-filled streets near the art center, he had imagined Chicago looked like the downtown shops or like the area around Wrigley Field. He knew that there was more to Chicago than that, but it never crossed his mind to explore those areas. He would have to be more open to exploring authentic places in the coming years, if he had them.

Nick's classmates, closest friends, along with a couple of instructors, selected twenty-five of Nick's pieces for the show including sketches and his most recognizable piece, *The Teacher*. All proceeds went toward creating a scholarship for art-oriented foster children.

In his video biography made during the school year, Nick cited only a few teachers who had really listened to him and allowed him to work within himself to complete assignments. He could draw any scene, a face with emotion, cartoon panels, but he struggled with language. Something went amiss when trying to write essays, he couldn't explain it. Reading was a struggle as well. The teachers were not how all teachers should be — supporters of the students. He stated, "High School was hell on earth. Like I had been thrown down into Dante's purgatory and put on a spinning wheel. But my first real painting, one of my best, came from this moment. One day, I had decided to take my life after school, but a teacher came to me, saw that I was hurting, and talked to me. He said, 'We all have our own paths to follow in life. Some are more alike than others and if ours is different, well then it is hard to take that first step.' Then he cited Thoreau, 'If a man doesn't keep pace with his companions, perhaps it is because he hears a different drummer. Let him step to the music which he hears, however measured or far away.' I thought about what he said all through the night. I couldn't sleep. I had this bottle of pills sitting on my nightstand. I could take the whole bottle, lay in my bed, and life would be over. But all I could do was draw and sketch in my notebook. The phrase, 'however measured or far away,' stuck with me. By morning I had made up my mind. I registered for the GED and printed an application for AAI of Chicago. I decided to march to my own beat. I decided that I had to make a change for myself and no one else could do it for me."

Williams watched as a harder, older, healthier Nick was projected on the wall in the foyer. His eyes misted as he read the words floating over the image. He remembered that day. The day when Nick had seemed so down, so low, so full of despair. Williams could only see the top of his head during class, strokes of his black pen quickly scraping over his paper. A black curtain of unkempt hair framed a solemn face, blocking out his classmates and his teachers. His eyes, black as pitch, with pinpoint stars glinting from the void within. Williams finally made eye contact as class concluded. Neither looked away and Williams new something was wrong. Nick's eyes were asking for help. It was the only way he would let anyone see his pain.

The bell rang and as his classmates filed from the room, but Nick stayed put sketching. Williams let everyone flow from the room then slowly approached the young, disheveled Nick.

"Nick," Williams remembered saying, "the bell rang, time to go home."

But Nick didn't move. He stayed with his head down, his hair blocking his vision, walling out Williams as he stood next to his desk.

Williams knelt down, one hand on Nick's shoulder.

"Nick? Is everything okay with you?"

A quiet broken voice asked, "How do you do it, Mr. Williams?"

"Do what, Nick?"

"How do you keep going day after day in a world where you don't know how to fit into it?"

"Well, we all have a place and that is why we were born. The world automatically made a place for us the minute we came into this world. Otherwise we wouldn't be here."

"But you lost your wife, your son, your role as a father and a husband. You had a place that was taken from you. And I can tell, Mr. Williams, you lost your place."

Williams rubbed his hands together as he leaned on his knee, "Yes, I lost them, a long time ago. I fought my demons and lived."

"But did you recover? Can anyone come back from that?"

"No, Nick, no one can completely come back from their past. Their past will stay with them forever, but it is the weight of the past that keeps people from finding their new place in the world. Can I ask you what you think you have lost?"

"I haven't lost anything, Mr. Williams," Nick said capping his pen. "But I feel lost. I feel like I haven't found my place or found anyone."

"We all have our own paths to follow in life. Some are more alike than others and if ours is different, well then it is hard to take that first step." Williams tilted his head to make eye contact. "Let me quote Thoreau here, 'If a man doesn't keep pace with his companions, perhaps it is because he hears a different drummer. Let him step to the music which he hears, however measured or far away.'"

"What happens when you have no companions?" Nick asked looking sharply at Williams.

Williams knew what he said next could make a world of difference, more to Nick, than to any other student.

"Then Nick, you must find them. And if they are not at North Wellington then you must go to them."

Nick nodded, his heavy dark hair swaying forward, "Thank you, Mr. Williams." Nick stood, walking directly to the door.

"Nick!" Williams said standing. Nick turned in the doorframe, still clearly haunted by the larger questions in life. "Are you going to hurt yourself?"

"No, Mr. Williams," he said flatly.

"I will be seeing you tomorrow then?"

Nick nodded, turned, and walked out of Williams' room for the last time. As Williams turned to straighten chairs and pick-up stray papers, he realized Nick had left something on his desk. He grabbed it and ran to the hall, but Nick was nowhere in sight. Williams looked down at the paper. A self-portrait drawn in pen. Williams only saw the eyes. They were so dark, black, and empty. No love or joy came from those eyes. Framed by dark flowing hair, Williams noticed words written in the hair — *infinite emptiness*. Nick's signature was scrawled in the right corner.

"Excuse me," a sharp voice snapped Williams from his memories. "Excuse me, do you have a ticket for this evening's event? We are having a private charity show this evening."

Williams looked from the tv monitor to the man in the heavily starched suit and slick-backed hair. He knew he was out of his depths in the big city. "Yes, thank you for asking. I am here for the Nick Logan art show."

"Very well, your name sir?"

"August Williams, I have my ticket here in my wallet, one moment." Williams began to dig into his suit coat for his wallet.

"No need, Mr. Williams. I have your name on the attendance list."

"Just like school, eh?" Williams interjected with a smile.

The doorman looked disinterested in any small talk or humous relays. "You may check your coat just inside the door to your right. Refreshments are being served throughout the exhibit. If you have special dietary restrictions, please discuss those needs with the waitstaff and they will accommodate you accordingly. The exhibit closes at 11 pm. Have a good evening." He swung the door open for Williams to enter.

A Nick Cave baritone flowed out the doorway. Williams stepped into what seemed like an entirely different world. The music filled in the void around each patron as they wandered through shadows and tunnels of light. Somewhere flashes of light were popping like bolts of lightning. Dropping his coat at the coat-check counter, Williams was met by a bubbly blonde, who slid a plastic chip toward him. He pocketed the marker and turned to see an 8x10 foot version of *Infinite Emptiness*. The eyes of the painting pulled him forward; he felt like he was drifting weightlessly through space; moving slowly, no atmosphere to push forward or rebound back; a moment lost; the body with no power, no will, no force; the arms flail, legs kick but the singular direction was predetermined by a choice we made long before.

A voice broke Williams' trance. "Mesmerizing isn't it," the bubbly blonde said.

Williams turned, "Oh! Yes. Pulled me right off my feet."

"It catches everyone. I get excited whenever a new person comes through the door," she said with a little more excitement than Williams felt was justified.

"Well, it caught me," he said, "have a good evening."

Williams remembered the day and the sketch that was left in his room. The full size version showed Nick's growth as an artist. No longer was the face a shape drawn on a piece of paper, but a figure seemingly coming through the painting. The sheer size itself would make the perspectives and depths extremely challenging to pull off. Williams stopped a passing server to ask for a glass of soda water with a splash of cranberry juice. He couldn't drink alcohol but he could certainly hold a glass as he walked through the exhibit.

Williams wandered from painting to painting, each piece seemed to capture not just the physical life of the subject but its inner soul as well. One portrait of a man's face showed every wrinkle and pain of a hard life; another captured a youthful man embracing a woman, both full with laughter; another showed tear-filled eyes bent in prayer.

Around another corner was a portrait of a homeless man wrapped in layers of tattered clothes, his shadow a tall respectful businessman holding a briefcase and talking on a cell phone. Another is a boy set apart from his peers, lost in the pages of a book, walled off from the company of others.

Williams stopped at a binder, each page an idea sketched out by Nick. Some were on napkins or pages ripped from paperback books or lined pieces of paper filled half with class notes, folded three times over like a middle school note passed to a friend. More plans than Nick had time to execute. His earliest plans were simply sketches of drawings and then as he grew over time at the school, Nick's art branched out to more complex paintings and a wider variety of mediums. One showed the plan for the large *Infinite Emptiness*, another for a 40' wire sculpture of Neal Gaiman's Sandman character. Taped to the pages was a thin piece of wire, thin enough to be mistaken as a light fishing line, along with the word *flowing* written along the side.

"He was good and he was going to be a great artist."

Williams turned to see a young man, pale and thin, with a black shirt and vest, black hair that wrapped around his head with gel, black pointy shoes, and burgundy pants painted on thin wobbly legs.

"Yes," Williams said, "I agree. Were you one of his friends and classmates?"

"I had been at the school with Nick for two years. He was about to graduate." The young man said taking another glass of red wine from a wandering waiter. "He submitted his portfolio to his advisor, the requirement to graduate, just the week before the accident. They graduated him shortly after the accident. But he knew that would happen, of course."

"Oh, really?" Williams said, "how so?"

"Oh, yes," the young man said. "He had shown all of us, and his advisor, the portfolio months before he submitted it for graduation. As for school, Nick didn't need to stay but he didn't want to leave last term."

"No? Was he afraid to graduate or something?" Williams asked.

"Well, once you graduate, you have to leave the campus, and you lose access to all of the art spaces and some of the supplies. Nick didn't want to lose that yet. He wanted to finish that big painting," he pointed back toward the entrance to the gallery. "He was going to enter it into the Art Prize contest in Grand Rapids, MI this fall. If he graduated in the spring, he would lose his funding and his ability to work in the studio last summer."

Williams nodded in understanding, "Clever, so he enrolls for a portfolio credit, finishes his painting in the summer, then used the funding to support his art for one more term."

"Yes, Nick was pretty smart about those things," the young man said. "He would always say, you have to find your way. No one will do it for you."

Williams smiled, "Yes, I suppose that's true. And what is your name? I am afraid we have been talking all this time, and I have no clue as to who you are exactly."

"Tristan McCallister. I work with digital media."

"Nice to meet you, Mr. McCallister. I am sorry for the loss of your friend."

"Thank you. And what's your name?"

"August Williams, I was one of Nick's high school teachers."

Tristan's eyes grew large and a wave of understanding washed over his face.

"Are you?"

"Yes, I believe I am probably that Mr. Williams."

"I have to introduce you to the others. Nick didn't talk much about high school but he said that you saved him, saved his life."

Tristan led Williams back through the exhibit to the final gallery, a small room with each wall filled with a single 5x5 painting. Standing in the center were four young artists, each staring straight at one painting until one of them would say, "shift" and the group would turn clockwise in unison.

"Guys, I would like to introduce to you Mr. Williams …. from Michigan."

They all turned to Gus, "*The* Mr. Williams?"

"The one from the painting?"

Gus smiled, "Quite possibly. I was a teacher of Nick's in high school and we had the exact conversation he described in the biography video."

"Wow!" a student said. "That is so cool you came. We didn't know how to get ahold of you or even who you were. How did you hear about the exhibit?"

"I get emails with news updates. The art show was in one of those updates. I happened to recognize the name and the rest is history as they say."

"Nick never gave us any specifics on where he was from, he just said Michigan and with Nick being from foster care, we couldn't get any family specifics."

"Yeah," another student said, "the funeral was tough. We couldn't do a thing because of the authorities."

"The state simply cremated his body because there was no

next of kin. We were able to collect his ashes after the fact with some help from some art patrons of the school."

"Yeah, they wanted to intern him in a pauper's grave at the cemetery with only a small little name plate."

"Nick probably would have thought of that as poetic," Williams said. "At least the Nick I knew way back in high school."

"Well, maybe," a young artist said, "but we thought of something different."

For the next hour, Tristan, Lux, Chen, and Maverick explained to Gus how they took some of Nick's ashes, mixed them with his paints, then traced each signature on every painting at the show and in his apartment studio. Then with some of the rest, they finished the last piece he had started titled *Self*.

"He had made several sketches then put several layers down to create the effect of him stepping down off of the painting," Lux explained.

"We just had to put on some finishing touches, some details he had noted in the sketches, and some things he mentioned to us in conversation," Maverick included.

"We put it in the show as the last painting," Chen said.

"Because it was his last," Tristan finished.

Williams stood before the ten foot painting of Nick, who seemed to be coming out of the painting toward him.

"He seems to be coming out to greet me," Williams said.

"Yeah, that was his idea. He thought that his true self was coming out and that anyone's true self would be bigger than our physical bodies," Tristan explained.

Lux started to cry, "He said he was finally becoming his true self."

As Chen comforted Lux, Williams turned to Tristan, "And you're saying his ashes are within this painting."

"Yes," Tristan said. "This one and all the others as well."

"I am not sure what to say. Part of me is upset at the

sacrilegious disposal of his ashes but then another part believes Nick's life was saved and made better because of his art. So, what better way to honor him than to help him live on through his work."

"We had many discussions, Mr. Williams," Tristan said.

"We didn't come to this decision lightly," Chen said rubbing Lux's back.

"Well, there is no going back now," Maverick said. "We can have a proper disposal of the rest of his ashes."

Williams looked a little confused, "So you are saying there are some left?"

"Oh, yeah," Tristan said. "We couldn't use all of the ashes in the paint or it would look really thick and full of texture."

"That would have ruined all his work," Lux managed to say between sniffles.

"Well," Williams said putting his hands in his pockets, "I would suggest a proper burial or at least a blessing by a priest, but if you raise enough money, a proper memorial."

"Where would we put his ashes?" Maverick said.

"If the proceeds of this event are going to fund a scholarship at the school, approach the dean with a tasteful, yet artistic way to display Nick's ashes on campus."

"That's a good idea," they said in unison.

"Let me know if you need help in this matter. My number is available through the registration, but as for right now, I am getting weary and tired. Thank you all for a wonderful evening."

"Good night, Mr. Williams," they said in unison.

As Williams left the art gallery, he felt a heavy sadness lifted from his shoulders, like a thick blanket made of chains being taken away. Nick had come so far in his short life — to find a perspective through his art, to craft a better future on the outside, to be satisfied with the internal workings of his mind. He was extraordinary. He took the initial step to leave a place as a young man barely older than a child in order to find a better life. Not only did he find a better life, he flourished. He became a leader, an adult, a trusted friend. His final project was to become his true self, the living embodiment of his art and his mind. He was successful. He truly became bigger than life.

Nick had done what Williams had not, moved on. But as long he was living, Williams had time to do the same.

37

"Mr. Williams?" Stacy advanced through the door, focused on his agenda.

Williams looked up from his computer and removed his reading glasses. "Yes, how can I help you?"

"All day today kids were talking about this holiday play and assembly. I have no idea what they are talking about. Can you tell me what and when it is, and what, if anything special, I have to do with my students?"

Williams recognized that Stacy was actually asking for help. This was the first time all year he had troubled to walk across the hall, much less ask for help. "We will probably find out the details at tomorrow morning's staff meeting, but the gist of it is every year the drama club puts on a Christmas play. It runs, usually, two hours in the afternoon on the Thursday before break. In the morning, the elementary kindergarten, 2nd, and 5th grades put on three little plays."

"What about middle school? No plays?" Adams asked with a smile.

"Well ..."

"Oh, don't tell me they have a day or time slot as well."

"No, they are a part of the high school play, and they also help with the elementary."

"So, what you are saying is that day is a lost cause, great!"

Adams threw his hands up in the air and spun around to leave the room.

"I wouldn't look at it that way. Look at it as a way for students to work together, using language, art, and music skills to spread a joyful holiday message."

Stacy turned back around, "Yes, I see that but couldn't they spread that message after school or in the evening? Why take up a whole day with it?"

"Stacy, you must realize by now that school is not just about academics, but about learning the social constructs of the society in which we live. Having a special day gives all the students something to look forward to, to participate in, and, simply put, to enjoy. What is the alternative? Looking forward to lectures and essays and multiple choice quizzes?"

"Point taken." Stacy said leaning back against a desk. "What does this mean for the next few weeks, business as usual with just the one day gone? Aren't we supposed to have finals that week? We are going to have to stay on task a little bit."

"Yes, finals are Monday, Tuesday, and Wednesday," Williams said leaning back in his chair. "You should expect that most teachers wind things down the last few weeks, wrap up the major unit, and prep for the exam. Friday is a half-day for students and staff gets to go home once their grades are in."

"So, most teachers give easy grades on the exams and leave right after the students on Friday, I suppose."

"Exactly."

"That's typical," Adams turned to leave in a huff.

"Just wait a second," Gus said moving out from behind his desk. "If you can have everything graded and back to the students by Thursday or Friday morning, any problems or questions by students can be answered BEFORE break. You don't want to wait until after the holiday to deal with this term's grading issues. The students will have trouble remembering their locker combination, much less your assignment criteria after break."

"Well, regardless of how everyone else feels around here, I think they will need to be prepared if they are going to make it in life."

"Make what, Stacy?" Williams was done with taking it easy on Stacy's hard-nosed attitude.

"To be successful in life, that's what."

"There is more to being successful than keeping your nose to the grindstone all year, every day, all day. The kids are also learning life skills here."

"That is what their parents are around to do, teach them about life."

"Many of their parents are not in position to do that and besides, we see these kids more each day than their parents. Think about it. Up at 6:30, out of the house by 7:15, classes until 3:00, then a club activity, work, or sports until 5:00 or later, then finally they get home for dinner if they are lucky. Then the good kids do their homework and maybe get some TV in before bed. When, in that day, is there time for life skills to be taught to them by parents?" Williams leaned on his desk across from Adams, "Maybe on the weekends they get to have some quality time, but more likely they are learning about life skills from living in this little made up world called North Wellington. We have to teach more than just reading, writing, and grammar."

Stacy was looking down, staring intently at the floor, his hand rubbing at his chin. "Yes, Mr. Williams." He slumped down into a desk, face in his hands. "I'm just not a very good teacher. The way I do things is not the way the kids like it or get it or learn it."

"Stacy," Williams said moving toward the slumped Adams. "No one, I mean no one, is very good their first year and the only reason any teacher feels good about their second year is because it is not as bad as the first."

Stacy let out a slight chuckle, "Jesus, Gus, I can't go through this another year. All the kids hate me, they cry, parents yell, students rebel. It's been awful."

Gus patted Stacy on the shoulder, "Yeah, it hasn't been easy to watch either."

They both chuckled. Stay looked up, "Thanks for that, it doesn't really make things better."

"Well," Gus said, "here is what I do know. As teachers we want, want, want to reach everybody all the time, but sometimes for any number of reasons, whatever it is, personality, gender, lesson plans, or content, we cannot get to every student, no matter how hard we try."

"But you seem to," Stacy said flopping back against the chair back.

"No, stop right there," Williams said holding up his hand. "I fail to reach students too. Right now, I could name five students, at least, that are just sliding by but if I push them, guess what happens -- more push back. So, I can coax and nudge until I am blue in the face but they have to decide to turn things around."

"Ok, so you have a handful of students, I have all BUT a handful."

"Hey," Williams said returning to his desk, "at least you reached a handful."

"Very funny," Stays said folding his arms across his chest. "But really, how do I reach more?"

"You already know the answer to that question, my friend."

"I do?"

"Yes, I have told you or shown you more than once this year."

Stacy put his face through his hands once again then ran them through his hair and to his neck. He sat like that, rubbing his neck with his hands before bringing his head down again.

Williams hadn't moved, "So you know what to do?"

"Yeah," Adams groaned, "I have to open up and ease off the gas."

"Yes!" Williams shouted standing up.

"But I don't know if I can do that," Stacy said slouching down.

Williams sat back down at his desk, "Why not?"

"I mean, I can give less work but I don't know about connecting with students."

"Ok, well start with giving less work. Pull back enough to where the students are being challenged but not burdened by the work."

Stacy nodded his head in approval and began to stand. His normal upright manner had been tarnished -- now his shoulders slumped and the crown of his head was what greeted people.

"Stacy," Williams stood again and leaned forward with one hand on the desk.

"Yeah?"

"A couple of weeks ago, after your mom came to visit, you told me that she wanted you to be this hardnosed lawyer. And I asked you if you wanted to be a teacher and you didn't answer."

"That's correct. I remember the conversation."

"And do you have an answer now?"

"No."

Stacy turned to gather his things, ready for the day to be over. Williams followed him across the hall. He knew now was the time to get to the bottom of this, well before the holiday play.

"You know, you can be a lawyer, any kind of lawyer, if you want to be one. Just because your mother wants you to be hardnosed, doesn't mean you have to be. I mean, you're pretty tough in the classroom, you might be a bulldog in the courtroom too."

Adams grabbed his jacket from the corner hook then looked Williams in the eye, "That's what I'm afraid of, being just like her."

"But you can just be yourself."

"Exactly, but what if I am just being myself and I turn out to be just like her. I don't know if I could stand it."

"Stacy, I have met your mother. She doesn't seem terrible."

Stacy looked at Williams, eyes going red, filling with water. "When did you meet my mother? Did she have something to do with me getting a job here? Is there anywhere that I can go that she doesn't have influence?" He rushed out with jacket in hand before Williams could answer.

"I saw her in the travel section at Barnes & Noble," Williams shouted.

Williams turned to see a few students still milling about staring at him. As he looked in their direction, they turned to their friends, giggling. Each time progress had been made, he felt like he had been pushed back two steps. At least Adams had come to him for advice about how to reach students. That was the first step with teaching, looking at the kids and wondering how can I get them to learn what they need to learn to be successful in the classroom and in life.

38

Williams pulled into the Steak and Egger eager to talk to his hospital friend. Since their conversation, Williams had done a fair amount of Googling Rex Chamberlain. It seemed that Mr. Chamberlain was a businessman economically and a poet spiritually. The two often didn't go together. Who would find lines of verse about mergers and acquisitions poetic? Which was why Chamberlain was such an enigmatic character in Williams' eyes.

He had purchased both of Chamberlain's collections of poems, published in small print runs in the 70s. Each were now out of print, but as with most things, if you look long hard enough, the internet will provide. He found both copies on Ebay. Chamberlain's name had been misspelled in the listing, so Williams had to dig a little. In the days leading up to their meeting, Williams poured over the collections. He felt they were good poems, a promising debut and follow-up.

He brought both collections with him although he didn't know why. With the books of poetry by his seat, he felt like a little kid about to see his favorite author. As he sat waiting in the window booth, looking out every so often to see cars pulling into the parking lot and checking the door whenever it opened, Williams read back through the poems. Each poem had clear images, always a turn at the end, and something held just off to the side or under the surface. When he was reading "Every Turn," Chamberlain arrived.

"Here is your table, Mr. Chamberlain."

As Rex approached, Williams closed the book of poems and slid it down into the booth beside him.

"Rex, I 'm glad you could make it. I have been wondering how you've been. Scans come back clear?"

"Afraid not, old boy."

Rex's demeanor had changed from the chipper upbeat man in the hospital.

"Oh, no! What did they say?"

"They ..."

Williams interrupted, "You don't have to answer that. I'm sorry for asking. That is a personal matter."

Before Rex could answer the waitress returned with a full pot of coffee. She flipped Rex's cup over and refilled Williams' cup.

Rex tipped a little cream into his coffee and then stirred it with a spoon.

"You get right to the nitty gritty stuff, huh, Mr. Williams?" Rex said taking a small sip.

"These things are what they are, Rex. We can do nothing about them but despair."

"You seemed to have changed your tune since a few weeks ago. What caused the change? Did you get good scans?"

"Hardly at all," Williams responded leaning over the table to sip his steaming coffee. "It seems my treatment needs to be more aggressive, so over holiday break, I will be taking an intensive two-week chemo regime at the hospital."

"Oh, wow."

Williams and Chamberlain continued to discuss treatments and the feeling of seeing the end of the journey. How knowing that death will be coming sooner rather than later can change the perspective of a person's life.

The breakfast came and went, like two old friends who had been meeting for years on Sunday mornings.

"Well, Gus, the bill is here. This is your last chance to ask me."

Williams smiled. He reached down to the seat beside him, where both volumes of poetry had been sitting for their whole breakfast. He put them on the edge of the table by the bill.

"I couldn't help but Google your name after our conversation at the hospital."

"And what did you find?"

"Well, a few webpages and articles about an energy company, philanthropy endeavors, and then a reference to a poet by the same name. I didn't know it was you until I received the books and found this grainy black-and-white photo of a long-haired, carefree man smiling back at me." Williams flipped to the back page of the book, showing Rex the picture. There he was kneeling down in a field next to a smiling Golden Retriever. "This is you, isn't it?"

Rex took the book from his hand and ran his fingers down the page. "Seems like a different life. In my 20s without a care in the world, I was happy just traveling the country with friends, seeing nature, meeting people, enjoying every flavor of life."

"Then what happened? Sounds like something changed."

"Well, ..."

"Shoot!" Williams interrupted again. "I did it again. You don't have to answer that question. I don't mean to pry. I am just used to asking questions as a teacher. I just blurt them out."

Rex chuckled, "No worries." He handed the book back to Gus. "People stopped looking inward and started looking at the war more and more. Then it was all about money, so I followed suit. I hooked up with a guy who needed someone in the office to help run phones and set meetings for a small electrical company he was starting. Then business started booming, and I got sucked in. Pretty soon, I had cut my hair, bought a closet full of suits, and was flying off to every tropical beach I could find with a different lady on my arm. We went for every job no matter how big or small."

"Sounds like a fascinating life."

"Oh, it was, but after the novelty wore off, it was terribly lonely. I had these shallow relationships that came and went with each vacation. The problem was that I was still the kid in that picture."

"You seem to have turned the corner some. You don't seem to be that shallow man now."

"No, I am not. But regret is a powerful emotion."

"I know," Williams said hanging his head. "I have my own regrets and shadows. But you gave up poetry? For all this time?"

"Well, no, not really," Chamberlain said. "I filled notebook after notebook when I was in these contemplative moods, but that was the extent. I polished a few ideas but mostly the notebooks became dreams unfollowed."

"How about now, don't you have the time to go back through those notebooks?"

"A young man's dream only."

"No, just a dream, Rex. You can still achieve your dreams and follow your passions no matter your age."

"No, I can't, Gus. I will be dead before spring."

Williams sat stock still, left without words. They never returned to their opening conversation about scans and diagnosis. Spring was too close.

Rex stood, sliding one arm into his jacket then the other. "Well, Gus. This was a nice breakfast. Shall we do this again?"

Williams was slow to answer, "Yes, I would love to. Maybe after my chemo treatment."

"Ok, see you in January. Call me to set a date and time."

And with that Rex was off toward the door, cheerfully greeting waitresses and customers on the way. On the table, Rex had left enough to cover both their meals two times over. Williams slowly slid from the booth, pulled his jacket over his shoulder, and pocketed both collections of poems.

In his Focus, Williams sat with the collections of poems in his hands. He thought about Rex's statement, "a young man's dream." Is that what he had, a young man's dream? He couldn't be a parent any longer, not a father to one of his own. That part of life had passed him by. Possibly like poetry for Rex. But Rex could still write poems, finish one more collection of poems, if he wanted. Gus couldn't go back and have one more family, not now. Maybe it was their age. Rex was much older, but both were senior citizens. Resigned to the fact that life was ending, why bother chasing a dream — was that the thought process? A symptom of old age possibly? Williams didn't want to accept it on Rex's behalf.

39

The holiday play was one of the students' favorite days, and Williams' as well. He donned his favorite holiday ensemble, a simple mossy green sweater with a maroon mock turtleneck.

The mood in the halls was merry and festive. Students had worn their holiday get-ups. More than one student had a Buddy the Elf costume, the girls had Christmas ribbons in their hair, several students wore fluffy white beards attached to Santa hats but, above all else, gaudy holiday sweaters abounded. Williams' classes would still have some substance as they read about the amalgam that is Santa Claus and about the Christian aspect of Jesus' birth.

"Mr. Williams, I thought you weren't allowed to teach religion in school?" Tony said flipping his paper around. "Do I have to do this?"

"Tony, that is a good question," Williams said turning to look Tony's way while handing out papers. "I am not teaching religion. If I were to give a sermon telling you to follow God's teachings or to follow the Torah or any other text, then I would be teaching religion."

"Then what is this paper about Jesus and Christmas?" Tony said flapping the paper out in front of him.

"I thought everyone would benefit by learning about the facts behind the holiday in order to understand one of the most celebrated days in Western culture. I am not telling you to follow it."

Williams continued to distribute papers. Tony slouched back in his chair, arms crossed. Williams turned to see the disgruntled look and felt like he should address this situation or risk a backfire of some sort later.

Williams approached Tony, "You don't seem too happy with that reasoning, Tony."

"No, I think it's just a bunch of whitewashing of students, holding back the culture of this school's minorities."

Williams knew he couldn't stand towering over the upset student who felt like he was being oppressed. He pulled up a chair next to Tony, holding the extra papers in his hand.

"So, you feel that I'm disregarding Hanukkah, Diwali, Kwanzaa and other holiday traditions?"

A look of slight befuddlement washed over Tony's face, "Yeah, that is exactly what I am saying."

"Do you think it is important enough to bring it to the attention of the principal?"

"Well, everyone should get to celebrate or be educated about all different types of cultures, especially the cultures of students in the school, no matter if it is one person or 300 hundred."

"Ok, great!" Williams said. He was aware that very few students were paying any attention to him. "Let's start with contacting other students that have a vested interest in these holiday traditions. Once you have this group contacted, make an appointment with Principal Anderson to ask for recognition of the holidays represented in your group."

"You gonna help with this?" Tony asked sideways.

"Tony, this has to come from the students. If you want something to change, you have to be the change maker. But I will be here to offer advice and lend you a meeting space in my room."

"So, you're behind the scenes."

"Yes, that's right. I won't be pulling on any strings like the puppet master, but empowering you to achieve what you want to achieve."

"Ok, I will let you know."

Williams stood, he had to regain control of the classroom or the students would get worked up and off task and once that happened, there was little hope. "Okay class, let's continue to learn about how Santa Claus is really and an amalgam of several different cultural figures including one depiction from the 1920s."

"Do you remember that, Mr. Williams," Jessica called out.

"Ha, ha, very funny, Miss Munoz -- ten points deducted from Hufflepuff."

"No one ever takes points away from Hufflepuff, Mr. Williams, they a bunch of wimps," Eddie said.

"They are not, at least read the books before commenting," Jessica snapped back.

"I read'em!" Eddie said.

"Don't lie," Natalie said. "You can't read."

Everyone started laughing at her comment, everyone except Eddie who just shook his head.

"Ok, everyone," Williams said holding up his handout. "Side one, the one with the picture."

During planning, Williams walked down to check out the elementary performance. He still remembered Danny in these plays. He was an elf in 3rd grade, followed by an ice goblin his final year in fifth grade. Danny and all his friends wanted to be the bad guys and destroy stuff, as most boys are wont to do. He wore blue tights and a long embroidered tunic with blue gloves and to top it off, he put blue gel in his hair. Janet twisted the top into spikes with a white gel. After the performance, the boys tore around the school like little heathens, adrenaline pumping and full of sugar. Williams just chuckled, then the principal caught them as they entered the early elementary corridor and told them that if they scared the little kids, they would be sure to have a month's worth of detention when they returned to school in January. Later the principal told Williams that it was like they all flipped a switch and suddenly acted like little angels instead of ice goblins. Holding hands with the kindergarten students, reading stories as they were poked, tapped, and pulled on by the Young 5s. The dubious elves had turned into blue Santa's helpers.

As Williams rounded the corner to the auditorium, he saw the lines of second graders waiting to go on stage for their part. The fifth-grade helpers guided the students onto the stage, directing them where to go and when to come off. Supervising the hallway was Beth Michelson.

"Hi, Mr. Williams," she said with a smile and a wave. "Coming to check out the performance?"

"Of course, haven't ever missed one."

"Well, it is standing room only," she said touching his arm gently. "But I have a reserved seat in the back row. You can take that one."

"Thank you, but won't you be needing it?" Williams said ready to reject the offer.

"No, not this year. We have quite a rambunctious group this year, and I'm afraid I am needed here." She smiled, touching a wiggling boy on the shoulder. He immediately stopped poking those around him. "Besides, I've seen this one before," she winked before turning to the line at her side.

"Ok, thank you. If you happen to change your mind, please just send me on my way."

She smiled and waved him off as she turned to the little elves getting ready to take their turn on the stage. The last thing he heard was her voice, "Please don't tug on my arm or tap me. You may wait your turn with your hand in the air."

Williams sat on the side in the auditorium. He watched as the children walked to the front of the stage to recite lines. Sarah Bilikin sat in the front holding cue cards for each speaker, directing the kids in each movement. The older students needed little guidance, while the younger ones needed much more prompting. While he didn't know a single student by name or by face, he knew some of his former students had children in the play. The laughter and excitement from each student filled the room with joy. Not much else could lift everyone's spirits like laughter from a child. As the play ended Williams, eyes glistening, he slipped out the side door to return to his classes in the high school.

40

As Williams returned from lunch, he could hear screaming from Adams' room.

"You can't make me stay here!"

Williams paused at the young man's voice. It was Cameron. There was only one boy with a voice like that at Wellington. A voice that loved nothing more than singing, fashion, and gossip."

Then he heard Mr. Adams, "Cameron, you need to retake the test. You completely failed it. You won't have time tomorrow in class."

"I don't care," Cameron shouted, voice trembling. "I will just fail."

"No, I can't let you do that, Cameron. You have one hour to work on this test, you may start now. You can catch the last half of the play if you stop fighting me on this and take the test."

"I'm the lead elf in the play, I can't be late," he pleaded.

Williams had heard enough. He turned the corner into Stacy's room. "Can I be of assistance? I heard the commotion from down the hall."

"No," Adams said firmly keeping an eye on Cameron.

Cameron moved closer to Gus. "Mr. Williams, can you tell Mr. Scrooge over there to let me go to the play? He wants me to retake the test right now."

"Is this accurate, Mr. Adams? You want Mr. Ides to retake his test right now?"

"Yes," Stacy said holding the test out to Cameron.

"And right now is the only time he can take it?"

"Yes," Stacy gestured with the test again. "As you know, Mr. Williams, grades are due over break and school ends tomorrow with a half-day." Adams smiled, "He won't have enough time."

Williams, hands clasped in front of him, turned toward Cameron, "Did you study for the test the first time?"

"Well, no," he said looking down at his jingle bell elf slippers, "I was too excited about the play. We made costumes, and we get to sing songs. It's just so much fun."

Williams looked to Adams and gave him a slight smile. One couldn't help but feel the joy coming from Cameron as he talked about the play.

"Well, Cameron," Williams said, "do you see how you not taking care of business then has caused problems now?"

"Yes, but I can't miss this. This play means everything to me. Please, Mr. Williams, Mr. Adams, I will do anything to make this play."

"Mr. Ides, let's see if this solution works for you and Mr. Adams." Williams glanced at Adams. "If the test takes an hour to complete, then you can come tomorrow morning at around 6:45 to take the test, which I will proctor."

"Ok, I will totally do that -- Can I go now?" Cameron started heading for the door.

"Cameron," Williams said, "if you don't show tomorrow, you will fail and have to retake the course, which means, according to school policy, you won't be able to participate in the Spring Musical."

Cameron stopped like a bullet had hit his chest. He turned to look at Williams and back to Adams, "Ok, I will see you in your room at 6:45."

"Thank you and have a good performance."

Stacy turned to Williams handing him the test, "Why did you

let him off the hook? He will never learn."

"Of course, he will," Williams said taking the paper. "He will either come tomorrow or give up the Spring Musical. Besides, he was so upset that you were going to hold him here that he would have failed again anyway."

"Let's hope this works," Adams said. "I'll come get the test from you in the morning."

"Before we go down to the play," Williams said leaning back against the desk, "were you really going to make him take the test instead of being the lead in the play?"

"Yes, why wouldn't I?"

"Come down with me to the auditorium. I don't think you quite understand what today is all about. Having kids miss their favorite thing is the opposite of taking your foot off the gas and getting to know them as people."

Williams walked to the door; Adams settled into his chair. Williams turned to see Adams sitting behind his desk, pen in hand, ready to grade papers. Williams cleared his throat and gave Adams the look only an experienced teacher could give. All the instructions that needed to be said were held in that one look. Adams dropped his pen and followed Williams as he made his way to the auditorium.

When Williams and Adams turned the corner to the auditorium, a wave of exuberance drifted toward them. Students bustled from one room to the next in full elf regalia. More than one Santa strolled the halls and a couple of Mrs. Clauses wandered around with frosted buns atop their heads.

As the pair, young and old, made the way through the bustling students, Williams smiled and pointed out the star athletes helping prep the young middle schoolers. The normally shy art students taking charge of the scene changes in the backdrops. And finally, they saw Cameron leading a throng of little blue and green elves in their lines.

"This," said Williams, "is just one part of what this day is all about."

"And the other?" Adams asked.

Williams moved aside a partition just enough so they could squeeze through to the other side.

"This," he said turning from Adams to the crowd bustling into the auditorium. "All the students who aren't in the play have already been seated. These are the alumni and community members who didn't get tickets for tonight's performance."

"Wow - for a play about Christmas?"

"Not just a play, Stacy," Williams said. "A feeling of connectedness that permeates this whole town. You see, North Wellington is like any small town. Everyone knows everybody and their business. We fight, we don't see eye to eye, but we support each other the rest of the time. And in the holiday season, the joy and love wash away any feelings of sadness, regret, and melancholy."

"Ugh, huh," Adams said, "but it seems to me that when push comes to shove, people will still do what is in their best interest."

"I think you have a limited view of humanity."

"I'm just not naive about people's true intentions."

Williams took his arm, "I've been around for a long time. I'm not naive, just hopeful that humanity will win out in the end." Williams guided Stacy to the auditorium door.

The lights flickered on and off cueing people to settle into their seats for the performance.

Williams kept his eyes toward the stage, smiling broadly as the students, young and old, told the fantastic story of a lost elf at Christmas time. Laughter and stories of hope filled an hour's time. The feeling of Christmas spirit sat heavy in his heart, full and warm. Life had its ways of seeing a person through to the end.

One look at Stacy and Williams knew he had won the day. His eyes were glistening with pure enjoyment connecting to the stage. Williams wondered if Adams had ever felt the holiday spirit. Had he ever felt part of a close-knit family? Had the joy of pure overwhelming love ever washed over him like the love rolling off the stage and through the auditorium? What Williams knew was one thing, but what he hoped for was another.

As the play ended, Gus signaled for Stacy to follow him out of the auditorium. They had to get back to their rooms to wrap up the day and, most importantly, beat the crowded exit or they would be stuck for another hour in the auditorium mingling with parents and students.

"So, Stacy, what are your holiday plans?"

"My mother would like to take me on a Caribbean cruise for seven days and then I have to make some decisions about law school."

"Well, a Caribbean cruise sounds like a nice, refreshing break. A little sun, a little fresh air, a couple of fancy drinks with umbrellas on the top."

"Yes, well, those things all come with my mother, which make them a little less refreshing."

"Not to get all serious on you, but where is your father in all of this? I haven't heard you talk about him at all."

"That is because I don't have one," Stacy said putting his hands deep into his pockets.

"C'mon," Williams said in a huff, "everyone has a father."

"No, not me," Stacy said shrugging his shoulders. "And I don't mean it in an angry emotional way or a he's-not-around-way or he's an asshole or anything like that. My mother, on one of her empowerment trips, decided to get artificially inseminated and have a child without a man involved."

"Well, then you have a biological father," Williams said.

"No," Stacy said turning in the center of the hall. "I have a sperm donor without a name."

"Classic question coming next," Williams said, "do you ever wonder who your 'sperm donor' is exactly?"

Adams continued to walk toward his classroom. "I used to wonder all the time growing up. Every boy wants a dad to play catch or wrestle or watch sports with and teach him how to shave and all that, but mom was pretty competent in most things. She made an effort to find men who would pal around with us. Some I think were actual love interests and others were just being paid for being a guy hanging out with us."

"That must have been a little disconcerting," Williams said.

"Well, once it is part of your existence, you stop questioning it and just accept it."

"I think I understand that part of it," Williams said rounding the corner to his room.

Williams waved to Adams as he departed for his room. He pulled his journal from his bag, stuck a holiday blend K-Cup into his Keurig, and settled himself down to write. He had accepted quite a bit in his life, yet there was still more he needed to accept, mostly having to do with the death of family. As he dropped a creamer into his coffee, Williams sat back looking out over his room. What would his life be like without North Wellington? So often he had seen teachers retire only to fall ill or slowly decline into a life not worth living. Mother Nature had told him his time was about up. Now he would have to start living for himself or bide his time until the inevitable.

41

Not even a full day back from the break and Williams was called to the principal's office. His first two hours with the students were pretty normal fare. Some light work to get the students back into the swing of school. Small side conversations discussing the events of the break. He had even taken a peek across the hall to where a tanned Stacy Adams was doing much of the same. The feeling of constant pressure and tension wasn't hanging over the room like it had been. But when a note from the office came at the end of second hour, Williams felt those pangs of nervous energy deep in his gut. The same the kids probably felt when they were summoned to the office.

"Mr. Williams, we are failing at keeping the young Mr. Adams from failing."

Principal Anderson paced back and forth from his desk to the printer, grabbing and organizing papers, shuffling back to his desk, then inserting each paper into a folder or onto a pile on his desk. Bent over his computer, Anderson clicked back and forth between his two monitors, as if playing a game of tennis between the two.

"You seem a little preoccupied, would you like me to come back in a few minutes?" Williams asked.

"No, I have to go to an admin meeting this morning with 'documentation' for adequate progress on certain district goals.

And this printing has taken me much longer than anticipated. I have had several interruptions and then I have to find all the right files." Anderson turned to Williams, "This is the last one." Williams watched the final manic hustle.

"Isn't it a little early in the new term to have to present information about district goals?" Williams asked, perturbed by his own presence in the office.

"I, much like you, don't have a say in some things, Mr. Williams. I just have to do what I am told."

"So, the superintendent needs to check some things off his list and his calendar is clear?"

"I suppose," Anderson said clicking through more files and tabs on his screen.

"Does he understand that today is probably not the best day to request a meeting about last term's numbers?"

"Mr. Williams, I am sure you have seen the superintendent's job done in many different ways, this is just his way."

"Todd, you are a young man. I can tell you want to do a good job and continue ascending the administration ladder, but don't emulate Snyder. He doesn't seem to think about people as much as he should."

Anderson looked from his screens for a brief moment. Williams could tell that Anderson understood the message but wasn't going to comment back. Williams wouldn't have either at his age. But the older he became the less inclined he was to keep his opinions to himself. Maybe it was that he didn't have much more time to form his opinions. As quickly as Anderson stopped, he started up again.

He slipped the paper, hot from the printer, into a file folder and then took the whole stack from his desk to his messenger bag by the door. Even the principal had pressure to meet the state guidelines, to follow through on board directives, and to follow the data commandments from the superintendent. Anderson hung the bag on a hook at hip level. He returned to his desk and sunk down into his high-backed leather chair, a small bit of relief seemed to drift away.

"I would just like to know what I can do to help you and Mr. Adams be successful in the coming months. We seem to have moved past the phone throwing and student berating, but students are still not happy. Trouble seems to be brewing. I saw a little red sky this morning and you know what they say, red sky in the morning, sailors take warning."

Williams chuckled, "Your use of mixed metaphors astounds me Principal Anderson. Were you an English scholar in your younger days?"

"I do like a good turn of phrase," he said leaning elbows first onto his desk, hands clasped together in a pyramid. "What can we, the administration, do to help him succeed?"

"The only thing we can do is give him time and support."

"That is what I am asking you, Mr. Williams," Anderson said leaning back into his chair, flinging his hands in the air. "What does that look like for Mr. Adams?"

Williams smiled. By asking how to support a new teacher, Anderson was basically admitting he didn't know how to support any teacher. And right now, he didn't even know that he was admitting it. But Williams also knew that he couldn't make that idea the point of the discussion. If he did, the whole discussion would turn into a mess of defensive posturing. Instead, he must guide Anderson. If he played his cards right, he could not only help Adams, but all the teachers at North Wellington and wherever else Anderson might end up.

"We support him by believing in him, telling him he has something to offer the students, and helping him see that the mistakes he makes in the classroom are mistakes. We can only nudge him in the right direction, we can't push or pull him. He is as stubborn as a mule."

"How long will that take?" Anderson's hands were now folded over his midsection.

Williams cocked his head to the side, "How long will that take?"

"You know, to nudge him in the right direction," Anderson said, grabbing a pen from his desk. He started tapping his left hand with the pen as he waited for Williams' answer.

"Mr. Anderson," Willams said, "good teaching isn't an end product or a final destination that is arrived at after a certain amount of time or a certain number of steps or a certain number of marks have been ticked off a list. Good teaching is developed through trial and error, contemplation, examples, mentoring, and other heuristics. Stacy Adams will be a good teacher when he becomes a good teacher, and he'll become one if we keep telling him that he is making a difference."

"We don't have a lot of time here."

Williams didn't like the idea of a timeline in play with Adams. "Time is irrelevant in this instance. No one likes confrontation or bad attitudes or feeling unliked. Slowly those things tell the teacher that what they have been doing isn't working, so they change. When the students are working in class, telling the teacher about their personal lives, the teacher will see their actions as 'good teaching' and continue to do those things."

"In this case, Mr. Williams, time is material," Anderson leaned forward, pulled a pad of paper from a wire file organizer, and began writing at the top before looking up over his non-existent glasses. "North Wellington has certain figures — this is between us, mind you."

Williams nodded in agreement, then Anderson continued.

"There are certain prominent figures in the community who," Anderson dropped the pen and threw air quotes in the air " 'don't give a rat's ass' who this kid's mom is in Ann Arbor, they are tired of his 'bullshit'."

"Are those," Williams threw his own air quotes, "air quotes directly from the mouths of the so called prominent figures?"

"I am just relaying what I have been told."

"So, what is the district's timeline?" Williams asked ringing his hands together. "Are they going to fire him mid-year? Because if you are asking me for a timeline, the reality is the timeline is all theirs. We have to have Adams in proper form, whatever that is, by when they say so."

"No," Anderson said, pen back in his hand, "I don't think they will fire him mid-year. But they are going to set a timeline of some sort and if Mr. Adams doesn't come around a little bit more than he has, they will let him go at the end of the year. And just to remind you and your union counterparts that the district doesn't need documentation or a cause to not renew a non-tenured teacher's contract."

"Yes, I know," Williams said leaning back in his chair. "I think the district should allow Mr. Adams at least the three years of probationary teaching that most new teachers are afforded."

"I agree with you on this one, Mr. Williams, but I don't have a choice in the matter." Anderson made a note on the pad of paper. "I am often at the mercy of the superintendent's office, who is sometimes at the mercy of the school board. If I push back too hard, I could not have my contract renewed, and if the superintendent pushes back, he could not have his contract renewed." Anderson looked directly at Williams. "We are all just employees that are replaceable, Gus."

"I know," Williams said. "But what I hope for is that you and the superintendent, who created this mess, would be strong enough not to topple over in a slight breeze. You know, hold your ground."

"Here is an analogy for your, Mr. Williams," Anderson put his pen on his pad of paper. "A strong oak tree can be uprooted and blown over, but in that same storm a blade of grass can bend to the ground then spring right back upright once the gale passes."

"So, you are bending?"

"I must," Anderson said. "We must."

"If a timeline is what you need, I would suggest giving Mr. Adams a full year. If not, reevaluate by Spring Break."

Anderson's pen scratched down Williams' timeline. "Thank you, Mr. Williams," Anderson said. "I will push for your first recommendation."

Williams stood to go realizing that he had given in, provided himself as the scapegoat. "One more thing before I go," Williams said. "You know if the district is to escape the wrath of Ms. Adams, you should document all you are doing to support her son, besides just asking an old man on his way out of the profession to guide him. After all, how would it look to her if all you did was provide an aging mentor and then fire the lad before the end of the year without so much as a principal conference, an action plan, a round of watching others teach, etc."

Anderson's brow furrowed. Williams' words tumbled around and around. He said, "We will take everything you have said into consideration. Thank you."

Williams turned to the door, "Thank you, Mr. Anderson, for giving me the opportunity to provide you with the recommendation of three years."

Williams walked, without a word, straight from the principal's office, past the secretaries helping students, and past the student assistants filing papers. Time was of the essence. Adams had to be nudged a little harder.

Williams knew better than anyone about the community and its citizens. On certain occasions they could be so supportive, but lately, with the onset of social media, the internet, and immediacy of information, everyone seemed to be a little less patient. Just like on TV they saw no qualms with firing someone. Professional coaches were fired after just a few seasons, regardless of wins and losses. CEOs were sent packing with golden parachutes. Actors and directors were blacklisted for comments new and old. Newscasters were fired for old mistakes now come to light. All the public attention regarding those firings had led others to believe that a short leash was best. Being unforgiving was the only way to be protected from litigious groups and people. Was it best to send Stacy on down the river? He was not a bad person. A demanding and unforgiving teacher, yes. But he could change over time; Williams had seen glimpses already.

Williams knew that not all teachers were good teachers. They were the ones who had little in the way of substantial lesson plans. They let the students "warm up" for ten minutes, then "cool down" for ten minutes at the end of class. The ones who let videos teach and worksheets provide feedback. They steered most of their grades to the top of the grading scale. No one complained about A's. Adams was not this type of teacher. He put time and effort into his lesson plans. He thought about what skill would fit best with what lesson. He gave honest feedback. His expectations and his relatability needed improving. Adams would be a great teacher given the time, the support, and guidance. But Williams knew that if he didn't help Adams turn the corner this year, it wouldn't happen.

42

The cold January wind blew through the Steak and Egger parking lot. Williams was running a few minutes late, which meant he was right on time for his 8 a.m. breakfast with Rex. A month had passed since he had seen Rex. Since then they had talked a few times on the phone and corresponded via email about a few different books they had been reading.

Williams had been coming to terms with his illness, with the disease that sat in his bones like a houseguest that would never leave. Having a terminal illness started to put everything else into perspective. Everyday decisions seemed a little more important now.

When Gus walked through the front door, Rex was already at the table, their table. He looked weaker, as if more life had been drained out of him in the last month.

"Sorry to keep you waiting. It takes me longer to get moving than I am used to."

"No problem, Gus. Although my time is running a little short these days."

"Yes, I know, mine too." Gus said pushing his jacket to the far corner of the booth then sliding in across from Rex. "How are you feeling? Things getting better with treatment?"

Rex looked up, peering over the brim of his coffee, eyes strong and unwavering. "There are no more treatments for me, only to make me comfortable, which means to rob me of any feeling in my final moments."

"What do you mean, are you refusing final treatments? Rex, you can't give up."

"No," Rex said holding his hands in the air to seemingly push back on Williams' idea of refusing treatment. "I am not refusing any more treatments, there are none to give." Rex's eyes glossed over, full with emotion. "The cancer has spread to all sorts of organs. No surgery can take it all out, radiation is not effective, and the chemo level would kill me first. So, I am left to make my final arrangements and say my goodbyes. I may have until spring if it keeps growing slowly."

"Oh, I am sorry, Rex," Gus said flipping over his cup as the waitress approached with a steaming pot of coffee. "We should talk about something else, no more discussion of cancer."

"There is no need on my account. I find solace in knowing that my time has come to an end. To know there will be no more walking amongst the freshly fallen leaves, listening to the rustle and crackle underfoot. Or the cold blast of air on a January morning. Though I do wish to see the first birds of spring, the children coming out to play in the street, and the smell of an April shower. And the last thing I long to see is a summer sunset over Lake Michigan. The sand beneath my toes, water racing up the shore -- just one more sunset, Gus. That is all I wish for, one more sunset over Lake Michigan."

"Rex, you are so strong. I know you will make it to that summer sunset. I will take you myself."

"You are a very kind man, Gus. My son wants me to go live with him in North Carolina. He is in human resources there. Makes a ton of money but has no poetic sensibilities."

"Is he your only child?"

"Yes, his mother and I had some trouble. It was a miracle he was born at all, but that romantic sentiment is lost on him as well."

"Sounds like you two don't see eye to eye."

"Well, we do on most things, but I am just trying to get him to slow down, enjoy some of the sweeter moments of life before they are gone. His mother was better at it than me. Now that she has passed, it is like two kings eyeing each other for the throne. But enough about me, how are you?"

"No, I am all alone. My wife and son passed in a car accident in '85, a few dark years followed and then just teaching."

"Devoted to your work, huh?"

"Well, yes and no," Williams said taking another sip of coffee. "I love the students and the community, they really bolstered me up when I needed it the most. Gave me a sense of belonging after Janet and Danny died."

"But you never married again or had kids. You were so young."

"Oh, I dated a few women but it hurt too bad, felt like I was betraying my wife and son. I decided to focus on myself a bit, read all the books I always wanted to read, write in my journal, and teach, really teach. And life just sort of floated by."

"As it does."

"So it goes."

The breakfast arrived. Rex and Gus continued to discuss one memory after another like two old friends. They found some friends they had in common and times when they must have been in the same place at the same time.

Rex's doctors didn't expect him to live into the summer, but Williams hoped he would so he could see his final sunset over Lake Michigan. As Rex's door on life was closing, Gus realized that his own door was still open for at least another five years. The grim reaper wasn't coming for him quite yet.

"Well, Gus, how did your chemotherapy go? This time was an aggressive approach, was it not?"

"Yes, very aggressive and it was awful. I was in the hospital for about two weeks and I was as sick as a dog the whole time. I had to stay in the hospital for multiple days. I felt like I was dying. One of the nurses said they hoped the chemo wiped out the cancer since it almost wiped me out."

"Well, that's good, I guess. Did you have family come with you to help listen to the doctors and take care of you?"

"No. No family around and I have only told one person that I'm sick."

"Oh, Gus. You have to tell people. They will want to help you, truly they will, just like I'm sure they helped you when you lost your wife and child."

"I don't want pity."

"It's not pity, but compassion and love."

Williams cut into his over easy eggs with his fork, letting the yolk run over his plate. He pushed a bite of hash browns into the yellow.

Rex looked on. "I know it's hard for an old guy set in his ways, a person who hasn't let anyone in for decades, but letting people in opens up your world."

"So says the poet who no longer writes poetry."

"Suite yourself." Rex took a bite of the last piece of bacon then pushed his plate toward the table edge. His meal half-finished.

"Rex, I am opening up. I'm opening up to you, aren't I?"

"Yeah, you did. You told a few small secrets to a dying man. Good for you. What about something deep Gus? Give me something that I couldn't read in a newspaper file or guess from talking to you for five minutes. Because that is what poetry is to me, the deepest, closest to the heart secrets."

Williams clenched his fork, knuckles turning white, "Right, but this isn't a competition between who can share the most. You are masquerading as a former businessman. You would rather be a poet but are too scared to admit it or try for it or something."

"Gus, you're right." Rex leaned back in his booth, placing his folded napkin on the table.

"What?" Williams looked at him in disbelief.

Rex started to cough. The fit lasted long enough to draw

attention from other tables. Williams called for more water as he ripped a stack of napkins from the dispenser, handing them to Rex, who was turning a little red. As the fit subsided, Rex caught his breath with big gulps of air and small sips of water.

"I think it's moving into my lungs," Rex said under labored breathing.

"I'm so sorry, Rex," Williams said pushing his plate to the side. "I shouldn't have gotten upset with you."

"But you are right, Gus. I'm scared. I sold my soul for money and I'm afraid I wasted my life in pursuit of it."

"No, you didn't sell your soul. You made money, provided for your family, lived a good life, but you don't have to quit now. You can finish the way you started."

"No, I took the wrong path. It was the most traveled but I thought it was the best and maybe it was."

"Oh, what does Frost know? As a hiker, I learned you never get off the trail in the woods unless you want to get lost. But I also learned the side trails have some of the best views. And some of them have the best water. So, either path is still a path." Williams drank the last of his coffee followed by a sip from his ice water. "How about this poem instead, 'Do not go gentle into that good night. Old age should burn and rave at close of day. Rage, rage against the dying of the light'."

"Yes! Yes! But I do not have the strength to rage any longer. The light is leaving me as I sit here; I can feel it."

"You are stronger than you know, Rex. Finish your poems, send them to your old publisher, leave the world as you want to be remembered."

"Okay, okay. Your passion is starting to fill me with motivation. But I will only finish my poems if you write your memoirs. Use all those old journals to share your story with the world."

Rex placed a used napkin off to the side on his uncleared plate.

"I don't know, Rex. I'm a nobody. Who would want to read

my memoirs?"

"It doesn't matter who you are but what you have to say, Gus. You have been pondering life for thirty years, you must have come to some conclusions in all that time. Send it out into the world."

"Now it is your passion that is motivating me, although with much more trepidation, I think."

Rex slid from the booth, holding on to the back of the booth as he reached for his jacket. He steadied himself as he slipped one arm through his sleeve then the other. Standing up, Williams saw how frail Rex was becoming. He was right, a little bit of life was leaving him every second. "Do you need help getting to the car?"

"No, but thank you. My ride is here." Rex pointed his ebony cane at a man in a black peacoat with a name tag.

Williams smiled, "Right you are. Well, thank you for another wonderful meal. I think it is my turn to get the check."

"Ok, Rex said smiling as he maneuvered between tables toward the door.

Williams sat back down in the booth, flagging down the waitress.

"Hi, Mr. Williams. Would you like more coffee?"

"No, no thank you. Just the check please." Williams reached into his back pocket for his wallet.

"Oh, Mr. Chamberlain took care of it before you got here," she said with a smile.

"How could he do that before we even ordered?" Williams stated in disbelief.

"He gave me $50 and said I could keep whatever was left." She stacked the dirty plates together to take into the back room. "Have a good day, Mr. Williams."

"Yes, thank you," Williams said slipping his wallet back into his pocket. "But Cassie, next time, please let me get the bill."

"Ok, will do, but just to let you know, Mr. Chamberlain always finds a way to pay. He thinks it's funny. Sometimes when he is here alone, he will pick a random person at the counter and pay for their breakfast but leave before they can thank him. It's like a Secret Santa or something."

Cassie took the plates back to the kitchen leaving Williams to think about all he had learned in the last ninety minutes. The life he had lived, the lives he had impacted, and what he had failed to do personally. Now, he had a project to start, journals to read, and more living to do.

43

At the end of January, school is starting to drag. Williams always thinks of a Gary Paulson interview about writing. He said something akin to writing is one long slog. To write a book is like walking miles and miles through a thick, thigh-high swamp. Teaching in January was the middle of the slog. The first few months were fresh, not so bad. Students had come back from the summer, tan, older, and with stories. They were ready to get back to the routine of class, the sports, the clubs, and their friends. Then before they knew it, Halloween distracted them, then Thanksgiving and finally the joyful holiday season of Christmas.

The first term was exciting. The students were motivated to learn, but then came winter. Like in the *Game of Thrones*, winter was often dreaded by many at school. In Michigan, the students started class before the sun rose and, if they were in a sport or a club, went home after the sunset. At first, there was a little excitement. What happened over break? Who got what presents? Which kids went to a tropical climate? Their tan bodies standing in stark contrast to the pasty white skin of their classmates. Unless students were involved in the ski club, there was little to look forward to on a weekly basis unless the basketball team was having a good year. Classes were just another step toward spring break and then summer. The only exciting things at

North Wellington were the basketball games and the drama that unfolded between students.

"Mr. Williams," Eric said, "are you coming to our game tonight?"

"Home game?"

"Yeah," Eric said closing his binder and piling his books up on his desk. "We play Christian."

"Oh," Williams said turning from his computer screen. "Are they any good? They usually run that 1-3-1 trap that gives teams fits."

"Yeah, we have been working on that all break. Coach brought in a couple of guys from his men's league that played college ball to really put some pressure on us. I think we should do pretty well."

"I will do my best to make it. You know I have a hard time resisting that concession stand popcorn."

"All right, I hope to see you there," he said turning to the door.

Williams hoped he could get Adams to go with him. It would be a step in the right direction for him to see the students in a different light besides in his classroom. Something changed when teachers saw students as a whole person and vice versa.

Across the hall, the students were trudging out of Adams' door. They were so clustered together trying to get out that they were getting stuck in the doorway. He peered over their heads to Adams who was still looking tan from his cruise, but no less stressed than before the break.

"Stacy," Gus said slipping through the last few students to enter the room, "I need a favor tonight."

"I don't know, Gus," Adams said shuffling his papers, flipping through his binders. "I have so much to do to get ready for this term. I haven't been teaching for years, you know."

"I know, I know. You have a lot to do," Williams said holding up his hands. "I just, uh, haven't been feeling so great since my treatment over the break and I wanted to go to the game tonight, but I feel like I should have someone drive me there."

"Gus, C'mon," Adams said turning from his work. "You know that is a crock. If you want me to go to the game tonight, just ask."

"You are too sharp for me."

"I think you need more adult interaction," Adams said smiling. "You are starting to act like a teenager."

Williams smiled. Adams might be turning the corner. "Fine, fine," Gus said holding up his hands again. "Some students asked me to go but I hate going alone, trying to find a place to sit or someone to sit by. I would rather go with someone I know."

"Okay."

"Okay, you'll go?" Williams asked.

"Yes."

"Great, pick me up at 6:30. 850 Merylton," Williams said. He slipped back through the tide of incoming students before Adams could object. Progress had been slow, but progress is progress. Hopefully, the two weeks off had helped Adams figure things out a bit or at least given him a little perspective.

Williams donned his green warrior sweatshirt under his black puffy jacket. Williams had never really liked the puffy jacket trend, but he had gotten so cold the older he had become. The down jackets were really the only thing that kept him warm. He understood now why older men were always wearing sweaters and vests and long pants in the summer.

When a black Cadillac ATS pulled into the driveway, Williams wondered if the person was lost and turning around. As the door opened and Adams started to step out, Williams flipped off his lights and pulled the door closed.

"I wasn't sure it was you," Williams said rounding the front of the car.

"Why's that?" Adams said standing half out of the door, "You don't like my ride?"

"It just seems more like an older person's car," Williams said sliding into the passenger seat.

Stacy slammed the door and revved the engine without looking at Williams, "You know, Gus."

Williams looked at Stacy, searching.

"That's because it is." Adams smiled, "My mother gave me this car and sold my old one without even asking me if I wanted it. She said the Cadillac is more reliable and more fun to drive."

"What was your old car?"

"That doesn't matter. What matters is that she didn't even ask me."

Williams was unsure of how to respond. Adams' blood was really pumping, veins had popped out on his forehead. Adams stomped on the accelerator. The tires squealed. Williams' head snapped back to the seat.

"Well, it really seems to get going pretty fast," Williams said grabbing onto the door. "I was wondering if you could make it go any faster. That take-off was pretty slow."

Stacy looked over. Williams was grinning from ear to ear.

"Sorry," Adams said backing down on the accelerator. "That sort of stuff gets me really fired up."

"Parents can do that."

"Yeah, but do you want to know the worst part?"

"There's a worst part?"

"Yeah, the worst part is that she was right. This car is way more fun to drive."

Williams started laughing.

"What's so funny?"

"It's the classic case of a parent knows best and the kid doesn't want to listen. And you're telling me that I am acting like a teenager."

"It's just this one time," Adams said.

"Sure," Williams said still chuckling.

Adams laughed as he turned the corner toward the school.

44

Inside the school, the heat poured from the gym doors. The odor of toil and fight lingered in the air. The buzzer sounded to signal the end of the JV game. Fans slowly slid down the bleachers. Williams and Adams slipped to the side as a large group of parents turned the corner. Williams smiled and nodded at each person. He overheard grumblings about playing time, complaints about the coach. Williams hadn't seen the scoreboard yet, but he knew if the parents were grumbling, the outcome was not in Wellington's favor.

"Jesus, it smells," Adams said leaning over into Williams' ear. "We are all going to smell like a gym when we leave here."

Williams turned, "Think of it as part of the experience."

"I guess."

Williams moved up to the admissions table where an elderly lady with short-cropped hair sat with an open cash box and a roll of tickets. "Hi, Peggy O! How are you this fine evening?"

"Oh, Gus, hi. Good. What a nail-biter that last game."

"I see, it must have been a good game, the aroma speaks of a good hard battle."

"Yes, I think so," she said with a small laugh.

"I brought along a new teacher with me. This is his first North Wellington game."

"Excellent," she said turning to Adams. "I'm Peggy O. and

what's your name?"

"Stacy Adams," he said shaking her hand.

"And what do you teach?"

"English."

Gus interrupted, "You're starting to get a line Peg, so we are going to go find our seats."

"Ok, nice to meet you," she said before turning to the next person in line.

Heading into the gym, Gus and Stacy were met with a small crowd gathered on the edge of the court. Williams spied the teams taking their spots in the open doorways of their locker rooms. Each was waiting for the other to start their warmups. They would have to wait until both teams took the floor before they could make their way to the other side of the bleachers.

"What's her deal?" Adams said nudging Williams in the side with his elbow. "I am guessing she's an old friend."

"Yeah," Gus said. "Something like that." He turned to look at Adams. "That woman has spent her whole life here. She grew up down the street, attended school here, went off to college and then came back to teach here for forty plus years. She retired because of health reasons but then ran for the school board and got herself elected. Her life is here."

"Wow, that is a lot of time in one place."

"She is not the only one," Williams said taking Adams' arm. "All over this gym are people that have made North Wellington part of their life, not just the school but the community. Little communities like this exist all over the Midwest but more and more people are losing their sense of belonging to a place. They are losing their connection to community."

Williams pulled Adams forward with the mass of people. The speakers blasted a heavy drumbeat as the Warriors took the floor. The way to the front cleared as fans clamored for seats. Williams and Adams found themselves standing on the corner of the court as the players rushed by. The strong young bodies pulsed with energy as they curled around the edges of the court before coming back together down the center to the basket. The lead player tossed the ball off the glass. Each player followed suit until the last player, a senior named Jessie, planted two feet, rose up, snatched the ball as it came off the glass and slammed it down. The crowd erupted. The student section jumped up and down, the energy already hyped.

"We need to go across the court to that side for a seat, past the student section," Williams said leading the way across the baseline to the other side.

At the edge of the student section, several students were standing on the sideline, bulging the fan section onto the court where the opposing team was going through warm-ups. Williams smiled as students yelled his name and waved in excitement over seeing their teacher at an extracurricular event. He slowly made his way around a pack of boys wearing capes and super suits, placing a hand on their shoulders to make sure they knew he was behind them. The last thing he wanted was to be knocked over with their rambunctious behavior. A fall could break one of his cancer-ridden bones. He made his way past three or four girls in homemade North Wellington crop tops. As he stepped to ascend the bleachers, a roar erupted behind him. He turned to see a pile of bodies.

A Christian player was splayed out on the floor. The rest of the Knights were running over. Some Wellington fans were yelling. Williams didn't want to get into the middle of things. He couldn't take getting knocked around, not with his condition. Then he saw Adams lying face down in a pile of bodies under a Knight player. As the player moved to get up, Williams saw a second commotion near the bodies on the floor. This one had elicited a different, more jovial reaction. Adams had landed on top of Jessica. Her cropped top had gotten pushed up in the fall and Adams had landed on her ample bosom. Her sports bra completely covered her, but the scene still evoked shock from the student body.

Jessica's face scrunched in disgust from being knocked to the ground, but quickly realized what happened and who was now on top of her. Adams, who was hit from behind, was slower to recognize what had happened. As he started to push himself up, Jessica slipped her top down then slung one arm behind Adams' neck. "Hello, again, Mr. Adams," she said with a sly smile. "If you wanted to talk, all you had to do was ask." Adams quickly jumped to his feet. Her friends all laughed at his embarrassment.

Williams reached down to help Jessica up off the floor. The commotion between the players and the fans had subsided as Stuart Jefferies herded students up into the bleachers and off of the floor. "I am so sorry Jessica," Williams said grabbing her hands. "Are you hurt?"

"No, I don't think so," she said standing up.

"I'm so sorry," Adams said, "that player slammed into me and I just flew forward. I didn't have any time to react."

"That's okay," she said straightening her top and skirt. "I know you didn't mean it."

"So embarrassing," Adams said.

"Please don't make a big deal out of it," she said. "It will be awkward."

"Right." Adams turned to Williams, "Well, let's get out of the way."

Jessica's friends surrounded her as Adams and Williams left. They could overhear them teasing her. Jessica pleaded, "Please don't make it a big deal." Her friend responded, "…unless it is a big deal." Then they all laughed. Williams kept moving forward. He would have to reinforce his point about proper student-teacher relationships at some point, although he didn't think it was needed in this case.

The game battled back and forth through the first half. Each team making runs then fighting back to even. Williams watched Adams and the crowd as much as he watched the game. Seeing the action but scanning the crowd on both sides of the court. He kept an eye on the student section. He saw his students interacting with each other. The underclassman interacting with upperclassmen. The JV players working their way into the fan section after they emerged from the locker room. Middle school students watched as costume clad high schoolers lead the cheers. Someday in the future, these middle school students would replace those they watched now. And the elementary students that were running through the halls, enjoying not the game but their friendships, would soon sit in the bleachers observing how the seniors did it.

"My high school was not like this," Adams said.

"Mine wasn't quite like this either."

"I can see why people come back here time after time. There is something special about this place."

Williams had won the battle. Adams saw that this was not just a job but a way of life. Teaching here, as it should be everywhere, had to be about the people and the people had to be about the community. "Let's go try the popcorn," Williams said. "My treat."

45

"Mr. Williams, you can come into my office," Principal Anderson said. His posture more rigid than usual.

"Todd, what can I do for you today?" Williams said taking a seat in the chair in front of the principal's desk

Anderson looked puzzled for a moment. "I am not sure I ever remember you calling me by my first name before. And now that's twice this year so far."

"Well, I feel like we have become more friendly this year with so many meetings about this and that. I thought maybe we could make things a little less formal."

"I am not so sure that this is the time for that, I am afraid."

Williams had been waiting for this conversation. Ever since the basketball game, students had been talking about "Adams' fall from grace." Apparently, some students had photos of Adams on top of Jessica with his face resting on her chest, and then others with her arm wrapped around his neck and a coy smile on her face. JohnnyFireball69's video made it on the evening news and ESPN even ran a spot with the video as part of the Top 10 Bloopers.

"Then let's get right down to it, Mr. Anderson. Why am I here?"

"We have to discuss your mentee, Mr. Adams."

"What about him? He has been doing really well in the

classroom. Students have been coming and going from his classroom with smiles on their faces. He has been trying to connect with students. Things seem to be going rather well, all things considered."

"Well, it's the 'all things considered' we have to talk about, I'm afraid."

Williams was tired of the pussyfooting around the subject. "You have said, 'I'm afraid' twice now since I've been in your office. Why don't you cut to the chase? What are you afraid of doing?"

"This sort of thing is not easy for me, Gus," Anderson said rubbing his hands on the arms of his chair. "I know you think I am some diabolical administrator working with 'The Man' to whammy all teachers. But that is not the case. I am just another member of this team trying to do what is best for the students and the community."

Williams looked at him in silence, hands resting on his lap.

Anderson continued, "We have made a decision, one that I am less than comfortable with at this juncture, but we have decided to not renew Mr. Adams' contract at the end of the year."

"Jesus Christ," Gus blurted leaning back in his chair. "So, this is it then. You are letting him go because of a video that you and I both know is nothing more than an innocent accident. He was blindsided for crying out loud. He had no way of controlling where he landed or how he landed."

"Gus, it is not just about any particular thing but about all the incidents this year. From the phone throwing at the beginning of the year to the student complaints to the parent complaints to the basketball incident. He is just a train wreck waiting to happen, and we are getting our car off the track."

"So, what am I doing here if your mind is made up already?"

"Well, we are concerned about his reaction. He has a volatile nature and we don't want any outbreaks in the school or the classroom."

"Oh, c'mon, Todd," Gus blurted out. "He has never hurt a

soul."

"Hear me out, Gus," Anderson held up his hands in a defensive posture. "I didn't mean anything by that, it was the wrong words. No one thinks he's going to hurt anyone. We are concerned with the repercussions from his family."

"What the hell, Todd?" Gus said crossing his arms. "I'm not firing him. You want this done, you do it yourself."

Gus stood up pacing behind the chairs, rubbing his hand down the back of his hair. "Maybe you could take him out for Valentine's Day, give him a box of chocolates and some roses then let him down easy. But one thing I will not do for you is your dirty work."

"Gus, Gus," Anderson was out of his seat reaching for Williams trying to calm him down.

"I don't want you to do anything of the sort. Please, sit down and hear me out."

"Fine, I'm listening," Gus said sitting back down.

"I just want you to find out if Stacy is thinking about returning to law school next year or if his heart is set on teaching here. If we don't have to let him go, that would be better for him and for us."

"You know, Todd," Williams said, "For someone who is supposed to be a smooth talker, you really fucked this up."

"I know, Gus, I know," Anderson said hanging his head. "There are certain things that never get easier. And having to let someone go is one of those things."

"Yeah, well, letting someone go is not always the answer. I will let you know if I hear anything about law school. But I hope you will have the courtesy to let Adams know in time so he can go back to law school."

"We put Spring Break as the cut-off time. If we don't hear from you or Stacy by then, we are planning on letting him go before we break. We are also putting in a Zero Tolerance Policy. One more thing that goes wrong with this kid and we are going to terminate immediately."

Williams stood to leave, strode toward the door, nearly knocking the chair over as he went. He then turned to face Anderson, "You know how it will look to fire the guy that got knocked down on national television. You talk about bad publicity. You guys are really trying to drum up some bad PR with this idea."

Williams opened the door to the office, flinging it a little harder than usual. Things just became a little more complicated.

In the hall, he ran into Johnny interviewing students for the approaching Snowcoming assembly. Williams started to pass them by, but Johnny stepped in front of him with his cell phone in hand.

"Mr. Williams, what do you think of the Warriors' chances of winning the conference this year? They have a few pivotal games this week against the Vikings and the Wildcats."

Williams put his hand up over the phone camera, "Get that out of my face. I am sick of you and that thing."

Johnny was stunned. He looked from Williams to the office. There in the office, Principal Anderson was standing in the door, running his hands through his hair. Johnny knew something just went down. He turned to follow Williams.

46

Williams made his way down the hall. He couldn't go back to his room for fear of seeing Stacy and spilling all the beans about what the front office had planned. He stopped to take a drink from a drinking fountain then continued on his way. Williams walked away from his room to the far stairs on the other side of the school. Following close behind with his phone ready was Johnny.

Williams rounded the corner. James was standing in the hall with Pete again. They were quietly whispering as Pete kept his eyes on his students from the doorway. Williams watched as Pete rubbed his chin, like he was deep in thought. He saw Williams coming down the hall. He waved him over.

"Gus, I want to ask you some advice," Pete said as Williams drew near.

"Hi, Pete, Terry," Williams said. "How can I help?"

"Well, Terry has been in quite a pickle since last November."

"How so?" Williams asked.

"To make a long story short," Terry said, "a couple of students claimed I kicked one of them."

"Right," Gus said. "I remember hearing something about that from a student."

"Yes," Pete said, "We handled that situation. The students eventually came clean that Terry didn't really kick anyone. He had stumbled over the student's feet multiple times before the student shouted out in pretend pain."

"Ok, so all clear," Williams said. "There is nothing more to be done. It was just a teenager being a teenager."

"Well," Pete said, "that's the problem. Another student has come out of the woodwork saying things about Terry."

"What are they saying now?" Gus asked.

As the three men stood in the hall discussing the latest development of Terry James, Johnny casually walked to a locker behind Williams. He opened the locker, pretending to rummage through its contents while holding his camera phone steady, aimed at the three men.

"There is another student, Sonya," Terry said.

"Oh, Jesus."

"That's right," Pete said.

"What is it she is saying?" Gus asked.

"She hasn't said anything yet," Terry said, "but she mentioned telling a few friends that we had been talking outside of class."

"Then she has," Gus said. "If she is telling her friends that she is talking with a teacher that means she spilled the beans. But what is more of a concern is what you both mean by the term, 'talking'."

"She will probably say it means we are in some sort of relationship. I would say that it means we had a few nice conversations about school and her future."

"What the hell, Terry?" Gus said rubbing his chin. "You really have to start getting ahead of this thing. I would write down a formal statement about what you heard and then the truth about your relationship to Sonja."

"That's what I was thinking," Pete said, "but Terry said it's more complicated than that."

The sound of a desk being dragged across a floor and a few loud shouts drew Pete's attention back to his room. Gus turned to Terry.

"Why is this situation more complicated than that?" Gus asked. "Are you in a relationship with this student?"

"I mean, I guess she could see it that way," Terry said.

"Jesus, Terry. What does that mean?"

"It means that during the kicking suspension, she reached out to me to ask questions about class material. She asked about how I was feeling and said that she wanted to make sure that I was okay. She seemed really concerned. I felt obligated to meet with her for her academics, but then we started talking about other things."

"One time doesn't constitute a relationship," Gus said.

"Then we met for coffee a few times."

"To discuss class material in a public place, that is called tutoring. Is there anymore?"

The look on Terry's face told Williams that there was more to the story. Pete came back from his classroom. The students had a new video to watch on the electoral college.

"So, I am sure Terry filled you in on this new development. She's delusional," Pete said. "No ground to stand on. We just make our statement and let the thing run its course."

Gus kept his eyes on Terry. He wondered if he had told Pete what he just told him. There was no getting ahead of this. Terry had just burned his career. If all they did was talk, he might be able to salvage a year until he was able to move districts. But if he had any sort of physical relationship with the girl, then he could be going to jail.

"I would suggest that Terry get himself a lawyer," Gus said. "A real lawyer, not a union rep or the overworked union lawyer, but a criminal defense attorney."

"Don't you think that is a little overkill?"

"No," Williams said. "And here is why. If it gets out that she and Terry are in a relationship then everyone will assume they are in a physical relationship. And a physical relationship is a criminal charge because he is in a position of power as her teacher. It doesn't matter if she is seventeen, eighteen, or nineteen."

"Won't that make me look like I'm guilty," Terry asked, "if I hire a criminal lawyer?"

"Are you?" Gus prodded.

Terry ran his hand through his hair, "Listen guys, all I did was talk to this girl over coffee. We talked about school, Netflix, and her future. Everything was innocent."

"I think Gus is right here, Terry," Pete said. "I think you have to be prepared. Just because you have a lawyer doesn't mean that you are going to come to the school guns a-blazing. It just means that you are prepared to deal with the worst case scenario."

"Thank you, gentlemen," Terry said as he turned to walk away.

Williams watched as he walked down the hall toward his room. Pete quickly turned to check on his students then faced Gus.

"What do you think?" he asked Gus.

"Well, if he's telling the truth then he will be reprimanded and told to use better judgment. In the court of social opinion, if this gets out, which knowing North Wellington it probably will, he is done."

"You're right."

"Try not to get too wrapped up in it yourself. Contact the union rep, set James up with him, and then you get out of the way."

The bell rang to end the hour, punctuating their thoughts. Williams turned to see Johnny striding away. The halls were flooding with students, Johnny simply could have been the first kid out into the hall. But if he had been standing close enough to record their whole conversation, James was in real trouble. There was nothing he could do about it now. All he could do was go back to his room for fourth hour. His thoughts turned to Stacy again and he hoped that Stacy could make the right decision.

47

Even though the halls were full of students and teachers bustling from one place to the next, Williams sat alone in his thoughts. The district had moved up the timeline considerably. Williams couldn't let Adams figure things out for himself so much anymore. He had to steer the situation. Everything hinged on Adams' relationship with his mother.

After the basketball game, Adams kept his head down. He couldn't find him in the hall or at the gym or hanging around before or after school. The basketball game incident had thrown him for a loop, Williams knew. He wasn't sure what razzing he was getting from his college friends or from his mother, all of whom had probably seen the video. The kids at school weren't saying anything to his face, but Williams heard plenty of gossip from side conversations. The pictures of Jessica with her arms around him circulated like wildfire. The rumor mill was not turning in Adams' favor.

Between Adams and James, this year was really turning out to be one to remember. So much drama could unfold over the next few months that his own story, the one that covered the last forty years, would be overlooked, which suited him just fine. The less attention he received for his time at North Wellington the better.

"Mr. Williams, what are we doing today?" Alex asked. "Are

we just reading?"

"Alex, I'm a little offended," Williams said putting his hands on his hips. "We are never just reading. We are reading."

"Riiiiight, sorry about that Mr. Williams," Alex said. "So, what are we doing after reading today?"

"I think we have to work on our public speaking abilities."

"Ugh, really? Like give a speech?" Alex said slumping down into a chair. "Are we going to have to do that today?"

"Probably not today," Williams said clicking through the attendance on the computer. "We will have to do some prep work today."

"Can we do the poetry thing that Mr. Adams is doing across the hall?" Liz commented from across the room. She must have been eavesdropping on their conversation.

"What?" Williams said, "You want me to do an assignment that Mr. Adams has done? You guys must be addled in the head."

"No, really, Mr. Williams," Andrea said. "He actually has a really cool assignment."

"Yeah," Liz said, "He has students writing poetry with their fiction books. Did you see the pages hanging up outside his room from the first two hours?"

Williams hadn't even looked in Adams' direction after hearing about the impending termination. Then with the James information, he had been lost in his own thoughts.

"We did something like that at our old school," Sophia said. "It's called Blackout Poetry, at least that's what my old teacher called it."

"I will have to take a look at it," Williams said. "You said there are some examples in the hall?"

"Yeah, go take a look Mr. Williams."

Williams set the class to reading. The timer on the projector screen ticked down from fifteen minutes. He sat in the back thinking. He had *The Nickel Boys* by Colson Whitehead spread open before him but he couldn't focus. He watched as the time ticked down. Most of the students were engaged in reading. A few sat biting their lips or chewing on their fingernails as they read through what must have been an exciting passage. A few put their heads down on the table, trying to focus solely on their books — the pages turned every so often. Others just put their head down on the table. Some looked up from their books to smile at friends and mouth a few words before they all giggled. Williams cleared his throat to refocus his nonreaders.

As it neared the end of reading time, Williams heard a commotion out in the hall. He feared the worst, a mass revolt for Adams. He hadn't seen such a thing since the walkout of '95 when students were upset over having a shorter lunch period. His students started to notice the noise. Williams closed his book, not that he was reading it anyway, and went to close the door. In the hall, students were streaming out of Adams' room.

"Noah," Williams said loudly above the din, "what's going on?"

"Hi, Mr. Williams," he said, "We are actually doing something fun in Mr. Adams' class."

"Oh, is it the poetry thing?"

"Yeah," Noah said, "I mean, I'm not the biggest fan of poetry, but anything other than writing another research paper or dissecting another piece of informational writing is good in my book."

"So, why is everyone in the hall?"

"We have to make copies of a page or two in our free reading books."

"Why so?" Williams asked. "What are you going to do with those?"

"Once we have our copies, we highlight certain words throughout the text to make a poem then we create a picture by shading the other words around it. Like those over there."

"Hmm?" Williams said looking toward the wall where, sure enough, examples of the assignment were hanging up. "Thanks Noah, I'll let you get back to your assignment."

"Thanks," Noah said already halfway down the hall toward the copy machine.

Williams walked over to where several copies of the assignment hung on the wall. The students were able to create poems from their book pages. The result, poetry crafted from another author's words. Some of the students really took pride in the accompanying art. Students had shaded faces, flowers, and fire, while others simply scratched out the rest with black marker or pencil.

Adams walked out of his doorway and looked in the direction of the copy machine. The students were chatty and casual as they made their way back to the classroom. He acknowledged them with a small nod and a smile if they were engrossed in conversation with a friend. When other students stopped to show him their page, he briefly talked with them. Soft music played from inside Adams' room. Williams could tell something had changed.

"This assignment is pretty neat," Williams said.

"Thanks," Stacy said walking over to where Williams stood. "I thought it would be a nice break from writing papers and a new way for students to think about word choice."

"Yeah, where to did you get this from?" Williams asked. "It looks like a great assignment."

"Over holiday break I had been reading *The Atlantic,* and I ran across a few words I didn't know so, I boxed them in until I could look them up later. When I went back later to look up the words, I just started boxing other words I liked. And I had the start of the assignment."

"How did you decide on poetry?"

"I had this teacher in high school, Mr. P. Everyone said the "P" stood for poetry because he loved working with poems. He had this one assignment where we had to write a poem and then work it into a piece of art, like if the poem was about freedom of expression, then it could be performed as graffiti on the side of a building. So, we had to draw a building and write the poem on the side. It made for visual art."

"So, you took those two ideas, the boxing out of words and the visual art, to make this assignment?"

"Yep, I sure did," Adams said. "Then I Googled it to see if anyone else had done something similar and sure enough the assignment was floating out in the Googleverse. It's called Blackout Poetry."

"Well, isn't that par for the course."

"That's okay though. I don't need to be a pioneer; I would just like to create some variety in my lesson plans. What are your students doing at the moment?" Adams asked while noticing some movement in Williams' class.

"Oh, they are probably doing very little at the moment. They were finishing reading when I heard the commotion."

"And you wanted to check to see if everything was okay."

"Yes," Williams said, "and I see that you're doing just fine."

"I think I'm getting the hang of this thing, no worries," Adams said turning to follow his students to the copier.

Williams walked back to his room. His mind was conflicted. Now that the district had plans to fire him, part of him wanted Stacy to fail so he would decide on law school. But what he really wanted was for Stacy to start becoming a good teacher, decide to go to law school — shaking off all the baggage from his youth — and reconcile with his mother. However, Williams knew all to well that we don't always get what we want.

48

February was always the bleakest of months for teachers and students. When a winter storm rolled in, the town shut down. Parents stayed home with kids, roads were left unplowed until late in the day, and teachers relished in the cherished snow day phone call. When Williams started teaching, he had to keep a phone tree in his night stand. If a phone call came, he would have to call the next person on the list. Now all the districts had automated calls. A simple code from a cell phone or computer and administrators could send phone calls to everyone on staff. When the snow day phone call came, Williams couldn't return to sleep. He slipped on his sweatpants and a sweater and headed down stairs to take in the sunrise.

The steam billowed off Gus' coffee and the cold blew through his clothes, chilling him as he stood in the open garage bay. Snow had piled up in front of his door making a knee-high wall. Nearly every snow day Gus would make a pot of coffee, slip on his boots, then head into the garage to see the havoc mother nature had wrought.

People have asked him, why stay in Michigan? He wanted to tell them that this was all he knew, his life was here in the quiet winter streets. In the summer, the streets came alive with ball players peddling to ball games or playing in the yard. The serenity of winter was always broken by the shouts and screams of children bundled in snow gear sliding down hills, building forts, and throwing snowballs across driveways. This morning a stillness fell over North Wellington. Williams could hear the faint sounds of a snowblower in the distance. Later when the children awoke to news of no school, they would emerge from their homes in snow gear and plastic sleds to take to the streets and hills. In these moments he could see Danny out with his friends, growing, gaining freedom. What made Williams really afraid wasn't the idea of moving away and meeting new people. He was afraid that if he moved, if he left this neighborhood, his memories of Danny wouldn't go with him.

So, when people asked him why he didn't move to a warmer climate, he smiled and said, "Someday, maybe, when I retire."

Williams dumped his coffee in the snow, staining the pure white with an acrid brown Rorschach splotch, and returned to the quiet and warmth of his home. Trapped in his house by the snow and the cold, Williams thought about his life and what little future he had left.

He had relished in the last snowstorm, reading with a fervor. He burned through title after title in a delirious haze. But now even with a to-be-read pile double-stacked by his bed, he had no desire to spend his time in another person's world. For too long Williams had not lived his own life.

Now with the state of emergency declared for vast portions of Michigan, all Williams wanted to do was leave. He could. He could walk out into the storm, down the side streets and into the nature trails and up into the dunes, where Janet waits for him. The snow would cover his tracks in a matter of minutes. He could call in sick for work. Email the principal that he had become ill and couldn't come back to work. He would retire immediately. A few short strokes of the keyboard and off he goes.

Mother Nature wouldn't take long to bring him to Janet. He would grow cold once he stopped moving. Blood would rush from his extremities into his core, tricking his mind into thinking he was hot. He would take off his jacket. Hallucinations would make his world come alive, but then eventually his heart would give out. When he laid his head back and dreamed of falling asleep next to Janet one more time, life would flit from his eyes. Snow would pile up next to his body inch by inch until all that had been August Williams was covered by snow.

Williams knew his life could end that way. He could do it. But he won't. Williams would go to work tomorrow, if it wasn't called off. He would finish the year, guiding Stacy the best he knew how. He would retire when the school year ended. School would carry on without him. In time, the students who remembered Mr. Williams would be no more. Then it will be as if he had never lived or taught.

But his legacy would last more than a lifetime, his work would last generations. He may not be remembered by name, but the impact he has made, the lives he has changed in the classroom, would forever have a ripple effect. And this, he feels, has made his life worthwhile.

The sizzle from his cooking eggs pulled him from his day dream. He turned from the window in the kitchen to the realities of life. Williams flipped over his eggs, pushed down the handle on the toaster, and waited. He always seemed to be waiting. He had been waiting for thirty years for something else to happen and now it had. If he waited any longer, life would be over. He had to start living.

The scene from outside the window told the same story as the one within. The house, quiet and calm, was also filled with loneliness. A solitary figure moved about the small rooms. No spouse would return his warm looks, no children would fill the halls with laughter, no phone calls would be received from loved ones. What was known without was also known within.

Williams pulled his journal from his messenger bag. He took his place at his kitchen table, opposite the stack of notes and stories from the October parent teacher conferences. Something about what Rex had said stuck with him as he turned from one page to the next in his journal. His ran his hand down each page. The slight indentations felt like small mountain ranges running east to west. His memoirs, Rex had said. Williams had pages and pages of his life written down in notebooks like the one he was holding. Not a day went by that he didn't write something down, after school during the year or with a cup of tea in the evening during the summer. But what was he to do with all of it?

His gaze shifted to the pile of notes from his writing session four months ago. His life didn't offer much in the way of adventure or profit, but he did know about teaching. He pulled the ribbon from the bottom of the journal, opening to a blank page. He took his fountain pen from its case and began writing what would hopefully become a plan for some sort of memoir.

As the cold winter storm raged outside of Williams' window, a fire started within. The same sort of energy that had captured Williams so many months before came barreling back. The organized papers started to find their way around the kitchen table. Williams shifted through different sticky notes and paper-clipped piles. He capped his pen and picked up his tea. He found the cup empty but his page full. Williams put his papers back in order, closed his journal, and rinsed his cup in the sink. Life would go on, Williams knew, at least for a little while longer. He climbed the stairs, past Danny's room, its door always open. This time when Williams stopped, a smile lit across his face. Down the hall, past family pictures and dusty portraits, Williams felt something different about how the rest of his life might turn out. A funny feeling, he knew, coming from a dying man. But sometimes, he thought, the end of the journey made the beginning that much clearer.

49

"Well, we made it one more month old-timer," Williams said as he sipped his caramel-colored coffee.

Rex looked like a ghost of himself. Stooped over the table, his breathing was labored but his eyes were sharp. "Yes, cruel months, January and February. Here in Michigan, the sun slips behind the clouds, hibernating like the bears and the squirrels. Whatever survives is given a rebirth in spring, a new life."

"So poetic, I am glad your spirits are up," Williams said. "In the spring you will be reborn as well - back to a poet."

Williams himself had transfigured. His demeanor, once drab and down about his cancer treatment, turned to one of at least considering the possibility of new experiences. Certain events change a person; his life was upended when Janet and Danny died. He no longer wanted to live for years and years punishing himself for what he had no control over. Now that death had come to tea, he had gained a new perspective.

"I don't know about a rebirth unless you are talking about going back to earth – 'to dust thou art, to dust returneth'," Rex said taking his coffee cup in both hands and sipping. Black coffee dribbled down the sides of the cup, filling the saucer. Williams placed a folded napkin down on the saucer to cover the drips. "I have enjoyed our brief friendship, the conversations over the phone and here at the diner."

"Rex, this isn't goodbye for cryin' out loud," Williams said. "Let's at least get some breakfast before we go off the deep end." He held up the menu to the waitress signaling they were ready to order. "How goes the poetry collection?"

"The last month has been wonderful in that regard. I dug out all my notebooks from the basement storage and went on a nice jog down memory lane. Life had been full of opportunities and wonder then."

"How were the poems?"

"Oh, mostly just bits and pieces. Early on I found some that were nearly finished, but as my business career took off, my writing stopped and those nearly finished poems remained unfinished. Eventually, I didn't even journal. There were these large gaps of time. I would have had to look at my bank statement to relive my life. What a waste."

The waitress came over holding her ordering pad. "How we doing this morning gentlemen? Ready to order?"

"Yes," Williams said, "I will have hash browns, well-done, bacon and two eggs over-easy."

She looked to Rex, "And for you, Mr. Chamberlain?"

"I will take the same, thank you, Cammie."

"Rex," Williams said leaning over the table, "life is a messy, complicated, busy, unclear, befuddling thing. We all just do the best we can."

"Yes, well."

"We can't go back, we can only go forward."

"No, that is where you are wrong, Gus." Rex gave Gus a hard stare. "For me and soon for you, there will be no more looking forward. Our days are numbered. All I have is looking back and …" Rex began to cough. His face turned red, Williams got up from his seat, and began to rub Chamberlain's back. He swiped Williams' hand away, "the end," he said. "All I have is looking back and the end. There is no more life left to live."

"If looking back is all we have left," Williams said, "then we must look at what we have cherished not that which we would banish. Those poems will be what live on, that and all the connections, interactions, and relationships you've had. The people you have employed. Your son. The lives you've affected from your birth until death. You live on, forever."

" 'All goes onward and outward, nothing collapses, and to die is different from what any one supposed, and luckier'."

Williams paused, coffee in hand, trying to place the quote. "Walt Whitman, *Song of Myself,*" he said sipping his coffee.

Rex smiled. He sipped his coffee, steadying it on his lip before tipping it to take a drink. "It seems we have switched demeanors. Your outlook has changed from when we first met in the MRI. What has made all the difference? Did you get some good test results?"

"Well," Gus said, "I started on the maintenance cocktail and I feel pretty good, but that isn't it. I started looking back through my old journals, thinking about my life, thinking about what I would have to offer others and I realized that ever since my family died, I have been coping and coming to terms with their deaths. I can't do that anymore, and I can't take that long to cope with cancer or I'll be dead by the time I'm ready to start living."

Rex nodded and took another sip of coffee, "And when did you come to this realization?"

Williams set down his cup and put his hands in the air. "I don't know, I guess just a few days ago during the big winter storm. I was sitting, looking out the front window at the snowstorm blowing and whipping snow, and then I went to write in my journal and all of a sudden, this notion broke into my head--and I mean broke. It was not a gentle coming to an understanding. But here was this idea that life is about over for me. Things are going to be what they are going to be. We can only move forward and carry all that we are forward with us. And how we carry it forward is on us."

Rex smiled weakly, "So right you are, so right you are."

As their usual orders came up from the kitchen, the two men continued to talk about their lives of literature. The symbolic nature of life was ever present. They talked of the Super Bowl and the miraculous run of Tom Brady, the Patriots, the Spartans, the Wolverines, the Tar Heels, and the Blue Devils. The glut of superhero movies and digital media. How artificial intelligence had become a reality, not just a movie theme. And maybe, soon, Arnold would be coming back from the future.

"I've read so many science fiction books over the years whose technology is now a reality that I wonder if ..."

"Gus, I'm sorry to interrupt but I am not feeling too well and need to go rest," Chamberlain said dropping his napkin down on his half-finished meal.

Williams panicked. He pushed his plate away from the table edge to help but Rex put his hand in the air, "I will walk out of here on my own."

Rex pivoted himself in the booth. He steadied himself on his cane, "You've been a good friend, Gus. I won't say goodbye until next time when spring sets things anew. But for now, 'Alone far in the wilds and mountains, I hunt, wandering amazed at my own lightness and glee, in the late afternoon choosing a safe spot to pass the night, kindling a fire, falling asleep on gathered leaves'."

Gus smiled as Rex headed toward the door, " 'I too am not a bit tamed, I too am untranslatable, I sound my barbaric yawp over the roofs of the world'."

Chamberlain, halfway to the door, turned with a smile, "About time."

The waitress returned to clear Rex's plate. She slipped the black padded bill holder onto the table. She smiled coyly then rushed off to dump the dishes and tend to more tables. Williams flipped open the bill holder, inside was his bank card with a note on the back of the receipt, "Already taken care of by Mr. Chamberlain" followed by a winking smiley face. The waitress walked by with two hot breakfasts, "He gave me fifty bucks just as a tip, said it would be worth it for me to see the look on your face."

"Well, was he right?" Williams said smiling.

"Totally."

She winked at Williams before striding off to deliver someone's breakfast. Next time he thought, next time.

50

Signs for the annual Snowcoming celebration were starting to appear in the hallways. The high school and middle school students played dress-up again for a week in the middle of winter. This time the culminating event was a boys' basketball game on a Friday night, where the alumni all came home to visit and partake in the adult evening festivities. Williams was nervous when talking to Adams about the event because of the lack of participation the last time and the debacle with the holiday play. If there were any disgruntled students or parents this time around, he knew there would be no hope for Adams to continue teaching through the end of the year.

Williams understood that this week was a pivotal moment. Such a silly thing to think about really. How could something so trivial as participating in a theme dress-up week be a linchpin moment when so many more pressing moments were out in the world? Williams sighed, this was the world of high school no matter if you were a student or a teacher. It all seemed the same. What happened outside of the community rarely had an impact on the feelings happening on the inside — it was a world unto itself.

Williams grabbed a flyer from the hall by his door. He read down through the days as he slowly moved towards Adams' room. He had finished his teaching; the students would be packing up their notebooks and computers. Williams shuffled through the door. A few students were already up, standing at the door for the remaining few minutes left in class. This never would have flown at the beginning of the year with Stacy. He would have them stay in their seats until the bell rang, and he would verbally dismiss them. Progress had been made, but would it be enough to save his career? Even though he had to leave Wellington, Adams could play off the move back to the Detroit area as move for family. No one would have to know he was being forced out.

“Mr. Adams, do you have a minute?"

"Yeah, they are just putting their, finishing their…they are actually packing up and getting on their phones,” Adams said frustrated. “They should be using this time to study for vocabulary.” He shouted, “Quiz Monday!”

The students let out a collective grown.

"I wanted to know if you had seen these flyers starting to pop up in the hallway."

Stacy took the flyer in his hands, "I have but I haven’t stopped to read what they say. This is some sort of homecoming event but in the winter, right? We had one in my high school too."

"Yes," Gus said, "It is exactly like it but instead of powderpuff football, the boys play volleyball. And the teachers get to play as well."

"Oh, wow," Stacy said. "And it looks like there are themes for each day of the week."

"Yes," Williams jangled the keys in his pocket, "Do you think you will be participating this time in the theme days?"

"Hmmm,” Stacy said as he looked down at the list of days: Mix-it Up, Toga, Powderpuff, Jersey, and Warrior Day. "I think I could manage one or two days. How about you?"

Williams felt a bit of pressure evaporate from his shoulders. "I think I can manage a few days as well,” he said turning to the students coming in through the door. "Now, I must go, I have to make it to the bathroom and back before class begins. Old age...”

"Get on that horse, Mr. Williams. Get on that horse."

Williams furrowed his brow as he left Adams' room. He leaned to the side to let students pass when Andrea collided with him, knocking him back into the door handle and slamming his shoulder blade into the edge of the door.

"Oh, my God! I am so sorry, Mr. Williams," Andrea said reaching her hand out to steady him. As she reached out, her pencil pouch fell to the ground, followed by her calculator, and math book. "I am just trying to make it to class on time and I went around this kid in the hall and boom, you were right there. I'm really sorry. Are you ok?"

Williams smiled but he felt a sharp pain in his shoulder and hip from where he had hit the door. "Yes, I am okay. Thank you for your concern." He bent down to retrieve her dropped materials. "Why are you in such a rush to get to class? Aren't most seniors living by their own schedule?"

"Oh, yes. Thank you," she said stacking her books and pencil case and calculator on top of her binder. "I have been waitlisted for Notre Dame and the guidance counselor said that they need to send my transcripts again at the end of the marking period."

"So, you are really hustling to math class.'

"Well, yes. You know how Mr. Calestra is about being tardy. If I'm not in my seat by the time the bell rings he says that you're late."

"Right," Williams said. The bell rang and Andrea groaned. "Let me walk you to class and offer a pass. I was going that way anyway."

"That's really nice but don't you have class? I can just go. I should have been more careful."

"Andrea," Williams said turning to walk down the hall, "Accidents happen. Let me help you."

"But I rammed right into you, aren't you mad?"

"Andrea," Gus said stopping outside of Mr. Calestra's classroom, "we can't let every mosquito wing throw us off the track or the train will never get to its destination."

"Thoreau, right? I think I get it."

Williams waved to Mr. Calestra, then pointed to Andrea and then to himself and gave him a thumbs up. Mr. Calestra nodded his head in acknowledgment, turned to make a couple of clicks on his computer, then turned back to the class.

"Ms. Lafeyette, your pass from Mr. Williams is about to run out. Please come in and join us for the class."

Andrea turned to Gus, mouthed thank you, then headed into class with the same determination that had knocked him over in the hall.

Williams watched as Clint began his calculus lesson. The exactitude of the subject matter astounded him. The precision needed to teach such a high level of math took a special individual, one who will hold the students accountable with a pinpoint focus. Teaching takes all kinds.

He turned to make his way to the staff bathroom. His hip and shoulder throbbed; tomorrow he would be sore. His bones couldn't take much of a beating.

On the way back to class, Williams heard teachers beginning their lessons. Some were having students turn in assignments, others were pointing out objectives on the board, others were directing students to get out lab equipment from cupboards. Williams sometimes wondered how schools managed to remain so organized. In this building, over 700 students were in classrooms with approximately thirty teachers. In less than an hour, all of those students would leave one room and make it to another. More people should stop to take in what was happening around them. Williams had been at fault for drifting through his days but now the wonder had come back.

He stopped to take a drink from the fountain; he heard some whispering. Williams stuck his head around the corner to see Johnny in an emphatic discussion with Kimberly from yearbook class.

"Johnny," she said, "I don't feel right about this. You don't even know the truth."

"The truth," he said slapping the back of one hand into the palm of another, "is that something fishy is going on and we need to expose it for the good of the students."

"I think you mean for the benefit of your personal YouTube channel," she said crossing her arms.

"Listen, Kim," Johnny said putting his hand on her shoulder, "this is on me. You won't have your name anywhere on it."

"But I'm doing it, Johnny! That means I will get in trouble because it is on my account in the lab and I will feel bad if something bad happens to them."

"If it's nothing," Johnny said, "I am pretty sure no one will get hurt. If there is something to it then we have made our school a better place."

"I don't know," she said.

Johnny looked down at his phone. "It's live."

Kim turned to go down the stairwell. Williams stepped back around the corner. Johnny was in a hurry to get to Adams' room. Williams watched him go. His own class was waiting for him. He could hear they were getting rambunctious without him. They would have to wait a bit longer while he checked Johnny's account on his phone.

"We should all be reading now," Mr. Williams said striding into the classroom. "You all know the routine and know what you should be doing. I'll start the timer with what's left of your reading time."

A student blurted out, "Can we have the whole fifteen minutes?"

Williams knew that if students ask for more reading time, he's winning the fight against computers, phones, and tablets, but he had to use it as a privilege now. "You were supposed to be reading. We will split the difference at 12 minutes this time."

The chatter started to die down as Williams walked around the room looking at titles, keeping track of what students were reading and the progress they were making. As he made his way down the last aisle, he slipped back behind his desk to retrieve his phone.

He swiped until he found YouTube then searched for JohnnyFireball69. A new video had just posted. He pulled out some earbuds he was given for attending a teacher training, affixed them in his ears and pressed play. Williams couldn't believe what he was seeing. It wasn't the usual prank or embarrassing moment, but a bit of hack investigative gossip.

Johnny had caught Williams coming out of the principal's office in a huff, then zoomed in on the principal who was shaking his head. He caught pieces of his conversations about James. He had James looking guilty. Then he had pictures of Terry talking quietly to Sophia Sternwood in the hall and then again at lunch and later in the library. *Jesus,* Gus thought, *he has the wrong girl.* The video ended with a question, "What's going on between Mr. James and Sophia Sternwood?"

Williams stopped the video. He flagged the video, hoping the YouTube people would find it in their hearts to take it down. He then reported the video, explaining the content to be damaging to a student and a teacher. He hoped the reporting would reinforce his point that it should be taken down. By the time he was done, reading time had elapsed. Williams would have to let Pete and Terry know about the video, maybe even talk to Johnny about taking it down, but for now he had to teach.

51

On the first day of Snowcoming Week, Williams wore exercise pants that made swishing sounds as he walked plus a button-down shirt, tie, and jacket. He hadn't heard anything back from Pete or Terry all weekend. After the five-minute bell, Williams walked down the hall to find Terry. His room was down the stairs and on the other side of the building. The lights were out and the door was locked. He gave the door another rattle, just to check. He stood there wondering if the video had caused some sort of ruckus. He turned to leave, hustling back toward his room.

"Yo, Mr. Williams," Anthony said, "we can hear you coming all the way down the hall."

"You better not go too fast or you'll catch on fire!" Harry shouted.

"If you stop, drop, and roll," Riley said, "we'll have to call 9-1-1."

"Help, I've fallen," Anthony cried out, "and I can't get up."

"Very funny, you guys," Williams chuckled. "You could have your own show at Second City."

"What's that?" Riley asked.

"It's, like, where all the Saturday Night Live people come from," Jessica said.

Everyone turned to look in her direction.

"What?" She said twirling her hair around her finger, "I'm not just a pretty face."

Everyone continued to stare.

"My dad always makes us watch old Adam Sandler movies and clips from Saturday Night Live with that fat guy who died."

"Chris Farley," Williams said.

"Yeah, that's the one," she said.

"Do you enjoy them?" Williams asked, "What would you recommend?"

"*Tommy Boy* is his best film by far, but I would start with his best of SNL stuff. Then you'll really appreciate his comic genius."

Anthony blurted, "You just got so much hotter."

The class laughed. His friends started hitting him and calling him an idiot. Williams himself couldn't hold back a grin. Jessica's face flushed.

"I am glad that someone is listening to her father at least in one aspect," Williams said opening the textbook next to his document camera. "Everyone turn to page 465 in your textbook. We are going to start reading about F. Scott Fitzgerald and the roaring 20s."

After class, Gus went across the hall to check on Stacy. He wore a striped tie with a plaid shirt. The students hardly noticed the mismatched attire, but Williams could tell Stacy was a bit uncomfortable with the fashion faux pas.

"You know," Gus said standing across the hall, "I wouldn't worry about standing out. The students hardly acknowledge a teacher's mismatch after the initial look."

Adams reached to smooth the tie down the front of his shirt.

"I thought this would be a good place to start, but I don't think the students are really noticing that I'm mismatched."

"Well, I'm glad that you did it."

"Did you see Terry James this morning at all?"

"No, why?" Adams asked smoothing his tie again. "Is

something up?"

"I'm not sure," Williams said. "Have you seen the video about him online?"

"No, but that doesn't sound good."

"It's not."

"I will look for him during planning if you really need to talk to him."

"No thanks, I'll just go talk to Pete, the union president."

"Alright, let me know. I will be in here."

Williams strode out of the room bumping into all sorts of mismatched students. Some wore crazy combinations. Some dressed like teachers. Some girls dressed as boys and some boys dressed as girls. Some nerds dressed as jocks and pretended to flex all day. Some jocks wore dark frames with white tape in the middle and hiked their pants up as high as they could go.

Williams did all he could to make it through second hour without running to find Pete. All through the hour he watched his students, trying to catch a whisper of some gossip about a teacher. He heard nothing. Right at the end of class, he rushed down the hall ahead of his own students. He strode into Pete's room and nearly bumped into the school's substitute.

"Hi Randy, is Mr. Jorgmander here today?"

"Yes, he's in a meeting with administration. I am not sure for how long. I was told that I should get comfortable because I might be in here for a few days."

"A few days?"

"Yeah, beats me," Randy said, "but there are all sorts of suits down in the office."

"Ok," Williams said turning toward the door. "Thanks for the information."

Randy was right. A big meeting was taking place in the conference room. Williams watched as the MEA lawyer and the district lawyer filed one after the other into the room. Sophia Sternwood was crying in the principal's office. He recognized Pete's voice through the door. Williams walked past the conference room, peering through the small rectangular glass in the door. He recognized Terry, Johnny, Principal Anderson, and Snyder. The other people in the room must have been Johnny's and Sophia's parents. Williams grabbed his mail. He stood as close as he could to the conference room pretending to read through an education travel brochure. He could only hear muffled sounds as different individuals took turns speaking.

Williams dropped the brochure into the recycle bin and walked out through the office. He could hear Sophia sniffling. Each secretary had a phone on their shoulder while typing away on their computer. The school office always had something going on. He would have to wait to see how things shook out.

52

By Thursday morning Williams still hadn't heard anything about the James situation. He woke from a fitful sleep determined to participate in "jersey day," but he couldn't find his old Warriors baseball jersey that he had made for these occasions. He couldn't remember the last time he wore it to school or anywhere for that matter.

Williams dug through his closet, but time was running out for getting breakfast and a cup of coffee before school. He pulled a button-down from a hanger and slipped his arms through, buttoning as he walked down the hall. He paused outside of Danny's room to finish the last button and from the corner of his eye he could see the Warriors jersey tossed over the edge of the footboard like he might have done with one of Danny's shirts. His fingers dropped from their task, languishing in the past.

Williams leaned in from the doorway, unable to step forward. How did the jersey get on the bed? He didn't remember the last time he was in Danny's room. It had been years. The room just sat open, memories spilling from the doorway like a river overflowing its banks. He hesitated and then walked in. He picked up the jersey from the bed. He undid the buttons on his shirt, pulled it from his shoulders, then tossed it down on the bed. He slipped on the Warriors jersey. He exhaled a deep breath. He was in Danny's room.

Williams took a seat on the bed. He ran his hands over the covers. He fumbled through the baseball cards and comic books on the dresser. Life had been so different. He pulled open the drawers. The clothes seemed stiff with age. He took a hat from a peg on the wall. He held it to his nose. Danny's smell was gone. Williams walked around the room. He was gone. Life with Danny and Janet had faded long ago from this room. He knew now that going forward, life had to be different.

At school, Williams was greeted by students and staff alike donning their favorite team jersey. Spirited conversations about which team was better at basketball, Michigan or Michigan State, bounced off the walls and down the halls. One student tried to settle the argument by pointing to his Duke jersey. A girl showed off her Connecticut Huskies women's jersey. She walked by the arguing boys then turned to say, "11 boys, 11."

The boys looked at her with confusion, their hands palm up at their shoulder.

"They have 11 National Championships and are a favorite again this year," she said before turning back into the crowd of students.

Another student turned to Williams, "Is that your old game jersey, Mr. Williams?"

"No," he said shaking his head in laughter. "I never went to school here."

"Hey, Mr. Williams," another student called out, "was it hard to catch baseballs with those old gloves that looked like puffy fingers?"

"Very challenging," he said pretending to tip his cap at the student before disappearing into his room.

With his bag and coat put away, Williams took out his journal. He had to write something about what he felt in Danny's room or it would sit with him the rest of the day, clouding his thoughts, filling him with anguish he didn't want any longer. He started with the word "Anguish," but before he could expound on those feelings, Adams came through his doorway, calling for him.

"Gus! Gus, are you here?"

"Yes," he said standing from his desk, placing the ribbon back into his journal and closing its cover. "I am here at my desk. Is everything alright?"

"Well, I'm not sure. Is what I am wearing ok with the professional dress code of teachers?"

Williams looked at Adams. He had a Detroit Tigers Kirk Gibson jersey on over a long- sleeved mock turtleneck with khaki pants and dress shoes. "I think the only thing that would offend anyone is the overtly dressy shoes," Williams said chuckling. "Today is a day to relax a little, so good for you to step out of your comfort zone."

"Ok, good," Adams said. "I didn't know if I had to wear a dress shirt under my jersey. I had one on but it just didn't feel right, but I brought it anyway."

"No, you're all good, Stacy," Williams said moving to the back of the room by the coffee machine. "Do you want a cup of coffee?"

"Sure, quickly, I guess we have class in about ten minutes."

Williams started the Keurig brewing the first cup and retrieved some small creamers from his mini-fridge. "How was the volleyball, did you go?"

"I didn't go," Adams said sitting down at a desk. "I had a thing."

"Oh, yeah?" Williams asked bringing over the first cup of coffee and setting it in front of Adams. "What were you up to last night? Hot date?"

"No, I'm afraid not," Adams said sipping on the steaming coffee.

"Well," Williams said bringing his coffee over to the desk and tipping in two creamers. "What are you up to? Or don't you want to say? Am I prying?"

"No, you're fine, Gus," Stacy paused. "I, ah, was at the homeless shelter, the Rescue Mission, helping distribute dinner and then talking to some of the old patrons."

"Wow, that is really something," Gus said. "Kind of awesome of you to spend your time in such a manner, especially as a new member of the community."

"Well, I always thought of homeless people as lazy, no-good members of society, probably because of how I was raised," Stacy said sipping on his coffee. "Not so much the influence of my mother, who usually just ignored the homeless, but that of my classmates at school. Many of them peered down their noses at anyone who wasn't financially at their level."

"And what did you discover last night?"

"I have been helping for the last month or so and I think the people that are truly homeless, not the ones standing on the corner asking for money because they don't want to work, but the ones who have been down for so long that they can't seem to find a way back to a job and a life, are just like you and me. They just don't know how to get moving in the right direction."

"So, they are all just down on their luck, like Orwell said, huh?" Williams sipped his coffee, careful not to spill on his jersey.

"No, don't misunderstand me here," Stacy said smiling. "There are some really crazy people there that need some serious mental care, but the average person is just so low that they have fallen into bad traps like drug use, alcohol abuse, and depression."

"Well, what can Wellington do about it?" Williams said looking Adams in the eye.

"I don't have any answers, but to start, the county should have programs that people can turn to for help," Adams said rubbing his chin. "They may have this already and if they do, it should be out there so everyone knows. And programs for mental health, programs for job training, programs for drug addiction."

"Well, that all costs. Does that come from the tax payers' pockets?" Williams asked trying to pull Adams further into the discussion.

“I’m not sure," Adams said standing. "All I know is that if Wellington and every other large community wants to have a prosperous, clean, and safe place to live, then they should have those resources for the struggling members of the population."

"True," Williams said standing and turning toward his desk. "It sounds like you want to run for public office."

"Maybe, but I certainly don’t want to do it for power or attention."

"Very good," Gus said turning to look at Adams. "A selfless leader willing to do what is right in the face of personal disaster. Sounds like a good candidate to me."

"Thanks," Stacy said retreating toward the door, “and thanks for the coffee. I’ll return the cup later.”

As Stacy walked out, students started to filter into Williams’ room, little by little, then in a few large groups. The last couple of students trickled in just before the tardy bell. Many still had wet hair from a shower and smelled of some fruity shampoo or musky deodorant spray.

“Mr. Williams, did you see Mr. Jorgmander is back today. What’s he been gone so long for?” Harry asked. “I, like, saw him in the building every day, was there some sort of meeting?”

“He is? I didn’t know,” Williams said. “I know that he had been in some meetings but I didn’t know for what.”

“I bet it’s for that James and Sophia thing,” Kendra said.

“What thing?” Williams asked.

“The video between James and Sophia. You should know, Mr. Williams, you were in it,” she said.

“I don’t think I was in a video,” Williams said knowing full well what they were talking about.

“That video can’t be right,” Harry said waving no at Kendra. “Johnny just makes that stuff up as he goes. Remember that video he did about finding a rubber glove in the school lunches?”

“Yeah, that was so gross.”

“Well, I watched him put the glove in his food before taking the video."

"Oh, but this is different," she said. "He can't make this stuff up."

Usually Williams would have put a stop to this sort of gossipy discussion but he couldn't help but want to hear what they all knew or thought they knew. Sometimes students would know more than the teachers in regards to town or school gossip.

"It's not all right," Jessica interrupted.

"What do you mean?" Harry said turning to her.

"I mean, Johnny was right about James talking 'intimately' with a student, but it wasn't Sophia, she's new."

"That doesn't mean James couldn't be creepin' on her," Anthony said.

"Then who was it?" Kendra asked.

"It was …"

"Ok," Williams interrupted, "Let's take out the papers from yesterday. We are going finish this prep work on Fitzgerald before we read *The Great Gatsby* next week."

The students shifted their conversations to whispers but moved to get out their class materials.

During his planning period, Williams went straight to Pete's room. He was at his desk, trying to make sense of all of his lesson plans after three days of substitutes.

"Pete," Williams said stepping next to him behind his desk, "what the heck is going on?"

"It's a complete shit show, Gus," Pete said turning to look at him with heavy eyes. "Everything is just f-ed."

"What do you mean?"

"Everyone has a lawyer in that damn room except me because I'm just supposed to record everything for the union, but right from the get go, it was bigger than that."

"Ok, so how did everything shake out?"

"Nothing has shaken out, everything is still in discussion."

"What?"

"Well, the school says Johnny's video is causing an educational disruption and his behavior is detrimental to the school, so they want to suspend him for ninety days."

"That takes him through graduation. He'd be done for the year."

"Right, well his parents brought in their own lawyer saying that the video hasn't caused a disruption to the educational environment. James has a lawyer, who says the video is causing defamation to his client's reputation or something like that, so they are suing Johnny for compensation." Pete took a breath before continuing, "Then Sophia's parents hired a lawyer and they are suing the school, stating the school didn't create a safe place for her from bullying. And they are suing the school and joining James' case against Johnny for compensation."

"Holy shit, Pete."

"Right, but, it's not done."

"No?"

"No, the school is also investigating James. They have video of him in the halls with Sonya and her going into his room after school on several occasions. The video shows them talking in a manner not appropriate to that of a student and a teacher."

"That doesn't prove anything though, right?"

"No, but the County Prosecutor and the police are going to interview Sonya to see if she is being groomed by him. They also have pictures of James and Sophia, mostly from the video."

"Shit," said Williams, slowly shaking his head.

"Right, he is probably done teaching, whether he is guilty or not."

"You are right, Pete," Williams said straightening a pile of papers in front of him, "that is a cluster."

"Just keep your nose out of it, Gus. They will contact you eventually for a statement about your role in the video."

"Okay, but I don't know much," he said holding up his hands.

"I mean it," Pete said with an unwavering stare, "you don't want to be close to this at all. As much as I want to see how this thing turns out, I excused myself from the proceedings. This will torch everything it touches. We didn't even have this conversation. And Gus, DON'T get involved beyond what they ask of you. DON'T breathe a word of this to anybody."

"Got it," Williams said turning toward the door. "I'll be in touch."

Williams strode from Pete's room. He didn't know what to think about the whole situation. He had never been a part of so much consternation.

53

The parking lot of the Steak and Egger was busier than normal for a Sunday morning in March. Spring had broken early, but no doubt it would be put back to bed before April. In Michigan, after three or four dreary months of cloud cover, when the sun decided to shine and the temperature hit forty-five degrees, people came alive, ready to embrace the rejuvenating properties of spring. Williams himself felt better after a few days of sunshine and mild weather. He was looking forward to seeing Rex again. They had talked last weekend of their writing projects and impending March Madness basketball tournament. Williams was sure spring would re-energize his friend.

Inside, the hostess directed Gus to their usual table. A middle-aged man who looked oddly familiar sat waiting. Williams turned to ask the hostess if there had been a mistake, but the man was already out of the booth approaching Williams.

"Hi, you must be Mr. Williams. My name is Wilt Chamberlain, Rex's son." Wilt extended his right hand out to Gus with a natural ease.

Gus smiled, "Like the basketball player?"

"Yes," Wilt said with a sigh, "like the basketball player."

"I thought you'd be bigger."

Wilt offered a hint of a smile but no friendly banter. He motioned for Gus to sit across from him in the booth as he sat in his father's seat.

"How's Rex? Is he here?" Williams asked picking up his cup to turn it over for coffee.

"No, I am sorry to say that my father passed away three days ago."

Williams eyes filled, his heart pounded heavy in his chest, and the coffee cup rattled in its saucer as he set it down.

"I'm sorry to hear that, Wilt," Williams said, voice quivering. "Did he at least get to see the spring weather? He wanted to see one last spring and summer sunset."

Wilt's hands shook as he picked up a manilla envelope from the table. "In his will, he had…"

Williams reached out his hand to stay the delivery of the package and anymore business about Rex's death, "Let's have coffee first. It is such a nice morning, and I was so looking forward to talking with your father. You look so much like him sitting there in his seat." Gus pulled the napkin down into his lap, "Will you have breakfast with me?"

Wilt's eyes glistened with memories and his lip quivered on his set jaw as he tried not to let his emotions break free. The waitress came with a pot of coffee and a bowl of creamers. Williams turned Wilt's cup over, letting her fill each one. The manilla envelope was placed off to the side next to the condiments.

"He," Wilt stammered, "he wouldn't let anyone administer pain medicine. Even in the end, he kept saying that he wanted to feel all that life had to offer with passion, excitement, and acceptance."

Williams smiled, "Lennon."

"What?"

"He was quoting John Lennon from The Beatles, 'When we are in love, we open to all that life has to offer with passion, excitement, and acceptance. We need to learn to love ourselves first, in all our glory and our imperfections." As Williams recalled the quote, he truly felt the message now, in this moment with Wilt. The entire passage came back to him. "If we cannot live ourselves, we cannot fully open to our ability to love others or our potential to create."

"He was always rambling off lines from somewhere, like a crazy old coot. I just sort of laughed most of them off."

"He was sharp as a tack, but seemed to start declining the last time we spoke. We often picked each other up when we were feeling sorry about our situations, either by phone or over breakfast."

"So, you have cancer as well?"

"Yes, a different kind than your father's, but cancer still."

"And is your cancer curable?"

"No, I will die from cancer." The finality of it still shocked him.

"I'm sorry to hear that," Wilt said.

"It's okay, I have come to terms with it."

"Well, about three days ago, dad called and said I needed to get on a plane, no excuses or delays. I heard the businessman in his voice, the voice I heard as a boy when he talked on the phone for work making million-dollar deals. He had been an entirely different man than the one who'd been showing up for the last ten years. I had almost forgotten who that other guy was."

"Your father and I talked quite a bit about his life as a businessman. He began to regret putting so much time into the pursuit of success instead of . . ."

"His poetry, I know."

"I don't think poetry is the right word here."

"No?"

"No," Gus said leaning over the table. "I feel like he was worried about not having enough love of ... life ... so that you could see the way he lived it for his first years and last ten."

"Are you sure you knew my father?" Wilt said sipping his coffee and then leaning back against the booth. "He was as shrewd a businessman as there ever was. He told me over and over again that you can't get caught up in another person's emotions or you'll never make a dollar."

Williams sipped his coffee, ready to listen.

"He would run the energy company by these standards and codes. All the transactions he saw were numbers. He never looked at the names attached to those accounts. He had this guy, Fred Machelonni, who would deliver these overdue notices. Fred would go to these people's houses and businesses with overalls and tools slung over his shoulder, ready to turn off their power unless they paid right then. Once the company started to work with the wholesaling of oil and then renewable energy sources, the codes were the same. Something was a little off with the work or the date or the delivery, he would take it out of their percentage."

"Wilt," Gus said leaning over the table, "the signs are there, can't you see?"

"See what? What signs?"

"Shutting off people's power bothered him immensely. Did you ever think about why he never looked at the names, why he had the code in the first place? He didn't want to hurt anyone. He didn't want to make those arbitrary choices."

"Then why did he do it?"

"You know the answer to that question."

"I do."

"Yes, you are in business, correct?"

"Yes."

"In your line of work, if the products or services you sell were given away for free or debts weren't collected, whose jobs would be on the line?"

"Everyone's job, mine included."

"And if you don't bring home a paycheck, what would happen to you and your family?"

"We would be out on the street."

"Exactly, so your father, while he had to draw the line in the sand for his customers, he was also protecting his family and the families of all of his employees."

"I guess," Wilt said slowly, staring at the tabletop.

"It doesn't sound like you are 100% convinced. Let me ask you a couple of questions."

"Listen, Mr. Williams, it doesn't really matter."

"Yes, it does. You have to believe your father was a good man through and through. There is no room for bad memories or ill thoughts of the dead. Now, what kind of car did your father drive to work every day?"

"He always drove a Cadillac, got a new one every five years on the dot."

"But did he have a bunch of fancy cars?"

"No, just a car for him and one for my mom."

"How about watches, did he have more than one watch, maybe a few Rolexes?"

"No."

"What about a second home or third home?"

"No."

"What about suits?"

"Off the rack."

"Do you see what I am getting at with these questions? Your father ran a business the best way he could. But he had to draw the line somewhere or else he would be putting his family and his employees at risk."

"I see your point," Wilt nodded. "Anyway, I got on the plane as soon as he called. I was in Oklahoma on a business trip. My connection went through Chicago, so I rented a car at O'Hare and drove here as fast as I could. He was outside sitting on his porch swing, letting the sun beat down on his face. His hands were black with dirt. He told me that the earth smelled new, the warm sun healing. "Hear the birds," he said, "life." I heard him but I was so worried because it was still kind of cold, I wanted to get him another blanket. I started to stand ..."

Wilt's tears ran down his stubbled cheeks. He wiped his face with his napkin then dabbed at his eyes. Williams reached out, placing a hand on his arm.

"He grabbed my arm with such strength, I was shocked. He said, 'Stay with me, son.' So I sat back down and I put my arm around him, something I don't think I had ever done before. He looked at me with such love in his eyes. He said, 'I love you, Wilt.' I told him I loved him too and then I kissed the top of his head. And you know what he said?"

Williams shook his head as he wiped tears from his eyes.

"He sat there for a bit looking out over the water then said, 'Wilt, you should do what makes you happy. All those years I spent working was to provide for our family and all the employees, it never really made me happy. Do what makes you happy'. I told him was a great dad and I couldn't have wanted it any other way. Then he looked at me with that businessman look and said, 'When I die, you will never have to worry about money again. So, be up and doing, with a heart for any fate'. And then he just leaned his head on my shoulder and slowly faded away. He held on against all the pain until I got home and then he just let go."

"Sounds like a beautiful ending to a great life."

Wilt nodded his head. The waitress brought their usual order.

"Here we go gentlemen, the usual for you Mr. Williams, and here is yours Mr. Chamberlain."

Wilt looked perplexed.

"Oh, I am sorry, darling. You are not my Mr. Chamberlain. I didn't even look when I delivered the coffee. I can get you something different, what would you like to have this morning?"

Wilt took a deep breath, "I am actually Mr. Chamberlain. Rex was my father."

"Well, you look like the spitting image, no wonder I didn't notice. What can I get for you young Mr. Chamberlain?"

"What was my father's usual order?"

"This here is your two eggs over easy with crispy hash browns and a side of bacon."

"That sounds delicious." Wilt slid his coffee to the side in order to have a clear spot for his breakfast plate. "I will take it. Thank you."

Williams smiled, unfolding his tear-filled napkin onto his lap. "Thank you, Cassie." Williams started to eat his breakfast, taking his time, watching Wilt, letting him settle his emotions with a hearty breakfast. "Before I forget to ask, I would like to attend the memorial service, is that soon?"

"The service will be on Tuesday," Wilt said ripping a piece of bacon in half. "I have the details all written down for you.

"If it would be all right," Gus said, "I would like to share with you how I met your father."

It was Wilt's turn to hold up his hand, "He told me. He met you at the hospital. He was nearing the end of his journey with cancer and you were just starting."

"Yes, that's right. He helped me understand how to live with cancer and look at life a little differently when it enters the fourth quarter."

Wilt continued to eat in silence. Williams finished his last bite of hash browns then pushed his plate to the side. The coffee was refilled, the plates were cleared, and Williams handed Cassie a fifty-dollar bill as she cleared the plates.

Wilt wiped his hands and his mouth on his napkin and then put it next to the condiments before picking up the manilla envelope. "Mr. Williams, my father really liked you. He told me so himself, said you gave him some inspiration to return to his first love, poetry."

"Thank you for telling me," Williams said nodding his head. "It's always nice to hear you make a difference."

"Yes, well, as per the norm with my father, he wanted to show you how much it meant to him by giving something back to you."

"Wilt, that is not necessary," Williams said waving his hands in the air. "I have all that I need, believe me."

"By law," Wilt said opening the manilla envelope, "I have to give you what is outlined in the will, what you do with it is up to you."

"What are we talking about here?" Williams said leaning over the table.

"The details are in here," Wilt said pulling the papers out of the envelope. "But the breakdown is about one million dollars."

Williams' hand shook as he set the coffee down on the table, "Did you say, one million dollars?"

Wilt looked down at the papers, "Yes, Mr. Williams. He left you one million dollars but in order to receive the gift, you must do three things. 1) You must start two scholarship funds in Wellington County. One for the study of poetry and one for the study of business and ethics. 2) Before you can disperse any funds, you have to write the introduction to his final book of poems. And 3) You have to finish your own memoirs, which can be published through traditional or independent channels."

"That's all, huh?" Williams said chuckling, "He didn't make it easy, did he? Is there a timeline? What happens if I don't complete all three tasks, for one reason or another?"

"It says upon your death, the money will be put back into the family account."

"Wow, that is about all I have to say about that."

Wilt chuckled, "He was always making sure money went toward the good things. Once in high school, he gave me a weekly allowance for gas and supplies while I played baseball but then once the season ended, he made go to the soup kitchen every Wednesday and Sunday to work it off at five dollars an hour."

"Well, good for him," Williams laughed. "I can only imagine the look on your face when he told you the backend of that allowance."

"Oh, man," Wilt said still laughing, "I don't think I would have taken the money if I had known."

"You don't seem too upset that your dad gave me a million dollars. You received some money too, I hope."

"Yes, don't worry about us," Wilt said placing the papers back in the envelope. "My father invested very wisely in certain companies over the years, which netted him a small fortune. A million dollars is just a fraction of his net worth. When he said I would never have to worry about money again, he was right. And neither will my children probably."

"Wow, that's great."

"Yes, but like your gift, it comes with some rules. Only so much per year. My children must work and have successful careers before receiving any inheritance besides college tuition, etc., etc."

"You know he only does it to protect you."

"I know, but it is still very frustrating at times to have so many strings."

"Or just one string."

"I suppose."

Wilt stood, laying the envelope on the table.

"All the details are inside. If you have any questions, the number for my father's attorney is included. And here," he said laying a second envelope on the table, "is a copy of his last collection of poems, so you can write the introduction. Details for the publisher are on the inside as well. There is a timeline for this one, so you should look sooner rather than later."

Williams nodded and then slipped out of the booth, "Thank you. It was nice to meet you and talk about your father."

"Thank you. I appreciate your friendship with my father. He knew many people but didn't have many close friends, at least not ones that understood him the way you did."

"Thank you," Williams said, extending his hand. "He made a big impact on my life."

54

Williams sat back in the booth holding the envelopes, unable to open them again. He slid from the booth, leaving the change from their bill on the table. Finally, he'd had a chance to pay. But he couldn't read Rex's final words here, not yet. There was only one place he could read those final words.

The road to the beach was long and winding, a dissection through the North Wellington district. The majority of residents lived in tightly packed houses, bracketed by large mansions and leftover plots from the timber era, the manufacturing boom, and the shipping industry. As the small suburb expanded, the forest surrounding Wellington shrank and premium developments took its place.

Slowly, the houses gave way to state parks and deciduous forests, filled with oak, maple, and pine. Williams entered the green tunnel through two towering dunes covered in underbrush and thick unmanicured lands. The canopy opened just over the crest of a hill to reveal a slight glimpse of blue, then a small curve in the road before the whole world seemed to open up with fresh blue water as far as the eye could see.

He turned down the road to the beach. Sand still covered much of the road in wide swaths of windblown berms. He maneuvered his car around each one until he found his way to the channel parking lot. He couldn't have asked for a better day to take in Rex's final words. He pulled the flaps of his hat down over his ears. He zipped his puffy jacket all the way to his chin. He grabbed the blanket that he kept folded in the backseat, a habit he got into when Janet rode with him in the winter. She was always cold.

On the benches at the edge of the channel, Gus settled himself down with Rex's packet of poems. He slid the stapled pages from the envelope. The first page was a letter from his publisher, Jon Martin. Williams read through the list of instructions about what to include and what not to include in his introduction. Williams didn't really want any of that information in his head; he wanted his friend's last words. He turned the page and there was the title, so simple, so obvious, and so true:

The End of Something
A Collection of Poems

by Rex Chamberlain
With a foreword by August Williams

As the sun rose high over Wellington Channel, Williams slowly read through Rex Chamberlain's last collection of poems. Each poem struck a chord so singularly. Since his last collection, Rex had lived a big life, full of adventure, love, and loss. All of those experiences were on display, along with a tighter, more commanding verse. Williams turned to the last page. A poem titled, "August in Twilight" with the subtitle, *for August Williams,* filled the page.

August in Twilight

for August Williams

He stood
in the drive

the clothes hung
on a line

the leaves laid
in the yard

the lamps glowed
in the windows

a day lived
sits alone
amid the dying light

55

Williams sat at his kitchen table. The Sunday morning had slipped away in fury of cleaning. He had been in one of those moods where he couldn't sit in his thoughts. He had to move. When trails weren't open, he cleaned. He had so much to think about: Rex's introduction, his memoirs, his retirement. When the house had been cleaned and the laundry finished, he sat down at the kitchen table with his journal and his stack of papers for his memoirs. He wasn't ready, yet. He had to keep on the move. He needed to go to school.

Mondays in March meant something much different than Mondays in January and February. Spring Break was just off in the distance. Michigan would sometimes drag the winter weather through until spring break, keeping families huddled in their homes. Sometimes Michigan would part the cloudy skies and allow the sun to shine down to regenerate life. Students would have just four weeks until spring break, scheduled for the first full week in April. It seemed to Gus that during spring break the entire state up and left, heading to Florida or Texas. Gus had gone a few times with Danny and Janet, but couldn't bring himself to travel all alone. But now, he was ready to see what the world looked like outside of Wellington.

Spring break meant something else for Williams this year, a deadline. He had to somehow figure out what Adams was going to do with his future. They had made a lot of progress in getting to know each other but not enough yet to invoke the confidence needed for Adams to lay bare his heart's desire. What Adams needed more than anything was to deal with the feelings he was having with his mother. Williams believed if their relationship were better, Adams would have a clearer mind to judge what he wanted for his future.

Williams parked on a side street, which was a closer walk to the school than the teacher parking lot. He didn't have any particular agenda; he just needed to keep moving. The halls stood silent. The school had a long standing commitment to family on Sundays. There were to be no sports practices, play rehearsals, or extra-curricular activities on Sunday at the school. But often times the varsity boys' coach could be found in the gym with his sons practicing with the shooting machine or the yearbook teacher could be found in her room editing pages for a deadline.

Williams climbed the stairs, pulling his keys from his pocket. He spread the keys through his fingers looking for the right one to unlock his door. As he rounded the corner, he saw the light on in Stacy's room. The door stood ajar.

In the room, Stacy and his mother were squared off like two prize fighters at a weigh-in. His mind raced. He figured this confrontation was what he, and Stacy, needed to happen in order to move forward. To Gus, it was obvious that Stacy needed to share his feelings with his mother, the bottled up emotions that made him rage on the inside and stew on the outside. As with most teenagers, the rebellious stage came in a slow building of angst and then exploded into a power struggle. Usually, the parents held on so tight until the child could show responsibility and break the stranglehold of childhood. Some families showed no obvious tension, while others offered the spectacle of a full-on brawl. Williams wondered how his relationship with Danny would've played out if the accident hadn't taken him away too soon. He saw Stacy, now boiling hot, ready to push free from his mother's guidance. He only hoped that their relationship could be salvaged afterward.

"Hi, I hope I'm not interrupting something," Williams said walking into the room.

"No," Stacy said. "She was just leaving. I am sure your car is waiting for you downstairs."

Ms. Adams replied sharply, "I thought you could show me your classroom. Your future."

Neither had turned to look at Williams. They were locked in an old fashioned stare down.

"Why don't we have a seat in my room," Williams said. "I can make us some coffee and we can sit in the office chairs for a nice conversation."

"The time for a nice conversation is long overdue," Ms. Adams said, "and a cup of coffee would be delightful." She turned to Gus, "Oh, hello. So, this is where you are a teacher. And let me guess, you are his mentor too."

"Yes, I'm afraid so," Williams said turning to the side to show Ms. Adams to his room. "I hope you are not upset that I didn't tell you."

"We hardly talked," she said. "When would you have had time to tell me?"

Stacy grabbed a Wolves coffee cup from his desk and whipped it into the brick wall. Gus and Ms. Adams jumped at the shattering of the cup. Suddenly, her demeanor was like a litigator.

"Well, Stacy, what do you have to say for yourself?" Ms. Adams stood in front of his desk, fingers splayed on the tabletop like she was ready to examine a witness on the stand, "Acting like a prepubescent child instead of an adult trying to teach children."

"What do I have to say for myself, what about you? So controlling all the time. What are you even doing here?"

"As a mother, I am allowed to come see my only child. Isn't it the mother's right?"

"Did you sue to make sure that was the case?"

"What are you talking about, Stacy? Where did all this vitriol come from? I have done nothing but try to support you every step of the way."

Stacy stood, "Support me, yeah. You sure have. I can't even take a step on my own without you telling me how to do it."

"That is ridiculous."

Williams strode to the desk, "How about we have a seat here? Let our emotions settle."

"Don't you start on me too, Gus. I can damn well stand if I want to and if I want my emotions to be unsettled then, dang it, they will be!"

Ms. Adams took a seat.

"I know you are feeling upset," Gus said putting up his hands to hold back the emotion flowing from Adams. "I think it is good that you are expressing your feelings here, just lay everything out on the table."

"What are you a psychologist now? Are you my shrink? Where is the leather couch Dr. Freud?" Adams pushed his office chair, sending it cruising across the front of the room before slamming into the edge of a desk and clattering to the floor.

Ms. Adams sat calmly with her legs crossed, hands placed on her lap as she absorbed the scene unfolding in front of her.

Williams put his hands in his pockets, "Stacy, this isn't for me. My hope is that you and Ms. Adams can reconcile your differences, that you can express your feelings and desires for the future. My hope is that your family can grow to become an asset to one another because I know how precious family is and how quickly it can be taken away."

Ms. Adams nodded, eyes glistening.

Williams continued, "So, I'm going to go across the hall to my room. And I will be there for the next couple of hours grading today's papers. You, either of you," he said looking at Ms. Adams, "can come over any time to talk or have a cup of coffee, but I urge you to get to the bottom of this business right now,

Stacy."

Williams then turned for the door. As he closed the door, he heard Ms. Adams start talking and then Stacy, both of their emotions running high.

Williams had been absorbed in a student paper about the use of weather in *The Great Gatsby* when he heard a door slam. He dropped his readers down on the stack of student essays. He waited. The sound of quick feet walking down the hall told him that Stacy had left. He waited. He heard the soft click of heels emerge from the room and pause in the hallway. Williams wondered if she would come over to his room or head down the stairs to the door. He began to stand, maybe she needed someone to walk her out. As he came to the door, Ms. Adams looked up. She folded a tissue blackened with mascara-stained tears, finding a clean corner before dabbing at her eyes again.

"Ms. Adams," Gus said stepping into the hall. "I was wondering if you would like me to show you out. I know this place can be a maze."

"Thank you, Mr. Williams," she said pulling back her shoulders. "But I think I can find my way out one way or another."

"You are as stubborn as your son," he said flicking off his light. "Sometimes we all need someone to do a simple thing with us for no other reason than to not be alone." He lifted his elbow to her.

She shook her hair back then slipped her arm through his as they walked down the hall. Their silence was understood. Two people walked arm in arm, both alone. One, the state's most powerful lawyer, the other, a simple teacher, but each with broken hearts and an uncertain future. They made their way through the barren hallways, amid the quiet hiss of the heating system, sensing the palpable feeling of the lifeless building, to the entrance where a car idled.

"Ms. Adams," Gus said turning to face her. "I," he paused,

"even though we know each other's names, I don't believe I have ever introduced myself properly." He stuck out his hand. "I am Gus Williams, please call me Gus."

She put her hand in his. "Amelia, Amelia Adams." Then a small smile escaped her lips, "Please call me Amelia."

"Well, it is nice to finally meet you. I have heard so much."

Amelia laughed, "I bet you have. Have you heard his ring tone? I can't imagine what else he has said about me."

Gus laughed, "I entertain by picking brains, sell my soul by dropping names, I don't like those! My God, what's that!"

"I object, I object," she said.

"On what grounds, counselor?"

"On the grounds that the song was written for a gay man coming out and doesn't have anything to do with a mother and a son."

"Fair enough, fair enough," Gus said holding up his hands in faux defensive posture.

"Mr. Williams."

"Gus, please."

She smiled, "Gus, thank you, not only for these few moments of brevity but also for being such a good mentor to Stacy. I don't think he would have been able to share all those feelings with me, as painful as they were, if you hadn't been talking to him all year."

"You're welcome, Amelia. I only want what is best for the young man."

"Yes, well," she said pulling her purse in front of her with both hands, "what he needs, what he has always needed, was a father. I tried my best to fill that role but I'm afraid things didn't work out."

"I think you did an amazing job," Gus said touching her arm. "A mother's job is often thankless, much more so when they bear the burden of parenting alone."

"Well, thank you for that. I think we have made progress today. My hope is like yours that I can have a whole family. I know that I am not the easiest person. I am strong-willed, I love to work, I love to be in control, and because of those things, I have been without love in my life for many years. The last thing I want is to lose my son. So, thank you so very much."

"You're welcome," Gus said opening the door. "I am sure you have many endearing qualities that make you lovable. You shouldn't be so hard on yourself."

She smiled and squeezed his hand. Gus handed her a folded note, "Here is my phone number, please call if you want to check in on Stacy."

"Thank you," she said slipping the note into her purse. "Is that the only reason I can call?"

Gus smiled, "Maybe we could talk about that hike you're planning."

"I'd like that."

Gus stepped back as the driver closed her door, hiding Ms. Adams behind tinted glass. As the car pulled away, Williams turned back inside. A small smile crept across his face. His heart beat a little faster and his pulse quickened. He hadn't felt that way in a long time, too long.

56

Williams went straight to Adams' room when he arrived at school the next day. The door remained open, students were milling about. Some students were standing against the wall around the broken cup. Stacy hadn't been back to school. Gus grabbed the trash can by the door. He walked over to where the cup lay in pieces on the floor, bent down, and started to pick up the mess.

"Mr. Williams," Johnny asked, "what happened to the coffee cup?"

Williams stopped, leaving the remaining pieces on the carpet, "No comment and please put away your phones."

"No phone this time, Mr. Willams," Johnny said holding his hands up.

"Johnny," Williams said putting his hand up, "I am still not going to comment. You burnt this bridge for the time being."

"I understand," he said. "I messed up."

"Ya think?" Gus said stooping down to pick up the remaining pieces.

Johnny knelt down to help, "I'm sorry, Mr. Williams. You were right about trying to do the right thing with my videos."

"Thank you," Gus said dropping more pieces into the garbage. "You can't make a living off of other people's problems or misfortunes or bad decisions."

"I don't agree with you, Mr. Williams. I see television news and YouTubers doing it all the time," Johnny tossed a final fragment into the garbage. "But I am not going to argue. What I do know is that I need to have a better check of my facts before publishing."

"What do you mean?" Gus asked turning to face Johnny.

"Well, Mr. Williams, I am not at liberty to say officially, but since you know more than the average teacher, I will say that I wasn't all wrong."

"What do you mean?"

"I mean I just had the wrong student in the video."

Johnny stood up. Williams followed him.

"Is that why you are back in school? Partial truth?" Williams asked.

"I suppose," Johnny said shrugging his shoulders. "There are some restrictions on my attendance, which I think are a little overboard."

"Like what?"

"I can't use any device with a camera until after I graduate unless it is directly supervised by a teacher."

"Which is why a camera isn't in my face right now, right?"

"Right," Johnny said. "Like I said earlier. I am sorry for making things hard on you. It wasn't really my intention. I just didn't like the idea of James praying on the female students at Wellington."

"That's a noble enough cause," Williams said sticking out his hand. "You sure are forcing yourself to grow up fast."

"Life does that to a person sometimes," Johnny said shaking Williams' hand.

Williams brought the garbage can back to the front of the room. The students were starting to take their seats. Williams wondered if Adams would show today. As he turned to leave, a substitute came barreling through the door holding a tub of pretzels.

"Hi, are you Mr. Adams?" she asked. "I'm here to substitute

for you."

"No," Williams said turning to the side, "I teach across the hall. I was just getting the room open for you."

"Great," she said, "I just picked up the job this morning."

"No problem," Williams said. "I'm Gus Williams. I teach across the hall. Come on over if you need anything."

"Thanks, I'm Shailene," she said. "I will, but I'm usually all set with my pretzels." She twirled toward the desk, purse and tote swinging, dropping a few pretzels on a student desk.

The student looked up in befuddlement before pushing the pretzels to the corner of her desk with the edge of her hand.

Williams left Stacy's room and headed down toward Pete's room, then turned back. He would have to wait until his planning to learn more about Johnny's story. For now, he had to finish teaching about MLA citations and works cited entries.

He walked into his room, "How many of you have had a driving citation before?" The students looked at him dumbfounded. "You know like a ticket?"

"I was with my dad once when he got a ticket, does that count?" Chase said.

"Sure," Gus said.

"What about a parking ticket?" Ella said.

"Sure," Gus said, "all those things tell you that you did something at a certain time. In this case, something you were not supposed to do. But what we are going to do is tell readers we did something in our paper."

"How does that work?" Harry asked.

"Yeah," Anthony said, "how do you get a speeding ticket in your paper?"

The rest of the class looked at Anthony with astonishment.

"What?" he asked.

"You are so stupid," Harry said.

"Shut up, you asked the same question," Anthony said sitting up straight in his chair.

"Ok, enough gentlemen," Williams said. "This can be a tricky subject. Let me explain further. When you borrow words from another paper to use in your own, you must tell the reader you didn't write them. You do that by using a citation and a works cited entry."

"If you don't give them a citation then you get a speeding ticket?" Anthony asked.

The class let out a collective groan.

"Sort of," Williams continued before any banter started. "You can get an F for a grade, kicked out of college, or even fired from a job."

"All for not citing your sources?" Jessica asked.

"Usually, the more serious the crime the more serious the punishment. For example, if someone cheats in here, they will get Saturday School and a zero on the assignment. Newspaper reporters that make stuff up get fired and, unofficially, banned from working at a newspaper again."

"Wow," said Jessica, "so, why is Johnny allowed to stay here? He made stuff up about that new girl."

"Yeah, but he told the truth about James," Harry said. "That dude was try'n to get with Sonya. The freak."

"Yeah, but she was all about it," Anthony said. "She snapped about it all the frickin' time."

"Ok, Ok." Williams said. "We are not going to make this classroom the court of public opinion. Let's refocus."

"Yeah, of course you don't want us to talk about it," Harry said. "You knew all about it and didn't say anything."

"Harry," Williams said, "that is quite enough. I found out the same way that you all did."

"That's not what the video showed."

"Wait, there's a video?" Anthony asked. "Were they gettin' busy?"

"No, idiot," Harry said.

"I've had enough of you calling me stupid," Anthony said getting out of his seat. "I wonder how stupid you'll look when I split your lip, you little shit."

"Whoa, boys," Williams said stepping in front of Anthony, putting his hands on his shoulders and trying to make eye contact. "No more name calling and definitely no splitting of lips."

"Anyway," Harry said, "there was a video of James telling Mr. Williams and Jorgmander about his thing with Sonya."

"Is that true, Mr. Williams?" Jessica asked looking hurt. "Did you really know and not say anything?"

Williams was in a bind here. He didn't want to lose these students. They had thought so highly of him and now, with one wrongly worded admission, he could lose them all.

"The day the video was taken," Williams said, "was the day I found out about the situation. My advice was for Mr. James to get a lawyer and cease all contact with the student."

"So, you told the administration?" Jessica asked.

"There was nothing to tell at the time," he said. "What we heard was that Mr. James heard rumors he was 'talking' to a student."

"But someone should have told," Jessica said. "I mean, he is like a predator."

"Ok, I think we are going off track here and I have probably said more than I should have already," Williams said handing out a worksheet on MLA citations. "What I want you to know, Jessica, and everyone else, is that I would never NOT disclose information if a student was at risk."

"Someone should give Mr. James a citation," Anthony said.

"I bet his cellmate in prison will give him plenty of citations," Harry said. "I heard they don't like pedophiles in lockup."

"Let's start on the side with the information box," Williams said drawing the students back to the curriculum.

After class, Williams felt like the students were all looking at him differently for what he had disclosed during first hour. More than likely, no one knew what he knew, but he would have to think of a different opener than the one he used first hour in case someone else made a repeat connection.

By third hour, Williams' anxiety was through the roof. He had to talk to Pete. Just as he was about to leave his room to head downstairs to find him, Shailene met him in the doorway with her jug of pretzels.

"Hi, it's planning right?" She asked.

"Yes," Williams said, "can I help you with something?"

"No, I just wondered if you would like some pretzels. During planning I usually just find other teachers with the same planning and talk about the school, that way I get to know where I'm working."

"Right," Williams said standing firm in the doorway. "I'm sorry but I can't chat right now. I have a meeting downstairs. I would suggest that maybe you select a book to read from my shelf and relax a little with your jug of pretzels."

"Oh, ok," she said. "Will you be back soon? I'll just read until you get back."

Williams passed by her in the doorway, happy to be off to find Jorgmander. The halls were eerily quiet for a Monday. Williams felt like this was the calm before the storm. March sometimes felt that way, the lull between sports seasons, between terrible weather and warm weather. As he descended the stairs, he didn't know what he wanted to hear from Pete. Maybe that James wasn't a creep, that Sonya was more willing, that James may have led her on but he drew the line.

Pete's students were working in groups creating some sort of poster. He was up walking around the room. When he saw Gus at the door, he made his way through the groups to talk.

"What's up, Gus?"

"Well, I saw Johnny was back in school today and then the students were making some comments, so I thought I should come to you find out what's going on."

"I can't really say much," Pete said leaning in to Gus, "but I know that Johnny has Saturday school for the rest of year and he has a technology ban. Sophia switched to Catholic, we paid her tuition."

"What? That's crazy."

"They both dropped the lawsuit against the school; it was a deal for Wellington."

"What about James?"

"That is a little more complicated." Pete said, "The county prosecutor has gotten ahold of it and is handling the investigation. You will probably be interviewed this week or next."

"Shoot."

"Right, well get your story straight."

"The story is the story, Pete," Gus said. "Thanks for the information."

"Yeah, no problem."

Williams needed to walk again. This time he wasn't going to stop to talk. With the weather creeping back into the 40s, he could get back out on the trails. He had his plan for after school.

57

Spring time often meant muck in Michigan. All Williams could do was lace up his hiking boots and tuck the bottom of his pants into his gaiters. Sometimes you just have to plow ahead to get to the other side even if your feet are going to get dirty. This seemed to be one of those moments for Williams.

The trail to Lost Lake steered Williams away from Wellington Lake and the bluff over Lake Michigan into the forest. Williams followed the trail into the undergrowth. The trail through the dunes sat naked most of the year; the trail through the forest path was equally sparse in the spring. But as the summer wore on, the forest path grew small and smaller as the plants encroached on the trail. Williams stood at the crossroads; the path to Janet and Danny's bench branched off to the left and the trail to Lost Lake ventured to the right. For years, Williams had been going to the left, up the forested dune then out into the sands or around the lake and up the dunes on the opposite side, but always to their bench. Williams lifted his foot to step toward Lost Lake then put in down again. Change was hard. He took a deep breath then lifted his foot, taking the path less traveled. His first few steps were hesitant, like he wasn't sure if he was going in the right direction. All new endeavors are the same, he thought. But in time he would hit his stride and the trail miles would be devoured.

Whenever he needed time to think, Williams always went to Janet. She kept him anchored. But now he needed Janet and Danny to be with him wherever he went instead of staying rooted to Wellington.

The trail to Lost Lake wasn't as familiar as the dune. In the forest, the trails crisscrossed every which way. The post pointed at two trails moving off in same direction, but Williams saw three. He took a right at the first fork. He remembered the path from years of hiking in the area. The trail took him to the highest point in the woods. At the top, there wasn't a bench or a view, just more trees, more undergrowth, more trail. Williams stopped to take a drink of water from his blue scuffed Nalgene bottle. The trail disappeared around a bend after about twenty-five yards. Just like life, Williams thought, the future is always disappearing around one turn or another.

The future for Williams wasn't going to be a wife, two kids, and a dog surrounded by a white picket fence. That dream had been snuffed out years ago, replaced with a nightmare. Now, at his age, his life should have been filled with trips to exotic locations, wintering in Florida, helping with the grandkids. Williams had none of that to look forward to. He only had what he had. Life was making him choose this time. Life had been patient for years and years. Not any longer.

The trail wound around different ridges before dipping down into the valley. The temperature dropped a few degrees as he descended and the trail grew muddy. He could see small piles of snow hiding under canopies built by fallen trees and evergreens. Each step left a small depression. The trail met Lost Lake on its east end, then wound around the northern side, skirting the edge. All along the path, benches for birders showed the way to the edge of the marsh. Some benches were lost to the high water levels and new paths had been cut through the undergrowth by hikers.

The rules were always to follow the trail in order to minimize impact on the local environment, but Williams always saw detours around nature-made obstacles. He had walked around beaver dams, flooded trails, downed trees, and washed-out bridges. He always looked for that original path. Sometimes it wasn't passable, but other times the new path was just for convenience sake.

What was convenient for Williams now? The convenient path would have been to retire last summer. But no, he had to carry on to fulfill his obligation. He knew no one would have cared if he retired. Life would have continued without Williams the teacher. Just like the trail would continue on and around obstacles. But now he was at a crossroads. Although Stacy didn't know it, he was just seven days away from the administration's deadline. Should he have pushed Stacy toward law school more? He saw no signs that Stacy was embracing or rejecting teaching. In fact, in the last few months, Stacy had become a much better teacher than he had been all year. Was he thinking about staying? His heart was about to be broken in a few short days if that was the case.

His path merged with a larger trail and Williams knew he was on the groomed, well-traveled route from the nearby lodge. He stopped to take a drink and laughed. Why did he always have to take the hardest path to any destination? The short walk to the viewing platform from the lodge was wide enough for a golf cart and covered with bark. Williams could have been to the platform and back to his car, clean, unburdened with a pack, fresh for whatever the evening would bring him, but that was not his way. He always took the path less traveled.

The viewing platform sat six feet above the marshy ground. A wooden bench and railing wound around the platform. Williams sat down, leaning back against the railing. He just wanted to stare out at Lost Lake, watch the spring birds flit about, maybe catch a deer walking elegantly through the woods, but the railing obstructed his view. Instead he looked down at his mud covered trail shoes and gaiters. Your feet can take you anywhere you want, Williams thought, but they can't help you see, not even what is right in front of your face.

Williams took a sip from his bottle, shouldered his pack then set off around the southern edge of the lake. After about twenty-five yards, the well-groomed trail narrowed to a small footpath that would be overgrown and unnoticeable by July. No benches adorned the shoreline on the rarely traveled south side. To a hiker from the northern shore, Williams must have looked like he was walking through the lake because the trail hugged the waterline so closely. Puncheons dotted the trail, lifting Williams up over segments that would have sunk him to his knees and destroyed the natural marsh.

The trail took an abrupt turn near the east end, bending sharply 180 degrees up a small ridge to start a switch back to the top. Once at the top, Williams couldn't tell that Lost Lake was just a few minutes away.

Maybe it was time for my own abrupt turn, Williams thought. Life had done that to him enough times. But what was he going to do? That had always been the question. The answer, of course, was anything he wanted. He would tell Stacy about the district's plans one day after school the following week. Then he would tell administration about his plans to retire. What happened after that, he didn't know, but his path would be set.

The sign post directing him back to his car appeared just around a bend in the trail. There was always a sign, if you knew how to read it. Williams followed the path off to the right, heading back down the way he came. The path stopped at a road. Williams walked up to the edge, watching cars head to the shores of Lake Michigan for a sunset walk or a quiet moment with a beautiful view. For as many times as Williams had walked this path, this road crossing felt different, like he was doing it for the first time.

I suppose, Williams thought, life would be different.

58

"Gus," Adams said, "I have my performance review this morning. Is there anything that I should do besides bring evidence for my goals?"

Williams' heart skipped a beat. He thought the review was the following week, right before spring break. Anderson must be leaving early for his vacation. Figures, Williams thought, teachers weren't allowed to bookend spring break with vacation days but administration could do so without batting an eye. Williams hadn't made the effort to talk about what administration was going to do. If fact, he had wanted to attempt to change the administrator's mind. Adams had been doing so well the last few weeks, ever since he had talked with his mother. The students had been coming and going from his class with laughter and smiles. He had seen some students return for extra help for essays and writing for other classes. Maybe this was good news. Maybe Anderson changed his mind. He hadn't been invited to the meeting after all.

"Stacy," Williams stammered, "let's walk down there together. We can talk on the way."

"Okay, let's go, old man." Stacy was light on his feet, almost eager.

"All right, hold your horses," Gus said moving out from behind his desk with slow deliberate movements. "Remember,

I'm not as swift of foot as I once was even a couple of years ago, much less at your age."

Stacy stood at the door waiting for Gus to make his way through the rows of desks. "So, what should I expect?"

"Well, first he will probably talk about your goals and if you reached them. Did you?"

"Yes, I have all the documentation right here." Stacy held up three colored folders with stacks of neatly aligned color-coded sticky-notes.

"Good," Gus said, "I figured that wouldn't be a problem for you. You like to keep your ducks in a row." Gus hesitated. "After you talk about your goals, he is going to talk about his observations and the teacher evaluation rubric. He should point out some positive traits and, possibly, some things to improve upon."

"Right, so be prepared."

"Stacy, you and I both know, if we are being honest, that much of this year has been rough in a number of ways. For quite some time the students and the parents were not happy with your teaching methods ..."

"But I have the data to support ..."

Gus cut him off, "Regardless of what you have in that folder, be prepared to listen to what Anderson has to say. And what I want you to understand is that you have started to become a good teacher." Gus stopped in the foyer outside the office and turned to face Stacy. "Becoming a good teacher takes time, time to find out who you are in the world, in the world of school, and how best to relate to the students in order to get them to learn. No matter what he says in there, you have made a lot of progress and next year will be even better for you, if you decide to stick with teaching."

Stacy smiled, "Gee, Gus, that sounds kind of ominous. It's not like I'm on trial for murder." They had reached the office. Stacy opened the door and turned to look back at Williams, "Thanks for all your help this year, with everything."

Stacy disappeared into the front office. Williams watched as he hesitated at Anderson's door, then stepped inside and closed it for their private meeting.

Williams took a seat on the bench outside the office. The same bench where he had waited for Stacy to arrive on the first day of school. He thought back to that first day, the terse interaction, the off-putting mannerisms. The fresh news of his cancer. The thoughts of retirement, his life after teaching, his past, and his future. It was as if this year began on this bench and now, it could end on this bench. This building had stood the test of time. How often does a school building get demolished? More often than not they get renovated. North Wellington was no different. This spot had held a school for nearly 100 years. When the old wooden structures burnt to the ground, the town rebuilt. First with wood, which was readily available from the sawmills that dotted the small peninsula. Each mill donated wood and let a few of their best carpenters spend time building the school instead of working at the mill. It took a village then as it does now.

Williams never worried about the school burning down. But he did worry about the students. More times than not he had caught himself having fatherly feelings toward some of the more needy students. The ones that maybe didn't have the best parental support at home. He tried to be their role model, offering advice and a helping hand.

Now, more than ever, he worried about how they were being influenced. First, television impacted children, then cable television, now YouTube and social media apps had taken the place of real people and real experiences. Williams didn't know how to combat it anymore. For him, teaching had always been about the student, not the subject matter. He could teach the nuances of creative writing or the structures of the essay or the finer points of proper grammatical structure, but none of that mattered unless the student was willing to learn. And Williams knew more than anything that he had never been an English teacher, but a teacher to students. His ability to relate to this latest generation was slipping away from him. It was time for him to retire.

The door to Anderson's office opened. Anderson was standing with his hand on the knob, nodding. Adams was still inside the room. He couldn't tell from Anderson's demeanor what had happened in the meeting. He wouldn't have fired him without union representation, that was a big no-no in education. He saw Adams stick out his hand to Anderson. Always business with this one thought Williams, always business. As Gus stood, he saw Pete sitting in an office chair. Shit, Williams thought, they fired him.

Williams went to the office door as Stacy stepped away from Anderson. Adams opened the door, "Gus, let's talk on the way up to our classrooms."

"What the hell happened in there? Why was Pete Jorgmander in there with you?"

"Relax, everything is under control," Stacy said putting a calming hand on Gus' shoulder. "Let's go up to your room to talk over a cup of coffee, maybe you need a decaf," he said smiling.

"I don't understand," Gus said.

"I will explain everything, let's just make it up to your room for some privacy."

The tables had been turned. Williams had been the calming influence, but now Stacy was the one with the rational behavior.

Back in his room, Williams picked up a coffee cup then a pod and set them both back down on the table. He turned to Stacy, "I can't make any coffee right now. I need to know what happened. Did they fire you? What was Pete doing in there? What did Anderson do, that cocksucker?"

"Whoa," Stacy said, "simmer down, you're boiling over, old timer."

"Calm down, calm down," Williams said starting to pace.

"Anderson has been in my ear about you all year and now, now he pulls a meeting without me, your mentor. I just don't understand."

Stacy walked up to Williams, put his hands on his shoulders to steady his mentor, his friend. "I told you downstairs I would explain everything. Are you ready?"

Williams took a seat at a desk. He looked the part of an eager student.

"First, I would like to thank you for all that you have done for me this year. I realize that I wasn't the best teacher nor an easy student. I can see that now as plain as day."

Williams smiled but he knew what was coming before Stacy even said it. He couldn't interrupt.

"After the long talk with my mother a few weeks ago, I have been doing quite a bit of soul searching, looking inside and then at the outside factors that made me such a bitter and angry young man. The truth is, all I have been given in life is nearly everything I had ever wanted, including love and support."

"What about the overbearing mother?"

"Well, I grant you that, she could be a little overbearing, but it came from a place of love, not control. She admitted as much to me. So, once I figured that out, I also had to realize my own part in the way I was feeling. If I wanted something, maybe I should have worked a little harder at convincing my mother that I knew what was best for me. And she said that she should have let me try things my own way, whether I failed or succeeded."

"Ok, that is all well and good, but what does that have to do with the meeting downstairs?" Williams said folding his arms over his chest.

"We are getting there," Stacy said. "I realized over the last few weeks that I could be a good teacher. I have the intelligence, and I feel that I could develop the patience and the classroom persona to really make a difference. But it would never feel natural, it would always feel forced."

"But," Williams said.

"But," Stacy said sitting down on the desktop in front of Gus. "I also know that I love the law, the precision of language, the argument, the justice system. I know that if I went to law school that I could become a great lawyer. And," Stacy said holding his hands like he is reaching for some tangible idea, "and it would provide me with resources to combat social inequalities."

"Like homelessness," Gus said nodding.

"Yes," Stacy said standing. "You understand what I am talking about."

"So, the meeting this morning was what? Some sort of firing slash resignation meeting?"

"No, no nothing like that at all, well, kind of like a resignation meeting."

"I had been talking to Pete recently about the contract. He heard that I had some connection to lawyers and wanted to know if I could run something past them."

"What, doesn't the union have their own lawyers?"

"Yeah, the literature says they 'employ several full-time lawyers' but Pete told me that we never get even a whiff of one around here. We only get to see the field agents, who are simply retired teachers, who have experience with negotiating contracts."

"And he thought it would be a good idea to get an opinion on contract negotiations from someone you may know?" Gus said quizzically.

"Well, I think he knew that my mom was a high-profile attorney."

"Right."

"Anyway, I wasn't so eager to help him out, but I felt I couldn't say no, you know."

"I know."

"Anyway, I kept putting him off and putting him off, hiding in my room, or leaving immediately, arriving right on time, I just couldn't do it anymore. After the big dust-up with my mom, I decided that if she really had my best interests at heart, she would help me with this Pete question."

"A sort of test?"

"Yes. I talked to Pete, wrote everything down, got the contract language, etc. then called my mom."

"And what did she do?"

"She had me fax over the information to her contracts lawyer then arranged for a conference call with me and Pete. She emailed back all the documents with notations on them for the union lawyers to look over when they had the chance."

"So, she came through for you."

"Big time," Stacy said with his hands on the back of his head. "Not only did she get Pete the information he needed to help with the contract, but the way she worked, explained the legal system, it was, it was, I was just enraptured by it all. I knew right then during the conference call that I wanted to be a lawyer."

"But what was Pete doing in there this morning? You didn't need him to be with you to turn in your resignation."

"No, I know. Pete was in the room when I went to have my meeting. I told him to stay for a minute."

"Bullshit!" Gus said standing, "I am not sure why this is so upsetting to me, but I know something fishy is going on."

"Okay, just relax," Stacy said patting the air with his hands. "Pete and I had something else to talk with Anderson about that had nothing to do with you or my resignation. And I would rather not say any more at the moment. The fewer the people that know about this situation the better."

"Ok, ok," Gus said. "I just, I was just a little panicked when I saw Pete in the room with you."

"You are definitely amped up about the meeting," Stacy stood rubbing his chin. "Was there something behind all of this? Did Anderson tell you he was going to fire me?"

Gus stood quiet but his eyes gave the answer.

It was Stacy's turn to pace the room again, "That motherfucker! All the time that I had been talking to him, he was just leading me along until it became late enough in the year to can my ass. Motherfucker!"

"Listen, calm down." It was Gus's turn to de-stress his colleague. "It's part of my job as a mentor to discuss your progress with the principal. When things weren't going well, and you have to agree that for a while things were not going so well, I worked on your behalf with the principal."

"Yeah, but to not let me finish the year. What the heck?"

"He set a timeline at some point."

"And that timeline ended this week."

"Well, next week actually. He was going to let you go if things hadn't been better but things had been great lately. You really started to figure this whole teaching thing out."

"Yeah, well."

"No, seriously," Gus said taking Adams by the shoulders, calming his emotional pacing. "You have really started to teach, not just distribute information."

"Really?"

"Really," Gus said, "right after you fell face-first into a student's bosom."

Stacy looked up from wringing his hands.

Gus held his gaze then a sly smile formed and they both started to laugh.

"Jesus, I thought I was done that night," Stacy said.

"Really, I couldn't tell."

"Oh my god!" Stacy said. "I went right home and started to pack my stuff. I couldn't sleep, I thought I would get called into the office the next day and be given my walking papers."

Gus just kept laughing, "You were so red. I couldn't believe it. I just hoped that you wouldn't make it any worse by trying to talk with Jessica."

"I couldn't even look her in the eye when she walked by into your room," Stacy said putting his face in his hands. "Ugh, I think what I will miss most around here is the life, the vivacity coming from all the students. Everything is so fresh."

"Yeah, me too," Williams said.

"Yeah ... Wait. Are you retiring?" Stacy said with a sly smile. "Good for you."

"Well, you know I have been sick all year."

"But you didn't seem sick. I mean, you had a few sick days here and there but you weren't gone for weeks or anything."

"No, no. I have been really trying to stay healthy for the students and for you. I just haven't felt all that great. I decided that I needed to do something else with my life for the few years that I have left."

"Have you told the administration yet?"

"No, I was waiting until the end of the term. I don't want a big fuss and if everyone knows, I feel like that is all everyone will talk to me about."

"Well, it's exciting for you," Adams said "Don't you want to talk about it?"

"No, not really. What am I going to say, 'well I had planned on traveling the world but I was so depressed over my family's death eons ago that I got stuck here and now I have this disease that is stealing my last few years'."

"Come on, Gus. You have to be more positive than that."

"Well, I just don't want a lot of attention, if you know what I mean."

"Fine," Adams said heading toward the door. "I plan to enjoy my last two months as a teacher, and I hope you do the same."

Williams smiled. His last few months would be much harder than Adams'. For forty years, he had come to North Wellington to teach. It was all he knew.

59

Spring break. Gus had not gone south for spring break since Janet and Danny had died. He just took his time as it came, enjoying the quiet streets when all of Wellington seemed to pick up and move to Florida or Gulf Shores, Alabama. Highway 65 was jammed full of cars with license plates from the Great Lakes State, bumper to bumper for twenty-four hours.

As students and staff hustled from the school doors, jumping into cars loaded with suitcases and car-top carriers, Gus remained at his desk, putting away his papers, filing lesson plans in his lone two-drawer filing cabinet. He remembered when he had three large four-drawer cabinets full of quizzes, readings, and tests. It was how things had to work before computers. Type it once, put it in a file folder, run it down to the ditto maker, crank the wheel, and file the copies away. Since then things had gotten progressively easier and easier. Now he could simply "push" his lessons out to his students through the internet. Each kid was connected via their Chromebook. Most had lost connection to tangible parts of the English-speaking world: the feel and smell of a new book, the crisp edges, the crack of a cover being opened for the first time. How ink flowed from the end of a new fountain pen, sliding effortlessly across the page. The loops and swirls of well-crafted cursive writing. The comfort of a well-read book, like an old friend stopping by for coffee and conversation. Now all that kids knew were thumbs, emojis, and acronyms.

This was how his grandfather must have felt as horses gave way to cars. The slow pace that allowed for contemplation and connection was traded for speed and instant access. The mile walk to the store was a good time for a talk with a friend or a loved one. The vacation to a secluded cabin for conversation around a fire or a quiet morning of fishing had become a thing of the past. Togetherness and connectedness had been traded for quick shopping trips with self- checkouts, all while listening to podcasts on AirPods. Then maybe a plane trip to a packed beach, ready for Instagram posts, Facebook memories, or Twitter conversations. Williams didn't want any of it. He would rather have a short conversation than a quick checkout, a quiet walk versus a popular jostling hangout.

At his desk, Williams looked out over his classroom. He knew that when he walked out the door at the end of the year he wouldn't be sure what would become of him. What would he take with him, what would he need? Nothing. He wouldn't need one pen, one book, one lesson plan, or a manilla folder crammed with a new curriculum to look over for the summer. But he would cross that bridge when the time came, he thought. For now, he put his journal back into his bag, slipped his fountain pen back into its holder, folded his messenger bag closed, and headed for the door. He flipped off the lights, looked back one more time. If anyone had been in the hall, they would have seen his eyes full of memories. But the halls were empty. The custodians were quietly making their way through each room, starting their holiday deep clean, but the rest of the staff had long since disappeared. Even Stacy was off on a trip with some college friends. A few had jobs now and were willing to host him for a few nights.

As Williams walked through the halls, he remembered the early days. How nervous he had been to teach. Janet sending him off in the morning; their life was just starting. How did he get here? So many years had passed. The same floors and same halls and same lockers. So many students had put their lives into these lockers. The books and assignments, their agendas, their cell phones. Each locker decorated in the senior hall with baby pictures, sports signs, playbills, academic honors. What would be on Gus' door if he were a senior? Would there be a bottle of bourbon, a few sports signs, a smattering of book covers, a contract, NHS stoles; he had done it all. But once those students graduated, all of it was wiped clean — no evidence of existence. His first senior class hadn't left any lasting impression upon the school but he remembered them, distant figures, blending into all the other students. A few had stood the test of time. He saw them at Meijer or in downtown Wellington. Many of his students were still in the area. Each one still called him Mr. Williams no matter how many times he corrected them and said, "Please call me Gus."

Would he be just a faint memory in all of their minds? Teaching is a noble profession, one that can really make a difference. That difference, Williams figured, was in the moment not in the memory. He knew those first students were better at English when they left than when they had arrived, but he also knows most of those students will only remember him as a teacher; "Who was our senior English teacher? Oh right, Mr. Williams." His legacy, a name only.

But there are an outstanding few, he thinks. Every once in a while, a student really needs someone, a teacher maybe. Nick Logan was one. He had made a real difference with Nick. Those were the ones you hung your heart on when you looked back at your career. Gus knew those didn't happen all the time and he also knew, that like Nick, you didn't always know how much of an impact you had until much later, if ever. First, life had to play out a little.

As Gus pushed open the door to the school, a cold blast, filled with the wet pungent smells of spring, brushed back the memories, keeping them within the brick walls of North

Wellington.

Williams pulled into the garage, letting the car idle as the door slowly lowered behind the back bumper. Williams was lost in memories again. He closed his eyes, Janet was getting out of her Dodge Omni. He laughed at that little car. But there she was, hair curled back, a bright smile, and those eyes he could fall into for hours. How could she be gone so early? What in life was so important for him to do without her for so many years? Without Danny? Her easy strides. The way her hips moved with just a little sway. The curve of her body. How had he gotten so lucky, he wondered as she disappeared into the house. The car idled.

Williams coughed, "Jesus!" he said before shutting off the car. He quickly grabbed his bag and hustled to the house door. He slapped the button to open the garage again. If someone had been outside, they would have seen a white fog roll out from under the door like it had just exhaled all the regret and sadness that it had built up over time. They would have seen a house rest a little easier on its foundation as if a great weight had been lifted. And they would have thought Williams was trying to kill himself. It would have been a different ending to his story, one that only he would know was an accident.

But inside Williams saw his home for the first time in a long time. The writing project he had started at parent-teacher conferences still sat listlessly at the kitchen table. He dropped his bag on a kitchen chair then draped his coat over the back.

The pantry was bare. Tupperware, bakeware, and kitchen appliances from the 80s were undisturbed in the lower cabinets. He didn't know how many times he had used those cookie sheets or the bean pot or even the casserole dish. How often does a person cook for one?

He walked through each room. He saw the living room full of books and an old sturdy reading chair. An unused study. A black walnut desk, an heirloom from his great-great grandfather engulfed the center of the room. He had it refinished after Janet's death. She hated that big desk, but he had loved it. He bought an old lamp with a pull chain that had a small gargoyle perched atop the stand holding the light. He bought a leather desk blotter, a holder for his fountain pen, a heavy octopus-shaped clock that reminded Gus of a creature from *20,000 Leagues Under the Sea*. The desk always looked so inviting that Williams never used it, which was ironic. The top was now covered with dust. The walls were filled with books of his reading life yellowing with age. His life was in decay.

The basement storage filled with items from another life stood out to Williams. The well-traveled path to and from the old washer and dryer seemed like such a small segment of the basement and yet for years it had seemed like all there was. Williams started to look through old boxes, wiping the dust from the flaps before opening each one. Old clothes from when he was younger. Clothes of Janet's. Infant clothes of Danny's. Some baby toys. Board games. Christmas decorations. A box of college papers. Old hiking equipment. A few books from their first apartment: *The Joy of Sex; Fear and Loathing in Las Vegas; Are You There God, It's Me Margaret; Zen and the Art of Motorcycle Maintenance; All the President's Men; The Shining*. Williams sneezed from the dust. He pushed the box back into its place. He headed back to the stairs, letting go of a life gone by. The boxes would all have to go.

He made his way up the stairs to the top floor. He turned toward Danny's room. He remembered the feeling he had when he found his Wellington jersey. The pain he had felt for so many years when he looked into the room had dissipated that day. He recognized the room for what it was, a life lived many years ago. It didn't have a place anymore. It would all have to go. Just the furniture would stay, a spare room for a guest, maybe, like it should have been a long time ago.

Finally, Williams made it to his bedroom. He took his normal path around to his side of the bed. He sat down looking out the window. He knew what he had to do but the summit seemed unreachable. He was too old, with too many problems to start fresh. He laid down on the bed, folding his hands across his stomach. He could hear a clock tick somewhere in the house. He reached over to where Janet used to lay. She wasn't there. She was never there, no matter how many times he called to her, envisioned her laying there with her mouth slightly open, snoring ever so softly.

He rolled over to her side of the bed. He opened her nightstand. The papers inside had yellowed and were becoming brittle. He swung his legs over the edge of the bed, stood up and then opened a dresser drawer. Inside the clothes looked old, some stiff with age. He went to the closet and ran his hands through her clothes. Some moved smoothly through his fingers but others were rigid, unwelcoming.

Williams went down the stairs to the kitchen, pulled a roll of garbage bags from under the sink. He started in his bathroom. He shook a bag open, flapping it in the air. He opened each cupboard, taking out Janet's makeup or face wash or hair supplies. He dropped them all into the garbage. He looked under the sink. He left the hair dryer but threw away the curling iron, a box of feminine pads, a make-up case, old shampoo, sunscreen, and foot lotion. Williams pulled out a bottle of Janet's perfume. He put it in the bag but then reached in to retrieve it. He looked at it a good long while. What if the smell had changed over the years? What if it wasn't what he remembered? He pulled off the top and started to bring the perfume to his nose and then stopped and tossed it into the garbage bag with the rest. When Williams walked out of his bathroom, his eyes were wet with tears.

He pulled the drawer on the nightstand all the way out. He fit one end of the drawer in the garbage bag and shook in the contents. He replaced the drawer then tied the bag closed. He set the bag by the edge of the stairs. He opened a new bag. Each drawer of Janet's clothes disappeared. Williams went to the closet. Hangers and clothes all. As Janet's half of the bedroom emptied, the pile of garbage bags near the stairs grew.

Williams pulled his car out of the garage. He started piling the bags by the garage door. He would have to call for a dumpster or wait until garbage day. Either way no one was coming on a Thursday night. Once all the bags were stacked in the garage, Williams stopped at the kitchen sink. He was tired. He took a glass from the cabinet and when he held it under the faucet, his hand trembled. He only filled the glass halfway thinking he might spill rest anyway. The clock ticked as Williams stood, steadying himself.

Thinking he might need to eat he pulled a banana from the bunch. Williams was starting to feel unsure about throwing everything away. Maybe he should give it to Goodwill. But he didn't want to see anyone running around town in Janet's and Danny's clothes. He had to keep cleaning. He took the last bite of the banana then trudged back up the stairs. He pulled open a garbage bag and went into Danny's room.

60

The next morning Williams woke up feeling a little different, like the night before had been a surreal dream instead of a reality. He rolled from his bed, sliding his feet into his slippers. In the bathroom he opened the cabinet to find that half of the shelves stood bare. The view from Danny's doorway made his heart skip a beat. Everything had been wiped clean. He frantically hustled down the stairs. He yanked the garage door open to find that a pile of garbage bags filled the spot where his car was usually parked.

He ran to the first bag and ripped it open. He pulled old shirts from the bag, then pants, and then uniforms. He pulled comics and cards. He started to open each bag, organizing as he went: shirts, pants, sweatshirts, shorts. Tears started to stream down his face, spotting the last item he pulled from the pile. Then he sank to his knees on the concrete, sobbing. He held an old shirt to his face then looked up to the ceiling.

I'm losing my mind, he thought. He dropped the shirt back onto the pile. He stood, pushing himself up on one knee. He brushed himself off, straightened his sweater, and headed back into the house. He had to finish this spring cleaning before he changed his mind.

By noon, he had carried all the boxes up from the basement. He stacked each one by the pile of garbage bags. He stacked the old books on a shelf before breaking down the box for recycling. He found a few boxes of old photos. He sat those on the shelf by the books. He wasn't sure what to do with all the stuff.

Janet's side of the bedroom. Danny's room. The basement. The life he had been harboring now filled the garage. It was Friday. He called Wellington Disposal and asked for a special garbage pick-up. He told them that he needed help disposing of several bags and boxes of garbage. For an extra fee they could be there this afternoon. He agreed. After he hung up he sat down in his recliner and promptly fell asleep.

A sharp pounding on the door startled him awake. He flipped the handle on his chair.

"Are you okay in there?" a voice shouted from outside, "Mr. Williams?"

Gus saw a man in a dirty North Wellington ball cap peering through the windows. "Mr. Williams," he shouted again.

"Coming," Williams shouted ambling toward the door.

Outside the door a man in stained jeans, sturdy work boots, and a thick black Carhartt jacket over a Wellington Disposal uniform stood waiting. His beard had been shaped to give his jaw an angular look.

"Wellington Disposal," he said. "You called for a special pickup."

"Yes," Williams said, "I thought they said the pick-up would be this afternoon."

"It is afternoon, Mr. Williams. It's 3 o'clock."

"Oh my God, really?" Williams looked at his wrist as if he were wearing a watch. "I must have fallen asleep."

"No worries, Mr. Williams," the man said.

Williams noticed something familiar about the man. "I'm sorry," he said, "let me get my shoes and jacket. The stuff is in the garage."

"If you could move your car into the street," the man said, "it would make the pick up a little easier."

"Yes, of course. I will be right out."

Williams sat down on the bench by the door to put on his shoes as the man returned to his truck. Williams slipped on his jacket and felt his keys in the pocket. He knew that man's face from somewhere.

Williams pushed the garage remote as he sat down in his car. The garbage truck waited in the drive across the street. Williams backed out, parking along the first yard bags to grace the street. The garbage truck slowly backed into the driveway, lights flashing and a warning signal beeping in the vacant afternoon.

The driver hopped from the cab, leaving the truck idling. He approached Williams where he stood next to the pile of boxes and bags in the garage.

"Spring cleaning, Mr. Williams?" he asked.

"Do, I, ah, know you?" Williams asked rubbing his chin. "You seem awfully familiar."

"I had you in class, Mr. Williams," the man said. "It's been almost twenty years now. The name is Simon Fitzpatrick, everyone called me Si."

"Oh, my goodness," Williams said sticking out his hand. "You were in Danny's grade. How could I forget?"

"Well," Si said, "the beard throws people. On most people it makes them look older but on me, it makes me seem young and hip."

"Right," Williams said looking at Simon more closely.

"So, spring cleaning," Si said again. "All of this stuff goes?"

"Yes," Williams said, "it has been long overdue."

"Ok, just give me a few minutes and I will be out of here. I will just tack the special fee to your regular bill."

"Wait," Williams said walking to the truck with a bag, "you own Wellington Disposal?"

"Yeah," Si said. "I started right out of high school when I was at community college. I had one old pickup with a wooden box built on the back of the truck. I offered to pick up everyone's garbage on my street for half the price of the competitor. They just had to make sure everything was in a closed bag."

"And now you own this huge company?" Williams asked tossing the bag into the truck.

"Yup, for the last twenty years, I have been building this company so that one day, I could leave it to my kids or sell it and do something else."

"Good for you," Williams said.

"You know," Simon said throwing the last of the bags into the truck, "I don't know if I ever told you how sorry I was about Danny. He was a good kid. It kind of made all of us grow up really fast. It was like we had to do something worthwhile with our lives because he was never able to, you know?"

"Thank you," Williams said. "You were so young. I didn't know what to do myself. I wasn't expecting anything from you kids."

"Well, I just wanted you to know."

"Thank you," Williams said taking a handkerchief from his pocket to wipe his eyes. "Danny would have been happy that you are so successful."

Simon picked up a box but the bottom dropped out before he could get it to the truck. Comics and MAD magazines spilled out on the driveway.

"I'm sorry," Williams said moving over to help. "I shouldn't have put so much in that box."

"That's okay," Simon said looking down at the magazines. "I haven't seen a MAD magazine since the 80s when I used to run around with Danny. Wow, this brings back some memories." He picked up a few, flipping through the pages.

"Well, you are more than welcome to them," Gus said. "I have had my fill."

Simon looked up at Williams, who began wiping his eyes again. "I think I will take them home to my kids. I have a son who is about the age Danny was when he passed and these will give me an opportunity to tell them a story about one of my best friends growing up."

"Sounds good," Williams said. "I will get some tape for the

bottom of that box."

When the rest of the boxes were loaded. Williams pulled his car back into the garage then went inside. He sat at the kitchen table waiting for the kettle to whistle. This spring cleaning didn't seem so refreshing.

But just then his phone rang. Flipping it over, he saw a number from Ann Arbor. Maybe Spring Break wouldn't be so bad after all.

61

A cold rain began to fall. Williams took off his jacket. He bent down to take off one shoe then the other. He wouldn't be doing any hiking today. When he was younger a rain wouldn't have deterred him from being on the trails, but since his diagnosis, he wasn't willing to risk any sort of sickness. Pneumonia would probably do him in at his age regardless of what else he had going on physically. The medicine seemed to be keeping the cancer at bay. His three-month scans were coming quickly, a reminder that he wasn't free to roam.

Wednesday of spring break was the worst, Williams thought. All those people who traveled to warmer climates would be starting to feel the pinch of coming back to Michigan. Wednesday was often the last free day. Thursday meant packing for an early Friday departure. Sometimes parents left on Saturday if they could complete the drive in just one day. Janet always liked to stop. She said it wasn't worth it to push themselves to drive through the night. They did it once at Williams' behest and were totally wiped for the next day.

Wednesday for Williams meant that he was getting bored. He had furiously cleaned the house as soon as school ended, finished two books, went grocery shopping, did the laundry, changed the oil in his car, hiked in the state park, went to see a movie at the theater, and ate at the new restaurant downtown that everyone had been talking about. Now he sat at the kitchen table watching the rain fall with nothing to do. He had remembered telling Danny that it was good to be bored. Use your imagination he would say. Alright Williams, he thought, use your imagination to entertain yourself. What are you going to do?

The first thing he did, he always did, was put the water on the stove to make some tea. He filled his stainless steel kettle halfway with water, set it on the back burner, and turned the knob to high. He wandered from the kitchen to his living room, to where his bookshelves filled the walls. He had spent so much time reading, living in a different world. Each book took him into a dream state, let him forget what had been bothering him. Now all the books were just markers in time. Were these more anchors holding him back from living his life?

He loved reading and loved the time that he had spent in those other worlds. But maybe he had spent too much time there instead of living out his own life, but those books had saved him for many years. Years he would have spent drinking or doing something else to starve his mind of the anguish of Janet's and Danny's passing. He didn't need these anchors anymore either, but what to do with them all? He went to his study, an office he never used. He ran his fingers along the books on the shelves. So much time. He pulled back his Herman Miller office chair and sat down. He had spent so much on that damn chair. He had refinished the heirloom desk, bought all the desktop ornaments, and then decided he needed the best chair so he could sit to write. Williams could count on one hand the number of times he had sat in the chair to write. He ran his hands over the top of the desk, pushing all the dust to the corners. The rain pounded outside. The kettle whistled. Williams pulled the chain on his desk lamp, casting a soft glow across the desktop. He stood, rolling his chair back against the bookshelf, fingers plugged into the desk, brow furrowed in deep thought. The kettle shrieked through the house.

He headed straight for the kitchen. He left the kettle to its screeching. He grabbed the stack of writing from the table, pulled his bag from the kitchen chair, and headed back into his study. He set his papers from the October parent-teacher conferences on one side of his desk. He pulled Rex's poems from his messenger bag and set them on the other side. He pulled his journal from his bag and placed it in the center of his desk. He placed his fountain pen in the holder. Williams returned to the kitchen, tossing the empty bag on a chair before turning his attention to the stove. He switched off the water, pulled a cup from the cupboard, dropped in a Rooibos tea bag, and filled his cup with hot water.

He carried his tea back into his study, being extra careful not to spill. He set it on the blotter and then sat down behind the desk. He opened one drawer and pulled out a laptop. Williams hardly had use for a computer at home. He worked with one every day at school: completing attendance, checking his email, Googling, and reading the news. While his computer booted up, Williams took his stack of memoirs and began to sort. He turned to the journal entry about his memoirs. He typed into a word document, *Letters to a Young Teacher*.

62

Friday morning, Williams awoke early as usual. He made his bed, showered, and dressed. He walked past Janet's empty closet and he walked past Danny's empty room without looking in either direction. The solemn movements were of a man resigned to a lonesome existence. He scooped the coffee grounds into the filter, added water, and pressed the start button. He took out McCann's Irish Oatmeal, filled a pot with water, and set the burner to medium heat.

He wandered back to his office where he had worked all through the last two days. He picked up his tea cup, his journal, and the notes from his writing sessions. In the kitchen, Williams dropped his cup by the sink then placed his journal and notes on the table. His oatmeal boiled and the coffee filled the pot. He rinsed his cup in the sink, filled it with coffee, and set it on the table by his papers. He scooped the oatmeal into a bowl, dropped in a spoonful of brown sugar, dried cranberries, and chopped almonds then sat down at the table.

He looked at what lay in front of him. Life had been like this for so many years. One quiet morning after another. The silence lingered. He had been fooling himself with the idea of Janet and Danny filling the house. Their stuff just took up space and kept anyone else from joining him. But they were never there with him, not for the last thirty years anyway. Now he was finally able to take a long, hard look at how his life had been and it made him shudder.

Williams slowly ate his oatmeal and sipped his coffee. He read through his notes, making comments. He had three days left to make more headway. He wanted to have a draft finished by the time school started up again. The timeline, truncated of course by his life expectancy, but also by his need to move on at the end of the school year. He would be done with teaching in two short months, and he planned to cut it away in one swift motion, never to go back.

This morning he had his three-month scans for his myeloma, an x-ray and an MRI. He cleaned his cup, his bowl, and the pot, setting each in the drying rack by the sink. He slipped his coat over his shoulders, pushed his wallet into his back pocket, lifted the keys from the hook by the door, and went to discover his fate.

The hospital felt different to Williams. No longer did he feel out of place or unsure of his future. His future had been set nine months earlier when he was diagnosed with an incurable form of blood and bone cancer. Life was just a waiting game. Cancer had set a siege upon his body and he had to fortify against it. Besides treatments, supplements, and healthy living, Williams knew the key had to be enduring optimism in the face of certain death, an impossible task.

"Mr. Williams," a nurse called, "you may come back and change now."

Williams smiled, sliding a thin stack of sticky notes into the pages of *Unbroken*. He ambled toward the door where the waiting nurse marked down his presence on a clipboard.

"Thank you," Williams said. "How are you today?"

"I'm good," she said. "Follow me. I will show you to a changing room."

Williams listened, but didn't pay much attention. He remembered the routines. An X-ray first then an MRI later. He would be here for a few hours. He returned to the waiting room where another patient sat silently, sullenly, as if death was going to come calling at any moment. Williams shuffled over to the younger man, sitting right next to him, "How ya doin', Sonny?"

He looked at him in a right-state of confusion.

"What's wrong, cat got your tongue?" Williams asked. "I'll start, that might make some things easier. I have multiple myeloma. It is a bone and blood cancer that will eventually kill me. They have found no cure."

"So, why are you so happy?" asked the man.

"I have a terminal disease. I can do nothing to get rid of it. My only choice is to live with it and I get to choose how to do that. Myeloma can't take that away from me. What is your name?"

"Jason," he said,"Jason Gossard."

"Nice to meet you, Jason," Gus said sticking out his hand. "Gus Williams."

"How often do you have to come here?" Jason asked.

"Every three months I get a scan and then they will meddle with my medicine if the cancer seems to be increasing too rapidly or if I don't feel so great on the medicine."

"That stinks," he said. "You're tethered to this place then."

"Well," Gus said smiling, "only if I want to be. The choice is mine to come back. What about you, what are you in for?"

Jason leaned toward Gus and whispered, "I have testicular cancer."

"Jesus," Gus said. "you'll be out of here and living like a king in no time."

"What?" Jason said, "I have cancer. They might have to do surgery, chemo, radiation."

"Jason," Gus said, "you should know that you have one of the most treatable forms of cancer. Buck up and whip its behind."

Jason just nodded. He looked at Williams, who looked more upbeat than most people - not just the dying cancer patients. Williams looked up as a nurse wheeled a chair in to the waiting room.

"Gossard, Jason," the nurse called.

"I'm Jason," he said. "I can walk. I don't need the wheelchair."

Gus smiled.

"House rules," the nurse said "You have to sit in the chair and I have to wheel you down the hall to your appointment. Now what is your date of birth."

Williams watched as Jason gave all the right identifying information then slumped down into the chair. He kept his eye on Jason. As the nurse started to wheel him from the room, they finally made eye contact. Williams said, "You can do this, just keep your eye on the ball."

Jason furrowed his brow then broke into a laugh that filled the waiting room. Williams sat thinking of other one-liners in case Jason came back, but another nurse opened the waiting room door. "Williams, Gus," he said.

Williams followed the same protocol as Jason, reading off his date of birth, address, and type of scan he had been scheduled to receive before he was wheeled out into hall to his appointment. Williams understood what Rex must have felt like coming back to the cancer center, meeting new patients, getting scans, waiting for the results. How did he do it? Now that Williams was on his way, fear started to set in. What if the cancer had progressed? What if he was all ready for the casket? He had to finish his writing, set up the scholarships, write the intro to Rex's book. He steadied himself as they turned into the X-ray room.

You'll find out nothing today he told himself. Today was just the scans. They will have to read them and compare them to others. Life would go on as normal until next week when he would receive a call from the doctor about what to do next. Life would go on.

63

When the students returned from spring break, the year took a different tact. No longer were they too concerned with their grades or projects, but instead they are were focused on the warmer weather that was just ahead. The kids who went to warmer climates on vacation came back with tan bodies and vibrant attitudes. For those who had to stay huddled in their homes for most of break, their pale skin seemed to mark their lot in life. Williams knew there were a few who couldn't afford to go away, those who couldn't go because their parents had to work, and few who chose not to go.

But the school couldn't get back into the swing of things. The State of Michigan mandated its standardized tests to occur for all grade levels the last three weeks in April. And specifically the SAT to take place the week following Spring Break.

Standardized testing meant that the entire middle and high school schedule would be disrupted as the administrators figured out a way to complete testing for all the grades. Williams always thought the school should just test the kids all at once but it wasn't possible with the accommodations needed for special education students. The school just didn't have enough certified bodies to proctor the tests nor enough rooms for each set of requirements. What happened then was a piecemeal effort to test a different grade every few days.

The testing would occur in one section of the school, so the teachers who normally used those classrooms would have to move each day to make room for the proctors and the students. Over the years, Williams watched as standardized tests became more and more of a priority in the school and were given more weight by parents and students alike. Williams thought it was a shame. Testing was just one barometer of students' capabilities. The real factor in whether or not students succeeded was their work ethic. So often Williams saw the brightest minds fail in life because they didn't push themselves hard enough. It was like they had no internal drive for success. Then he saw students who weren't as capable go on to do amazing things because of their work ethic.

He had tried to impart this wisdom into his students each year around standardized test time. He wanted to alleviate some stress. He didn't think it was necessary for the kids to have to give up their evenings and weekends and summers to do standardized test practice. It just seemed wrong, but then again, the students pointed out year after year that they were working hard to get a good score, which is what he had told them would make them successful, wasn't it a Catch-22?

Wednesday morning, Williams found his testing materials in his room locked behind his classroom door, as the instructions stipulated. He was to test a group of juniors, allowing the senior class to skip out until after lunch. He pulled the answer sheets from the box and started laying them out on the desks alphabetically, guided by the precoded labels affixed to each test booklet. He put two number two pencils next to each test. He scanned the room for any prohibited posters or projects that might aid the students. He erased the board. He followed the directions to write the school address, school code, and testing room number on the board. He also wrote "start," "5 minutes," and "stop" on the board. He surveyed the room to ensure compliance with the state guidelines.

He made two cups of coffee in his Keurig, dropped a couple

of creamers into his pocket, and headed across the hall. He made sure to press his door shut so no students could enter the room before testing began. Adams' room was wide open, kids were flowing in and out. Stacy was nowhere to be found. He set the coffee down on the desk then sat in the front row. He casually pulled out his creamers, emptying two in his cup and tossing the other two onto Stacy's desk.

Williams scanned the room. Stacy still had instructional posters on the wall along with sample papers. He watched as students came and went freely throughout the room. Each desk was bare except for two pencils laid neatly side by side. Williams watched as some students checked the list in the doorway of the room then looked inside and then back at the list. Martin, a brash student with little tact, walked in and stood in front of Williams.

"Are you our proctor in here today, Mr. Williams?"

"No, I don't believe I am. I am just waiting for Mr. Adams to return. You must not have seen him recently?"

"Nope," he said looking around. "So we sit anywhere?"

"I'm afraid not, Martin," Williams said standing. "I think you have to sit alphabetically according to who is in your group."

"Oh."

"You should probably wait outside until Mr. Adams comes back. I'm sure he will be here shortly."

"Alright," Martin said. "I am going to leave my stuff on this desk and then I'll move it."

Martin dropped his stuff on a desk by the door then joined the mass of students moving out in the hall. Williams started to get antsy, Stacy only had about one minute before the tardy bell rang and students were expected to move into their testing rooms. Just as Williams was about to get up, Adams came through the door with a box of testing materials.

"They gave me the wrong test," Adams said out of breath.

"Really?"

"Yes, I was checking my materials like the instructions said when I noticed that the answer key and the test books didn't match. The answers said SAT and the test said PSAT. I rushed down to the counseling office and ran into several other teachers with the same issue. We just got it sorted out. You should check your box."

"Good call," Williams said. "I will check before I hand them out. Do you need any help getting prepped? Like taking down these posters?"

The tardy bell rang.

"Shoot," Adams said looking up at the clock, "I totally forgot about all those posters, what a pain."

"I know," Williams said, "it almost makes you want to not put any up to begin with."

Williams busied himself by pulling down the posters. He carefully laid them on the counters in the back of the classroom. Adams put the test books down, one on every other desk. He wiped his board then wrote out the time stamps along with the school code.

"Wait one minute, please," Adams shouted toward the door as students started to peek their heads in to see if they were allowed to enter.

Williams laid out the last set of exemplar texts on the back counter then returned to the front of the room to gather his coffee cup.

"Well, just in the nick of time."

"Thank you so very much," Adams said picking up his coffee. "And thanks for the coffee."

Williams leaned in to Adams. Quietly he said, "Here is to your first and last test proctoring experience."

Adams laughed and held up his coffee cup in an agreeable salute, "Yes, the last for both of us."

If the students were wiser members of society, they might have seen the look on each teacher's face as they stood side by side at the head of the classroom. On the face of one, they might have seen the excitement of a future that had no limits. On the face of the other, they might have seen the reminiscences of a past that stretched for decades.

"Yo, are we taking the test in here today?"

Adams furrowed his brow and turned to the student.

"Ellis."

"Yeah?"

"Could you please wait in the hall with all the other students? And I will come get you when we are ready for you to enter, thank you."

Ellis turned back toward the door mumbling under his breath.

"Nice job, Mr. Adams," Gus said finishing his cup of coffee. "At the beginning of the year, you probably would have snapped at that oblivious young man if not at his initial interruption, but also at his mumbling."

"Well, I have learned from the best to pick my battles and not let every little thing get under my skin."

"Bravo."

"What do you say?" Adams said draining the rest of his coffee, "Shall we proctor a test?"

"I suppose so," Williams said holding out his hand for the empty cup.

Adams handed over the cup then walked to the door. "Excuse me," he said, "I would like everyone to make a path for Mr. Williams to get to his door. We won't start until you make a path, which means you'll be here later in the day."

The students grumbled. A few moved out of the way.

"Remember," Adams shouted, "You get to go home as soon as the test is over. Move, please, so we can start."

The students parted like the Red Sea for Moses. Williams and Adams ushered their students into their seats with little cajoling, read the directions, and started the first test as others were still going over directions.

Test proctoring is a boring endeavor. Williams used to read during the test, but now the rules specifically stated proctors must actively monitor test takers during each section. So,

Williams started the timer and then wandered up and down the rows, pausing at the end of each row just long enough to recite a poem from memory. Each year he tried to remember a new poem. He'd keep a copy in his pocket and would sneak peeks during each pause to double check the lines. This year the poem was by Henry Wadsworth Longfellow, "The Psalm of Life."

Williams was just on the second stanza, "Life is real! Life is earnest!" when Principal Anderson appeared in the doorway. Williams smiled and gave the thumbs up sign to signal all was well, but Anderson stood watching him pace the room. It was as if he wanted to ask him something but couldn't form the words or way to do so.

Williams walked down the last row, hoping Anderson would leave before he had to stand next to him. As Williams approached, Anderson smiled. "Gus," he said, "are you all set?" Williams smiled and nodded, mouthing the word, "yes." At that, Anderson promptly turned and left to find another testing room. Maybe Anderson isn't so bad after all, Williams thought, maybe he just wanted to double check that there weren't any more testing screwups.

64

Many teachers complained about proctoring a standardized test but Williams always found that it was one of his easiest days teaching. He read the directions, followed the time frame, and collected the booklets at the end of the time period. Nothing much to it. What he never cared for was the teaching to the test, which was the game all teachers had to play. For example, if the students had to write an analysis essay on the test, Williams would have to teach analysis on and off throughout the year until the testing day. Throughout the year, the teachers were obligated to ask students questions that were formatted in the same manner as the test questions. Likewise, the reading had to cover the same type of information, fiction or nonfiction, as they would see on the test. The game, Williams called it to other teachers. You have to play the game. He had told Stacy on more than one occasion about making sure he was not only aligned with state standards, but also SAT standards.

As the testing finished, Williams walked row by row collecting the answer keys in alphabetical order. Then he reverse-pivoted and collected the test booklets. Williams put all his materials back into the box then walked down the aisle asking students to drop in their pencils and scrap paper. Then he released his students to lunch. As the last student left the room, Williams followed behind to drop off the materials in the counseling office. He met Stacy in the halls.

"Everything go okay in there?" Williams asked.

"Yeah, easiest day of the year," Adams said.

"I have always thought so. Are you going to be a little sad that you are not doing that anymore?"

"Not really," Adams chuckled. "How about you? Any pangs of regret or remorse or nostalgia in there?"

"No, over standardized testing, I think not," Williams laughed. "There will be things that I miss, but days like today will not be one of them."

"I suppose not," Adams said pulling open the door to the counseling office. "What will be some of the things you'll miss?"

"Well, I'll miss the life in these halls," Williams said setting his box on the table with all the others then holding the door open for Adams. "I mean, look at all the potential futures that are ahead of these kids. So much possibility."

Adams and Williams stood side by side, watching as students streamed down the hall in both directions. Some students were laughing, others were lost in their own world, blocked in with earbuds. Groups of students laughed in conversation. A middle school student knocked another in the shoulder then took off running, zig-zagging through and around others. Boys and girls held hands. Best friends hung on each other in close conversation.

"Each life," Williams said, "has so much possibility left. That is what I'll miss and the vibrant youthful energy."

"They do have energy," Adams said.

"I'll miss it for sure but ..."

"Wait!"

Williams heard a familiar voice behind him. He turned to see Andrea standing near the counseling office door.

"Are you retiring, Mr. Williams?" Andrea said, "I didn't know that."

Stacy looked at Andrea then at Williams. He didn't know what to say.

Williams approached Andrea in order to have an intimate conversation, "Andrea, I wouldn't want to lie to you, so I am going to tell you this in confidence."

"Oh my God!" she said. "You are."

"Yes, Andrea," Williams said rubbing his hands together. "I am thinking about retiring but nothing is official."

"What does that mean, nothing official? Does that mean you are not retiring?"

"As of right now I will be employed here again next year."

"But you might not be?"

"Correct."

"Ok," she said.

"Are you trying to drop something off in the counseling office?" Williams said pointing to the paper in Andrea's hand.

"Yes, I have a scholarship application to turn in for the Daughters of the American Revolution."

"The doors will be locked until all the test materials have been sorted and packaged for the mailman."

"Oh!"

"You will have to find Mrs. Carcetti and deliver it directly to her."

"Alright, thank you."

Andrea turned to join the throng of students slowly dispersing into doorways. Williams wondered if she would get into Notre Dame or have to settle for another university. Any school would be happy to have that girl. She worked so hard. For the longest time, Williams had been convinced that the number one attribute that helped students to succeed was hard work. The students who could stay focused on the smaller details of an assignment, who could follow up with questions, and who could spend time thinking about their school work outside of class were the ones who succeeded in college and in life, no matter the field.

"Andrea," Williams called. She turned, frowning a bit. "Let's keep that conversation between us, shall we?" He smiled and winked.

Andrea suddenly lit up, as if a small secret was all she needed to brighten her day. Williams wasn't sure how long she would last without starting a rumor, but a rumor about his retirement wasn't that farfetched. Not this year and not any year before.

Williams returned to his room, his lunch cut short by the testing schedule. In years past when the seniors were asked to come in late, many legally called in of their own accord because they were eighteen, while others had their parents call for them. Gus never really understood parents who allowed their children to skip for no reason. When did a teacher or instructor ever really "do nothing" in class? Teachers were always going to use the time to their advantage and besides, students with nothing to do usually started trouble.

His plans for the day were to return their spring break reflections and discuss how to revise them for a better grade. The students who showed up would get a head start on their classmates. It was a lesson he wouldn't have to repeat. He would offer to make them coffee or hot chocolate, even give them cookies from Meijer. Every year the students who came to school would tell their stay-at-home peers and a few would seem disappointed that they had missed out, while others responded with a common retort about playing video games or watching Netflix or eating whatever they wanted at home. Those students missed the point. It wasn't about the cookies, but it was about making the effort to do what they were supposed to do to get ahead. As a teacher, Williams understood that the success of students largely depended on going the extra mile because most would do only what was required but the best would see the need to go above and beyond the basics.

Students came and went year after year, some leaving indelible marks in his memory while others quickly faded. Many years ago, he started to view his students as characters in a novel, allowing their actions to be part of a larger narrative arc.

Those students whose characters quickly faded were often the most ordinary. They would come and go through the days, minding their own business, doing the required assignments, standing out in no particular manner. But then there were students who left lasting impressions for one reason or another. There was Harry who was always listening to music; Johnny who made videos; Anthony had his bombastic personality; Andrea had a serious dedication to knowledge and justice; Jessica who showed her peers that a girl can be both fashionable and intelligent. And then there was Frank, Big J, and Mighty K. Of these three seniors, two planned to play college football, while Frank, the third of the trio, was probably the smartest kid in the school and also the strongest per pound of bodyweight. For most of the hour the three were in a heated discussion about the benefits of the traditional versus the sumo-style deadlift. Williams, unable to really add anything to the discussion, just listened from time to time as he helped others with their papers.

"Well, my powerlifting brethren," Williams said, "I am not sure I can help you in your debate, but I can help you revise your papers. What say you?"

"Well, Mr. Williams, I bet you could help our debate," Big J said. "Let me ask you this question."

"Ok," Williams said settling into a chair at their table. "Go for it."

"If you were practicing to be the best, wouldn't you want to practice what would ultimately be the best practice, not practice with different techniques all the time?"

"It is hard for me to give you an informed response with so many vagaries, but I would suppose that the old adage is true, practice makes perfect."

"See," K said. "J is right."

"But with the sumo-style deadlift, the lifter is able to lift a shorter distance."

"Yeah, but all the deadlifts over 1000 pounds use a conventional stance."

"You are not going to lift over 1000 pounds, J," Frank said pulling his hair out sideways from his head. "I am 140 pounds and I can lift almost as much as you."

"You can not," J said laughing.

Williams stood to leave the table but first he leaned down, "I think all three of you should be proud of what you accomplished in your time here. And I know that if each of you put the same energy into your future profession as you have with lifting weights, you will all be very successful."

"Thanks, Mr. Williams," all three said in unison.

Big J then turned to Frank, "After school, I will deadlift more than you."

"I can't lift heavy today," Frank said. "I lifted super heavy yesterday."

"Right," K said. "Talking trash but can't back it up."

"Friday," Frank said standing up. "Lift off."

"Where you going?" J said.

"The bells going to ring," Frank said going toward the door.

In an unbroken stride, Frank was at the threshold of the door as the bell signaled the end of the school day. Williams pushed in chairs as he followed students toward the door. He grabbed his garbage can and then wiped the leftover napkins and hot chocolate cups into the trash. After making his way around the room, he stopped behind his desk for a can of Clorox wipes. He wiped down each seat, scrubbing the spilled drinks from the tabletops. There was a knock at his door.

"Yes," he said, "how can I help you?"

"Mr. Williams," Andrea said striding into the room. "I'm the class president this year and one of my tasks is to find a speaker for graduation. I was wondering if you would like to speak at graduation."

"Andrea," Gus said turning in her direction. "I would be honored to give the last lecture to the senior class."

"Thank you so much!" she said, "I will see you tomorrow."

Andrea quickly turned from the room ticking off another task on her to-do list.

Williams wiped down more desks, scrubbing intently where the students had created artwork with their pencils. He had dumped the last plate into the garbage when someone knocked again. As he turned toward the door, he saw an unexpected visitor, Amelia Adams. She was holding a tray with two cups of coffee from Starbucks.

"I was wondering," she said, "if you would like to have coffee with me this afternoon."

Williams smiled, "I would be happy to."

65

As April rolled into May, North Wellington fought to come back to life. Williams stood, grasping the railing on the fishing pier, looking out over the lake and then back over the town he called home. The wind strengthened then roared against the mid-day sun. Thick clouds blanketed the rays of warmth, the temperatures dropped, and Lake Wellington became angry against the sky, tossing white waves over the shore, filling walkways and parking lots with dead reeds and murky water.

The lake gave back all the debris and trash that man had discarded into its waters. Williams thought about his own life. As the waves crashed against the pier, spraying him with water, he held on as he always had. Life seemingly tossed everyone around, uncaring and unbiased. But at some point amid the discarded styrofoam cups, worm cans, bait lines, plastic toy shovels, candy wrappers, bags, broken flip-flops — amid man's refuse — life had to continue.

Even in nature, the downed trees, stumps and ripped cat tails that adorned the shores edge, gave life or came back stronger. Had Williams come back? Or had he just given his life to others?

When the wind died down the lake calmed itself, but the debris remained. A small current pulled some refuse back out to greet unsuspecting boaters. Large logs would drift idly by, waiting to punch a hole in a speeding power boat.

But the storm passed, as it always does, and the lake calmed its churning waters. Williams smiled. In nature, as in life. April and now May, life began anew.

Last week, he told Anderson of his intention to retire. He had deliberately waited until after the last board meeting of April to turn in his letter of resignation. He asked that they keep the information a secret. He wanted no fanfare, no parties, no retirement celebration. By the time the school board would vote on his retirement only a few short weeks of school would be left, with graduation consuming one week. He truly hoped that there would be no awkward celebratory moments.

Williams walked down the boardwalk from the fisherman's landing. The high water started creeping up into the parking lot as the winter snowmelt came rushing down the Lake Wellington tributary. Now in May, the parking lot had turned into a home for ducks instead of for cars. Williams side-stepped the goose droppings, slowly making his way. Every spring he liked to walk the edges of his community, to see what had changed over the course of the year.

This time he felt he had changed more than his community. A fact he had overlooked for many years. When his life ended, the community of Wellington would continue on and on for years to come. The old families would move on and new couples would start their lives. Life would go onward and outward, ever expanding and contracting. Williams' timeline would end, closing off one branch in the world, but his legacy would continue on. Each interaction, each teaching moment, would gain new life like a piece of beach sand finding a new home in wet hair or clinging to the bottom of a cooler or in an unsuspecting fold of a book. His legacy would spread out in the world like the millions of pieces of sand that left the beach each year.

As he walked away from the waterfront, Williams felt more content than he'd ever felt before. Life would be different from here on out, for however long it lasted.

66

In a final act of gratitude, Andrea, after learning about Williams impending retirement, had the senior class ask him to speak at graduation. He had felt terrified and excited and grateful all at the same time. He spent evening after evening pondering what to share and how to share it. His yellow legal pads filled with ideas, starts and stops, and then, eventually, his story. He wanted the truth to be told. It was his swan song. His salvation. When graduation day finally arrived, Williams felt confident in his message. He walked out in front of students for the last time in his life to share with them his truth in order for them to hopefully, one day, find their own.

First, I would like to thank all of you for inviting me to speak at your graduation, to be a part of one of the biggest days of your lives, here in front of your family and friends. This is truly an honor. Just a few weeks ago, shortly before being asked to give this speech, I decided to retire from the teaching profession. To many of you, this is no surprise, expected more so than not. But to be honest, I wasn't sure until holiday break that this was going to be my denouement. You see, this job saved my life.

In 1985, a terrible car accident claimed the life of my wife and son. An accident where I could have been the driver. I have often thought back to that fateful morning when Janet and Danny climbed into the car to take an innocent shopping trip. If I had "put my foot down" or said "no" to Janet or even gone along for the drive, she would still be here today and Danny would be here with his own children. But those of you who remember Janet know that it was damn near impossible to force her to do something she didn't want to do. It was one of the many things I loved about her.

For ten years, I lived every day for our family. They were my everything. Their matching sleepy looks in the morning. Their smiles. Their laughter. Their love. And this job, this teaching career, was simply a vehicle for me to be with them and to support them. I know this sounds like I wasn't invested in the students here but that wouldn't be true, I was. It was just that everything else came second to Janet and Danny — our little family unit.

Since I decided to retire from teaching, I have thought quite a bit about my years in the classroom, each and every one. This year as much as any other has taught me lessons about life. At the start of my career, like at the start of yours no matter what field it is, you will be learning, pants-on-fire learning. If you are lucky, time will fly by because you have found a career you truly enjoy. Then, if you are like me, you'll meet someone and life will change. The job will still be important but not as important as the people you come home to every day. I was lucky. I had a career that allowed me to spend as much time as I could at home or out on adventures with the ones I loved.

So as you embark upon the rest of your lives, I want you to not, I repeat, not think about what career you want to have or how much money you want to make but how, HOW, you want to spend your days, HOW you want to live your life. Decide first how you want to live and then find a way to support yourself. If you do, then you will live a very full and fulfilling life.

When I was in studying in school, I had no one to tell me that advice. I guessed at my career and got lucky. But after Janet and Danny died, I didn't want help or advice or anyone, for that matter. I lived five dark, dark years. I found myself wallowing in the bottom of a bottle. I conditioned to be sober during school but as the dismissal bell rang, all governors were off. I wallowed. I sat looking out the plate glass window, watching life being lived by everyone else. I sat atop the Dune Ridge Trail until well after sun down. I would wander down to Echo Rock at 3 am. More than once the administrators or teachers or police officers would find me stumbling down the street in the early morning hours and drive me home. The saying goes, "It takes a village to raise a child," but sometimes it takes a village to take care of one of its own.

When everything you have lived for is taken away, your whole being is shattered. The bottom is the only place to go and that is where I stayed for five long years. Then, with the help of friends, friends who should have abandoned me long before, I sobered up and regained my perspective.

So, as you go through life, something or someone may knock you down, dump you in the gutter, and take all your joy from you. Life doesn't care who you are or how much money you make, life is indifferent. So, when that time comes, whatever form it comes in, you must look inward, look to friends, and take steps to right the ship, to pick yourself up by the bootstraps, to put yourself back together again, to simply get well.

Many nights in those five years, I contemplated giving up on life and there have been days since where I wished the good Lord would take me home to see my family again. But He has had other plans. If you are feeling like I have felt, you are not alone. You don't have to remain broken or alone. Call a friend, find a reason, a why, to start living again.

After I sobered up, I started to read again and teach, really teach. Books became my why at home and you became my why at work. For the last twenty-eight years, I have lived a purposeful and content life. I have travelled across the universe in spaceships, lived within the realm of Middle Earth, stayed with the Russian families of Tolstoy and Dostoyevsky. I became a member of Lord Chamberlain's Men. I rode through the Wild West with a six-shooter strapped to my waist. I survived alien invasions, a zombie apocalypse, a pandemic disease, World War III and the recreation of dinosaurs. I followed presidents on the campaign trail, learned about the science of everything, witnessed the perfect storm, climbed Mount Everest, and became a wolf on Wall Street. I have as many books in my home as the school has in its library and now, with my recent donation, you will have twice as many. But the hours of 3-10 pm weren't just for reading, I spent many of them here with you, coaching, cheering, being awed by your talent, humbled by your compassion toward others, and much more.

More than books, the staff and the students gave me joy and a reason to live. If I didn't really teach for the first ten and was drunk for the next five, then I hadn't really taught at all. So for the last twenty-eight years that is what I did. I gave myself to North Wellington, heart and soul.

In the last forty-three years, I have witnessed happiness and heartache, joy and sorrow, life and death. Each year the students move down the hallway from kindergarten to senior year, flowing like the lifeblood of the building. The culture and the atmosphere are made not by the adults in the building but by the students, from seniors down to kindergarten. If the seniors are combative and destructive another class down the line will be also. If the seniors pride themselves on sports, the younger students will as well. If the seniors put an emphasis on higher education and studying, so will others. Life is what you make it and high school is no different.

Parents like to say, "wait until you get into the real world" as they wag their finger, but high school is the real world, just a smaller, more intimate one. A world where a dirty look from someone in the hall means something. A breakup means being surrounded with friends but also having to live with seeing that "other" person every day for the next two years. In high school, you must live with your mistakes; they stare back at you in the halls and in each class. In high school, you learn how to go about life. Not everything is bad. You are taught how to celebrate at pep assemblies and create lasting bonds through hours and hours of friendship and experience. You learn, hopefully, how to be yourself. You learn that in order to be successful, you have to work for it. You learn that having strong people to rely on is invaluable. You learn that teachers and administrators are not the enemy but are mentors. You learn all of this and more here at North Wellington.

But there comes a time when you must leave this place. You understand, that time is now. You have no choice in the matter. Your time is up, as is mine. Later in life, you will have to choose to stay or to go, but that is a lesson for another day. Today, beyond those doors awaits another "real world" as you head off to college or work or the armed forces. You will find yourself equipped only with the skills you learned here and at home in the last twelve years. You will be fine. You are more prepared than you think you are for this adventure. Sure, you will make mistakes and fall down, but you will get back up and make better choices next time. You will find your next community. You will find your next set of friends. You will discover how to live. Then you will have to do it all over again after college or after work or after a tour in the armed forces. And how you choose to live the rest of your life is up to you. You can choose to never start over again and to stop challenging yourself. You can choose to stay within your comfort zone. You can play it safe.

Take it from me. I have been playing it safe, hiding behind my career since 1990. I never really got back up. Life was easier that way but also, to be honest, rather sad and lonely. Every once in a while, you need to push yourself out of the nest. The fall will be swift and the landing painful but you need to go after your hopes and dreams. Discover something new about who you are. You will not be the same person twenty years from now that you are today. Don't be afraid to step out of your comfort zone, you've done it before. You'll do it again.

By tragedy or by choice, keep growing, keep living, and keep smiling. For life is only what you decide it to be. Thank you and God Bless.

67

Williams backed away from the podium, eyes glistening. The seniors stood and cheered. Slowly the former students of Mr. Williams stood as well, followed by the remaining audience, school board, and administrators. Williams placed his notes inside the lectern. He stepped to the side of the stage and placed his hand over his heart. Then he mouthed the words, "Thank you" and took a slight bow.

Someone shouted, "We love you, Mr. Williams."

He smiled and waved. Stewie from NHS waited for him by the stairs. Principal Anderson took to the lectern to introduce the school choir conducted by Sarah Bilikin. The senior members filed from the seats to the risers. The alma mater was to be their last song played at North Wellington.

Williams returned to his seat next to the bleachers, hands shaking. Classroom speaking was one thing; speaking in front of a gym full of people was another. The rush from being in front of all those people started to fade and he felt his face cooling. His hands were tingling less but his emotions were swelling. As the song concluded, Williams' cheeks were wet with tears. He watched as one by one the students of the graduating class ascended to the stage to receive their diplomas, shake hands with the superintendent, and be photographed one final time as a student of North Wellington.

Finally, the superintendent stood before the senior class. "We have a saying here, 'It is a great day to be a warrior.' And I think today is definitely one of those days!"

The crowd roared its approval.

"As superintendent of schools, I am pleased to accept the certification of requirements for the class of 2019 as duly prepared to receive their diplomas for graduation from North Wellington High School. On behalf of the staff, administrators, and North Muskegon Board of Education, we acknowledge that you have met all the requirements set forth by the State of Michigan. I now pronounce you the 2019 graduates of North Wellington High School."

As the audience stood to applause, the graduates filed back out through the gym to the front of the school where they would gather together one more time to throw their tasseled caps into the air before they dispersed amongst family and friends. Williams watched as the last graduating class of his career moved down the aisle smiling and full of joy at their accomplishment. The teachers followed in line behind the seniors. Williams slipped behind Pat, who was chatting away to Tom about the student speeches. In three more steps he was out the back door to the gym. Five more steps and he was out in the fresh spring air. In fifty yards he was past the throng of students, parents, and friends milling about in front of the school savoring the night's celebration.

As he walked down Merylton Lane, he wondered what could have been. He wondered about Janet and Danny. He wondered what life would have been like if he had been stronger after their deaths. Would his life have been filled with love again? Would his life have been filled with another child's laughter?

During his mile walk home, Williams could only be certain of one thing. He was moving on, stepping outside of his comfort zone. This time by his choice. He wasn't sure what the future held, but he knew one thing, life wasn't over.

As twilight set over North Wellington, William took a long look at his home. First, he saw the freshly cut grass and mulched garden, then his eyes drifted to the For Sale sign stuck in the yard. Finally, he saw the idling black SUV in the driveway. As the driver exited the vehicle he said, "Good evening, Mr. Williams."

Gus smiled, "It is. It is indeed."

Climbing inside, Gus wasn't sure of much but he was sure that the rest of his life would be an adventure.

THANK YOU: I heart felt thank you goes out to my wonderful children, who understand that language and books and storytelling help make me a happy man. Without them and without stories, I would be lost. And to my brother and sister who never stopped believing in me and sharing life's joys and sorrows. Always knowing someone has your back is a blessing no one should take for granted. And to my parents who gave me a solid foundation the best way they could, from my father reading me Shakespeare before I could walk to my mother who showed me the life changing place called the library.

I also want to thank the first readers of this book: Mike, Brett, and Caleb. Your notes and motivation to finish my first test of novel writing pushed me to make the final corrections and continue on this journey. Thank you so much.

I have had many teachers and many students in my life. All of which inspired me to write this story. I want to thank the teachers for being patient with a wild, often distracted young man in the classroom, and I wanted to thank the students who had a seemingly busy young teacher at the head of the class. I keep learning and I keep sharing what I know. And someday I will take the those final steps like Gus and walk away, leaving only my lessons in the lives of those who took my classes.

The writing of AUGUST IN TWILIGHT was a multi-year journey that saw many starts, stops, and life changes. The goal was always to finish and be proud of what I accomplished, and I am.

Finally, I want to thank everyone that has bought, read, and shared this book. You are helping make dreams come true. God Bless.

Made in the USA
Monee, IL
27 January 2021

58875451R00215